Praise for the novels of Jude Deveraux

"Jude Deveraux's writing is enchanting and exquisite."

—*BookPage*

"Deveraux's touch is gold."

—*Publishers Weekly*

"A steamy and delightfully outlandish retelling of a literary classic."
—*Kirkus Reviews* on *The Girl from Summer Hill*

"[A]n irresistibly delicious tale of love, passion, and the unknown."
—*Booklist* on *The Girl from Summer Hill*

"[A] sexy, lighthearted romp."

—*Kirkus Reviews* on *Ever After*

"Thoroughly enjoyable."

—*Publishers Weekly* (starred review) on *Ever After*

JUDE DEVERAUX

As You Wish

mira

mira

ISBN-13: 978-0-7783-0761-7
ISBN-13: 978-0-7783-0769-3 (International Trade Paperback Edition)

As You Wish

For questions and comments about the quality of this book, please contact us at
CustomerService@Harlequin.com.

BookClubbish.com

Printed in U.S.A.

Look for Jude Deveraux's next novel

A WILLING MURDER

available soon from MIRA Books

For more from Jude Deveraux,
visit her website at jude-deveraux.com.

As You Wish

Prologue

"GET STRONG. GET TAN. THINK YOU'RE SMART ENOUGH to do those two things, kid?"

The man was as tall as Kit, a couple of inches over six feet, but he was very wide. Kit wondered if three of himself, glued side by side, would be as wide as this officer. With his short black hair, he looked like a cartoon bear.

"Yes, sir." Kit's back was so straight it was like steel.

"And when we pick you up in the fall, if you pull your pants down, I don't want to see your shiny white ass. Do I make myself clear?"

"Yes, sir. I'm to sunbathe in the nude." As soon as he said the words he knew they were wrong. They sounded too elitist, too much like who he was, which was not "one of the guys." His father didn't lube cars. Dad had stopped a couple of tribal wars in the Middle East, but that wasn't something Kit could brag about.

When the big man leaned closer, as much as Kit wanted to step away, he didn't. "Was that a remark? A joke? Are you laughing at me, kid?"

"No, sir!" Kit practically yelled the words. Sweat was running down the back of his neck.

It was 6:00 a.m. and he'd been pulled out of an early training session to go to this man's office. But he hadn't minded. At nineteen, he was the youngest of the recruits—some of whom had spent a couple of years in Vietnam—and he'd been hassled the most. *"You been weaned yet, kid? Potty trained?"*

"Miss your mommie, do you?"

"A few years back I had a one-nighter with a girl named Montgomery. Think I could be your daddy?"

Kit had smiled through it all, but each barb had made him more determined to do a job that he was uniquely qualified for.

The big man took a step back from Kit. "You...bathe—" his tone made fun of the word "—however you want to, but in September I want you and that big nose of yours lookin' like you've always lived in the desert. Do I make myself clear?"

"Yes, sir, you do."

The man took another step back and looked Kit up and down in contempt. Like all his father's family, Kit was tall and lean, built more like a runner than this guy, who could probably bench-press cars. "I don't know what they were thinking when they got you," he muttered. "You're just a boy, and you're so skinny you could slide through a keyhole." He shook his head. "Do I have to remind you that no one—not even your famous daddy—is to know what some idiot picked you out to do?"

"No, sir, you don't."

"You think, Montgomery, that you can hang around your kinfolk and not tell them why you are—what did you call it?— sunbathing in the nude?"

"I won't be with them, sir." Kit wasn't looking at the man directly, but staring over his shoulder.

"Oh, that's right." The man had a sneer in his voice. "You're rich. Own lots of houses, do you?"

Kit wasn't sure if he was supposed to answer that or not. Some

time ago he'd realized that he couldn't spend the summer before
he shipped out with his family. They were too perceptive and
too nosy. They'd know he was up to something and they'd do
whatever was necessary to find out what it was. And knowing
them, they just might make sure it didn't happen.

No one was to know that he was training to go undercover
in Libya. A young man named Muammar al-Gaddafi had just
taken over the country and Kit was to find out what he planned
to do. Thanks to his life with his diplomat father, Kit was fluent
in Arabic in all its dialects. From the classic, to the Lebanese that
was half French, to the Arabic spoken by the Saudis that came
from inside a person's throat, he knew them all.

And Kit had inherited the hawk nose of his father's family and
the dark eyes of the Italian ancestry of his mother. With a tan
and in the right clothes, he could sit in a souk, smoke a bubble
pipe, and no one would pay any attention to him.

Months ago, one of his father's friends, a former American
ambassador to Syria, had spent a week at their house in Cairo.
Kit had seen the man watching him as he played kickball with
Egyptians, ate schwarma from a street vendor, and as he got into
a loud argument in Arabic with a cabdriver. Just before the ambassador left, he'd asked to speak to Kit in private. He started by
asking if Kit would like to help his country. It had been a dra-
matic opening that appealed to Kit's deep patriotism. Without
hesitation he'd said yes.

It hadn't been easy to lie to his family and say he wanted to
take a year off from college to bum around the world. Only
his father seemed to guess the truth. He'd stared at his son for
a while, then said, "What can we do to help you prepare for
this…this trip?"

"Get me away from here," Kit said before he thought, but his
father had nodded in understanding.

Two days later, Kit received an invitation to spend the summer at Tattwell, an old plantation owned by relatives of his mother, the Tattingtons.

When Kit was silent at the question, the big man waved his hand. "Go on. Get out of here. Just remember that I'll be one of them that picks you up and you better be fit and dark. Now go!"

The next night Kit arrived in Summer Hill, Virginia, and the next day he looked into the eyes of the woman he would love for the rest of his life. But Miss Olivia Paget didn't feel the same way about him. In fact, she felt exactly the opposite. As though his life depended on it, Kit worked to change her mind.

Chapter One

REGRET, OLIVIA THOUGHT AS SHE LOOKED ABOUT THE little restaurant. On a TV talk show she'd seen that morning, the young, perfect-looking interviewer, her hair unnaturally shiny, asked the old actor if he had any regrets about his long life in show business.

Of course he said no. He'd had a great life and wouldn't change a thing. What else could he say? That he regretted his marriage to wife number two, who took everything he'd worked for during his forty years in film? That he wished he hadn't made the three really bad horror movies when he was broke? What about the twelve years he'd wasted when he was in a drugged-out, alcoholic stupor? But then the critics agreed that he was a better actor when he was drunk. After rehab, he became serious and dull. A costar notoriously said that bourbon seemed to be his fuel to joy.

But he said he regretted nothing. *I'll drink to that!* Olivia thought.

What would she say if that interviewer, her dress tighter than

the skin of a snake and about the same size, asked Olivia what
she regretted in her life?

"Sex," she'd say. "I missed out on those precious years of
young sex. Shoved up against a wall, slamming away in the front
seat of a car with the gearshift ramming into your back, sweat
dripping off your noses, the sun coming up and you've been
at it all night, and the next day you're so sore you can hardly
walk. That's what I regret missing in my life. One summer of
it was not enough!"

She imagined the interviewer's face, her HD makeup that
made her look plastic, freezing in place. Would she be stern and
say, "That's *not* what you're supposed to answer"? Would the
network bleep out what Olivia had said? Would Robin Williams
smile down from Heaven and say, "You go, girl"?

To Olivia, one of the great mysteries of life was why young
people believed that sex wants, needs, thoughts, cravings—any
and all of it—disappeared with age. When did a person go from
being "hot" to "cute"? "They're such a cute couple." That's what
kids automatically said about people past the age of… She wasn't
sure when that was reached. And at what age were you supposed
to forget that you'd ever had sex? Forget those days you spent
naked by the pond. The smell of the grass crushed under your
body. The water so warm and seeping into crevices, then him
licking it away. Kids were shocked if a person over fifty mentioned anything sexual. At what age did a person revirginalize?

"Hello."

She looked up to see a big, tall young man—at least young
to her—midthirties, possibly older. He was quite good-looking,
and his eyes had a kind of feral energy that Olivia guessed would
get him whatever he wanted. The shirt and trousers he wore
looked casual, but she could tell that they'd been custom-made
for him. But the smooth outward appearance of him seemed
studied, as though he were an actor playing a role.

"Are you Mrs. Montgomery?" His words were spoken in a

newscaster's voice, with no real accent. But she would put money on it that it wasn't the way he spoke when he was a kid.

"I am. And you're from Dr. Hightower?"

"Yes. Do you mind?" Politely, he waited for her to motion for him to take the chair across from her. He sat down, then nodded for a waitress to come to him. As Olivia had guessed, the young woman arrived quickly. When he gave his order for black coffee, Olivia was glad to see that his eyes didn't linger on the pretty young waitress. Nor did he speak until she'd left. "Jeanne—Dr. Hightower—said you would take us to the house."

"I will, but we need to wait for the other tenant, Elise, to get here. I got a text from her and she should be here in a few minutes."

When the waitress put the coffee before the man, she set down a plate of little lemon cookies. "They're on the house. For "

She glanced at Olivia. "For both of you."

Olivia knew the girl's mother and it took only a quick squint of her eyes to make the girl go away. When she looked back at the man, she wondered if he was as oblivious to the attention of the waitress as he seemed.

"I guess Jeanne told you that I'm Ray Hanran."

"I was told little more than your names, but I did assume that you and Elise are friends."

"Oh no," he said, "I've never met my new housemate. There was supposed to be an older woman staying with us, but she dropped out."

Olivia couldn't help frowning. "I know that the other guest is quite young."

"Is she? I have no idea. You know Jeanne. She tells you little about anything."

"Actually, I don't know her. It was my husband, Kit, who asked me to escort you two to the Camden Hall estate."

"Estate? That sounds bigger than I thought it was."

"Jeanne's summerhouse is one of four small houses on what

used to be a fairly grand property." Olivia was concerned about the arrangements. "Does this young woman, Elise, know that she's spending the weekend with a man she's never met?" She gave a pointed look at the wedding ring on his left hand.

The way he smiled showed that he knew what was in Olivia's mind. "I don't know what she's been told. None of this was my doing. It took Jeanne weeks to make me believe I should stop work and go to some cabin nestled in the woods." His eyes widened. "You don't think this is like a dating service, do you? Meant to match me up with some lonely young client of hers?"

The way he leaned back in his chair made Olivia think he was going to leave—which would disappoint Kit greatly. "I really don't know anything," she said quickly. "My husband was called away to DC and he sent me an email saying a psychologist, Dr. Jeanne Hightower, was sending two of her clients here for a long weekend. He asked if I would please meet you two in this restaurant and lead you there. It's not easy to find."

Ray frowned. "I don't understand any of this. I'm having…" He took a drink of his coffee and seemed to consider whether or not to confide in her. "I'm having some serious marital problems and Jeanne was recommended to me. I've been going to her for weeks, but I haven't made any progress in my decision about what to do. I was planning to quit therapy, but then Jeanne started nagging me to go to Virginia to spend some time at her summerhouse. I finally gave in and here I am."

Suddenly, a look of abject terror came onto his face. "This isn't one of those retreats, is it? Where I'm supposed to wear a white robe and talk about my…my *feelings*?"

Olivia couldn't help a laugh at the fear in his voice. "It's not. The house is a pretty little three-bed, three-bath, and it was empty for years. I wasn't even aware that it'd been sold. I've lived in Summer Hill all my life but I've only been on the grounds of Camden Hall once, and that was many years ago. But now that I live there—"

"You *live* there, but you've only seen it once?"

Olivia didn't like talking about her personal life, but she knew she had to say something to keep this man from leaving. In her calmest voice, the one she often used with strangers, she said, "You see, I'm a newlywed." She waited for his astonishment. Young people seemed to think older women were born married. He did look surprised, but he recovered quickly. "At our wedding, my husband gave me the deed to a house on the Camden estate. He and I were together years ago when we first saw the old River House on the property so he knew I liked the place." She paused to remember that blistering hot day when the two of them were naked. Young, strong bodies glistening in the sun.

She looked back at Ray. "My husband bought the house for me, but I didn't see it. We left from the wedding to go on a six-month-long honeymoon to see the places where he'd worked during his life as a diplomat." *Places I should have seen with him*, she thought, but didn't say. Kit had also recently introduced her to people she should have known for the last forty-plus years.

"As soon as we got back to the US, Kit got a call from someone in DC and had to leave, so I returned to Summer Hill. I spent last night at the house of a friend. After I get you and young Elise settled at Dr. Hightower's house, I'm to go to the home my husband bought for us. It's at the other end of the estate."

He looked at her for a moment, seeming to consider this information. "Isn't a groom supposed to carry his bride over the threshold of the new house?"

If Olivia hadn't asked herself that very thing, she would have laughed. But her disappointment showed on her face. The first time she saw the inside of the house she wanted to be with Kit. Part of the reason for their long honeymoon had been so the old house could be repaired, painted, and furnished. Every day they'd delighted in seeing the photos the decorator and the work crew sent them. They'd begun with cobwebs and mice, a raccoon in the attic, and 1940s electrical. But underneath the filth had been beautiful old beams and stone fireplaces, and giant windows that looked out onto a pretty pond with an island in the middle. It was all going to be perfect!

But as much as she'd enjoyed the traveling and buying things for their house, there were times when such deep waves of regret flooded Olivia that she'd been unable to move. Kit and she had known each other for so very long and they should have been together all that time. She should know the best places to shop in Istanbul. She should be able to speak Arabic because she should have lived with Kit when he was stationed in Egypt. She should—

When she looked at Ray, sitting quietly and watching her, his eyes were almost glittering with interest in her every word. It took her a moment to recognize that look. "You're a salesman, aren't you?"

Ray let out a laugh that almost sent coffee spewing, but he grabbed a napkin and covered his mouth. "What gave me away?"

"'A lean and hungry look,'" she said, quoting Shakespeare. "So what is it that you're using all this concern to try to sell me?"

"Stay with us."

"What do you mean?"

"Jeanne sent me here to give me time to think. When I'm at work in the city or at home with my wife, Kathy, I can't stand back and look at what's going on. Jeanne said she wants to give me time away so I can make what will be the biggest decision of my life."

He paused for a moment. "But things have changed. I thought two women were going to be there and they could…"

Olivia watched him take a cookie and slowly eat it. "They could do the cooking and entertain each other so you'd be free to do whatever you want."

Ray laughed. "Sure you're not Jeanne's sister? So yeah, I'm spoiled. Kathy and I have no kids so I'm sort of…" He shrugged.

"You're everything to her?"

"Pretty much. Kathy doesn't really have a life of her own. It's just *me*."

"So what's wrong? Something at work?"

Ray took a deep breath. "I want a divorce but I don't know how to tell my wife."

"Oh," Olivia said. "That is a problem. And I can see your need to think long and hard about that."

"Yeah, but if I'm alone in this house with her, that girl might get the wrong idea about me."

It was the opposite of what Olivia had thought, but he did have a point. He seemed to attract women to him.

"Stay with us," Ray repeated. "It's just for a few days, then when your husband gets back, he can carry you over the threshold. As he should do."

"Hmmm." For a moment, Olivia acted as though she were contemplating the idea. She leaned toward him. "Are you dying to ask me if I can cook?"

Ray was serious. "If you can't, I'll be condemned to live on pizza."

"And mess up that perfect waistline of yours? That would be a true tragedy." Olivia was making jokes to cover what was going on in her mind. When she first saw the fabrics and colors that she and Kit had chosen, she wanted him to be with her. She wanted laughter and…

Memories, she thought. The two of them were in their sixties now. How many years did they have left to make the memories that should have been theirs for the last forty-plus years? She well knew that was time enough for children to grow, for grandchildren to have reached their teen years. But she and Kit had missed out on all of that. Those memories didn't exist.

"Are you all right?" Ray asked.

"Sure," Olivia said. "I think we should wait for Elise to get here before we make any decisions."

"Good idea," he said. "But just so you know, if she's some little lost lamb looking for a daddy figure, I'm out of here."

Olivia blinked at what he'd said, but she knew he was right. She'd seen the way the waitress glanced at him. That Ray wasn't returning the girl's looks of I'm-willing-if-you-are raised him in her estimation.

When his cell phone buzzed, he pulled it from his pocket and looked at the ID. "This is Kathy, so I…" He was asking her permission to take the call in private.

"Of course. Take your time."

When he spoke into the phone, his face changed to one of concern—and unless Olivia missed her guess, there was love. As she watched him go out the side door of the little restaurant, she didn't envy his situation. He was married to a woman who had dedicated her entire life to him. Olivia had seen that many times. The woman had no children, no job, no close friends, so the husband became her reason for living. No doubt every decision she made, everything she did, was controlled by *Will Ray like this?*

From Olivia's experience, men tended to like that. And way too often, men demanded that kind of subservience.

But she'd never thought of it from the perspective of a man who didn't want that clingy attention. A man who didn't want a wife who depended on him for everything. Olivia imagined the wife's panic when her husband got home late from work. Hysteria at a creaking floorboard. The incessant phone calls. The constant need for his approval.

And there would be misery if Ray didn't give her his total attention. Would there be tears over Ray's neglect? "I spent all day cooking this dinner and you can't even give me a compliment?"

As Olivia ate one of the lemon cookies, she thought about Ray's problem. Yes, it would be a difficult decision to leave a woman like that. Walking away from anger would be easier than dealing with all those tears.

. Olivia looked out the window to see Ray on his cell phone. He was smiling in a gentle, kind way, as though talking to a dear friend. Yes, he had a very difficult decision in front of him.

When she turned away, she saw a young woman enter the restaurant through the front door, and Olivia was sure she was the other tenant. She was in her twenties, tall, thin, and naturally blonde, with a very pretty face. She had on worn jeans, a T-shirt, and sandals. The regular attire of her generation.

But this girl was different. For one thing, she was perfect. Not just physically perfect, but in that flawless way that only a lifetime of money could achieve. When the girl turned, Olivia looked into her extraordinarily blue eyes and saw nannies and cooks, heavy silver serving pieces, Ivy League schools, and a girls' lacrosse team.

It was in that second that Olivia made her decision. Yes, she'd stay at the summerhouse with Ray and this girl. Maybe he thought he had no interest in other women, but she'd seen the ambition in his eyes. It was better not to tempt him.

The girl came to her table. "Are you Mrs. Montgomery?"

"Yes, I am."

"Great. I'm Elise Arrington." She dropped her small canvas bag to the floor, took Ray's chair, then saw the coffee cup. "Is someone sitting here?"

"Your housemate." Olivia nodded toward the big window. Ray was still on the phone, his handsome face smiling in a sweet way.

Olivia watched Elise when she saw Ray. Would she be like the waitress? But the only sign Elise gave was a slight widening of her eyes. *She has those deeply ingrained manners, learned from childhood*, Olivia thought.

"He's rather large, isn't he?" Elise said. There was a tiny bit of disdain in her voice.

Olivia was glad there was no attraction. "I don't know if Dr.

Hightower told you, but one of the three occupants dropped out."

Elise leaned forward and lowered her voice. "I'm to share a house with just him?"

"Ray asked if I'd mind staying there too. If it's all right with you, that is."

"Yes, I'd like that." With a sigh of relief, Elise turned to the waitress—who made a point of ignoring her.

Olivia leaned back against her chair. She wasn't sure if this was getting interesting or if she should run away. Actually, she'd been dreading this time away from her new husband.

They hadn't yet figured out what they were going to do with their lives. Kit was retired—sort of, since he still got called back to DC now and then. Olivia had spent most of her life managing some appliance stores and trying to make a home for her late husband and his son. She'd thought she'd done a good job, but on her husband's deathbed, she'd been told that he'd willed the stores to his son, which meant that she was without a job.

Olivia watched as Elise got up and went to the counter to place her order. The woman at the register, who Olivia knew owned the little restaurant, apologized for the lack of service. The moment Elise turned away, the owner went to the waitress and snapped at her.

When the waitress glared at the back of Elise's head, Olivia had to repress a smile. Ah, the age-old fight for the dominant male. Ray was a man to be won and the waitress saw Elise as a rival.

As Elise sat back down, she nodded toward Ray. "Who's he talking to?"

"His wife."

"I'm glad he's married." The owner put a tuna salad sandwich on whole wheat and an iced tea in front of Elise, who thanked her. After the woman left, Elise said, "If you don't want to stay, please tell me of a hotel or a B and B in town."

"I think I'd like to stay with you two, but you should know that Ray seems very nice. Not a predator at all."

"But he's here as part of his therapy, so there has to be something wrong with him. I wonder what he did to get sent here?"

"Not to be unkind, but couldn't the same be said about you?"

Elise had her mouth full and waited while she chewed. "I didn't do anything. Jeanne rescued me from a mental institution."

"Oh." Olivia tried to keep her eyebrows from going skyward. She wanted to fire questions at the girl. Was she bipolar? Schizophrenic? Did she have violent episodes? "Should you…?" she began, but didn't know where to go from there.

"It's okay," Elise said. "I didn't hurt anyone. They think I tried to commit suicide so they had me locked up."

"Who did?"

"My parents and my husband. This sandwich is really good. Quite fresh."

"You tried to commit suicide?" Olivia's voice was soft and caring.

Elise took a long drink of her tea. "No, I didn't. I was so angry at my husband, Kent, that I couldn't sleep, so I took one of his sleeping pills. What I didn't know is that he had crushed *four* of them and put them in the drink he made for me. When I woke up in a hospital, Kent was crying and begging me to forgive him for slipping me the extra pills and nearly killing me. I told him I wanted a divorce. In the next minute, in came my parents with a therapist who was telling them that I'd tried to commit suicide. My throat was so raw I couldn't talk but I looked to Kent to tell them the *truth*. But he lied and said I'd taken the pills by myself. And of course no one was going to believe *me* because I'd just tried to kill myself, right? So anyway, I was locked away for 'protection' and talked to for weeks about my suicidal depression. Only Jeanne believed me when I said that if I was going to kill anyone it would be my husband and not myself. Do you think they have any pie? I haven't eaten much lately because I was hidden inside the trunk of Jeanne's car for so long, then I was too angry to eat. Is there a restroom here?"

Olivia was blinking so hard she had trouble reacting. Hiding in the doctor's trunk? She very much wanted to hear this story. She pointed out the restroom door, then raised her hand to the owner. She came to the table as Elise left.

"What do you need, Olivia? And I'm sorry about the waitress. She broke up with her boyfriend and is looking for a new one." She glanced up as Ray came back in. "Is he available?"

"No. Not at all. Could you bring us a slice of every kind of pie you have?"

"There are six of them."

"That's great. One of each, and put everything on Kit's bill, with a twenty-five percent tip."

"You got it." She was watching Ray as he started back inside. "If I were ten years younger…" With a sigh, she took the empty dishes and left.

Ray sat down across from Olivia, then looked at Elise's glass of tea. "Did she show up?"

"She did." Olivia was still trying to digest all that she'd heard.

"Is she crazy? I mean, she is one of Jeanne's patients."

"She's not crazy at all," Olivia said. "Would you like to have some pie? I've ordered rather a lot of it."

"I'd love some."

Chapter Two

"ARE YOU SURE YOU'RE OKAY?" KIT ASKED. "IS ESTELLE'S house comfortable?"

Olivia held the cell phone close to her ear as she watched Ray and Elise looking at the flowers in her friend's garden. Ray was big and handsome in a rough sort of way, while Elise looked as fragile as a butterfly. The two of them were so different they didn't seem to be the same species.

"Are you still there?" Kit asked.

"Yes," Olivia answered. "I'm here and listening. I heard you say you might have to stay in DC for a whole week. Which country are you trying to save?"

"I, uh—"

She cut him off. "I know. You can't tell me. What do you know about Dr. Jeanne Hightower?"

"Nothing, really. My cousin Cale's friend Ellie Abbott swears by her."

"Ah, I see. Two mystery writers."

"Yes." Kit lowered his voice. "Has something happened? You sound...well, distant."

"I just ran into a couple of very interesting problems, that's all."

"You're going to stay with Jeanne's patients and help out, aren't you?"

Olivia gave a sound that was half groan, half laugh. "I'm not sure I like someone knowing me so well."

"I may have missed out on a few years, but I remember everything. So tell me what's going on."

"Ray is a big guy, midthirties, who probably grew up on the wrong side of the tracks, but it looks like he's pulled himself up in the world of sales. Now he wears Bond Street clothes, but I'd bet that he has a gang tattoo somewhere on his perfectly toned body."

"I hope you don't go searching to find out," Kit said. "And the girl?"

"Money and manners. She dresses like a street kid but she probably went to Miss Porter's and Bryn Mawr. I haven't heard the whole story yet, but I think she tried to buck the system and she got locked up for it."

"As in jail?"

"No. As in being held in a mental institution under lock and key. But it seems that Jeanne broke her out, hid her in the trunk of her car, and drove her across the country."

Kit was quiet for a moment. "I thought what I was doing was exciting, but you have me beat. My concern is whether you're going to miss me at all."

"I don't want to see our house until you're with me," she blurted out.

"Good! I like that. It's you who was the practical one and wanted to stay there alone."

"Are you saying you're the romantic one?"

"Peacocks, well house, moonlight parties in the nude. They were all from me. Yeah, I think I'm the Emperor of Romance."

Olivia smiled at the images of long ago that he brought up. "I'm not so sure. When you get back, you need to prove it to me."

"I look forward to doing just that."

They were silent for a moment, just breathing. "I better go," Olivia said. "The warrior and the fairy princess have stopped talking. Ray might start trying to sell her a mountain that may or may not be full of gold."

"What's his problem?"

"He's trying to get the courage to tell his wife that he wants a divorce. Poor thing. My heart goes out to her. He's her entire life but he's going to drop her."

"You think it's another woman?"

"Probably. You know the saying. Men divorce because they have someone else. Women leave because they're fed up."

"No, I hadn't heard that one." He paused. "Did you get fed up with me?"

"You know I didn't. What happened between us was an accident. Just fate."

"And two bratty kids and a peacock and...and Gaddafi."

Olivia laughed. "Good idea. Let's blame him. I do have to go. Ray is looking at his watch, and Elise looks like she might drift away into a fairyland of her own making."

"Ah, my wife the brilliant people observer. How I could have used your expertise when I was working in Morocco. We could have—"

"Don't," she whispered. They had agreed not to dwell on what they'd missed in not being together all those years. At least not out loud.

"You're right. I better go too. The prez is waiting for me."

"*The* president? No! Don't answer that. Just go. I love you."

"And I love you more. Keep me up to date on this. It's interesting."

"I promise." Reluctantly, they hung up and Olivia went into

the garden. Ray and Elise were standing on opposite sides, lost in their own thoughts.

Their silence made it flash across Olivia's mind that this woman she didn't know, Dr. Jeanne Hightower, had planned for Olivia to be with them. That would have taken some detailed organization, but it could have been done. As it was, the situation reeked of too much coincidence. An "older woman" was supposed to have been with them, but she'd dropped out. Was it just an accident that Olivia had been asked to accompany these two? She didn't think so.

"If you're ready to go, we can leave now." As she led them through the house, Ray picked up Olivia's suitcase from beside the front door and followed the women outside. He put the case in her new BMW, another gift from Kit.

Olivia glanced at Ray's sleek Jag, something more suited for a bachelor than a married man.

He closed the trunk. "I'm getting rid of it and buying an SUV."

"Girlfriend pregnant?" she said before she thought. "Sorry, I shouldn't have said that."

But Ray gave a snort of laughter. "You *are* Jeanne's sister. Not yet, but I'm working on it, and I refuse to feel guilty about it. I've always wanted kids and my wife isn't able to have any. If that makes me a bad guy—"

Olivia put her hand up. "I know all about wanting children. And, Ray, I don't judge. You can say what you want. It's my guess that the reason Dr. Hightower put you here with strangers is so you *can* talk."

Ray groaned. "This *is* going to be a touchy-feely weekend, isn't it? Where's the nearest bar?"

"Not allowed." She was smiling. "Did you and Elise talk?" She nodded toward the young woman who had politely stepped away from them.

"Nothing but about how pretty the flowers are. I get the idea she came from money."

"You think?"

Ray laughed. "She kind of oozes it, doesn't she? What's her problem? Daddy wouldn't buy her a jet of her very own?"

"Now who's judging?"

"Okay, I'll back off. But it's my job to quickly figure people out so I can sell them things. For her, it would be Chanel and Cartier. Bet she has a black Amex."

Olivia didn't want to reveal confidences, but sometimes assumptions needed to be stopped. "Elise escaped authorities by being locked inside the trunk of Jeanne's car. No color of credit card would have helped if either of them had been caught. You ready to go?" As she walked away, she called for Elise, who got in the seat beside her, and they left for the summerhouse. When she looked in the rearview mirror, she was glad to see that Ray still wore a look of astonishment. Good! Looking at someone else's problems often helped you solve your own.

It wasn't until 3:00 p.m. that Olivia was able to get away from her housemates. She had driven onto the grounds of Camden Hall, Elise beside her, Ray in his sleek car close behind. At the gate, Young Pete—past eighty years old—waved them in and Olivia went left to what had been the gardener's house. There was a plaque on the door that read Diana's Cottage. She figured it was probably named after Diana the Huntress. Her mother said there had once been pheasants on the property, so maybe the little house had belonged to the gamekeeper.

Whatever it had been, the cottage was now so cute it almost hurt a person's eyes. It was stone, with a tall roof punctured by two windows. One of them was round, like an eye watching over the estate. Olivia hadn't been surprised when Elise wanted the upstairs bedroom with that window. It was small enough to be difficult to see into, but large enough for her to watch for anyone approaching.

Olivia took the second bedroom and was glad she would have her own bath. There hadn't been any discussion of the matter, but Ray seemed to know he was to stay downstairs.

She was glad to see that the refrigerator and the small pantry had been fully stocked, and wondered who'd done it. Jeanne, who owned the cottage? Or had Kit called someone and asked them to do it? Olivia was learning that her husband had become a person who made others jump to do his bidding.

It hadn't always been that way, she thought. When they'd met, he'd been a boy of nineteen, and all the world had been a wonder to him.

By the time Olivia got her housemates settled, all she wanted to do was escape. Ray looked like a bull with four red flags being waved at him. Now that it was time for him to start making his decision, he had no idea where to begin the process.

As for delicate, ethereal-looking Elise, for all her pretending that being signed into a mental ward and escaping inside a car trunk didn't bother her, she'd gone around the house pulling the shades down. Even with that, she sat on the far end of the couch, a pillow on her lap, and kept looking toward the back door as though she were ready to run through it.

Olivia nearly ran outside, then stood there for a moment breathing in the fresh air. Did she really and truly want to take on these two needy…well, children? Big Ray with his wild-eyed looks. Tall, fragile Elise with eyes that darted about the room. Could she deal with them?

She'd had to reassure Ray that he could indeed make a sandwich all by himself, and had to show Elise that her bedroom door could be bolted. Olivia tried to calm herself and look around. She was standing on a pretty flagstone terrace that was in a little garden with a short wall around it. She had an idea that the area had once been used for vegetables, but now had only a few shrubs. Surrounding the little enclosed garden were trees that needed pruning.

Beyond that was a tall stone wall that encircled the entire property. Everyone in town knew that in the spring Young Pete hired brawny high school kids to assess the winter damage and repair the old wall. "Roofs and walls," he said. "That's the key to maintenance." Nowadays, he rarely left the grounds that his family had looked after for three generations. Old Pete, Pete, Young Pete. No one in the next generation of the family wanted anything to do with taking care of some old houses.

As Olivia looked about the bit of garden with its scraggly shrubs, she thought how she'd like to divide it with crisscrossing paths. She'd use bark rather than gravel so walking on it would be silent. In the middle would be an arbor with a bench under it. Along the sides—

She broke off her thoughts. Was this derelict garden part of the enticement to get her to take on these damaged people? If so, who had thought of it? Kit? Or the unmet Jeanne?

When Olivia heard a noise from inside the house, she left through the little gate and hurried toward the road they'd driven in on. But she avoided it. She didn't want to be seen. Both Ray and Elise had looked as though any second *the* question was going to come from them: "What do you think I should do?"

Olivia dreaded hearing it. Maybe in other circumstances she could come up with an answer, but right now her own problems filled her mind.

As she walked past the old stables, she looked toward Camden Hall. It was a big, sprawling Edwardian house, three stories high, "more glass than wall" as the saying went. It was a beautiful house, but it had that hollow look of a place that had been unoccupied for as long as anyone could remember.

Behind the house was what was once a pleasure garden, all flowers and little ornamental trees. It was neatly trimmed, but was now mostly bare.

Ahead of her was what she'd been looking for, the tall fence that Kit had recently had replaced. The old roses had been carefully pulled away from crumbling bricks. After the new fence was up, the pruned branches had been tied back on. In another year, they'd return in full, glorious color.

The fence enclosed River House—the place Kit had bought for her and they had restored while they were on their long honeymoon.

Olivia had told Ray that she didn't want to see the house without her husband and that was true. What she did want to see was the tiny island in the shallow river that ran in front of the house. It was where she and Kit had made love back in 1970—and been caught doing it.

Even now, so many years later, the memory made her smile. How Kit had protected her! Back then, Young Pete had only recently taken over the caretaker's job and he was zealous at it—and *very* serious. That day he'd heard voices and had run home to get his shotgun.

Olivia and Kit, both naked, their clothes on the ground, had looked through the trees and shrubs to see Young Pete standing on the other side of the water. He was coming toward them with a gun in his hand.

They looked at each other, arms entwined, bodies bare, eyes wide. Did they call out and tell Young Pete that they weren't trespassers? But actually, they were. Had it been the father, Olivia would have identified herself. But the son was a different matter. Who knew what he would do?

Kit took over. He grabbed a handful of mud, smeared it on his face, and stuck a big, leafy branch into his hair. Yelling at the top of his lungs and looking very scary, he ran, stark naked, over the bridge and toward the wall that surrounded the estate.

Young Pete was so flabbergasted at the sight of the naked, wild-looking man that he stood and stared, his shotgun lowered.

Kit was almost over the wall before Young Pete recovered

enough that he raised the gun and took aim. Olivia, who'd been on the girls' softball team in high school, picked up a rock the size of her fist and threw it. It hit Young Pete in his lower back. As he spun around, the shotgun accidently went off, and the unexpected recoil sent him facedown into the water.

Olivia, naked as the day she was born, grabbed their clothes, ran across the bridge, and headed for the wall. She leaped onto a stump and propelled herself up. As she knew he would be, Kit was leaning over, both his arms held out to her. He pulled her up and over. With clasped hands, they ran through the wooded area. When they reached the edge, they stopped and looked at each other. She used Kit's shirt to wipe the mud off his face and he kissed the bloody scratches on her body that had been made by the stony wall.

It wasn't until after they'd made love on the grass that they saw that Olivia's brassiere was missing.

They halted, fear in their eyes. Would they be identified through that? Arrested for trespassing?

But then, Kit's eyes began to sparkle. How could a piece of underwear identify its owner? "Was it that pink one with the rosebud in the center?" Kit asked.

"The very one," she answered.

They began laughing and didn't stop until they got back to the huge old plantation, Tattwell, where they were both living and working. After that, just the mention of the word *rosebud* sent them into peals of laughter.

As for Young Pete, when he went to the sheriff with the pink satin brassiere and demanded that they find the owner, he set off laughter that didn't die down for twenty years.

The sheriff said, "We'll have a town-wide search to find out who it fits."

"Like Cinderella's shoe," the deputy said. "Just a different body part."

"When duty calls, we must serve," the second deputy said.

The men looked at Molly, the dispatcher, who had on her usual tight sweater. She was a thirty-six triple D and the bra was a thirty-four B.

The men were smiling at her, as though to say, "You first."

"In your dreams," she said, and went on typing.

The story spread as only gossip in a small town could. Young Pete was constantly asked if he'd identified his trespasser yet. Asked if he needed help in looking at mug shots of possible suspects. Some wit took a photo of the found article and made it into a wanted poster.

$1000 reward for the Satin Bandit. Please call me.

One by one, every male in town had crossed out phone numbers and put his on it.

It was *that* place Olivia wanted to see. The house held no memories, except that she and Kit had thought it was beautiful. She saw the back of the house first. Three stories with a long, one-story addition to the side. They'd agreed that would be Kit's office. The idea was that he'd work there, but the truth was that neither of them could imagine being in the same house but rooms apart. They had so very much time to make up for. They'd been together for one glorious summer, then separated for decades. Too much time lost!

Quietly, slowly, she walked past the house, then looked back at the front. There were lots of different heights of roofs from all the additions that had been tacked on over the years. One tall window had a rounded top. It was said that in the 1930s that had been an artist's studio. In the '50s it had been made into a kitchen and that's the way she and Kit had left it. They hadn't wanted an island—which to the two of them was a modern concept—but a table where one could sit while the other cooked. She wasn't tempted to peek in the windows to see the restoration work.

To her right was a little round brick building. It had been used to store garden equipment, but Olivia and Kit agreed that it was too pretty for that. So far, they hadn't decided what else to use it for.

Ahead of her was the old bridge. It was weathered and splintery, but caught in the grain of the old wood were flecks of the blue paint that had once covered it. That day she and Kit had made love on the island, he said, "It should be lacquered red. Twenty coats of it." Laughing, kissing, she'd agreed with him. Lacquering the bridge red was on their list of things they planned to do.

She took her time crossing, remembering every second of that long-ago day. She'd ridden piggyback on Kit across the bridge. The island was small, created by the man who built Camden Hall. The river, deeper back then, had been widened to form a large pond in front of the house. The excavated dirt had been piled in the center, the edges reinforced with stone.

In its heyday, it must have been a fisherman's dream.

At the far end they'd found the remains of what may have been a hut, something to sit in while waiting for unsuspecting deer to come to drink.

Kit had said it was a place for lovers to meet.

At their age, all it had taken was the mention of "lovers" to get them to tear off their clothing. They'd tossed them on the ground at the far end of the island, then fell down on the mossy surface that had once been a fisherman's hut or a place for lovers to meet or the purpose Olivia liked least: a place to hang deer carcasses.

When she got to the end of the bridge, she looked around. The landscaping had changed. Years ago, it had been kept mowed and there was a path edged with little woodland flowers. Now it was just weeds and overgrown trees that darkened the place.

She raked her shoe through the grass until she saw the bits of gravel. Stepping over some stout fallen branches, she went to the far end of the island. The foundation stones of the little building were nearly covered now, but they were still there.

Bending, she touched one, smiling at the memory of that day. She could almost feel their lovemaking. Hear it. Smell it. Feel the sun coming through her clothes. Kit's strong young hands on her breasts. Her head was back, wanting more and more of him. To become one with him. Body, mind, and soul.

Suddenly, she became dizzy and had to sit down on the stones. A bit of sunlight came through the trees and she held out her hand to it.

How different! she thought. In her mind, she remembered smooth, pink skin. But the sunlight showed lines, veins, and a couple of those brown spots that no amount of sunscreen could prevent.

She snatched her hand back. Balled it into a fist and for a moment, she closed her eyes.

Over forty years, she thought. That's what she and Kit had lost.

She stepped up onto the stone foundation. On impulse, she lay down on it and looked up at the trees. On their honeymoon, Kit had talked about his diplomatic service, even about the three scary years when he'd infiltrated young Gaddafi's new regime. He told her of the months in the hospital after an armored vehicle had rolled over with him in it. His pain and rehabilitation had been excruciating.

Olivia talked of running the appliance store and how she'd opened more stores. She'd discovered that she had a knack for business.

What they didn't talk about were their marriages. They'd decided that one afternoon in Paris. They were sitting at one of the lovely outdoor cafés having coffee and Kit started telling about the birth of his son.

"When I held him in my arms, I didn't know I could feel such love. He was red faced and hairless, but I thought he was the most beautiful thing ever put on the earth. And Gina was—"

He broke off when he looked across the table at Olivia. She was smiling, but there were tears running down her cheeks. His son had not been *their* child. It hadn't been Olivia in that bed.

Kit took her hand in his and kissed the palm. "There was no one else," he said softly. "It has always been us. Together or apart, just us."

Olivia was swallowing hard, trying not to let the tears overwhelm her. They'd had full lives. They just hadn't been with each other.

Kit kissed her index finger. "What..." He kissed her second finger. "The hell..." Kissed her ring finger. "Am I going to do..." He put her little finger between his lips. "With that bloody theater?"

His question made her laugh and the tears disappeared.

It was a relative who'd brought Kit to Summer Hill in 1970, and it was another relative who brought him back many years later. Kit told her he hadn't been worried about returning and possibly seeing her. He'd thought that if he did meet her, he'd feel nothing. Surely, all those years apart, with the lives the two of them had experienced, would make that one summer seem long ago and far away. Maybe they could even laugh about it. Become friends.

But it was the opposite. Kit saw Olivia walking on the street and everything fell away.

To his eyes, she was as beautiful as she'd been when he met her.

He was afraid to approach her, afraid she'd tell him to get out of her life. And too, Kit knew himself well enough that he feared his pride might make him leave and never return.

Instead of direct confrontation, he set up a trap to lure her to him.

"Like a spider," Olivia had said later.

"Exactly," he said. "A huge and *very* hungry spider."

During the first, long-ago summer they'd spent together, Olivia had been preparing for a Broadway show. She was to play Elizabeth in *Pride and Prejudice*. She would have been on the stage that summer but there'd been a fire in the theater. While it was repaired, the play had been put on hold until the fall.

In his attempt to rewin Olivia, Kit bought an old warehouse in Summer Hill and turned it into a theater. He then set about casting the play—*Pride and Prejudice*, of course—even finagling his famous actor cousin into playing Darcy.

There were a lot of hiccups along the way, and one of the players ended up in prison, but Kit got what he wanted. He and Olivia married not long after the final performance, and that day they set out on their long honeymoon.

"Really," Kit said. "That warehouse cost me a fortune and the remodeling cost even more."

With his every word, Olivia was smiling more broadly. What sixty-plus-year-old woman had a man do all that to win her?

"Want to run it?" he asked.

"Me?" Olivia sat back in her chair. "You mean be director, producer, stage manager, and…?"

"Actress. All of it. Why not?"

"No," she said. "That's not for me." In that long-ago summer they'd spent together, she'd believed she wanted to become an actress. When she'd won the lead role, she was sure that was the beginning of her glorious career. But once she was there, all she thought about was home—and Kit. He had disappeared without a word and it had taken the heart out of her.

She looked back at him. "We'll have to find someone to take it over. Don't you have some relatives who'd like to run a little local theater?"

Kit smiled. Olivia had teased him about his huge family and he had been as glad to get away from them as she was. "I'll put out the word and see who wants the place. Maybe the town will

have a new play every few months. It could bring in some rev-
enue. Are you ready to go?"

She realized he'd done what he'd planned to and had replaced
her tears with a smile. It was why he was so good in the diplomatic world, why "the prez" called and asked his advice. "Thank
you," she said as he pulled her chair out for her.

"Anything for you." He took her arm in his.

After that day, their boundaries were set. They would never
mention the very personal things that had happened to them in
the years they'd been apart.

But still, Kit had said that he'd come to despise his ex-wife,
Gina. "Every rotten thing she screamed at me was true—and I
hated her for so clearly seeing the worst parts of me."

"When you don't love someone, everything they do is intol-
erable," Olivia replied.

"Exactly!"

That had been the extent of their discussion of his marriage
and divorce. As for Olivia's marriage, she never mentioned it
and Kit didn't ask.

She was glad of that because she didn't want to confess that
her husband had had a long-term affair. Actually, he'd had a
whole other life. What was especially humiliating was that
Olivia was sure it was *her* fault.

The year after her summer with Kit, Alan Trumbull, a re-
cent widower, had hired her to work in his family's appliance
store to answer the phone and take care of the accounts. She
saw that he was overwhelmed with a baby and a store that was
going downhill. But Olivia meant to keep to herself and not get
involved in other people's problems. She just wanted to work
hard enough that she wouldn't have the time or energy to think
about the rotten deal Life had handed her.

But after weeks of sitting quietly in the store, she broke.
Watching Alan fumble with a baby and invoices and salesmen
made her admit defeat. She couldn't continue to sit there and

do nothing. She pulled the baby from Alan and began directing his life, his business, his child, his house. As the months went by, Alan stepped back and let Olivia handle it all. He never actually proposed. He just mumbled, "I guess we better make it official," and two weeks later, they were married. Their wedding night had been quick, perfunctory. Loveless. She'd stayed in bed until Alan went to sleep, then she got up and went over the quarterly tax reports. It was either do that or spend the night crying. Night after night, she thought, *Kit, Kit. Where are you? Why did you leave me? Why was I not enough for you?*

Over the years, she'd used work and domestic duties to try to block out those questions, but her lack of help made her anger rise. Alan used to say, "You're so much better at business than I am, Livie. You don't want me holding you up." Then he'd go off to play golf.

It was only when he was dying of cancer that she found out that Alan didn't know which end of a golf club to hold. She'd sat beside him in the hospital and listened to his story of how he'd had a secret life with a quiet, plump, sweet-tempered woman named Willie. They'd had a daughter together. And it was Olivia's hard work with the appliance stores that had supported mother and daughter. There'd even been enough to send the girl to a good university.

His confession about his love for his other family had so shocked Olivia that she couldn't speak. Alan had taken her hand in his. "Please, Livie, don't be angry and punish me. Let me see them. Please."

But she hadn't been angry. She'd stood up and looked down at him. "Alan, I never knew you had such courage in you." She started to leave the room, but then turned back and kissed him on the forehead.

She would never have predicted it, but she was *glad* to find out that he'd had some joy in his life. Heaven knew *she* had never given him any. She'd fulfilled all the work and duties,

but nothing she did came near to achieving true happiness—
for him or herself.

Willie came to the hospital, her pretty daughter drove in from
Florida, and Alan's son, Kevin, put his arms around all of them.
In an instant, Olivia became the outsider.

She wanted to walk away and leave them alone, but Willie was
as incompetent as Alan was. The two of them, Alan dying and
holding on to Willie with her endless tears, looked to Olivia to
take care of everything.

And she did. Doctors, medicines, alternative treatments that
for a while gave them hope. They all fell onto Olivia.

After Alan's death, she made the funeral arrangements, and
she was the one who held Willie while she cried herself to sleep.

At the funeral, Olivia knew there would be questions about
who Willie and her daughter were. If she told the truth, all sympathy would go to the wife. Olivia was the wronged woman.
She'd given her life to Alan and his son, Kevin—and everyone
in town knew that. And what thanks did she get? Her husband
had set up housekeeping with a woman who was older, plainer,
and less intelligent than Olivia. Unappreciative bastard!

Yes, Olivia could have made people hate Alan Trumbull.
She could have played the martyr and gained lots of sympathy.

But only she knew the truth about her part in it. She decided
not to sully her husband's memory.

It was only when the will was read that Olivia got a true
shock. With the help of a prestigious law firm in Richmond,
starting the moment he knew he was dying, Alan had managed
to get everything put into his name—and he'd left the entire
business to his son. Olivia got the house that she had found and
remodeled, and she got the retirement plan that she had set up.
But everything else went to Kevin. As for Willie and her daughter, Alan had made a trust fund for them years before.

For a while, Olivia had been so angry at how he'd tricked her
into signing papers, that she was tempted to tell people about

his second family. To destroy the memory of Alan being a "nice guy" would get him back in a big way.

For the second time, she didn't do it. Alan, so very cowardly in life, had found the courage to tell Olivia what he thought of years of being on the receiving end of her managing his life. In death he'd taken away what had kept Olivia so occupied that she couldn't think about the summer of 1970—and the aftermath of it.

She turned the keys over to her stepson, then tried to occupy herself. Gardening, church work, cooking for fund-raisers. She did them all. She became the person who was asked for help whenever anything was needed.

The town considered her a saint. She'd done so much for Alan and Kevin, and now she was dedicating herself to the town. Did the woman ever think about herself? they wondered.

As for Kevin, Olivia did her best to stay out of his life. When he left the stores to run themselves, she said nothing. When he married a woman who ordered him about, Olivia felt it was her fault. It's what she had made Kevin think a wife should be.

Nor did she speak out when she saw Kevin and his wife, Hildy, spend masses. House, cars, trips, lavish wardrobes. The appliance stores faltered, then failed—and Kevin was left deeply in debt.

When Olivia sold her house, cashed in her retirement plan, and bailed her stepson out of debt, the townspeople began to speak her name in whispers. A true saint of a woman.

Olivia moved into a back bedroom of Kevin and Hildy's big house—the one Olivia had paid off—and "helped out," meaning that she more or less became their unpaid servant.

That had lasted for fourteen months, then Kit Montgomery had returned to town, put up his theater, and everything changed.

Except for the damaged lives, Olivia thought. Broken lives could never be fully healed.

Chapter Three

"HI."

Startled, Olivia sat up and saw young Elise standing a few feet away.

"I didn't mean to scare you. I was out walking and I saw a bit of yellow and..." She shrugged.

Olivia's blouse was a pale yellow, her slacks a dark brown, not bright enough to be a beacon that was easily seen through the trees. It looked like Elise had been searching for her. "Are you hiding from Ray or your husband?"

Elise smiled. "Both. Ray is stomping around, looking for something, but I can't imagine what. And..." She hesitated. "By now my family knows I'm missing. They'll be searching for me."

Olivia tried to imagine the enormity of being pursued by... What? The police? Had the girl been labeled as an escapee from a mental institution? Said to possibly be dangerous? "What will happen if they find you?"

"I don't know. Jeanne said that what they're doing is illegal, but my father paid for a wing on the clinic, so I don't think anyone will listen to me. I have no money of my own, and—"

She broke off because Olivia put her arm out to the side. Elise sat beside her on the little stone wall and let Olivia hold her.

"What did your husband do to make you so angry?"

"He loved someone else," Elise said simply. "He married me because our mothers have been best friends since college, and my father gave Kent a job and a house and…"

She was crying and Olivia guessed that she'd done a lot of that.

"I'm sorry." Elise sat up straight. "I don't mean to dump my problems on you. You're so perfect and elegant, while my life is as sordid as something on *20/20.*"

"Doesn't that show deal with murders?"

"I'm sure Kent has thought about that with me," Elise muttered. Olivia looked at her in alarm.

"I'm kidding. Kent would never kill me. If he did, Dad would probably fire him. Maybe. And if I wasn't his cover, Kent wouldn't get to screw around with Carmen. And who would he present to the world without *me*? I'm the image he wants people to see. Not the gardener's sister."

"Ah," Olivia said. "Carmen gets the passion while you get the ladies' luncheons that further your husband's career."

Elise groaned. "I'm twenty-five years old and already I'm a cliché." Olivia couldn't help laughing.

"It's not funny." Elise sniffed. "Well, maybe it is a little." She gave a bit of a smile, then buried her face in her hands. "What am I going to *do*? I don't know how to solve this."

Olivia took Elise's hands in hers and looked at her. "We're going to fix this. There are many lawyers in my husband's family and we'll set all of them on this. They'll be like wolves going after lambs. How does that sound?"

"Can I go after Carmen too? She came to my wedding. I felt so sorry for her because she kept throwing up. I knew she was pregnant, but I had no idea *my* husband was the father."

"She didn't, by chance, have a girl, did she?"

Elise's pretty eyes widened. "She did. How do you know

that?" She jerked her hands out of Olivia's grasp. "You aren't with them, are you? Did you—?"

"No," Olivia said calmly. "But it appears that you and I have some things in common. Alan, my late husband, has a daughter named Alana. She was born four years after we were married. I worked six days a week running the appliance stores that put Alana through college."

"Oh," Elise said. "I've put on dozens of dinner parties for Kent's clients. Every morning he gave me a list of things to do for him. I spent my life in a car as I ran errands for him. And it was all so he'd have more time to spend with Carmen."

"Alan told me he was playing golf. He was so passionate about the game that he went on several trips to play on fabulous courses. It wasn't until he was dying that I found out that he didn't even own a set of clubs."

Elise let out a full laugh, then leaned back on her arms. "My husband complained about how much I spent on groceries, but he was buying Escada for Carmen."

Olivia leaned back beside her. "Alan bought a vacation house for us. It was a cute little place just fifty miles away in the mountains. But every time we planned to go, he came down with some illness. I found out that his girlfriend and daughter lived there."

It was Elise's turn. "While I was locked away, my parents came to visit and I said I knew that they'd known about Carmen all along. Guess what they said?"

"I can't imagine."

"My mother said, 'Darling, Kent couldn't marry the gardener's sister, now could he? She'd probably serve tacos at a dinner party. How would Kent's career progress with a wife like that?'"

Olivia blinked at the coldness of Elise's parents and she couldn't top it. But giving sympathy might make Elise feel worse. "I don't know about you, but I love tacos."

"Me too." Elise was smiling as she sat up. "Thank you. You're making me feel better." She looked around. "What is this place?"

Maybe it was having just shared confidences, or maybe it was because Elise had called her *elegant*, but Olivia told the truth. "It's where my husband and I made mad, passionate, all-consuming love back in the summer of 1970. When the caretaker came after us with a shotgun, Kit and I climbed over the stone wall in our birthday suits and escaped."

Elise looked at her for a moment, eyes wide. "I wish I could have an adventure like that. But Kent saves everything for Carmen. I'm the one who picks up his dry cleaning."

Olivia smiled. "It *was* an adventure, and a bit dangerous. But back then, I would have followed him anywhere."

"Even past firearms." Elise sighed. "That's what I want. A man who'd brave a shotgun for me."

Olivia looked serious. "I bet if you broke into the dry cleaners at night, there'd be all kinds of guns involved."

Elise laughed. "You *are* making me feel better! You think we should go back and see if Ray is starving or not?"

"It's funny about men. They're only helpless when they're sure someone who will wait on them is nearby."

"So what's his problem?"

Olivia started to tell but thought better of it. "Let's go back and ask him."

As they started toward the bridge, they heard a car door slam, then a woman's voice.

"Kevin! I told you she wasn't here, now let's *go!*"

Instantly, Olivia stepped back into the trees, and Elise moved behind her. "Who are they?" Elise whispered.

Olivia's face fell. "My stepson and his wife. They are very, very angry at me."

"What dreadful thing did you do?"

"I got married and moved out of their house. No more free cooking and cleaning."

"I had no idea you were such a selfish person."

Olivia put her hand over her mouth to keep from laughing out loud.

"Come on, Hildy," Kevin said. "I brought a picnic basket and two bottles of wine. You know her plane gets in today and of course she'll come here. Let's wait."

"Why she'd want to give up our beautiful new home for this horrible old place, I'll never understand. Or why she married that old man."

"He's rich—you know that," Kevin said. "Olivia has always loved money. When I was a kid she was always working. If it hadn't been for having a home with Willie and Alana, I don't know how I would have survived my childhood. *They* always had time for me."

Just a few feet away, across the narrow piece of water, Olivia's whole body stiffened. This was something she hadn't heard before. She'd *had* to work. She had to support all of them. She had to—

"So who the hell does he think *paid* for that home?" There was a great deal of anger in Elise's voice. "Who gave them the time to do nothing?"

When Olivia turned to look at her in gratitude, she saw that Elise was pulling her T-shirt off over her head. "What are you doing?"

"I'm going to escape by going over that wall in my birthday suit. I *need* an adventure."

Olivia hesitated for only a second. She didn't have the beautiful body she'd once had, but she'd kept in shape. She had a wooden ski machine in her office and spent twenty minutes a day on it. Expending the pent-up energy kept her sane, and vendors were used to talking to her when she was out of breath. She unbuttoned her blouse. "I'm with you."

Under her T-shirt, Elise wore a very pretty white bra made of lace. As she unsnapped it, Olivia said, "If you leave that here,

Young Pete can add it to mine that he found so long ago. I've been told that it's in a frame and on his wall like a trophy."

With a wicked little smile, Elise dropped the bra to the ground, then removed the rest of her clothes and tossed them over her arm. She unabashedly watched Olivia undress. "My mother would kill to have a body like yours. But lying on a table and having gorgeous men run their hands over her and calling it a massage hasn't helped." She nodded toward the house. "Are they still there?"

"Oh yes," Olivia said. "But they're looking the other way. I think we can make it across the bridge without being seen." As she stood there naked, she felt silly and embarrassed, but also a bit excited. She'd had her clothes off for most of her honeymoon, but this was different. This was someone else's fantasy.

Elise picked up a stone. "What are you doing?"

"I'm going to throw it at the end of the terrace to distract them."

Olivia took the rock from her. "Let me." It had been a while since she'd thrown anything, but she'd kept her arms strong— and well, maybe Kevin's ungrateful words would help her aim.

She drew back into a pitcher's stance, leg lifted, and threw the rock. It sailed over the strip of water and hit the bottle of wine standing on the cooler. The bottle hit a rock and made a loud sound as it broke into pieces.

"Impressive!" Elise said.

"What the hell was that?" Kevin shouted as he jumped up.

"It's this horrible old house," Hildy yelled back. "It's falling down. I *told* Olivia that man was a charlatan. He's put her in this house and he's left her—just like he did before. Kevin, we *must* get her out of here. If we have to move into this place, we're going to be here when she gets back. I bet if we look hard enough we can find a key hidden somewhere. We must do whatever we have to to make her see reason."

"Is there a key?" Elise whispered.

Olivia gave a nod. "I think I've just seen the gates of hell."

"Come on," Elise said. "Race you across the bridge."

Olivia started to follow, but on impulse, she tossed her pretty blue and white satin bra through the trees. Naked, clothes over her arm, she ran after Elise, across the bridge, then took a sharp left over a shallow part of water that lapped about their bare ankles.

At the tall stone wall, Elise hesitated, unsure of how to get over. Olivia came up behind her and began throwing clothes over. The stump she'd used so many years ago was gone, but a thick tree branch hung down low and ended on the other side of the wall. Olivia jumped up, caught it, swung herself up, then looked down at Elise on the ground.

Bits of sun sparkled on their bare bodies.

"Come on." Leaning down, Olivia stretched out her arm to Elise. "Don't back out now."

Elise grabbed Olivia's arm in a grip so secure that it felt as though she'd rehearsed it, then propelled herself upward. The two women scooted across the branch.

Olivia groaned. "I do *not* want my gynecologist to see what I've just done to my nether regions."

"A gyno would be the *only* one to see my injuries."

"I don't know. Ray seems to like you."

"Bad Olivia!" Elise said as she came to the end of the branch and dropped down beside the older woman.

As soon as they were on the ground, they began running, body parts bouncing. In spite of their age difference, both of them were tall and thin, and as pretty as wood sprites.

Abruptly, Olivia grabbed Elise's arm and stopped her. Silently, she pointed. Houses had been built on the land since she and Kit had run across there.

With muffled giggles, they pulled on their clothes and, braless, they started to walk around the old stone wall to the entry gate.

"It's getting late and I'm hungry," Elise said. "Do you think part of Ray's gang membership was to be able to make a tuna casserole?"

Olivia let out a snort of laughter. "You saw that in him too? That's exactly how I saw him. I told Kit I bet that on what looks to be a very fine body he has one or more gang tattoos."

"And what did your husband say?"

"That he hoped I didn't go searching for them."

Elise laughed. "I love a man with a sense of humor."

"Let's see… You want passion and humor. What else?"

"Are men capable of more than two good traits?"

"Ooooh," Olivia said. "So cynical at such a young age."

"I have my father and my husband as role models. According to them, what makes a man is how much money he has."

"I understand that. In that case, my late husband was powerful. He had all the money I could provide."

"Now who's being cynical?"

"Truthful, my dear. I'm just being truthful."

"Anyway, when it comes to Ray, I'm allowed to say anything I want. He looks at me like I'm some brainless rich girl who's never had a problem."

"Then change his mind," Olivia said.

They had reached the main gate to the Camden Hall estate. To the left was Young Pete's small house and to their right was a three-story stone tower. Decades ago, the neighborhood kids had named it Pete's Spy Tower. Three generations of the family had watched through the open porch on the top, and it did resemble a prison guard's eyrie.

When Elise and Olivia stepped onto the property, Young Pete was standing there. His long, unsmiling face was wrinkled from a lifetime of being outside in all weather. His blue eyes were watery, but it was said that he could see a fly at a hundred yards.

As calmly as she could manage, Olivia asked how he was doing and introduced Elise. Young Pete said nothing, just gave a sort of grunt and nodded.

As the women walked toward the cottage, they suppressed their giggles. If Young Pete had seen them just a few minutes earlier...

The man's voice came to them. "Well, Olivia, I see you've been up to your old tricks."

Olivia froze in place. He was telling her that he knew what she'd done today *and* who the culprit was so long ago. She could feel her entire body turning red. Deeply embarrassed, she started running so fast that Elise had trouble keeping up with her.

In the cottage, Olivia barely let Elise inside before she slammed the door behind her.

Ray was sitting on the couch reading a trade magazine. "You two look like you've been up to no good."

Elise started to laugh, but the look on Olivia's face stopped her.

"If he knows, the whole town does," Olivia muttered. "The church, the quilting circle. Oh no! Maybe my parents knew."

Elise turned to Ray. "Do you know how to make a drink? Not one of those nasty tea-colored things on ice, but something that tastes good?"

Ray gave Elise a slow glance up and down, as though he was seeing her for the first time. When his eyes met hers, it was with a look the waitress at the diner would have loved. He was interested.

But Elise didn't budge. She glared at him.

With a nod of concession, he went to the kitchen and they heard ice tinkling. In minutes, he returned with two of those wonderful glasses that were a big triangle on top. Two olives on toothpicks were in each glass.

"Girlie enough for you?" Ray asked Elise.

She sipped hers. "Delicious. You must have had bartender experience."

Ray shook his head in disbelief. In a sentence she had taken away his years of success and put him back to going to school during the day and bartending at night. "Daddy cut your allowance off, did he? Terrified you'll have to get a job like the rest of us?"

Before Elise could speak, Olivia held out her empty glass. "Another one, please."

"I hope you two floozies don't get drunk. I've got a tuna casserole in the oven."

That was too much for the women. The drinks on an empty stomach, the memory of what they'd done, Young Pete's knowledge, and Ray's casserole made them fall on each other laughing. They could hardly stand up.

Chapter Four

BARTENDING IN A COLLEGE TOWN HAD GIVEN RAY A lot of experience with drunken females. He put his big hands on their shoulders and half pushed, half pulled them into the kitchen and set them down on the long seat that ran under the window. They were laughing and saying nonsensical things like, "Will he put the two new ones in the frame with my old one?"

"Maybe he'll have three separate display cases."

"I have a scrape on my right cheek—and I don't mean my face."

"I have a *scar* on my leg from the first time! That damned wall needs to be sandblasted so future adventurers are protected," Olivia said.

"Explain that one to a contractor," Elise said. "Oh. Wait! Carmen's brother might be able to do it. Think I could get a discount? For services rendered?" They collapsed in laughter.

Ray was shaking his head as every sentence made them go into more laughter. They were nearly hysterical with it.

Opening the oven, he pulled out the big casserole. It had been a long time since he'd cooked anything, but he'd remembered rather easily. Boil the noodles, drain, flake the cans of tuna. Add cheese. It wasn't difficult.

Behind him, the women were now on people named "Kevin" and "Hildy." Whatever had happened, he wished he'd been there to enjoy it with them. But then, if he, a male, had been there, he doubted if it would have happened. From their laughter, it sounded like one of those girl things.

He got out some plates and forks, dumped a bag of salad mix into a bowl, pulled a bottle of dressing from the fridge, and put it all on the table.

Elise was now lavishly complimenting Olivia for having hit a wine bottle with a rock. "I was aiming for that big metal planter three feet away." That made them laugh harder.

Ray poured Coke into three glasses. Maybe the caffeine would sober them up. But as he picked up the bottle he realized that he was jealous of their merriment. There wasn't anything in his life right now that came close to happiness. His wife was a wonderful woman. She kept a beautiful home. She was his boss's daughter.

If he went through with what he planned, he was going to lose it all. His wife, who was his best friend, his home, and probably his job would all disappear.

And for what? For love? Was it worth it?

He looked at the two women by the window. All he knew about the girl, Elise, was what Olivia had told him—and that seemed fairly horrifying. As for Olivia, when he'd first seen her, he'd thought her eyes looked haunted. She smiled and was gracious, but there was something else there too, as though a part of her was missing. Not complete.

He looked at the three glasses. "What the hell," he murmured, then opened a cabinet and pulled out a bottle of rum. Maybe this cottage was magical and he could get drunk enough that he could laugh as hard as they were. Too bad that experience had shown him that alcohol only made him worry more.

"Here you are, ladies." He set the drinks down. "More booze. I'll keep them coming all night if you'll tell me what you did that was so funny."

"Do you have any tattoos?" Elise asked, then laughed as Olivia shushed her.

"I'll show them to you if you tell me everything," he said in a low, sexy growl.

"Ewwww," Olivia and Elise echoed. Then they looked at each other. "I'm in," they said together.

Ray quietly smiled as they drank their rum and Cokes and decimated the huge casserole. As he listened to them, most of it told in disjointed phrases, he managed to pick up the story. It seemed that the two of them had stripped off and run across a forest together.

He wished he'd been there—not to see them naked, but to see their happiness. He deeply wished he could share it with them.

After they'd eaten all they could hold, he got up from the table, pulled it out about three feet, then held out his hands to the two women. Olivia took his hand but Elise didn't move.

Both of them had that unmistakable look of drunkenness in their eyes. "You still have your shirt on," Elise said.

"And you want it off because…?" His tone was suggestive.

"A shirtless man reminds me of the best part of home." Elise's words were a bit slurred and her eyes dreamy.

"Your husband?"

"Heavens no!" Elise said. "Carmen's brother. He works in the garden and has his shirt off rain or shine. He's prettier than the delphiniums." She took a drink. "And he's my friend."

Both Olivia and Ray were aware that Elise wasn't telling everything, but neither of them asked for more. This wasn't a time for seriousness. They all needed the great cure of laughter.

With a one-sided smile, Ray pulled his expensive knit shirt over his head and tossed it on the window seat. "Will I do?" His words were smug; he knew he looked good. He was thick and muscular, with little body fat. Four hours a week with a personal trainer kept him in very good shape.

"Turn around," Olivia said, and he obeyed.

On his upper left shoulder was a tattoo of a scorpion and the number 283. Elise put her hand over her mouth to suppress her laughter.

"Were you a member of the Scorpions?" Olivia was trying to hold in her laughter, but it was in her voice.

Turning back, Ray shook his head at them—but he was smiling. "Two snobby little girls. Can I sell you two some diamond-encrusted watches?"

"Ever the salesman," Olivia said, and she and Elise laughed some more. When Ray held out his hands to them, they took them.

"Can you ride a motorcycle?" Elise asked as she followed him into the living room.

"Like I was born on it. And no, I've never participated in a gang war. Sounds like you two have all the same questions Kathy did."

"Your wife," Elise said as she and Olivia plopped down on the couch.

Ray went into the kitchen and got a big bag of tortilla chips and a container of freshly made guacamole dip and set them on the coffee table. He was still shirtless and didn't seem inclined to re-dress. He sat in the big chair to the side. "I suggest that we each tell our favorite sex fantasy."

Olivia laughed, but Elise nearly choked on a chip.

"Come on now, you two have been teasing me ever since you came back, and this is after a day of running around like a couple of Lady Godivas. Maybe I should break into the care-taker's house. I'd like to see his trophies." He narrowed his eyes at Elise. "And yes, Miss Got-Rocks, I have broken into more than one house. And before you start trying to wheedle the rest of my story out of me, I'll tell you that after my best buddy was killed in one of our burglaries, I quit. Cold turkey. I put myself through school. Clawed my way to the top. Married the boss's daughter—who I now want to divorce. You have any more questions?"

Elise looked at Olivia. "Not me. You?"

"None. I've had a recurring dream." She looked at Ray. "I'm back to the sex fantasy idea. That is, if you can imagine an old woman like me involved in sex."

"Olivia," Ray said slowly, "I can imagine you doing acrobatics naked."

She gave a little smile. "I am a bit limber."

"Should I leave the room for you two?" Elise asked, half-serious.

"Naw," Ray said. "Jeanne told me Livie's husband had single-handedly brought down governments. I don't think I'll risk it."

"I can tell you that I like flirting better than young men asking me if I need help carrying a bag of groceries." Olivia took a breath. "Okay, back to fantasies. It's a very simple dream, but since it's appeared off and on for about four years now, I sometimes think it's a premonition. I'm in bed—"

"Great start," Ray said.

"Be quiet, Mr. Scorpion." Elise leaned back on a pillow and looked at Olivia. "What did you do in bed?"

"I woke up to several men kissing me."

"That's all?" Ray asked.

"They have different colors of skin. Black, brown, red... I'm not sure. Maybe blue. I had some very pleasant thoughts about those blue men from that movie. Anyway, the actual color isn't important, but there is a contrast." Leaning back, she said nothing else.

Ray spoke first. "What happens after the kissing?"

"I don't know. There was never a dream sequel, but I would expect that there is a lot more kissing." She looked at Elise. "What about you?"

"I hope it's better than the first one," Ray muttered.

Elise took so much time in replying that Ray went to the kitchen to get rum, Cokes, and ice, and refilled glasses. Within seconds, the women were again smiling.

"After I was married," Elise said, "I spent a lot of time thinking about my wedding day. I had so many thoughts about it, that I even, uh… I…"

"Come on," Ray said, "out with it."

"I rehearsed my fantasy."

"So now you must tell us," Olivia said.

"My wedding dress cost $48,781.82." She waited until they'd lowered their eyebrows. "It was a ghastly thing. My mother seemed to think I was so bland that if I didn't have a dress big enough to use for a tent, no one would actually *see* me. It was heavy and awkward. I could barely walk in the thing. But what I could do was spread my legs under it and no one could see me."

Olivia and Ray had equally wide eyes.

"No, no, not like that," Elise said. "My mother never knew it but I wore a pair of white yoga pants underneath that hideous dress. It was just defiance on my part and nothing came of it, but as I stood at the altar, those pants made me feel that a little of myself was there. But anyway, after I was married, I was so…disappointed, I guess, that I became obsessed with the idea of 'What if it hadn't happened?' I thought of awful things, like car wrecks, and tornadoes that took Kent away, and even once I thought 'What if I had said no?' That was the scariest idea I could imagine."

She took a swallow of her drink. "Somewhere in there I began to fantasize about what could have happened. I imagined that just before I was to say 'I do' to Kent, a man would ride a black horse down the aisle of the church. Of course, everyone would be stunned into silence—me included. When he got to the altar, he'd put his hand down to me. He wouldn't say anything, but I'd know what he meant. I'd grab his arm and vault onto the horse behind him and we'd gallop out of the church."

"Then what?" Ray asked.

"I'd like to think that we'd go somewhere and have sex like I see in the movies. Not what Kent and I did for eleven minutes every other week, but real sex, the kind that raises a sweat."

"Hear! Hear!" Olivia said.

Ray smiled. "How did you rehearse *that* part?"

"I didn't dare practice the sex, if that's what you mean, but I did say that I wanted to take riding lessons. Kent's mother had ridden as a girl so that meant it was okay for me to do it. Whatever Mummy did was the height of perfection and therefore allowable for me to do."

As she took a deep drink of her rum and Coke, Ray and Olivia were silent as they waited for more of her story. It felt as though she was leaving something out.

"So I started riding lessons and it was weeks before I got up the courage to tell my trainer that I wanted to learn how to leap up behind a man. He agreed instantly. I think he was bored teaching rich girls how to stroll through a park on a horse. For weeks we rehearsed.

"He'd ride up to me, then lean down. I'd grab his arm as high up as I could, put my foot in the stirrup, and leap. It was a really hard thing to do but I managed it. Maybe it was silly, but it made me feel, well…prepared."

"For when a naked woman bent down from atop a tree branch and held out her arm to you?" Ray asked. When the women looked at him in surprise, he said, "I listen. I have to so I can sell things to people."

At the memory of her day's adventure, the sad look left Elise's pretty face and she smiled. "Exactly! If I hadn't rehearsed I couldn't have swung up, and that old man might have hit us with a shotgun."

"You presaved our lives," Olivia said and the two women started laughing again.

Ray's groan halted them. "I hope you women are aware that neither of your little daydreams has to do with sex. A *sex* fantasy involves tongues on flesh and being tied to a bed and orifices and—" He broke off because they were looking at him with great interest. "I think you two want *romantic* fantasies."

Olivia and Elise looked at each other, then back at Ray. "No, we'll take the sex," Olivia said.

"I agree," Elise said. "Tell us about the sex. Do bad boys… you know…do things in different ways?"

"No," Ray said. "We don't." He was grinning. "Bad boy. No one's thought of me like that in a long time. I think all the suits I have to wear rub the edge off a man."

"True. You look like a stockbroker now." Elise was smiling at the naked upper half of his body.

"If I didn't think I'd break a little thing like you in half, I'd demonstrate what I know. I could—"

Olivia cut him off. "I think you have enough problems with two women in your life. Tell us your sex fantasy—unless it involves your wife and your mistress together. That's too close to home for me to be able to stand."

"No worries," Ray said. "Kathy and I don't… Anyway, as for the sex fantasy, get your mothers to buy you a book. My *romantic* fantasy is to be myself around a woman. Not an image but the real me. And she still likes me as I am."

Olivia sighed. "Unfortunately, I know exactly what you mean. My late husband never really *liked* me."

"After all you did for him?" Elise said.

"I think maybe it was because of all I did for him."

Ray refilled their glasses. "Now don't go getting maudlin on me. Drink more rum and eat more guacamole. There's ice cream in the freezer. Want some?"

"How did you meet your wife?"

"I guess you'd say it was through my overwhelming ambition."

"Because her father owned the company where you worked?" Elise's voice was hard.

"No. Not that. I could learn about the business, but Kathy knew things I didn't." He smiled at the looks of interest on the women's faces. "Three forks on a table, that sort of thing."

Elise grimaced. "I put on dinner parties with four forks. Kent's family loves to impress people."

"Kathy knows all that. She's really great. She and her mom lived in a big place in Connecticut, but her dad mostly stayed in his apartment in town. Considering Bert Cormac's temper, we all understood."

He took a breath. "I knew Kathy had a sort of crush on me—she was always hanging around my office—but I was afraid that underneath that outward sweetness she might be like her father. Bert in a dress? No thanks! So anyway, I didn't actually think about her as wife material until the annual office party. Black tie, lots of clients."

"Clients of what?" Olivia asked.

"Advertising. We have some big accounts. Whatever is said about Cormac, he's one of the best. Anyway, that night I was supposed to be out of town, but Bert wanted me at the party so I flew back—and I had only hours to come up with a date. I had an old girlfriend, Dolores, who I'd known most of my life, so I called her."

Ray lifted his hand. "Big mistake. She was out of her element. She got drunk, then spilled a drink on Kathy, and said some awful things to her. I tried to get her to shut up, but I wasn't fast enough. But then, it turned out that Kathy could handle herself."

"What happened?" Olivia asked.

"As I said, before that night, I'd never paid much attention to her. She has a really pretty face but she's a bit... What's that German word? *Zaftig*, that's it. Not my taste and besides, she was so overwhelmed by her father that I thought she had the personality of a wet noodle."

He smiled in memory. "But that night she surprised me. I swear she was about to laugh at the awful things Dolores said. *Laugh!* Then Kathy put her arm around Dolores and walked out of the room with her. I was truly impressed. Now *that's* class, I thought."

He shrugged. "But later, I saw Kathy crying. Not a lot, but just enough that I knew what Dolores said had hurt her feelings. We talked for hours that night and that's when I began to think maybe we could help each other."

"And now you want someone else." It was easy to see that Elise was thinking of her own marriage.

Olivia was sipping her drink and looking at Ray. "My guess is that you've found a woman who is more like you. Or what you grew up with."

"Dr. Jeanne's going to lose her job," he said. "You girls mind if I...?" He waved his hand over his bare chest. He didn't wait for an answer, but got up and went into the kitchen to get his shirt, put it back on, then poured himself a glass of straight Scotch. He took the bottle into the living room.

Olivia said, "You mentioned a man whose death changed your life. Does your big decision have anything to do with him?"

Ray finished his drink and poured himself another one. "Yes. Everything to do with it. That was Carl. Rita—the woman I fell for—is his little sister."

"Tell us your whole life story," Elise said. "Take our minds off our own problems."

Chuckling, Ray leaned back in his chair. "I grew up in a rough neighborhood in Brooklyn. No dad, a saint of a mother who did the best she could at two jobs, but I was alone a lot. From the second grade, Carl Morales and I were best friends. We were taller and bigger than all the other kids." He sipped his drink. "When you stand a head taller and twenty pounds heavier than the other kids, you can go either of two ways."

"Be a bully or...?" Olivia asked.

"A savior. A protector. Carl and I saw ourselves as kings and it was our job to watch over our subjects."

"With that philosophy, how did you get into a gang?" Elise's voice was disparaging.

"We were big, not smart," Ray said. "Actually, that's not true. I've always been smart, just not very wise. And I was ambitious. Carl was my follower. Wherever I led, he went with me. By the time I was twelve, my goal in life was to become the ruler of the Scorpions. I thought that was the highest a person could reach. Carl and I quit school at fifteen and joined the gang. Then we spent three years showing them we were the best."

"By robbing houses," Olivia said.

"That and a lot of other crimes. Grand Theft Auto, B and E, all of it. We got to be so good that we became careless. When we were barely eighteen, the owner of a house had a gun and..." He stopped for a moment. "Carl threw himself in front of me and he died for it."

Ray closed his eyes for a moment. "I'd never imagined my life without him. We were rarely apart, had no secrets. We were..." He took a breath. "He left behind a mother and a little sister. At Carl's funeral his mother told me her son's death was my fault, that Carl didn't have the brains to get into trouble on his own. She said, 'You had a choice. You could have led him to *do* something with his life, but you chose to teach him how to be a criminal.'"

Ray put his drink on the coffee table. "She was right. Carl had turned his life over to me and I'd led him the wrong way. The next day I got out. I had to smack a few noses to make my point but I did it. I got a job as a mechanic, earned my GED, college—" He shrugged. "A professor said I was an inch away from being a con man so I should take advantage of my talent and go into sales. I did."

They were silent for a while, then Olivia said, "And Rita was the little sister."

Ray grinned. "Yeah. From the day of the funeral, I sent money to Carl's mother. I sent everything I could afford and the amount increased as I did better. She never thanked me, never even acknowledged me, but the checks were cashed."

He sighed. "His mom never came close to forgiving me, but Rita grew up and went to a community college. When she got out, you'll never believe what her mother did."

"Sent her to you for a job?" Olivia asked.

"Close, but no. She sent Rita to Kathy. I think she knew that I wouldn't hire the kid. She brought back too many memories and too much guilt. But Kathy didn't know any of that. She just heard a sad story so she gave Rita the job as my assistant."

"Your *wife* hired her?" Elise asked. "I never did anything for Kent's work."

Ray shrugged. "Kathy's a better judge than the employment department. She helped me with a lot of things."

Both women waited for him to elaborate but he didn't. "Did she know about you and Carl?" Elise asked.

"No," Ray said. "I never wanted someone as sweet and innocent as Kathy to know about my sordid past. When she asked me questions about my childhood, I'd play a romantic Bad Boy part. I'd tell her about motorcycles and black leather jackets, that kind of thing. I didn't tell her about breaking windows and stealing kids' Xboxes."

"What happened after Kathy hired Rita?" Olivia asked.

"I hadn't seen her since she was a child, but I instantly knew who she was. She and Carl had different fathers, but they both had their mother's eyes, a weird blue-green that could turn to ice. Carl could freeze a person with those eyes."

"And you fell in love with her," Olivia said.

"Not at first. I was so angry that she'd been hired that I had it out with Kathy. Every time my assistant would get good, my wife would step in and help her move to another job. It used to make me crazy! I knew Kathy was jealous, but I swore to her there was no reason to be. At one point, I wanted to ban her from the office, but since her dad owned the place, I couldn't very well do that. And besides, Kathy was my sounding board for every idea I had. When it comes to business, she and I are partners.

"Anyway, I was so angry that at first all Rita and I did was argue. The only thing she shared with her brother was his eyes. She wasn't a follower like him. Rita was bossy and ambitious and kept telling me I was stupid and wrong."

Olivia laughed. "True love if I ever heard it."

"Yeah." Ray's voice sounded faraway. "It was. It is. Rita and I share it all. With Kathy, I had to learn everything. Nothing was natural. Meals, clothes, teeth brushing. Everything we did was different from each other and we had to figure out how to mesh. But Rita and I are alike. It's all *easy*. I know what she wants for dinner, for her birthday. I know how to *please* her. Does that make sense? I love Kathy, but I don't think I've ever done anything that genuinely pleased her."

Olivia spoke up. "You said—and I quote—'Kathy and I don't...' You didn't finish that sentence, but I assume that meant sex." She waited for his curt nod. "What about you and Rita?"

Ray hesitated.

"Go on," Elise urged. "Tell us the truth. No secrets and no judgments."

"It's not something I'm proud of, but yeah, there was a lot of sex."

Elise looked at him with wide eyes. "Walls? Tables?"

Ray's eyes sparkled. "We used the big oak desk in my office so much that it got wobbly. Is that what *you* want?"

"Perhaps," she said cautiously. "It would be— Oh hell. Yes!

It's exactly what I want. Kent treats me so delicately that I want to scream. I'm willing to bet he doesn't do that to Carmen."

Olivia was beginning to sober up and she looked at Ray. "Did you ever think that that passion is what Kathy would like to have?"

Ray gave her an intense stare. "Everyone talks about the unfairness between the sexes, but in this area the women win. A woman can fake it, but if a man has no desire, he can't perform. I truly love my wife, but I have as much sexual desire for her as I did for Carl."

"Poor woman," Olivia whispered. "I've been her."

"So have I!" Elise said.

"Look, I can tell you guys are on her side, and you're right. Kathy is wonderful and she deserves only the best. Her father bullies her mercilessly, and she cowers in front of him. If I left her, she'd be at his mercy. It's hard for me to think of doing that. The problem is that for the first time in my life, I'm in love with someone. Deeply in love, and I went to Dr. Hightower to help me figure out what to do. Should I leave Kathy and watch her come apart?" He looked at them as though begging them to throw him a life preserver.

But neither Olivia nor Elise knew what to say. Elise stood up. "I don't know about anyone else, but I need to go to bed. This day has been all that I can handle."

Hesitating, Olivia looked at Ray. If she stayed up, she knew they'd talk more and she couldn't deal with that. The dreaded question of "What do you think I should do?" was going to be impossible to answer. Part of her identified with Ray being married to someone he couldn't love as anything other than a friend. But part of her also went with Kathy. His wife was in a passionless marriage. Is that why she'd dedicated her life to her husband? To try to make him want her as much as he did the hometown Rita?

If that was so, when Kathy found out she'd failed, there was going to be a lot of anger released. If she was anything like her formidable father, that could be very bad.

Olivia stood up beside Elise. "Me too. I'll see you in the morning."

"Cowards," she heard Ray say under his breath.

Olivia gave a little smile, but she didn't turn back.

Ray sat alone for a while, sipping his whiskey, then he reached into his pocket for his phone and turned it on. There were eight emails from Kathy. He knew from experience that that many meant something bad. It was either an accident or death—or more likely, Bert Cormac was throwing one of his legendary fits and he was sure that only Ray could fix whatever the problem was.

He skipped the earlier emails and looked at Kathy's latest one.

I SHOULD BE THERE BY SEVEN A.M. I HAVE EVERYTHING YOU'LL NEED WITH ME, INCLUDING YOUR PLANE TICKET AND PASSPORT. BE PACKED AND READY TO LEAVE. CAL TALKED DAD OUT OF GOING WITH YOU. YOU OWE HIM AN AUSSIE HAT.

"Damn!" Ray muttered. Australia meant the Hanberg account. It was a really big one, and if Cal had talked Bert out of handling it himself, Ray owed the man more than a hat. The older Bert Cormac got, the harder he was to deal with. For the last few years, his bad temper came to the surface within seconds. If he went to Australia, the account was as good as lost.

I'LL BE READY, Ray emailed back.

When he went to his bedroom, he thought about packing his bag, but he didn't. He knew Kathy would do it for him. As he headed to the shower, he thought how Rita would *never* pack a suitcase for him. She'd say, "So now I look like your maid?

You want me to put on a little uniform? Something short and cute? Hold your breath."

Just the thought of her smart mouth made him miss her. When he got out of the shower, he called her, and they had a lively bout of phone sex.

For his wife, he didn't read the rest of her emails, didn't thank her for making the arrangements, or for all she'd done to save the account. But then, it was the kind of thing Kathy always did for him. He no longer even noticed.

Chapter Five

OLIVIA AWOKE EARLY AND LAY IN BED LISTENING TO the silence of the house. She and Kit were going to be living just a few yards away, past the big Camden Hall, at the River House. She wondered what would have happened if they had stayed together after their summer in 1970.

Would they have retired to that house? Even to this town? Or would they have chosen somewhere they'd seen on Kit's world travels? Would they have said something like, "I loved the island of Moorea. Why don't we settle there?"

Yet again, she had questions she couldn't answer. Kit said that places didn't matter, that only people did. She knew he meant that they could live anywhere and they'd be happy as long as they were together. But she also knew how much family meant to him.

Last night she'd called her husband. He sounded tired and although he didn't say so, she guessed that he hadn't slept in a while. She'd tried to cheer him up with an amusing story of the rivalry between Ray and Elise, but she didn't burden her new husband with the more serious aspects of it all. She left out Ray's poor wife, Kathy, and what was coming for her, and Elise's fear of the future. Nor did Olivia tell him about Kevin and Hildy saying they were staying in River House. Kit's temper was fierce enough that he might send the sheriff.

No, she wasn't going to put more on him than the US government was already doing.

However, when he said he would have someone look into Elise's predicament, she was grateful.

Between Olivia's silence and the secrecy that came with Kit's job, they didn't have much to talk about. After they said good-bye, she knew that after she went to bed, Kit would go back to work.

Olivia got up, dressed, and left the room. Elise's door was shut and Olivia wondered if it was bolted from the inside. She tiptoed down the stairs, glanced at Ray's closed door, then went outside. The morning was cool and the air smelled good.

It was a bit odd to be inside an area that was fully enclosed by a tall stone wall. Across the entranceway, she could see Pete's Tower. It seemed to be empty, but he was sneaky enough to be hiding and watching.

When she remembered that he'd let her know he'd almost caught them so many years ago, she again started to blush. But she stopped herself. Yesterday had been such an extraordinary day! Sliding bare bottomed across the tree branch, scraping her skin on the stone wall, running through a forest naked. Who did those things at her age?

People who'd missed out in their youth, she thought. From the moment she'd walked into Trumbull Appliances so many years ago, it was as though her life had not been her own. Taking care of Alan's son and trying to figure out how to revamp an old appliance store had taken all her time. And she'd had to look after Alan. He was one of those men who never remembered where he'd put things, who forgot where he was supposed to be when. Olivia had become a human calendar.

And Kevin was just like his father. He had to be checked for homework, reminded of what was due when. She'd tried leaving it up to him, but Kevin's tears at not being allowed to go on a field trip because he'd forgotten to get the permission slip signed had broken her. In frustration, Olivia had given a huge discount on a major appliance to Kevin's teacher in exchange for being told directly about her stepson's assignments. The next year she did the same thing. She'd heard that at the end of each school term the teachers drew papers out of a bowl. All but one was blank and it had Kevin's name on it. The winner got her stepson, a quiet, rather lazy little boy, and the appliance of their choice from the store.

Olivia never tried to find out if that was true or not.

She walked on the dew-damp grass, trying to stay out of sight of the tower in case Young Pete was up there.

What she'd overheard Kevin say yesterday had hurt more than she wanted to admit.

Parents often made jokes about how ungrateful children were, but Kevin's statement that Olivia had always "loved money," had even married for it, hurt deeply. And it was very unfair!

It had been Alan who'd come up with the idea of opening more appliance stores. Olivia had said that they couldn't compete with the big national franchises. And besides, how could she work more than she did?

But Alan said he would run the new stores. He'd reminded her that it was his family who had started Trumbull Appliances. "It's in my blood," he said.

And of course Alan was backed up by his mother. She believed her only child could do anything.

Olivia had done the work to start the first of the new stores, telling herself that Alan would soon be helping. But just after the store opened, Alan said he'd hurt his back while unloading a truck full of Wolf ranges. He said that as soon as he got well, he'd go back to work. He never got well enough to help with the stores. But his mother did. Together, she and Olivia ran the business.

Six months after the grand opening of the first new store, Alan bought a place in the mountains that he said was for him and Olivia. But she only went there once.

She shook her head to clear it. Why had she put up with it all? she wondered. Why hadn't she...? But the truth was that these questions only came from hindsight. She didn't like what it said about her, but she'd had no idea that Alan and Kevin were so very unhappy.

While it was true that she and Alan had never had much of a sex life, she hadn't minded. She'd never felt that raw passion for him that she'd had with Kit, so she didn't hunger for it.

Maybe she had been too harsh with Kevin. She was always trying to teach him to...to... What? Be less like his father? To not always depend on others to get him out of messes?

Olivia couldn't help giving a snort at that thought. Like his father, Kevin landed on his feet. He'd married Hildy, a woman who made all their decisions. When the two of them were nearly bankrupt, Olivia had bailed them out. Thanks to her, they'd not lost so much as a teacup. Today, they still had their huge house, two cars and a pickup, their twice-yearly vacations, the country club membership, et cetera.

She knew that now they were again racking up bills, but she had no more money. Did they think that next time they got in debt that Kit would save them? She dreaded when that show-down came. The anger on both sides would—

Olivia broke off her ugly thoughts because Elise was sitting on an old bench behind Camden Hall and smiling at her. She looked so young and so fragilely beautiful that Olivia stopped frowning and smiled back. "Hungover?" she asked as she sat down beside her.

"No, I'm not. I think Ray's story of his friend's death sobered me up. And also, what he said about his wife was too much for me."

"Poor Kathy," Olivia said.

"Exactly. She sounds like a great wife. She takes care of him, helps with his work, but there's no sex between them. He 'can't' do it."

"Not with Kathy anyway, but for Rita he's damaged the big oak desk." Olivia sighed. "How I remember those days."

"And how I wish I had them to remember."

"So who's the Adonis of the Delphiniums?" Olivia asked.

"What do you mean?" Elise's fair skin blushed almost purple.

"You're going to keep this from me? After what we've shared?"

"Okay, so maybe there is a guy who…I've spent some time with. Kent knows Carmen because her older brother takes care of our big shared gardens." When Olivia looked puzzled, she explained. "My parents and Kent's live next door to each other, and he and I have a house in the back."

"That sounds dreadful!"

"You have no idea. I have no privacy. Anyway, Carmen does the bookkeeping and runs errands, whatever, for her brother's landscaping service. They do the gardens for a lot of our neighborhood."

"And that's the brother who you, uh…?"

"Heavens no! Diego has three kids. It's the younger brother, Alejandro, who I got to know. He's…well, he's rather nice looking."

Olivia looked at her. Elise's face had faded to a lovely shade of pink. "Drop-dead gorgeous, is he?"

Elise gave a great sigh. "Black hair and dark eyes. Skin like honey and a body… Not that I've looked, mind you."

"I see. What binoculars do you use?"

"The kind made for watching eagles from a mile away. I could identify any three square inches of his bare upper body. I could pick out his jeans-clad lower half by centimeters."

"And was your interest returned?"

"Let's just say that I spent a lot of last summer in a rather small red bikini."

Olivia raised an eyebrow.

"Don't look at me like that! I've never broken my marriage vows. Alejandro and I are friends. He helped me with my Spanish, and we planted a garden together." As she spoke, she didn't look at Olivia. "Anyway, it's his sister, Carmen, who is the love of my husband's life. It's hard to imagine now, after all I've learned, but a few weeks ago, I asked Kent to bawl her out on my behalf."

Olivia looked at her in question.

"Carmen pushed a huge flowerpot off a low wall and it almost landed on my foot. If the thing had hit me, it would have broken bones. When I told Kent about it, he said it was my imagination and that Carmen certainly hadn't done it on purpose." Elise's voice was rising in anger.

"Unwed mothers can be vicious to their lovers' wives. There should be laws."

A bit of a laugh escaped Elise. "I'm going to have to deal with all this soon and I want you with me."

Olivia took her arm. "Of course. I'll be there and I'll bring a garden truck full of my husband's lawyer relatives."

"That sounds perfect. Mind if Alejandro drives?"

"With or without his shirt on?"

"Interesting question since I've rarely seen him in a shirt. When we went to the nurseries together and that last night..." Her head came up. "I don't think he owns many shirts."

"You could buy some for him."

"That would be like putting a cover over the statue of David. Repainting the Sistine Chapel. Covering —"

Laughing, Olivia said, "I get it."

They sat in silence for a moment, enjoying their camaraderie.

"You came to see if your stepson and his wife are still here, didn't you?"

"Yes." Their air of merriment was gone.

"They are," Elise said. "I couldn't sleep so I came out before daylight and I peeked. They're inside the house. I should call the sheriff." But they both knew she wouldn't. Olivia would be exposed and probably, so would Elise. It was too much to risk.

There was something in her tone that made Olivia take her hand and squeeze it. "What woke you?" she asked softly.

"I thought I heard a car door slam. I tried to go back to sleep but I envisioned men in white coats surrounding the place. The longer I lay there, the more vivid my images became." She shrugged. "I gave up."

"Last night my husband said he'd have someone look into what's going on. And he'll find out if Jeanne is in trouble."

"Is she in hiding?"

"I don't know. I wish…"

"That all this hadn't happened?" Elise said. "Me too. I lie awake and wonder why I didn't see it coming. I was always so in love with Kent. He's so tall and handsome and I was the scrawny kid who lived next door. When I was about twelve, he was playing football with his friends, and as always, I was hiding in the bushes and watching. The ball hit me in the chest so hard I nearly passed out, but when Kent asked me if I was okay, I said I was fine. My whole chest turned black and blue, but that was okay because Kent had actually *looked* at me."

"And you thought things would change after you married him."

"I did. I believed that I'd become the center of his attention. We got married, just as our parents wanted us to, but I was still the kid hiding in the bushes." She sighed. "Your kitchen is nice."

Olivia looked at her.

"I saw it when I looked in the window. My mother chose my kitchen. It has black cabinets."

"I prefer white," Olivia said.

"Me too."

"Did you see anything else in the house? Hear anything? But I think it's too early for Hildy to be up."

"Actually, I spied because I heard loud voices from inside. They were having a heated discussion about the papers on the table. It was checkbooks and bills, that sort of thing."

Olivia groaned. "Oh no. They *are* having money problems. I was afraid of that. I told Hildy I'd take over balancing the checkbook, but she said no. That made me suspicious. She never stepped away from someone else doing her work."

"I think they plan to stay in your house until you get back."

"I'm sure they do. Hildy called me as soon as Kit and I got back to the US, and I stupidly told her he had to go to DC so I'd be returning alone. I even told them when I'd be arriving. But then Jeanne called Kit and I returned a day earlier."

"So they know you'll be here alone without your husband?"

Olivia nodded. "They're probably practicing the tears they're going shed. Kevin used them on me as a kid. I've told them a dozen times that I have no more money."

"But your husband does."

"Yes," Olivia said. "But I don't want to start off our married life with an ugly scene with my relatives. If the two of them would just stop spending so much there wouldn't be any problems. An interior designer doesn't need to be hired to put up the blasted Christmas tree! And a fourth fur coat isn't really necessary. If—" She broke off at the unmistakable sound of a car door closing.

A look of such fear came onto Elise's pretty face that Olivia's heart seemed to lurch. "It could be someone else."

"This early in the morning?"

"We'll climb Pete's Tower and see who it is. And if Young Pete is already there we'll throw him over the side."

The two of them took off running, going on the far side of Camden Hall to reach the tower that stood guard by the front gate.

Elise bounded up the stairs like a young colt, while Olivia followed.

At the top, Elise looked down the stairs. "You are never going to believe this!"

"What is it?" Olivia stepped onto the open platform. They could clearly see the cute little summerhouse. In front of it was a black town car, the kind that came with a driver. Ray was standing by the back door talking to a woman. Even from this distance they could see that she was very pretty, with lots of red-blonde hair, and she was round and curvy. Not at all fashionably thin.

At the back of the car, the driver was putting Ray's big leather suitcase in the trunk and taking out a couple of bags that had an elegant brown on brown design.

"I'll bet that's Kathy," Olivia said.

"If those are her cases, why's the driver taking them out of the car?"

"Maybe she's going to drive his car back to New York."

"Then why doesn't she drive him to the airport?" Elise asked.

Olivia shrugged and they watched Ray set his wife's suitcases inside the house.

"She's staying." There was anger in Olivia's voice. "He's leaving that poor woman with *us*. How are we going to look at her without pity? She's going to know something is up. We can't hold in this huge secret."

Elise narrowed her eyes. "He wants *us* to tell her. That SOB thinks he's won us over, and now he's giving us the job of telling her that her cheating husband wants to dump her."

"There's a gate on the other side of the pool. We can head him off on the street." Olivia was the first one down the stairs and she almost outran Elise's young legs.

The side gate was hidden by azalea bushes, but Olivia knew

where it was. When the swimming pool had been put in years before, an exit had been cut into the wall.

Both women had to pull on the old door to get it open and when they heard the crunch of the car on the gravel drive, they became frantic. They burst through just as Ray's car rounded the corner.

Elise leaped into the road in front of the vehicle, making the driver slam on the brakes.

The driver threw open the door. "What the hell do you think you're doing? I almost hit you!"

When Olivia tapped on the back window, Ray lowered the glass.

"Olivia." His voice happy. "I left you a note. I have to go to Australia. If I don't, Bert will and we'll lose the account. Listen, it was *great* meeting you two. You'll have to come to dinner someday, but right now I have a plane to catch."

Elise had come around the side and she shot her hand through the window to grab him by his necktie. Ray seemed quite amused by her action. "You left your wife with us!"

"I did. Kathy wanted to stay and I didn't think you'd mind. You'll be three ladies together and you can do lots of complaining about us men."

Elise yanked on his tie. "You expect *us* to tell her, don't you?"

"No." His face was serious as he removed Elise's hand. "I don't want you to say anything. Just let her have a good time. Make her laugh. Take her out shopping." He looked at Olivia. "Does this town have any stores? I know, take her to Richmond and you two can buy yourselves some things. My treat. Now I really do have to go." He nodded to the driver.

"We can't—" Elise began, but Ray was putting up the window and she jerked her arm back.

He waved to them, then he was gone.

As they went back through the gate, Elise looked at Olivia.

"If I call my father, he'll send men in white coats to get me. I'd almost rather do that than face Ray's wife. What about you?"

"I could go listen to Kevin and Hildy cry poverty. Hey! I could write them a check. It would be days before they were told it was insufficient funds."

"That might make them so angry that they'd have you jailed."

"I know the sheriff. He'd protect me. I have to consider that. What's your decision?"

"Well… I could use some new clothes. I only have what Jeanne and I bought."

"I bet we could run up a whopper of a bill on Ray's card."

"But is it worth it? Kathy's unhappiness versus Armani." Elise's hands were like a balance scale.

They sat back down on the bench.

"This isn't going to be pleasant," Olivia said.

"You're an actress so you can pretend, but everything I feel shows on my face. Truthfully, I don't think we should leave these grounds. Someone will see you and tell that you're here. And for all I know, my so-called family has put me on CNN. Catch the crazy woman. I'll be turned in for a reward."

Olivia looked around the place with its high walls. What had seemed like a sanctuary suddenly felt like a prison. "All right, here's what we're going to do. We are going to be nice to Ray's poor wife. This may be her last time of peace before her life falls apart. Think how you felt when you heard about Kent and Carmen."

"Murderous." Olivia gave her a sharp look. "But not to myself."

"I know. Okay. Deep breath. Calm nerves. Let's smile and be as nice as we can be, but let's not even hint that anything is wrong. That poor, poor woman."

"Agreed," Elise said and they started back to the summerhouse.

Chapter Six

KATHY HAD NEVER FELT SO EXCLUDED IN HER LIFE. All morning she'd done her best to befriend the women Ray had told her were truly wonderful. "They're very funny," Ray said. "And we talked for hours. I told them some very private things. Those women got more out of me than Dr. Hightower ever did."

Kathy hadn't commented on that because he'd kept his visits to Jeanne Hightower so secret that she'd come to resent the woman. What was he talking to her about? Kathy had her hopes, but she wouldn't be sure until he told her.

But these women! What about them had made Ray say they were so easy to talk to? She could hardly get more than ten words out of them. She'd tried to get them to leave the house and go into Summer Hill with her, but she hadn't succeeded.

She couldn't help but wonder if the problem was her weight. Both of them were so skinny that at any moment Kathy expected them to "suggest"—in that superior tone skinnies had perfected—that if she ate "healthy" she would, you know, lose weight. They probably thought she ate doughnuts four times a day.

This would, of course, be followed by their suggestion that she exercise, as though she sat around all day eating bonbons. Skinnies always believed they knew the answer to every weight problem. Eat less; move more. In their minds, it was oh so simple.

All this would be said while the skinnies were eating and eating, then eating some more.

And their idea of exercise was three leg lifts and a brisk walk to their car. Kathy's favorite suggestion was that she park her car far from the store and walk. Her reply was a deadpan "Should I give up my daily three-mile jog to do this?"

Kathy had three personal trainers, one for boxing (guaranteed to make a person lose weight, ha!), one for HIIT—high intensity interval training—that had her pushing a steel sled full of forty-five-pound plates, and one for yoga (Kathy could bend over and slap her hands on the floor).

As for food, she gained on Weight Watchers, barely maintained on twelve hundred calories a day, and never lost no matter how much she moved, lifted, or stretched. Or how little she ate. Whenever a skinny followed Kathy around for a day, she'd sit down and say, "I have to have something to eat or I'm going to pass out." Kathy was then supposed to feel sympathy for her thirty-six-inch butt.

But these women barely spoke. When they did, it was impersonal. Politely, kindly, Olivia told her the history of the estate. Elise told about River House, where Olivia was to live with her new husband, and how there was a pretty little island in front of it.

Kathy didn't miss the fact that during this last bit the two of them were twitching with some shared secret about the island. They did *not* share it with her.

Olivia chatted about gardening and church, and told of a play the town had put on last summer. Elise said that in the last year she had become very interested in gardening. In fact, she'd spent hours each day just watching the plants.

Again, there were the little smiles of secrets shared. And again, Kathy was excluded. Right now the skinnies were sitting in the living room, each with a book, and silent.

Suddenly, the thought came to her that maybe the problem could be with whatever Ray had told them.

That idea nearly made her heart stop. Had he told them—please no!—about their nonexistent sex life? How women everywhere came on to him? Kathy had seen and heard a thousand versions of *What's a gorgeous guy like you doing with a fatty like her?*

What could her reply be to that endless question? My father owns the company where Ray works? Perfect. That would make it clear that a hunk like Ray wasn't passionate about a chunk like her.

What could Ray have told them? It had been odd that he'd said he was going to Virginia by himself. He liked people around him. After Ray left, his secretary, Rita, called and told her about the situation at work, and Kathy knew he had to go to Australia.

When she finally got him on the phone last night—he didn't answer her emails, and her first two calls went to voice mail—he'd raved about the women so much that Kathy wanted to meet them. It was her idea to go to Virginia and stay for a while.

Oddly, Ray had suddenly started discouraging her visit. He'd said the house was "too small to move around in" and he disliked the grounds with an empty mansion and a wall around it. But she'd very much wanted a vacation, and he'd made the women sound fascinating.

She should have known it was too perfect to be real. Maybe these women were like so many others and had fallen for Ray. Maybe young Elise was after him. Was that why they were looking down their noses at his less-than-svelte wife?

By lunchtime, Kathy had decided to repack her bags and

leave. She was used to women falling for her husband, but this was ridiculous!

"Is anyone hungry?" Olivia asked. "I am." She was standing in the doorway, and unless Kathy missed her guess, there was pity on her face.

Kathy had had it! "Shall we order in three supersize pizzas? A slice for each of you and I'll eat the rest of them? And let's not forget the huge bottle of regular Coke and those cinnamon bars." Skinny Elise was standing next to Olivia. "Better than delivery, I'll go get them so you two won't have to be seen with me." She went to the stairs.

"What's wrong?" Elise asked. "What did we do?"

It was Olivia who realized that they had unintentionally been *too* reserved with Kathy.

They'd not meant to, but they had excluded her. Olivia spoke loudly. "My stepson and his wife have camped out in my house at the far end of the estate. They're planning to hit me up for money, so I don't want them to know I'm back in town. And the police are probably after Elise, so she can't be seen outside the grounds. That's why we didn't want to go into town with you."

Kathy halted at the doorway but kept her back to them.

Olivia continued. "We were too embarrassed to tell you so we kept quiet. I apologize."

"Me too!" Elise said. "I wanted to go shopping with you, but I'm afraid that if I use a credit card, my dad will send men after me and I'll be put back in a loony bin."

Kathy turned to face them.

"And if I go out," Olivia said, "someone in town will tell my daughter-in-law, then she'll be over here nagging me to death. And crying. I know I'll eventually have to face up to it, but…" She shrugged.

Kathy was trying to understand what they were telling her. "You two are also patients of Dr. Hightower?"

"I am," Elise said. "She broke me out of the mental institution where my husband, Kent, and my father had put me."

"Jeanne got her out by hiding her in the trunk of her car," Olivia said. "There may be legal repercussions. I'm not one of her patients but I think she arranged for me to be here."

"Do you?" Elise asked. "You didn't tell me that."

"It's just a theory I have and if I ever meet the woman I plan to find out."

"She's—" Elise began, but Kathy cut her off.

"You two haven't been excluding me because of…" She motioned to her body.

"Of course not," Olivia said. "What a dreadful thought."

"But I ought to," Elise said. "You look like a taller version of Carmen. But your face is prettier and what do you use on your hair? It looks great. Oh, and Carmen is the woman my husband dumped me for. They have a little girl. He didn't want to start a family with me."

As Kathy sat down on the couch, she named a salon shampoo. She was staring at Elise. "I'm not understanding this. Your husband…?"

"Had a second family," Elise said.

"And so did mine," Olivia added.

They looked at Kathy—and waited. They knew that her husband was on the verge of starting a new family, but they didn't tell her that. And if Kathy knew, she gave no indication of it.

Elise broke the silence as she looked at Olivia. "Do you think Jeanne put us together because you and I have the same problem?"

"I have no idea, but it makes sense," Olivia said. "I have come to believe that this is supposed to be a therapy weekend."

"We spill our guts, that sort of thing?" Elise asked. "Actually, I'd *love* to tell my whole story. As long as no one even mentions suicide."

The two women turned to Kathy, silently asking if she'd like to hear of Elise's problems.

Kathy could just blink. Maybe it was all the zillions of diet programs she'd been on in her adult life, but they made a person feel that if you just lost weight everything would be perfect. If you had marriage problems, thinner thighs would resolve the issues. And a skinny you would stand up to the Mean Girls of the world. Hey! You might even be asked to join them.

But that didn't seem to be true. Tall, model-thin Elise's husband preferred a woman with meat on her bones. "Please," Kathy said, "I'd like to hear whatever you want to tell."

"But wait!" Olivia said. "I have to get sandwich makings and wine. That all right with you two?"

"Perfect," Elise said. "I think maybe I should start at the end and go backward. I want you to know what was actually going on while I was so innocently frolicking in the dirt with Alejandro."

"Alejandro?" Kathy asked.

"Our family's gardener's little brother. The most beautiful man on earth."

"I have another candidate for that title," Olivia said, and they looked at Kathy.

"Still looking for mine."

"What about—?" Olivia began, but stopped herself and looked at Elise. "Please begin."

"When I look back on it," Elise began, "it seems that everything—Kent, Alejandro, Carmen—were all caused by Tara. I knew her in school and she was an absolute bitch. About two months ago, on a lazy afternoon, she showed up at my house, uninvited. I could tell by the wild look in her eyes that she had something dreadful to tell me. It was always some gossip about someone we both knew. It would be a divorce, or that she'd seen a husband with a pretty girl. Something salacious and mean."

"What does she do?" Olivia was on a pillow on the floor on

the far side of the coffee table. She began slathering bread with mayonnaise and loading it with cold cuts and lettuce.

"She's a lawyer—which she loves to rub in my face." Elise's voice changed to falsetto. "'How I wish I could be like you, Elise, and spend my days doing nothing but enjoying myself. A stress-free life.'"

"Zinger there," Kathy said.

"Jealousy is what that is." Olivia handed Kathy a plate with a thick sandwich. "Did she make a pass at your husband and get turned down?"

Elise gave a little smile. "Not that I know of, but two times she told me she was expecting an engagement ring from a guy she was dating. But it never happened. That day, I could tell that she had Big News. She didn't say a word, just handed me her cell phone. It was a photo of Kent out shopping with a pretty woman and a little girl. I handed her phone back and said that was Carmen, our gardener's sister. Mostly, I was annoyed that Kent was at a mall when he was always telling me that he never had time to leave work."

Elise took a breath. "Tara opened her briefcase and pulled out a thick folder. It was full of photos and documents—all of them about my husband. It looked like she'd been working on it for quite a while. She left it all with me and scurried away."

Olivia reached out and took Elise's hand.

"I sat on the couch and went through the papers. Over and over. At first, all I could see was the money. Somehow, Tara had tapped into a bank account that I didn't know Kent had. He was always on me to save money. His favorite words were 'How much did it cost?' But his secret account showed that he earned more than he said he did, and he was spending a lot on…on…them."

Elise was trying to get her emotions under control. "It was a while before I saw that there was a birth certificate listing Kent as the father of Carmen's daughter. I remembered the week she was born. It was just a few months after our wedding, and Kent had to go away to a two-week conference. He didn't call me while he was away because he said his phone broke and he didn't have time to fix it or get a new one."

She paused. "After a while, I realized that the money put into the account was direct deposit. That meant his boss, *my father*, had to know about Kent's other family."

"You were being betrayed by everyone," Olivia said.

"Yes, I was."

"What did you do?" Kathy asked.

"That night when Kent came home—it was after eleven—I was still sitting on the couch with the papers on my lap. I hadn't moved in hours. I got up and handed him the folder. You know what he said?"

Both Olivia and Kathy shook their heads.

"I can quote him as it's burned into my memory. He said, 'I bet Tara did this. She's always liked sticking her nose into other people's business. Elise, baby, you ought to stay away from her.'"

"Yeow," Kathy said. "That was cruel."

"That's the voice of a man who is scared." Olivia was frowning. "And what did you reply to that?"

"I lost it," Elise said. "I started screaming. By that time Alejandro and I were…" She stopped talking.

"You told him about Alejandro?" Olivia asked.

"No. I had enough sense not to mention Carmen's *brother*."

"Ah," Olivia said. "But part of you wondered if Alejandro was a decoy."

Elise took a drink of her soda. "It certainly did seem to be a huge coincidence that he and Carmen were together, and that Alejandro and I were…were friends."

"How was Kent during all this?" Kathy asked.

"He seemed calm, but he wasn't. He made me a drink and he was shaking so much that he spilled half of it."

"And he put pills in it," Olivia said softly.

Kathy gasped.

"He did." For a moment, Elise's jaw clamped shut. "I was pacing back and forth and yelling so I didn't see him do it. I wanted to grab something and hit him with it. He had no idea how much I was planning to give up for him! I had such a deep sense of loyalty that I hadn't... I never..." She swallowed. "Anyway, I was so angry that I couldn't see or hear much. When he handed me a drink, I gulped it. It was almost straight vodka and I hadn't eaten all day. It went straight to my head. I was so dizzy that Kent pushed me toward the bedroom and I fell down on the bed. He left the room."

Elise stood up, paced for a moment, then looked back at them.

"As soon as my head stopped whirling, I got up, went to the door, and opened it. Kent was on the phone. I heard him say, 'She knows.'"

"And that's when reality hit you," Olivia said.

Elise nodded. "I finally, at last, saw that my husband was never going to really love *me*."

"It was about love," Kathy said. "You weren't angry about money or even another woman, but about *love*."

"Yes. That's true."

Again, Olivia squeezed Elise's hand. "That's when you wanted oblivion, so you took a pill."

"Yes, but only enough to calm me so I could think," Elise said. "There was a bottle of Kent's prescription sleeping pills on the bedside table. He said that the stress of his job kept him from sleeping."

"Maybe it was his guilty conscience," Olivia said.

Kathy grimaced. "Or worry about how to afford everything."

"That's more likely," Elise said.

"You took a pill." Olivia's voice was encouraging. "But you didn't know that Kent had already given you some."

Elise nodded. "When I felt sleepy, I was glad. It was all horrible, but at the same time it was a relief. I thought about how in the morning I'd contact a lawyer."

"Would it be Tara?" Kathy asked.

Elise smiled. "She certainly would know the meanest, most soulless lawyer there was. When I drifted off to sleep, I was almost happy."

"You were thinking about Alejandro," Olivia said.

"I was *hoping* about Alejandro. Maybe he didn't know about his sister and my husband. But then, he and his brother had said things that suddenly made sense. Had everything between us been to distract me? Or could it have been some huge, cosmic coincidence that my husband and I had fallen for two people from the same family?"

"Or just old-fashioned proximity. They were both there, near you two," Olivia said. "I can attest that youthful hormones tend to guide people, not wisdom. What happened when you woke up in a hospital?"

"Kent was holding my hand and he'd been crying."

"Out of fear of going to jail?" Kathy's voice was angry.

"My guess is that he was genuinely sorry," Olivia said. "I doubt if he meant to harm you."

"He didn't," Elise said. "He was just stupid, that's all. He was kissing my hand and saying he was sorry. And he was telling me that from now on he'd be a better husband and we'd start over fresh. We'd forget about the past and go on from there."

"Did you believe him?" Olivia asked.

"All I could think about was his cute little daughter. He was going to abandon her? I didn't think so—and I didn't want that. My throat was raw from the tube that had been stuck down it, but I managed to say, 'I want a divorce.'"

"What did he say to that?" Kathy asked.

"He started pleading. I knew he was afraid that a divorce would make my dad fire him. But Kent could see that I wasn't going to back down. That's when my parents and his arrived."

Elise looked at Kathy. "A therapist was with them and she was talking about my suicide attempt as though it were a given. She was telling them how to 'handle' me to make sure I didn't do it again and talking of a place where I'd be 'protected.' I could hardly speak but I kept saying no and trying to get Kent to tell them the truth."

"But he saw his opportunity and took it," Olivia said.

"He did. I think he was afraid that I'd press charges against him. Putting pills in somebody's drink is a crime."

"What did your parents say?" Kathy asked.

"My mother—as always—was disgusted with me. I don't think I've ever pleased her in my entire life. But my father..." Again, Elise's jaw clamped down. "My father was giving Kent looks as though to say, 'I knew this was going to happen.'"

"Do you think he knew Kent had put the pills in your drink?" Olivia asked.

"No. I think my father thought I'd found out about Carmen and had tried to kill myself. He wanted me put under constant care so I couldn't try to do it again. He and Kent signed papers and I..." Elise shrugged.

"You were put in a psychiatric ward," Olivia said.

"And no one there believed me when I said I hadn't tried to kill myself. One of the doctors said I was so angry that he was afraid that if I were released I might harm Carmen and her child."

"That's horrible!" Kathy said. "*You* were made into the villain. And meanwhile, Kent was at home like nothing had happened."

"Then you met Jeanne," Olivia said.

"She wasn't my doctor so she couldn't release me without the permission of my father *and* my husband. The, you know, sane people."

"So you escaped in the trunk of her car."

"I did. She let me out after we crossed the state line, and I sat in the front seat. We took turns driving."

"What did you talk about?" Olivia asked.

Elise smiled. "Jeanne said, 'Just so you know, I think your whole family is a bunch of douche wads and I'd like to see them locked up. But let's talk about happy things.' So we did. Food, gardens, and places we'd been. The next day she dropped me off at the diner in Summer Hill. She said, 'I'm going to see that you will be given a chance to fix all of this.'"

"With lawyers," Kathy said. "I know some."

"I guess so, but I got the idea that she meant something else."

Olivia smiled. "I'm on Jeanne's side. I want to hear about happy things. I want to know about your shirtless hero."

"Who may or may not have been spending time with me to cover for Carmen and—"

Olivia put up her hand. "Tell us the story, then let Kathy and me be the judge. How did you meet Alejandro?"

"Through Tara," Elise said. "At least she's the one who made me actually *see* him." She shook her head. "It's hard to imagine now but I was so involved with my husband that I paid no attention to the gorgeous, half-naked man sauntering through the garden two days a week. But then, Tara showed up and—"

"Wait!" Kathy said. "When and where was this?"

"Long Island, the summer before I found out about Carmen and their child. Back in the days when I still believed that Kent and I could possibly be a happy couple."

"I want to know how you and Kent acted when you were together," Olivia said. "And especially what you were like."

Elise grimaced. "I was perfect because that's what I thought it took to make a man love me."

"Been there, done that," Kathy said. "With every diet I hoped that— No. This is your story. Tell us about you and Kent, then we want details about you and the beautiful Alejandro."

"We were and are nothing but friends. That's all." Elise's voice softened. "It never went past that. On that last night, I tried, but he said no." Her eyes seemed to fade as though in a dream.

"Does Alejandro have dark eyes?" Kathy asked.

Elise came back to the present. "Like a stallion at midnight."

"And you *never* went to bed with him?" Kathy asked.

"I was never unfaithful to Kent. Not so much as a kiss. But there was one night with Alejandro when I was tempted to the point where I nearly broke. Moonlight and margaritas. We'd had an argument and he was leaving the country. I had some decisions to make and..." She looked at the women. "I guess I better start at the beginning."

"Yes, you should," Olivia said and the women settled back to listen.

Chapter Seven

ELISE HAD ON WHAT LOOKED LIKE A 1950S NIGHTIE. Something out of a Sandra Dee movie. Physically, she didn't have a lot on top but she knew her long, slim legs often sent men's eyes into spirals. As usual, this morning, she was trying to entice her husband to actually *look* at her.

"The Becketts are a very important couple so cook something special, will you?" Kent said.

Elise leaned against the kitchen counter, her legs extended so they looked even longer. "Like what?"

"I don't know. I'm not a cook. Have you seen my keys?"

"Behind you."

He turned. "Where?"

"There. In that red lacquer box."

He picked them up. "No wonder I couldn't find them. Why did you put them inside that thing?"

"It's a Japanese *tebako* box and I would never think of putting car keys in it. It might damage the finish."

"If you didn't put them there, who did?" When she started to speak, he put up his hand. "It doesn't matter. I have to go."

"Wait! I was wondering if you like what I have on." She twirled around. It was a very short garment, covering the upper half of her with yards of semitransparent pale pink silk, and leaving the bottom half of her bare.

"It's cute. How much did it cost?"

Elise tried to not let her fallen spirit show. "Nothing. I've had it since before we were married. Part of my trousseau."

"That's good." He stood there, staring at her, waiting for her to release him. "Out with it. I can tell that something's on your mind."

"I want to get a job."

Instantly, there was laughter in his eyes. "Doing what? I understand that you're bored, but really, what kind of job could you get?"

"I was thinking about an art gallery."

"There aren't any galleries near here—unless you count the local craft fair."

"Maybe Dad could lend me the money to open one."

Kent gave a snort of laughter. He was a handsome man, tall, with dark blond hair and blue eyes. He looked best in tennis whites, with a sweater tied around his shoulders. He was the epitome of good health and ancestors who went back to English aristocracy. Whereas Elise's family had had money for generations, it was Kent's that brought in the illustrious lineage.

"Sorry, babe, but you know your dad. He's not going to do anything that won't make a ten-times profit. Why don't you take some classes?"

"More cooking?"

"That's a brilliant idea! You could make something fantastic when we have Mr. and Mrs. Beckett over. Duck a l'orange. How about that? Doesn't that sound good?"

"Such fun!"

Kent gave a sigh. "Okay, so you don't want to take any more cooking classes." He looked at his watch—a gold Piaget that her parents had given him as a wedding gift. "I have to go. We're working on a big merger today and I have to be there. Tonight we'll sit down and talk about everything and I'll try to find something for you to do."

"Then you'll be home tonight before dark?"

"Of course. No. Wait. Today's the eighteenth, right? I have to attend a…well, something tonight. Take a bubble bath and curl up with a book. Use my absence to enjoy yourself." He gave her cheek a quick kiss, then hurried out the door.

Elise stood by the window and watched him drive away in his 700 series BMW, a car owned by her father's company. Across the lawn, through the trees, she could see the side of her parents' house and wondered if her mother was watching as Kent left.

Where they lived had once been a guesthouse, used for overnight clients of her father's management company. But when Kent and Elise got married, everyone—except Elise, that is—thought it would be great for "the children" to live there.

Turning, she looked to the right and could see the corner of Kent's parents' house.

They were kinder, less financially ambitious than Elise's parents.

The two mothers had met in college and they were so opposite that they were a perfect match. Elegance and ambition were their overriding characteristics and they learned from each other.

When they met men like themselves, they snatched them up so fast the men weren't sure what had happened. The women got their husbands to buy two big houses next door to each other. The wives acted as though they were one property and loved to call the place "an estate."

There was great disappointment when one got pregnant and the other one didn't. A boy was born, Kent, then two more children. It wasn't until years later that Elise was finally born. She would be an only child.

From the time she was a year old, her mother was disappointed in her. Elise was a quiet, ethereal, dreamy child who was more interested in art than in being better than the other kids in her class. She wasn't competitive, didn't seem to have any ambition, and liked to step back and let other people win. "It makes them so happy," she said, and that was enough for her.

The only thing that pleased her mother was Elise's blind adoration of Kent. Whenever he was near, Elise would put her paints and crayons down and watch him.

"I think they should marry," Kent's mother said one sunny afternoon as all the children were playing in the pool, their nannies close by.

"Agreed," Elise's mother said, and that was that. They never spoke of it again. But then, they didn't need to. It was settled.

As Elise looked out her window at both houses, she felt trapped. She couldn't figure out why her husband was so distant with her. She couldn't put her finger on what was wrong, but there was something missing. There was a gap in their marriage and she had no idea how to fill it.

With a sigh, she got dressed in knee-length shorts, a sleeveless linen blouse, and sandals, then cleaned up the kitchen that she'd never liked.

On the wall was pinned a list of things she was supposed to do that day. Pick up Kent's dry cleaning. Call Mrs. Beckett to ask if she or her husband had any food allergies. Take Kent's shoes to the shop to be repaired. Go to a department store and find a gift for one of Kent's clients—who Elise had never met. Drive twenty miles to the fishmonger Kent liked and get their red snapper.

Elise pulled the list off the wall and had an impulse to crush it, but she didn't. She tried to put it in order of what to do when. Feeling defiant, she dropped the list on the little kitchen desk and picked up a novel she'd had for a week, and went outside.

There was a small patio at the back of the house that couldn't be seen from the big houses. It was a haven to Elise. There was a larger stone terrace to the side, where they had a grill and the obligatory fire pit. It was what the designer Kent had hired called an "entertainment area." It was only used for clients he wanted to impress.

What Elise liked most about the guesthouse was the small patio. It was shaded and had a short stone wall around three sides. It made her feel safe, protected.

When they'd moved in, Kent had wanted to tear it out. "We'll bring in a dozer and flatten the area and make it five times as big," he'd said. The landscape designer—a very nice older man—had seen the way his young bride looked like she was about to cry. He told Kent that was a terrible idea and the new entertainment area should be on the sunny side of the house.

When Elise had mouthed "thank you," he'd smiled.

Last summer, she and Diego, the Mexican man who took care of the gardens for all three houses, planned how to make the little area beautiful. She sketched her vision of it on a drawing pad, but she didn't know enough about gardening to make her ideas reality.

"My brother knows about plants and he's coming here. He'll tell me what to put in to make it look like your drawing," Diego said.

She smiled at him; she'd always liked him. He'd been working there since she was in middle school. His sister, Carmen, was often there and they'd shared a few laughs—until the first time Elise came home from college, that is. Carmen had glared at Elise as though she were an enemy. Elise asked her what was wrong but Carmen wouldn't say.

By the time Elise and Kent were married, Carmen was so hostile that Elise stayed away from her.

Late last summer she and Kent returned from a trip that was supposed to have been a second honeymoon, but he'd spent most of the time on the telephone. While they were away, Diego had finished her little patio. The beauty of it had cheered her up considerably. "These are lovely," she told Diego as she touched the vines that trailed down the low wall. "You are a plant genius."

"It wasn't me. My brother, Alejandro, did this."

"Tell him thanks from me," Elise said, and went back inside the house. She had to sort out the household accounts and take care of the mail and do the laundry and go to the grocery and... She had to do *all* of it.

The rest of that summer she'd been overwhelmed with all the things Kent gave her to do. Dinner parties and barbecues and Kent's clients stopping by for cocktails.

Sometimes she got fed up. "Why can't you take them to a restaurant?"

"Everyone takes them to restaurants. They want to feel like they're part of a family, *our* family." He put his arms around her, clasping his hands behind her back. "Come on, baby, all of this is for us. For you and me. So we can get closer to the time when we start that family you want so much."

Kent held the promise of a baby in front of her like a carrot before a donkey. It *always* made her back off.

This was the beginning of the third summer they'd been married and Elise was determined that this year would be different. She had to get something to do besides pick up Kent's dry cleaning. As for cooking, she'd taken enough classes to know that it wasn't a skill she wanted to develop further.

She stretched out on one of the thickly padded chaises and opened her book, but she didn't see it. She needed to figure out what to do about her marriage.

"You look like you're fascinated by that book." The voice dripped sarcasm.

Elise tried to keep from showing an expression of horror. Tara! The school gossip. The girl who found out secrets and happily blabbed them. She lived in New York City, but her mother had a house nearby. "Hi," Elise managed to say. "What brings you out to the boonies?"

"Mom wanted New York bagels and whitefish salad so I had to drop everything and take them to her."

Elise understood. Tara's mother subsidized her daughter's New York apartment—with the stipulation that her daughter be at her beck and call.

Tara plopped down on the chaise next to Elise. "So what's up with you other than staring into space? Recovering from the night? With a hunk like Kent you must have a great time in bed."

Elise gave what she hoped was a mysterious smile. "Yeah, sure. We never get enough."

Tara seemed to be satisfied with that answer and looked back toward the little wall.

Behind it was lawn and trees that Diego and his men kept trimmed. Suddenly, Tara sat upright. "Good Lord! What was *that*?"

Elise looked but saw nothing. "I don't know. Sometimes we get foxes, but—"

"No! Him. The man."

"Diego? One of his men? They're the gardeners."

Tara got out of the chair and looked along the side of the house. "Hey! Yeah, you," she shouted. "Come over here."

"Tara, let the men work."

"He can work on *me*," she said under her breath.

"Most of the men are married and have children. I don't think you should—" She broke off because a truly gorgeous man was standing at the top of the wall. He had on dirty cotton trousers and heavy boots, but from the waist up he was naked. Long, lean muscles, stomach divided into ridges, honey-colored skin. But as beautiful as his body was, his face was from the cover of a magazine: high cheekbones, full lips, dark eyes surrounded by thick black lashes. His coal-black hair reached down the back of his neck.

Elise had no idea who he was.

"Do. You. Speak. English?" Tara asked loudly.

He jumped down to the patio with the grace of an athlete, then oddly, turned his back to Elise as he looked at Tara. Elise's face was about a foot from his sun-warmed skin. If she put her hand up, she could touch him.

When he reached behind him, it took her a second to see why. Tucked into his waistband was a copy of *The Lord of the Rings*. He was showing her that he could indeed speak English.

Elise moved around him to stand beside Tara. She was looking up at him like he was a meal and she was starving.

"Do you think he can speak?" Tara asked out of the side of her mouth.

Elise saw the man's eyes sparkle. "I have no idea. I've never seen him before. He's probably one of Diego's relatives."

"There are *two* of them?"

Elise saw the man try to keep from smiling. "No. Diego isn't like him at all."

"What. Is. Your. Name?" Tara asked. "Me Tara. You…?"

"Tarzan?" Elise suggested.

Tara frowned at her. "Really, Elise, how can you make jokes about this? This man is hanging around your house and you don't even know who he is."

When Tara looked away, the man glanced at the wall behind them and nodded slightly.

She understood. "He's Diego's brother. He chose the plants along the wall. What was his name? Alex? No. Alejandro."

"*Si, si*, Alejandro." The man grinned, showing even, white teeth.

Tara went to the chaise to reach inside her handbag. "I like men who speak no English."

When Elise looked up, he winked at her in conspiracy.

Tara handed Alejandro her business card. "This is my address on Long Island. Why don't you come by tomorrow afternoon? You and I can talk about you doing *my* garden."

Alejandro made no reaction.

"Do you think he understands you?" Elise asked.

"Probably not." Tara smiled up at him. "*Mañana*. Get it? Tomorrow at two. *Dos*."

"*Mañana. Dos. Si,*" Alejandro said.

"Good boy." Tara took a step sideways. Another one, and she'd see the book at the back of Alejandro's waistband and know he'd been playing a joke on her.

Elise had seen Tara do some nasty things to people who laughed at her. She whipped out her hand, pulled the book out of Alejandro's waistband, and held it behind her own back.

Sure enough, Tara looked behind him, admiring the view. There was just lots of skin, no book. She stepped away. "I need to go." She ran her hand down Alejandro's arm. "You, cutie, come see me. *Mañana*."

"*Si, si. Mañana. Tres.*" Alejandro looked like he was trying hard to understand her.

"No, no. *Dos*. Two. Come tomorrow at two p.m." She rolled her eyes at Elise, and whispered, "Beautiful but dumb." She gave one last look at Alejandro, then left.

Elise stood beside him in silence until Tara was out of sight. "I'm so sorry." She handed him back his book.

"That's all right," Alejandro said. "It's the most fun I've had for months."

"By the way, that's one of my favorites." She nodded at the novel. "I feel like I owe you. Would you like a glass of lemonade?"

"Yes, but no. My brother would kill me. I bet that right now he's glaring at the back of me."

Elise looked around him and there was Diego staring at his brother's back with fire in his eyes. "He is," she whispered, then stepped to the side. Loudly, she said, "Would you show me? I have no idea what that looks like. It's around the other side of the house."

As soon as they were out of Diego's sight, she held out her hand. "I'm Elise."

"And I'm Alejandro."

They shook hands. His was big and work calloused and very warm.

He broke the hold. "I really should get back to work." He took a step away.

"Why are you here? You don't seem like a..." Elise realized she was putting her foot in her mouth. "I mean... Your English. It's so good, but I mean..."

"It's all right. I understand. At home in Mexico, I teach Spanish to English people. I need to speak the language well."

"And you know about plants, right?"

"I do. I studied botany. My brother thinks it's a useless subject to know."

"My family feels that too! My degree is in Fine Arts. Try to get a job in that!" They smiled at each other.

"I don't mean to be an elitist, but if you have a degree and a job, why are you here?" She raised her hand to indicate the garden. "Doing this?"

"I must reveal my secret. I got into trouble at home and my big brother rescued me. Got me out of the country and gave me a job."

"Oh. Trouble as in drugs?"

"I wish. Then I'd be rich. Maybe dead, but rich."

Elise laughed.

"I'm sure you have other things to do than listen to a gardener's life story."

"No, I can't say that I do. My husband wants me to cook some exotic dishes for his clients. But all of them just want beef. And lots of it. So no, I don't really have anything else to do. What kind of flowers are those?"

"Peonies. *Paeonia california*. And those over there are *Paeonia corsica*."

"Wow. I'm impressed. And based on my little garden here, I think your degree is quite useful."

"Thank you. I was hoping you'd like it."

His eyes really were extraordinary. "I should have studied domestic management."

"And I wish I'd learned how to get a wheelbarrow loaded with a hundred-and-fifty-pound dogwood up a hill. First time I tried it, the thing fell out twice."

"And you picked it up and put it back in?"

"You can bet Diego wasn't going to help me. He—"

"Alejandro!" It was Diego—and his tone was a command.

"My brother wants me to get back to work. I have to go."

She frantically searched for something to say that would ensure that they'd talk again. "If I take Spanish lessons, will you help me?"

He was walking backward. "Yes. Most of my clients were women. Bored wives of rich men. Like your friend Tara. *They* were the problem."

"Oh, I see. And she's not my friend." Her head came up. "I guess I'm like them." She couldn't keep the deflation out of her voice.

"You are far away from being like *any* of them." The way he said it was so nice that she smiled.

"Alejandro!" Diego bellowed.

"I'm in trouble now. To *mañana*."

Smiling, she watched him walk away until he was out of sight.

Chapter Eight

ELISE HAD BEEN TAKING SPANISH LESSONS FOR A month but she'd not seen Alejandro. Diego and his other men had been there as usual. They mowed and trimmed and pulled weeds with quick efficiency, then left in a couple of old trucks.

She didn't dare ask Diego where his brother was. She didn't want him to think she wanted something more than someone to talk to. Which she assured herself that she didn't.

One Sunday at the joint family dinner, her mother said it was time for Elise to start taking responsibility in the community. She kept her groan to herself. To her mother that meant joining committees and trying to show interest in whatever the other members—all of them over sixty—had to say.

She hadn't told anyone she was taking Spanish classes three mornings a week. She was sure her mother would complain that it wasn't French.

Her teacher was a Mexican woman in her fifties, very nice, and she was constantly feeding Elise. "You are too thin!" Elise ate everything she was served but she didn't put on weight. But then she never sat still long enough to let calories settle.

One day her teacher's three young grandchildren were there. Elise took one look at them and forgot about the teacher. She spent two hours with the kids and they delighted in telling her that every word she said in Spanish was totally wrong. Elise learned more from them than from any formal lesson.

After that, her teacher made sure the children were always there. Elise made a great babysitter. She and the children cooked Mexican dishes, played Mexican games, and spoke only in Spanish. By the end of the month she wasn't fluent in the language, but she was on her way.

It was when her teacher said her father was ill and she had to return to Mexico that Elise again began to feel the loneliness of her life. Kent was always gone, girlfriends all seemed to have busy lives, and her mother was pushing her into joining the dreaded committees.

Elise began to have dreams—both real and made-up—of a man on a horse who rescued her from—from everything. One morning she woke up startled. In her dream, it had been Alejandro on the horse.

She finally got up the courage to ask Diego where his brother was. She was told he was on "another job." His tone was unmistakable. Alejandro was off-limits to her, a married woman.

That Sunday, Elise was standing by the door waiting for Kent to finish a call so they could walk to her parents' house for the weekly dinner. Or, as she called it, the What's Wrong with Elise? dinner.

"Come on, it's not that bad," Kent said when he joined her.

"My mother wants me to join her committee about cleaning up the parks."

"Sounds like a worthy cause."

"It would be if we did some actual cleaning. But I'm to help some other women decide how to deal with the people who have been assigned by the court to do community service. Like any of us know how to do that."

"I'm sure you'll do fine." Kent was looking at his watch.

"Need to be somewhere?"

"Don't start on me! For once, let's have a nice meal without you starting a fight. Maybe it would be good for you to join a committee or two. *Do* something instead of sitting around here all day and complaining."

The unfairness of his accusations took her breath away. "I spend my life doing things for *you*."

"And I spend mine doing things for *you*, so we're even. Are you ready to go? Let's get this over with. I have to—"

"Go back to the office," Elise shot at him.

"You're hopeless. You have everything any woman could want but you're still not happy." He walked out the door, leaving her behind.

Elise leaned against the wall and closed her eyes. He was right. She had everything in life but she was miserable. Her only happiness was when she was at Spanish class. The children, the home life, the laughter. Even the sadness of someone ill. It was *life*. And it made her happy.

She stood up straight, put her shoulders back, and went to the dinner. It was always a formal affair. Her mother had the Sunday dinners catered and served. She believed in what she called "polite conversation." That meant that everyone was to agree with her. Disagreement of any sort was not allowed.

Usually, Elise made an effort to participate in whatever the others were talking about, but this time she was silent. She kept asking herself what she really and truly wanted to *do*. If she could wave a magic wand, what would she change?

She looked around the table at both sets of parents and her husband. Everything, she thought. I'd change it *all*.

"Elise!" her mother said sharply. "Would you be so kind as to join the adults in conversing?"

Elise looked across the table at her. "I was thinking about herbs and horses."

Her father gave a chuckle. "Horses don't eat herbs."

"I think I should take riding lessons and I need an herb garden. Mrs. Beckett said she could tell that I'd used dried basil. She said she could taste the difference." *Pretentious little woman,* Elise thought. She'd seen the jar on the counter and wanted them to think she was above such crass things. Elise was pleased that everyone was looking at her in surprise.

"Beckett Steel?" her father asked.

"Yes, that's them. I thought I'd have the gardeners dig a hole or two in the back, just past the oak tree, so I could plant a few things."

"A 'hole'?" her mother said.

"Just so it's deep enough for a pot or two. I don't need much."

Her mother shook her head. "Really, Elise, sometimes I think you were raised by the staff."

I saw them more, she thought, but didn't say.

"Tomorrow I'll call Leonardo and he can design something for you," her mother said.

Elise suppressed a grimace. She couldn't stand the little man. He teased and flirted with the women until they were in giggles, so they hired him. She looked at Kent in wide-eyed innocence. "Isn't he really expensive? I thought maybe I could sketch something, then have our gardeners do it." Her father paid the gardeners but a professional designer would send the bill to Kent.

"I really don't think—" her mother began.

"I think that's a great idea," Kent said, then looked at his father-in-law with pleading eyes.

We are children living in a dictatorship, Elise thought. *We still have to ask our parents' permission for everything we do.*

"Yes," her father said to his daughter. "That's an excellent idea. Use some of that expensive education I paid for."

"Edgar! Really," her mother said. "Elise can't possibly—"

Kent, who *never* contradicted his mother-in-law, spoke up. "I believe she can. Sweetheart, you go ahead and make your little garden. It'll give you something to do all day."

"And riding lessons?" Elise pressed.

"I see no reason for you to—" her mother began.

Kent's mother, by far the quieter of the two women, said, "I took riding lessons until I went to college. I think it would be a lovely thing for you to do."

She might be the quiet one, but she knew how to get her way. Elise smiled at her in gratitude. "Thank you," she said softly.

Kent left right after the meal and Elise lost no time in getting started. She spent hours on the internet researching herb gardens.

By Monday morning, when Diego and his men arrived, she had a drawing she liked.

She met him as he was getting out of his truck and held out her sketch. It was a big circle, with an X of walkways, a bird-bath in the middle.

"I need an herb garden," she told him. "But I don't know what to plant in it. My mother wants it to be beautiful and elegant and smell good." That was a lie but she felt it was for a good cause. That she hadn't considered where it might lead wasn't something she wanted to think about.

Diego looked into her eyes so hard that she felt the blood rushing up her neck.

He seemed to reconcile himself that there was nothing he could do to stop this. He took out his cell and made a call. She knew enough Spanish to understand that he was warning his brother that if he so much as touched the little gringa, Alejandro would be sent back to Mexico. And further, Diego would marry him off to the girl who lived next door to their mother.

Elise had to turn away when she heard Alejandro's cry for mercy.

Diego clicked off and told Elise that his brother would help her choose the plants she needed.

When Alejandro got there, for a moment they just stared at each other—and she knew he'd thought about her too.

"So how's Tara?" she asked.

Alejandro's face didn't change. "Doing well. We're getting married next week."

Elise laughed. Tara had called and been quite angry because "that idiot gardener of yours" didn't show up. "Sorry to take you away from your other job."

"Diego had me putting in a hedge of Pyracantha—all those thorns—around some garbage cans. And he had me drive to New Jersey to pick up some bromeliads that they sell four miles from here. It was like he wanted me to stay away. I can't think why."

His innuendo made Elise frown. "I'm not really... I mean..."

"We're to be friends."

"Yes," she said. "*Amigos.* How about if we speak Spanish while we do this?"

"All right. Except that if my brother gets too bossy I may have to speak to him in English curse words. They're quite the best."

"Are they?"

"Oh yes."

"Then I'd be honored if you used my language."

"Now where's your plan and where do you want this garden put in?"

"You don't have to do this," Alejandro said.

They were digging the big circle for the garden they had marked out with string and stakes. Beside them in the shade, a garden hose nearby, were over a hundred plants they'd chosen. In the two weeks that they'd been together, their talk had gradually taken on a flirty intimacy. "It's just my big brother showing me that he's the boss."

Elise jammed the shovel into the ground, and tossed the big clod into the wheelbarrow. "I'm enjoying this."

He looked skeptical.

"Okay, so maybe not actually happy at having to dig a giant circle, but it gets me outside." The sun was bright and she really hoped she didn't sweat off her sunscreen. She knew she should change into pants and a long-sleeved shirt, but being near Alejandro made shorts and a tank top feel, well, right. And what was a little sunburn? She wouldn't have to pay for the sun damage for another thirty years. Besides, Alejandro was, as always, bare from the waist up.

She looked across the widening space they were digging. Diego had declared that the whole herb bed had to be dug by hand—and he couldn't spare *any* men. He'd meant to keep his little brother so busy that he wouldn't have time to socialize with their employer's wife. He hadn't counted on Elise volunteering to help Alejandro dig.

"Tell me about your home," she said.

"I did. There was a problem with—"

"I know that part," she said quickly. "Randy older woman, beautiful young teacher. She couldn't control herself. The end."

Alejandro smiled as he dug deep. "Beautiful, huh?"

"So far, it seems to have caused you more problems than it's helped."

"You don't know the half of it," he mumbled.

"Then tell me. Give me something to think about besides bashing your brother over the head with this shovel. Has he always been so stubborn?"

"Since he was born. He and our father used to have arguments that rocked the roof."

Elise sighed. "I'd like to have the courage to stand up to my father." She wiped sweat off her forehead and picked up her bottle of water. "Is that why Diego's here in the US?"

Alejandro leaned on the shovel to watch in admiration as she drank half the bottle of water. When she finished, he went back to shoveling. "My father broke his leg."

She could tell that he was about to start a story. "Tell me as much as possible in Spanish and please help me with the translation."

He gave her a smile of such pleasure that Elise almost lost her balance.

They went back to digging while Alejandro started telling of his life in Mexico. When he was a child, his father broke his leg and couldn't get to his bookkeeping job at a trucking firm. His parents were worried about how they were going to support the family. In frustration, his mother said that the only thing she knew how to do was cook.

"Is she any good?"

He rolled his eyes. "The best. Everyone said so. She pushed out a window in the kitchen and put up a sign that she was selling burritos. Everyone came running. A year later, Dad and Diego built a cover and set out four tables. The next year they rented a building with a covered terrace, and..." He shrugged.

"And you had a five-star restaurant."

"A *New York Times* critic did stop by and he wrote a rather nice article." He had to help Elise to understand all the words in that sentence.

"Wow! A *New York Times* restaurant review. Did you work there? Can you cook?"

"A bit. It was Diego and my brother Ricardo who got the most out of the place." The way he was smiling made her want to know more.

"My mother hired a sixteen-year-old girl just out of school, then spent two years training her. She—"

"Let me guess. She became Diego's wife."

He grinned. "Right. Then my mother hired a second girl. Young, pretty, smart." He looked at Elise.

"Your brother Ricardo took her?"

Alejandro laughed. "He did."

"So that left you. What happened with the next girl? Or were you too young?"

"By then I was old enough, but my mother always said that I was going to university. No wife for me! To make sure I didn't fall in love and take away her help, she hired a woman in her thirties who had two kids."

When he stopped talking, Elise looked at him. "Are you blushing?" She drew in her breath. "You didn't!"

Alejandro looked at her from under his lashes. "She taught me a lot."

Elise leaned on her shovel and laughed. "Did your mother know?"

"I'm not sure. But one day I was yawning and she said, 'At least you aren't getting *married*!'"

"She knew."

"Probably so." He was smiling. "The next year I went to the University of Mexico."

"And studied plants."

"And English and literature and some other languages. All of it, according to Diego, useless."

She suddenly realized that he hadn't said a word about his sister. "What about Carmen? Did she fall in love with some gorgeous young man?"

"No." He said the word in a way that showed he didn't want to talk about that.

She lowered her voice. "Did she get into trouble and that's why she's now with you and Diego?"

Alejandro took a while before speaking, as though he was considering how to answer. "She just wanted to come to America. She's like our father and good with numbers, so she does the bookkeeping for Diego."

"I don't mean to pry, but it seems like she's changed. When we were teenagers, we were almost friends. I used to buy cinnamon gum and give it to Carmen because I knew she liked it.

But one day she told me that she didn't want any more of my charity. I apologized but I didn't see it that way. I used to buy Kit Kats for my friend Lisa. It was just..." She shrugged.

Again, he took his time before speaking. "She...uh...she..."

When Elise's phone rang, he looked like a weight had been lifted off him. "You'd better get that."

"It's not important. Did something awful happen to Carmen? Is that why she changed?" Her eyes widened. "An American didn't do something bad to her, did he? Or she? Is that why Carmen suddenly seemed to think that *I* was an elitist and a—?"

"Your phone! It keeps ringing. Maybe something is wrong."

Frowning, Elise wiped her hands on her middle and picked up her cell off the towel on the grass. "It's my mother," she said with a groan, then accepted the call. "Yes, I'm here." She listened. "Now? This minute?" She let out her breath. "Yes. Of course I will." Elise's eyes brightened. "It so happens that one of the gardeners *is* here. No, I'm sure he won't mind. Yes, I'll tell him to take off his shoes." Elise shook her head. "Mother! He won't get dirt on anything. If I have to, I'll make him strip naked and when he goes up the stairs, I'll watch his every step to make sure he touches nothing."

Alejandro coughed to cover his laugh and Elise held the phone away as her mother bawled her out.

She turned back to the phone. "Yes, I apologize for my rude, vulgar remark. It was insensitive of me. I will make sure the gardener is clothed and clean. And yes, I'll be there in minutes." She clicked off. "We have to go to the house."

Alejandro looked down at his bare chest. "I need to get a shirt."

"No!" She blinked. "I mean, you don't have to get one. My parents are leaving to spend the weekend in the Hamptons with some friends. I have to go back to the house and gather roses for my mother to take with her."

"And you have to cut them for her?"

"Mother doesn't like the thorns."

"When do I walk up the stairs?"

"After they leave, of course."

Alejandro looked at her with one eyebrow raised.

"I'm not old enough for you so quit hoping. Mother wants you to move a chair to my house and she's worried you'll get dirt all over everything. Come on, I have to go now or she'll make my life miserable."

"I'm not sure your mother would like to see you and me together."

"She won't notice, and besides, you have to take the thorns off the roses." He was frowning. "What's wrong?"

"I think I should get a shirt out of the truck."

Elise narrowed her eyes. "If you want to cover up for *them*, does that mean you're half-naked for *me*?"

"You think your bare legs are going to get burned?"

"Touché. We—" Her phone was ringing again. She looked at the ID. "It's Mother. Race you there!"

Alejandro outran her but just as they reached Elise's mother's big rose garden, he faked a leg cramp and let her win.

Laughing, she went to the little shed on the far side and got out gloves, secateurs, and the wooden trough.

"Funny little basket," Alejandro said.

"It's an English trug."

He said the word a couple of times. "So what do you want first? Damasks? Hybrids? Grandifloras?"

"Show-off. I want fat pink smelly ones."

"Your mother has some nice bourbons."

"My mother doesn't know half what you do."

"About roses or her daughter?"

"I'm not answering that," she said. "Here! You hold the trug while I cut, then we'll sit down over there and take the thorns off."

As Alejandro followed her down the rows, he glanced back

at the house. "Are you sure your parents won't mind that I'm here? Your mother doesn't like us getting too close to the house."

Elise felt a pang of guilt at her mother's callousness, at her snobbery toward most people.

It took them twenty minutes to cut the flowers and another twenty to remove the thorns. Elise stabbed herself twice and when Alejandro looked like he was about to kiss her hand, she glared at him.

"Can't blame a man for trying."

Between them was an unspoken agreement that they wouldn't step over the line. She was married and therefore off-limits. But their teasing of each other let them know they were wanted—and oh, how good that felt! To know that a man thought she was pretty and desirable made Elise stand up straighter and put her chin out. She chose her clothes more carefully, was concerned about her hair and makeup. That it was all for the wrong man was something she didn't want to think about.

"I'd better take these to her," Elise said. They were sitting side by side on a wooden bench in the shade, and she was reluctant to leave him. "You should go with me."

Alejandro stretched his arms across the back of the bench. "Call me when you're done so I can do some stair climbing." Obviously, he didn't want to face her mother.

Laughing, Elise went to the front of the house, where one of her parents' staff, Edward, was loading the back of the big SUV. "Hi. They ready to go?"

Edward smiled at her. He'd worked there since she was a baby. "Your mother has changed her clothes about a dozen times. So who's the naked guy you've glued yourself to?"

"Him? He's Diego's brother. I've told him over and over to put on some clothes but he won't do it. I think the poor boy has very low intelligence."

Edward grinned. "That's why you were sweating in the sun

beside him? I was shocked to see that you know how to use a shovel."

"He's my new gay friend and he showed me how."

"Gay! That's a good one. That boy's eyes are eating you up."

Elise got serious. "How much has Mother seen?"

"None. I told her Diego sprayed the grass with poison to kill the snails. She hasn't stepped outside once. I don't know if she fears the poison or the snails."

"Thank you."

Edward closed the van door. "You sure you know what you're doing?"

"Just trying to keep my sanity."

"I think—" Edward began, but the front door opened.

Her mother looked her up and down. "What a disgusting outfit you have on. You look like a farmer. And is that sunburn on your nose? Really, Elise, you are an embarrassment to our family."

Behind her, Edward rolled his eyes. He'd always been a strength to her in surviving her mother's diatribes.

"Your roses." Elise held out a deep basket full of them. "And we removed every thorn." She drew in her breath at her slip. Would her mother ask who "we" was?

Her mother didn't take the basket. "I think the least you could have done was put them in water. We have a long drive ahead of us. Oh no! I forgot my pearl earrings." She went back into the house.

It was several minutes later before the car pulled away and Elise went back to Alejandro. He was still sitting on the bench. The sun had moved enough that a ray of sunshine touched his face. His eyes were closed, and she stood there looking at him. The black whiskers on his cheeks, his hair down the back of his neck. The color of his skin, the way his chest curved out, then was flat.

She knew the strength of him, the speed of his movements.

Earlier, she'd stepped wrong and had nearly fallen. In one swift movement, Alejandro had dropped the shovel and caught both her arms before she fell.

But the instant she'd looked up at him, he'd released her. She understood. It was one thing to tease and flirt but another to actually touch.

"Are they gone?" he asked, but didn't open his eyes.

He is as aware of me as I am of him, she thought. "They are. The staff took the afternoon off for a well-deserved rest. The house is empty."

Alejandro stood. "If my brother hears that you and I were in a house alone he'll send me home."

"To marry the girl next door?"

"You heard that, did you? You go up, toss the chair down, and I'll carry it away."

"Come on, coward. What are you doing?" He'd unfastened the button at the top of his trousers.

"The stairs. I'm to be naked, remember?"

Laughing, Elise told him to keep his pants on and to follow her.

They went to a side door, not through the kitchen in case some of the staff were lingering. But she doubted that they stayed two minutes after her parents left.

The big house had that silent, eerie feel of being empty. They walked softly and didn't speak. When they got to the big entry hall, Alejandro halted.

It was an impressive area, with a marble floor and big Chinese jugs perfectly placed. In the center was a round table that was suited to be in a museum.

"One time I kicked a soccer ball across this room. My mother was not pleased." His expression showed his pity for her.

The stairs were wide, and curved, and carpeted in deep red. Elise went up first, then turned to face him and kept going up.

"In case you ever need to know, you can sneak down these stairs in silence. And the freezer always has ice cream in it."

"I'll remember that."

At the head of the stairs, she went past two closed doors, then opened the one on the left. Inside was a large room created for a little girl. There was a four-poster bed with a domed canopy. Behind the bed was a silk hanging embroidered with a tree. White cabinets had shelves full of books. A bulletin board had notes about homework due.

"It's all pink," he said.

"Peach. A much more subtle color, according to the designer." She opened two big louvered doors to expose a wide, long closet packed full of clothes.

"These are all yours?"

"Every dress, shoe, necklace, and headband." She put on a pink Alice band to demonstrate.

"I like your hair loose better. Or pulled back. Maybe with a rose."

"Like a flamenco dancer?"

"Like a pretty girl who is happy with her life."

"In that case, no roses for me." She took off the headband. "Sit down while I look through things."

There was a big round hassock in the corner and he sat on it, watching her as she opened and closed drawers and tossed things onto the floor near him.

"Why are your clothes here and not in your house?"

"Not enough room over there. And Kent's suits—" She broke off. They never mentioned his name. It was as though they didn't want to remember that he existed. Saying it aloud put reality into the day.

Alejandro picked up a blue-and-white dress. It had wide straps at the top and a gathered skirt. "This is pretty. You could dance in it."

It took her a moment to bring her mind back to the present.

"I wore that at a garden party my mother had. It has a jacket. Ah. Here it is." She held up a short, dark blue bolero.

"Very nice. I like it. So how are you going to get all of this to your house?" She gave him a sweet smile. "I'm a man. I don't carry dresses. At least not empty ones."

"I'll stuff them full of other clothes, then you'll just have to carry one."

He groaned. "Where's the chair I'm supposed to take?"

"It's— Ow." She'd tripped over Alejandro's feet as he sprawled on the hassock. He caught her arm, but instead of the usual flirtiness, he was looking around the big closet and frowning.

It was as though she could read his mind. "I don't need all these things to be happy."

"But it's what you're used to. It's your world. It's where you belong."

He said this in Spanish and his deep voice made it beautiful. He was still holding her bare upper arm. Without thinking what she was doing, she put her hand on his warm chest and leaned forward. To kiss his lips was all she could think of.

He hesitated, but then he pushed her away and stood up. He seemed to be trying to act as though nothing had happened. "Are you sure you need *all* these clothes?"

The intimate moment was gone. Behind him, Elise closed her eyes. When she opened them, Alejandro was looking at her in the mirror over the dresser. For a flash of a second, she saw the longing in his eyes. The deep wanting of something that he knew he could never have.

Elise wanted to go to him but couldn't. He was right. Her life; his life. They weren't alike. They didn't even run side by side.

"If we could meet on common ground," she whispered, "as equals, we could—" Turning, he gave her a look that made her stop talking. They both knew it was no use.

If they began something they couldn't finish, the pain they felt now was nothing to what it could be.

She gave a quick nod of understanding and stepped away from him. It took a deep breath to bring her back to the present. Away from what might be and back to what *was*. "How many shoes can you carry?"

He gave a slow smile, glad she understood. "One pair and that's all."

"I bet we could slide a dozen pair of sandals over your arms."

"Like a horse harness?"

Elise's gasped. "Horse! My riding lesson. I've got to go!"

He started toward the door.

"You forgot my clothes."

"I thought you were in a hurry to leave."

"Not so much that I'd forget my dresses. Hold out your arms and I'll pack you."

"A horse, a mule, a Christmas tree," he muttered as she slid sandals over his forearms, and they smiled at each other.

Chapter Nine

BOTH KATHY AND OLIVIA WERE STARING AT ELISE IN wide-eyed shock. Kathy recovered first. "You didn't go to bed with him?"

"No. And now I deeply regret it."

"I know all about regrets," Olivia said. "If I'd only said or done what my heart told me to, I would have had a lifetime of... of happiness." She looked at Elise. "What was your excuse?"

"Guilt. Kent was working so hard. *For me.* At least I thought he was. But I was playing around with the gardener and..." She shrugged. "Maybe I was afraid of the intensity of what I felt for Alejandro—and I didn't know if I actually liked him or just lusted after him."

"Did you find out?" Olivia asked.

"I think so." She swallowed. "No, that's not true. The lust I could handle. Whether I did or didn't go to bed with him, that was cut-and-dried. But liking him, maybe even..." She paused. "Maybe even *loving* him was what I couldn't bear."

She looked at them. "I knew Alejandro was right. We came

from two different worlds. It's romantic to say 'We'll live on love' but it's not very practical."

"I know about the struggle to pay the bills," Olivia said. "Sometimes money becomes the number one thing in life."

"Hmph!" Kathy said. "With a father like mine and married to his clone, I'm well aware of the importance of money."

"After the time in my closet, I began to think about what I was doing."

"I wish I'd been that smart with Ray," Kathy said.

"At the time I didn't feel smart. I felt cold and calculating. I thought about the truth of divorcing Kent and running away with the beautiful Alejandro. Then what? I have no job skills so I didn't think I could help financially. And forget the money, there were our families. My family would disown me for sure. And I can't imagine that his family would accept me. One of us was going to have to give up his or her entire life, friends and family, places, *everything*! For one of us, all that we knew would be taken away. When I looked at it, I could only see it ending badly."

Elise put her hands over her face. "I felt awful about my thoughts, but all I could see was that Alejandro and I would come to hate each other—and it would be *my* fault."

"So what did you do?" Kathy asked.

"I knew I had to end it with him. Stop it before the word *love* was spoken."

Elise looked away and squeezed her eyes shut in an attempt to stop the tears. "I made all these decisions before we finished the herb garden. It was so cute. Very simple with its little gravel paths and the birdbath in the middle. We had such a good time doing it! He and I went to the nurseries to buy the plants. We had glorious, wonderful, divine days of laughter while riding around in Diego's old truck. There was no AC, and the wind whipped in through the open windows. We'd arrive at a nursery sweating and happy."

Elise took a moment to calm herself. "We enjoyed each other. That's my highest compliment. We never ran out of things to talk about, and we slipped in and out of Spanish and English until it seemed like we had our own language."

She looked at them. "Everything was *fun*. It was all so easy. I'd never had that with Kent. With him, a dynamic was set up when we were children. He was the older one, and therefore smarter, more knowledgeable, and infinitely wiser. I was the little girl who looked up at him in adoration—and kept her mouth shut."

"But you and Alejandro were equals," Kathy said.

"Yes. We agreed on fundamentals, things like..." She put her hands up. "I don't know how to explain it, but we were the *same*."

"I know what you mean," Olivia said. "Kit and I were like that. Every idea one of us had, the other one liked it."

"Exactly! We'd go into a nursery, separate, and twenty minutes later we'd meet and both of us would have a wagon full of the same plants. Diego got sick of us. One time he tried to stick his nose into what we were doing. He said we needed to plant some red flowers around the border. I told him no, that I wanted blue. Later, Alejandro said he'd told his brother the exact same thing. Diego threw up his hands and said we were both crazy."

Elise looked away. "It was all too good. Too perfect, too wonderful. And I realized that I had to stop it."

"While you still could," Olivia said.

"Yes. When the garden was finished, we looked at each other and I knew he was thinking what I was. What was our next project to do *together*? But I'd already decided what I had to do."

"And that was?" Kathy asked.

"To end it in a way that there would be no mistaking what I meant." Her voice lowered. "I was horrible. I was a monster. I was..."

Olivia squeezed her hand. "Tell us."

"I said, 'Thank heavens *that* is finally done. Now I can do something worthwhile. See you around, Alejandro.' Then I turned my back on him and walked away."

"How long did you cry?" Olivia asked.

"Off and on for a week. I tried to give my attention to Kent. I asked him out on a date. Cooked for him. Tried to entice him into sex."

"While you imagined being with Alejandro?" Kathy suggested.

"I wanted to do that, but in bed, Kent was so fast that I didn't like to think that's how Alejandro would be."

"Is this when the red bikini and the binoculars came into play?" Olivia asked.

"Yes. I wouldn't allow myself to be near him, but I watched him from behind the curtains. I saw his muscles play against each other, saw him spray himself with water."

"I assumed he knew you were watching," Olivia said.

"Oh yes. He weeded the flower beds in my line of sight twice a day. And I began swimming." Elise gave a one-sided smile. "In a tiny bikini. Not a string really, but close to it. And to make sure I looked good, I went to the gym every morning. I'd seen Alejandro looking at my legs so I did a lot of legwork."

"And he watched you?" Olivia asked.

"Yes. There's a big hedge that surrounds my parents' pool, and one day when he came around it, I was sitting on the end of the diving board. I pretended I didn't see him. I've always been good in the water so I stood up, walked to the end, ran down the board, and did a perfect swan. I swam to the other side of the pool and got out. I looked to the opening in the hedge but he was gone."

"You're cruel." Kathy's smile showed her delight.

"Young lovers *are* cruel to each other," Olivia said.

"Did you two spend the rest of the summer pining over each other?" Kathy asked.

"No. Our separation ended when Kent and I had a fight. It

was at the last of the summer and the air was growing cool. I was feeling very sorry for myself. I was a martyr. I felt that I'd given up everything for Kent, but I hadn't received much in return. I'd begged him to please, please go away with me for a couple of weeks. Just the two of us, but he said he was too busy to leave."

"Too busy with his other family," Olivia said. "Been there, done that—except I certainly never begged Alan to spend more time with me."

"And I never asked Ray to go away with me." Kathy shuddered at the thought. "He needs lots of action, lots of people. Go on. What happened?"

For a moment, Elise and Olivia stared at her. This wasn't the impression that Ray had given them. He had insinuated that Kathy wanted to be near her husband every minute of every day.

"What happened?" Kathy repeated.

"I blew up," Elise said. "Maybe it was because I knew that in a few days Alejandro was returning to Mexico. Diego didn't need him in the winter, so Alejandro was going home."

"You might never see him again," Olivia said.

"That's what was bothering me. I may have met a man I could love, but he might leave my life forever."

"*Could* love?" Kathy said. "Sounds to me like you were heart and soul gone to him."

"Maybe," Elise said, "but nothing had changed. I thought about jumping in bed with him, but if I did that, I was afraid that later, after he left, I'd be in even more pain."

"Some pain is bearable," Olivia said. "And I think you could have lived with that one."

Elise nodded. "After all that's happened and what I know now, I deeply and truly wish I'd sat on his face."

Kathy's and Olivia's laughs deepened and it cleared the air of misery. "So what *did* you do?" Kathy asked.

"I got angry at Kent and said that he'd spent the whole summer working and I never saw him."

"And his reply?" Olivia asked.

"He gave me a very hard look and asked me what had happened to make me so needy."

"Yeow! A bit too close to home," Kathy said.

"It was. I wanted to scream at him that I'd given up the love of my life for him and he was accusing me of being 'needy'?"

"And you were," Olivia said.

"Deeply so, but Kent did nothing to help me. He went off to work that day in anger. And that afternoon, he sent me a text. He said he was bringing home a dozen people for dinner and I was to serve something 'special.'"

"Punishment," Olivia said. "Plain, old-fashioned *punishment*. He's the grown-up and you're the little girl and you're not to make demands on him."

"You're right. Yet all I wanted was his arms around me...and comfort. I think that if he'd given me that, then things could have healed between us. But he did nothing." Elise took a breath. "I went outside, sat down on my little patio, and started crying. I think I was realizing how bad my marriage really was. I don't think I was loud, but Alejandro heard me."

Olivia and Kathy were smiling. "The arms you needed."

"He didn't touch me. He sat down on the end of the chaise and listened. When he heard about the dinner, he said, 'Will you let Diego and me fix this?' All I could do was nod."

"They made dinner, didn't they?" Kathy said.

"Yes. All the men who worked for Diego were his relatives and they'd all helped his mother. They took over my kitchen like they were professional chefs."

"What did they make?" Kathy asked.

"Chicken cordon bleu."

"I've made that," Olivia said. "Flattened chicken fillets rolled around ham and cheese."

"I had the chicken breasts in my freezer and while Alejandro thawed them in the microwave, Diego gave a grocery order to the men. We were soon chopping and stirring and tasting."

"What about you and Alejandro?" Olivia asked.

Elise smiled. "It was like the barren months had never happened. It turned out that *he* was the cook. Diego was the manager. He told the men to set the table and get out serving bowls. Alejandro and I were at the stove and I followed his directions. It was…" She closed her eyes for a moment. "It was wonderful. All of us were working together and I was part of it. I got shouted at in two languages for doing things wrong—and each time, Alejandro told them in English to back off."

"Because we have the best curse words," Kathy said.

"And he can use them!" Elise smiled. "Fifteen minutes before Kent and the guests were to arrive, Alejandro told me to go get dressed for dinner. I was a mess and said I didn't have enough time. He said that even one minute was more than enough time to make myself into the most beautiful woman in the world."

"Awwwww," Kathy and Olivia said.

"And he told me to wear red—but more of it than I usually did. Meaning—"

"Your tiny red bikini," Olivia said. "I like your Alejandro."

"Me too," Kathy agreed.

"The dinner party was lovely and delicious. I was in such a good mood that I was an excellent hostess. I entertained and fed them and made sure their wineglasses stayed full."

"I'm curious as to how Kent reacted to this," Olivia said.

"He didn't like it. He was barely above a sulk all evening. And whenever anyone gave me a compliment, he made a snide remark, hinting that I was usually inept. He made it clear that what I'd pulled off that evening was quite unusual for me."

"Any guest comments?"

Elise smiled. "Oh yes. They took *my* side. One of the women cut Kent a couple of times. She and I clinked glasses across the table. It was a magical evening."

"All because of Alejandro," Kathy said.

"That summer, every laugh, every good happening, was given to me by him."

Olivia and Kathy looked at each other, then back at Elise. "Was that the last time you saw him before he left the country?"

"Oh no," Elise said with a grimace. "The next day I managed to make him so angry I thought he was never going to speak to me again—or me him."

"Anybody want more wine?" Kathy asked. "We may need it because I want to hear every word of *this* story."

"Fill 'er up," Olivia said. They leaned back to listen.

Chapter Ten

AS SHE MADE DINNER, ELISE KEPT LOOKING AT THE little shopping bag. Kent was going to be very angry when he saw the bill. So far, she hadn't come up with a plausible explanation. She didn't think "I wanted to thank one of the gardeners for being so nice to me" would calm him down. She could almost hear him. He'd talk in that kind, patient voice. He was a wise guru and was teaching her about life. "Elise," he'd say, "you do not buy a five-thousand-dollar gold watch for the gardener. A tip of, say, fifty dollars would be more than sufficient."

As he lectured, his voice would rise. He'd tell her how she didn't understand the value of money because she'd never had to earn it. "Everything has always been given to you. My parents and I have had to work for what we have."

This is where Elise would have to bite her tongue to keep quiet. Her father was the moneymaker. He had an eye for a deal. When he got married, he was aware that his wife was a package deal with her best friend and her husband. Since the foursome got along well, it hadn't been a burden.

It was Elise's mother who insisted her new husband give a job to their friends. "So we can buy big houses next door to each other." Kent's father was dubbed an executive vice president and put in charge of... Well, no one was sure of what exactly. But he was paid well and the two men were good friends.

Whenever Kent brought up what a hardworking family his was, Elise knew she couldn't say anything. To stand up to him with the truth made Kent go into a rage—then leave. One time he stayed away for three days.

Tonight she was preparing his favorite meal: meat loaf and mashed potatoes. For all his illustrious ancestry and an Ivy League education, his tastes tended toward the ordinary. Kent's idea of a good time was a football game and buffalo wings.

She took the meat loaf out of the oven just as she heard his car drive up. She grabbed the shopping bag and shoved it under the pot holders in the towel drawer.

He entered, frowning, and Elise went to him to kiss him hello. "Don't start on me. I'm not in the mood."

She stepped away. He'd been this way since the dinner party. Angry, sullen, and as though he was deep in thought about something.

In the past, she would have tried to coax him out of his bad mood, but tonight she didn't feel like doing that. She went to the kitchen, made herself a plate, then went outside to sit on the little patio to eat alone.

Where was Alejandro? she wondered. In just a few more days, he'd leave to return to his own country. Would he fall in love with some beautiful girl with black hair and a red rose behind her ear? Would he return in the spring or stay there? If Diego had his way, by this time next year, Alejandro would have a new bride and a baby on the way.

She could hear Kent inside the house as he opened drawers and slammed them. He wasn't used to having to serve himself.

"I have to *do* something about my life," she whispered. "Really and truly *do* something." Before she was married, she thought that by this time she'd have a child to care for. She'd be one of those dedicated mothers who arranged playdates. She'd be head of the PTA and make sure the other mothers showed up when they were supposed to. She'd—

There were tears running down her cheeks. No children; no job; a husband who could barely stand her. Yet she was constantly being told that she had "everything."

That night she slept in the second bedroom. She had a fantasy that Kent would come to her and apologize for being "such a beast." Then he'd make love to her. And in the morning some deep intuition would tell her that she was pregnant.

But he didn't so much as tap on the door. The next morning she stayed in the room until she heard him leave. He was going to be away for the night and he banged his overnight case against the door frame. It was the first time that she hadn't packed for him.

When the house was quiet, she left the room and dressed carefully. She put on dark linen pants, a white blouse, and ballet flats. She got the little shopping bag out of the drawer and opened it.

Inside was a gold Cartier watch. It was simple but elegant. When she'd seen it in the shop window, she thought it was like Alejandro. He may seem like an ordinary man, but to her, he was pure gold. She knew she had to give it to him. Something to remember her by. When he wore it, she wanted him to think of her, to close his eyes and remember the laughter they'd shared. Digging together, sitting in her closet while she tossed clothes at his feet, being at the nurseries and pulling wagons full of plants. She wanted to give him something so beautiful that he never forgot her. Even if he married someone else and she never saw him again, she wanted a tiny bit of her heart to be his.

When she left the house with the box bulging in her pocket, she didn't have to look far for him. He always seemed to stay nearby. In case she fell apart again and was crying? He'd run to rescue her?

First, she went to Diego and invited them to her house at three for a thank-you party.

She didn't want to keep them after five so they could go home on time.

Diego said they'd be there but he looked cautious, as though he thought she was up to something—which she was. Elise wanted more time with Alejandro. As much time as she could get.

Finally, she went to Alejandro. "Hi," she said. He stopped shoveling mulch and smiled at her.

She hadn't seen him since the dinner party, the night they'd all had so much fun. The night Kent had sulked like a spoiled child. The night that Elise had *not* played her role of being less than he was.

She looked around to make sure they were alone. "I can't thank you enough for what you did for me. The party went very well."

"They liked the food?"

"Very much."

She sat down on the grass near him and watched as he went back to work. The sun hit his golden-toned skin, glistening off the coal black of his hair.

After a while, he stopped shoveling and turned to her. He didn't say anything but there was such longing in his eyes that it made her breath catch.

She wanted to go to him, slide into his arms, and never let go. But her whole life of doing what she should and not what she wanted to held her back.

He saw what she was thinking, gave a nod, then he put his shovel into the mulch and withdrew a scoop.

Elise got up and went to stand by him. "I know you're leaving soon." She stepped closer. "My Spanish teacher and her grandchildren—mostly the kids—taught me how to cook some

Mexican dishes. I told Diego that he and the men are invited to a little party at my house today. At three. Is that all right?"

He put down his shovel and faced her. "Of course. That's very kind of you."

His voice was so formal, so distant that it felt as though he'd already left. "I wanted to give you a gift, something special. From me."

His eyebrows drew together. "A gift?"

She pulled the box out of her pocket and handed it to him.

Taking it, he frowned deeper. He opened the box, barely glanced inside, closed the lid, then shoved it back into her hands. With his shoulders straight, he swiftly walked away from her.

For a moment, Elise just stood there. He looked as if he was *angry* at her. But how could that be?

She hurried after him, but he was moving so fast that she had to run. When she was close, she grabbed his forearm, but he jerked away and kept going.

"Will you please tell me what's wrong?" He didn't slow down or answer.

When she saw that he was heading toward the back fence, she realized that he was going to the trucks. He was going to *leave!*

Elise ran faster than she ever had and just as he reached the gate, she threw herself in front of it. She was out of breath.

He didn't speak, just crossed his arms over his chest, and glared—at the fence. He wouldn't meet her eyes.

"What...?" Pant, pant. "...did I..." Pant, pant. "...do?"

He cut her a look of such anger that the hairs on her neck stood up. Then he looked back at the fence.

To Elise's surprise, she didn't relent. When her parents or Kent got angry at her, she felt like a failure and skulked away. *Maybe it has to do with...with caring,* she thought. She was always afraid of losing their love.

But with Alejandro it was different. She wasn't afraid of anything about *him.*

"Is that all you're going to do?" Her teeth were clenched. "Stand there and glare at the wall? You can't even *speak* to me? I wanted to give you a gift to remember me by. *You* are the one going away. This time next year you'll probably be married and have a kid, while I'm—"

When he didn't look at her, she broke off. "Oh, go away! I've had all the sulking, ungrateful men I can stand. I'm going to become a lesbian. The hell with all of you."

She stomped away, but got only a few feet before he halted in front of her. She stepped around him and didn't slow down.

Again, he put himself in front of her. "Is that what you think of me? That I've done so much for you that you give me a *tip*."

She was still holding the watch box. "A *gift* is completely different. It's—" She waved her hand. "You won't listen so why bother? You and your sister are just alike. Cinnamon gum, Cartier watches, whatever. You twist them around so they're something bad." She looked him in the eyes. "If you think I have some ulterior motive for this—" she held the watch box in front of his face "—then I'd rather throw it in the lake than for you to have it."

She looked at him with all the anger she felt. Her rage at Kent, her parents, what her life should be and wasn't, all of it was in her eyes.

He stepped to one side and she started toward the house.

"Don't come to my party this afternoon," she said over her shoulder. "It's for people I *like*." When she got to the house, she slammed the door shut.

For hours, Elise worked like a demon on speed. She cooked and cleaned while playing music at a deafening level. Anything to keep from thinking about what had happened.

"Why am I always *wrong*?" she shouted, but the music was so loud that she couldn't hear herself.

By three, she had huge bowls of guacamole with a tub full

of warm tortilla chips. She'd made chili rellenos, burritos, and rolled enchiladas.

She did her best to smile when Diego and his men arrived, but her eyes were showing her anger. She turned the music down.

"Maybe we should come back," Diego said.

"No, of course not. I made lots of food. Eat. Take the leftovers home."

Miguel turned to Franco and said in Spanish, "I'm glad I'm not Alejandro."

Elise whipped around and in Spanish said, "Alejandro is a steaming pile of dog poop. You like the guacamole?"

The men stepped back, eyes wide. "*Si, si.* It's very good."

"Then eat it!" In the house, she leaned against the refrigerator. She really did need to get herself under control. She'd put out only beer as the men had to drive home, but now she pulled limes out of the fridge. It was time for a margarita—or twelve.

Two hours later, Elise was laughing and dancing with one man after another. They took turns twirling her around. The music had changed to songs from Mexico that blared out from the cell phone of one of the men.

At six, Elise shouted that the men should go home to their families, but they said their wives and kids were in Mexico. She knew Diego's family was, but not the other men's. She raised her full glass, the rim coated in coarse salt. "To loneliness," she yelled in Spanish.

They all drank to it.

Diego, the boss, the serious one who looked out for everyone, was the last to relax and enjoy himself. The men kept saying he was the best dancer but it was nearly dark before Elise could get him onto his feet.

He was good, moving around so easily that Elise glided across the stone terrace. "Is this how you got your wife?" she asked.

"I promised to get her out from under my mother's rule. She

ran to me." He spun her around at arm's length. "You are destroying my little brother."

"Good! He's ripping my heart out and it's bleeding all over my feet. I may drown in my own blood."

She'd said this in Spanish, with such drama that Diego laughed. "There are things about my family that you don't know. We keep our secrets to ourselves."

"So tell me your biggest, baddest one."

"Maybe I should. Maybe we should tell you."

"I'd like to hear of someone else's problems."

"Then I must be silent," Diego said.

She started to ask him what he meant, but he whirled her away again, then Miguel took her hand, then Franco, then…

She was in Alejandro's arms, her breasts just touching his chest. He had on a shirt of pure white, with ivory embroidery down the center, and pearl buttons. His hair was washed and slicked back. There was little light on the patio and the dusk made his eyes even darker.

She pushed away from him, but he didn't let go. "I hate you."

"I know." He pulled her to him so that her arms were folded onto his chest. His heart was beating against her cheek. The music changed to slow and he swayed to it. "I have to go back."

"To your real family?" she said.

"No, it's not. Part of me will never again belong there."

"You're going to make me cry."

"Good. We will weep together."

For a while they danced. She put one arm around him, one folded against his chest and he held her fingers in his.

"We both have problems we need to solve," he said.

Elise stiffened. "You have a girlfriend."

He chuckled. "I wish it were so simple."

When the music changed to a hard beat, Alejandro took Elise's hand and led her into the garden, away from the men. They teased, but Alejandro didn't slow down.

He stopped at the bench by the herb garden and they sat down. He didn't let go of her hand.

When she looked up at him, her eyes begging him for a kiss, he didn't lean forward. He smoothed her hair behind her ear, then put her hand on his chest.

"We cannot start what we will not be able to stop." He stroked her hair. "We both need to be sure," he said. "I could not bear to be something you use then toss away."

"I wouldn't do that."

"Not intentionally, but I see you with your husband. There is a part of you that if he called, you would go. I would die if that happened."

Her body was still but her heart was about to leap out of her chest. He seemed to be saying he loved her. And he seemed to be *very* sure of how he felt. But for Elise, just last night she'd been hoping to have Kent's baby.

"I am leaving in the morning."

"No! You can't—"

He squeezed her hand and smiled. "I will return in the spring and we will see what has changed."

"You mean I'm to choose between you and my husband?"

"You must decide much more than that. Your life, your home. You have never been away from your parents. Your husband treats you as a child. He has secrets that…"

"That what?" When he was silent, she leaned back to look at him. "Diego was hinting at something and now you. What are you trying to tell me?"

He took a while before answering. "I am going to see that you know. When you have the facts, you will need to choose what you want to do."

She could tell that he wanted her to know something but she couldn't figure out what. "I'm not sure I have the strength to do what you want of me."

He pulled her head back down to his chest. "You were very

strong when you saw the truth of what could happen. You were right to stop it."

"You mean when I ran away from you after we finished the garden?"

"Yes. You were stronger than I was. I was to the point where all I could think of was getting you in bed with me."

"Really?" She sounded so enthusiastic that he laughed.

"It was after you ran away that I missed you."

"Did you?" she asked.

"Every minute of every day, I longed for you. To hear you laugh, to talk with you, just to be near you."

"I felt the same way," she whispered.

"How could you feel anything other than cold in your tiny red swimsuit?"

"Can't really swim in that thing. It tends to come off."

Alejandro groaned. "You are wicked to tease me so. We need time to figure out all of this."

She waited for him to continue, but he didn't need to. She understood what he meant.

How could they blend their lives together? Elise needed to be absolutely *sure* of what to do about Kent. And what about her parents? Could she get a job somewhere? "Yes," she managed to whisper. She didn't know she was crying until she felt the wetness of his shirt.

"I will come for you in the spring. Then you can tell me what you've decided."

"What about you?"

"I know what I want. I've always known. From the first time I saw you, I was lost." His arms tightened on her. "I will pray. I will wish on stars. I will buy potions." He paused. "I will *hope*. When I return and see you again, I will know what you have decided."

He leaned away from her and put her hands on her lap. "I must go now or I'll not be able to control myself."

She put her hand on his cheek. "Alejandro, please stay. Just tonight. One night." Holding her hand to his face, he kissed her palm, then released it. He stood up, stepped into the dark, and was gone.

Chapter Eleven

ELISE LOOKED AT OLIVIA AND KATHY. "THAT WAS months ago and I haven't seen or heard from him since then."

"Wow," Kathy said. "I would have ripped off his clothes that night."

"I wish I had," Elise said. "Now I'll never get a chance. By now he's probably returned and been told that I was locked away because I tried to kill myself."

"Since he's Carmen's brother, I imagine he knows more than that," Olivia said. "Of course she's what the men were trying to tell you about."

"That my husband and their sister..." Elise took a breath. "Now I'm on the run from the law and I doubt if I'll ever see him again. But it wouldn't matter. I still don't know how Alejandro and I would *live*."

Olivia's head came up. "Alejandro said he'd see that you found out. Do you think he had anything to do with Tara starting to investigate Kent?"

"I don't know," Elise said. "But it's possible."

"Alejandro did have Tara's card," Kathy said. "Maybe he sent her something."

Elise closed her eyes for a moment. "That would mean that he chose *me* over his sister. He gave his loyalty as well as his love to me. But what did I do? Up until the night before I found out, I was still hoping that Kent and I could... I don't know, start over? Alejandro was more loyal to me than I was to him. I wish I could change... Change it *all*!"

"Me too," Olivia said.

"And so do I," Kathy added.

It had begun to rain and the sound was nice in the house. The women got up, took bathroom breaks, straightened the kitchen, and pondered all that they'd heard.

Elise kept smiling, relieved to have at last been able to tell someone about her and Alejandro. When it was happening, she'd told herself that it wasn't serious, but saying it all out loud had made her see that there was more there than she'd realized. What had Kathy said? That she was "heart and soul gone to him."

Maybe she had been. Maybe she *was.*

"So who's up for a game of Scrabble?" Kathy asked when they were back in the living room.

When they looked at her, it was as though they were holding a sign. You're Next.

But Kathy was hesitant. "Olivia, your husband's a diplomat, right? Have you traveled a lot?"

Elise started to say something, but then Kathy looked at Olivia, and there was something in her eyes. But what was it? That she felt sorry for Kathy? But why?

It took her a moment but she began to realize that Ray had told them something about her. But what in the world was it? When it came down to that, what did he really *know* about his wife? Their eyes seemed to want some information, but they were afraid of the answers.

In a lot of ways, Kathy was Bert Cormac's daughter. She'd

inherited her mother's sensitivity, but there was enough of her father's personality in her that Kathy could, well, survive the two men in her life. And one of the ways she'd done that was to keep her mouth shut. She never truly confided in anyone. She let others see one thing while she kept the truth to herself.

But these two women, these strangers, had confided in her. More than that, they'd entrusted her with some deep secrets. A call to the police could change Elise's life forever. And Olivia…

"Maybe Scrabble would be good," Olivia said. "Has anyone seen a board around here?" She opened a corner cabinet.

The truth was, just as Elise had, Kathy *wanted* to talk. She wanted to tell these women who'd been through so much about her life. She took a breath. This was going to be hard for her so she'd better start with something easy. "Did Ray tell you how we first got together as a couple?"

Both women stopped opening cabinet doors and smiled.

"His date spilled a drink on you and he said you handled it graciously," Olivia said.

"With class," Elise added. "He didn't say so, but I think he fell in love with you at that moment."

Kathy looked from one woman to the other, then let out a loud laugh. "How funny! Ray didn't 'fall in love' with me then or at any other time."

"He *does* love you!" Olivia was serious.

Kathy leaned back in her chair. "Yes, he does. He loves me very much. More than he knows, but that's not why he married me."

Olivia and Elise were staring at her but they didn't seem shocked by her words. "I bet Ray told you that after the spilled drink he saw me crying."

"Yes, he did," Olivia said. "He said his date had hurt your feelings."

"Ray is an idiot! Smart, brilliant even, but an idiot. The truth is that she and I set that whole thing up."

"I want to hear this," Elise said.

Olivia agreed. "This is a house of stories and you're next. Elise, get the wine and the glasses. Are there any more of those chips?"

"Oh no," Kathy said. "I gain weight even looking at food. You have any club soda?"

"Kathy," Olivia said, "I don't know who has messed with your mind but you look great."

"I wish I had boobs like yours," Elise said.

"You wouldn't be able to stand up," Kathy shot back, then put her hand over her mouth. "Sorry."

But Elise and Olivia laughed and got up and went to the kitchen. Minutes later, they had a banquet of wine and chips and dip on the coffee table.

It had been a long time since Kathy had some good, old-fashioned girl time. Between her father and Ray, both of them men who demanded a lot—and got it—she didn't have much of a chance for girl talks. To those two men, if it wasn't something that would lead to making money, why bother discussing it?

Now these women were watching her in silence, waiting for her to tell them what happened. Elise had poured her heart out and Kathy knew she should do the same. But she'd never told anyone the truth about what had happened. But then, who could understand the power of Bert Cormac and Ray Hanran? The few times Kathy had tried to describe them to women friends, they'd thrown up their hands in horror. "You should get away from them," they'd said. "Stand up to the tyrants." "Be good to yourself." On and on. Sometimes women's "support" lacked understanding—or variety.

Kathy didn't dare tell anyone that there was a part of her that loved the challenge, loved the fireworks that a life near those men created.

Fireworks, she thought. Yes, that described Ray exactly. In the rare moments when he was quiet, he was like an unlit bomb.

And the endless attention he gave her—even if it was to find his lost papers—was exciting.

Kathy took a breath, picked up the glass of cold white wine that Olivia had poured for her, and took a sip.

"Poor Dolores," she began. "It was one of Dad's black-tie balls, two floors down in our building, and meant to impress his clients. Not that Bert Cormac would know a white tie from a clown's bow tie. He left arranging the entire party up to *me*."

She took another sip. "You have to understand that my father and my husband love each other. Father-son love. Fishing buddies love. Besties. Clones, actually. So when Dad realized that he had to go a black-tie event without Ray there, he had me send for him."

"Wait," Olivia said. "Ray said you helped him, but I didn't realize you worked for the company."

"You mean get a paycheck, dental, that sort of thing? I don't. Bert Cormac believes in family—or that's what he says. To him that means I do the work of three employees and never receive acknowledgment or pay. And certainly not any thanks."

Olivia was looking at her in disgust.

But Elise was smiling. "That silk shirt you have on is Italian and retails for over a grand. And the stones in that necklace are real. I think you're compensated."

Kathy gave a slow smile. "I am my father's daughter."

At her tone, Olivia snuggled into the couch. "I think I'm beginning to like you, Kathy Hanran. So Ray was told to return from his business trip and he called a girl from Brooklyn to be his date."

"Exactly," Kathy said. "And I found her in the restroom crying. Not to be catty, but she should have cried. She looked horrible! She had on a purple polyester dress with a set of rhinestone jewelry that came from the Dollar Store. Literally. And her hair! Ghastly. But Ray had given her three hours to get ready—which included buying a dress—and she'd done the best she could."

"Why didn't she say no?" Elise asked.

Olivia spoke before Kathy could. "I have a feeling that when Ray turns on the charm it's almost impossible to say no to him."

"You're right," Kathy said. "The first thing I did was get her out of that public restroom. I had a key to Dad's office and I kept a box of cosmetics in his bathroom. I thought I'd take a shot at repairing her face. I couldn't fix that dress, but I could get rid of the purple eyeshadow."

Kathy drank more wine. "I think I should add something about that night. I thought I had a boyfriend, Larry. We'd met a couple of months before and he was so attentive that he'd almost blocked Andy out of my mind."

"I take it Andy is the unattainable one?" Olivia said.

"The one who never looked at me. His office was near Ray's so I hung out nearby every time I went into the city. I was hoping that Andy would notice me. But he never did."

When Olivia glanced at Elise, Kathy understood. "Let me guess. Ray told you I was near his office because I had a crush on *him*."

Elise and Olivia nodded.

Kathy gave a little laugh. "I do know my husband. Anyway, that night I was feeling great, full of love for the world, so I wanted to help the girl. She was short, so I had her sit on the bathroom counter while I fixed her face and we began to talk."

Chapter Twelve

"RAY WON'T LET ME BREAK UP WITH HIM." DOLORES was sniffing. "I've tried. He agrees but then he shows up at my door and..." When she shrugged, the hideous dress nearly fell off her bony shoulders. She was only about five feet tall and didn't weigh a hundred pounds. Next to Ray she looked like a lost child.

Kathy was using a Q-tip to remove the mascara from under Dolores's eyes. "Ray is like my dad. He wants to win, no matter what the prize."

Dolores looked surprised, as though she couldn't believe someone like Kathy could know him so well. "That's Ray, all right!"

Kathy began to replace the eyeshadow with four shades of brown, blending each color into the other. "What Mom and I used to do is figure out a way to make Dad do what we wanted him to. You need to make Ray stay away from you."

"How do I do that?" Dolores looked like she was going to start crying again. "I've yelled at him. Slammed doors in his face. There isn't a name I haven't called him. But it doesn't matter

what I say because he does this thing to my ear, then it's panties gone. It's like they just drop off of me."

Kathy's eyes were wide.

"Now you're shocked. I better leave."

"No!" Kathy said. "I'm not shocked. I'm jealous. I wish my
boyfriend did that."

Dolores sighed. "That's the way it always is. You want what
Ray gives me and he wants me to be elegant and refined, like
you are. You think any people who match ever get together?"

Kathy stepped back to look at her work. *Much* better! "Not
that I've seen. Just to be clear, my boyfriend's parents think I
come from low-class working stock. To them, I'm one step up
from being the garbage collector's daughter. They're surprised
that I don't eat peas with a knife."

Dolores laughed. "You're nice."

"I try to be. What if you and I do something so awful that
Ray has to break up with you?" Kathy wiped the red rouge off
Dolores's cheeks and put on some peach-colored blush. "Is there
someone else at home who you like?"

"Yeah. Donnie. But he's seen me with Ray so he's too scared
to get near me."

"If this works, invite me to the wedding."

Kathy looked back at Olivia and Elise. "We made a plan to
wait until Ray was on the far side of the room, then she'd spill
her drink on me—it was club soda—and she'd bawl me out. It
almost failed because when Dolores said I looked at her like she
was the garbage collector's daughter who eats peas off a knife,
I choked up. I had to leave the room so nobody would see me
laughing."

"If all that worked so well, what made you cry?" Elise asked.

"I…" Kathy took a breath. "This is a difficult memory to
go back to."

"And my story was easy for me? Leaving Alejandro? Hearing him tell me I still needed to make up my mind? That I should—?" She broke off at Olivia's look. "Okay, sorry. But you need to confess."

Nodding, Kathy took another drink of her wine. "I'd left my clutch in my father's bathroom so I went back to get it." She looked at Olivia. "Have you ever had a single moment in your life that changed everything?"

"I have," Olivia said. "Someone asked me to go to Richmond and I said yes. When I got back, the man I loved with all my heart was gone. I didn't see him again for over forty years."

"Oh." Kathy paused, blinking as she thought about that. "I guess you do know. I was in the bathroom when Larry—who I thought was *my* boyfriend—came in with Felicity, Cal's girlfriend. She was—"

"Wait!" Olivia said. "Who is Cal? And how old is he?"

"Calvin Nordhoff, management director. He's about the same age as Ray, I guess. Dad says he couldn't have a company if it weren't for Cal keeping everything in line. He's the balance between the flamboyance of Ray and the rock-hard stubbornness of my father."

"One man who can balance the two of them," Olivia said. "The third leg of a stool. Remove one and it collapses. Interesting."

Kathy blinked a few times. "I never thought of it that way, but I guess you're right. The truth is that I've never known exactly what Cal does. I always had the idea that he disapproved of me. The boss's daughter sticking her nose into every department. I avoid Cal whenever possible. Anyway, Felicity was like everything I feared in one very skinny body. She used to look me up and down in a way that made me want to hide in a closet."

"Why were Larry and Felicity in your dad's office?" Elise asked.

Kathy sighed. "Funny how, even after years, things can still hurt." She looked up. "They were in there to have sex on my father's big, gaudy show-them-I'm-the-boss desk."

She paused a moment. "I knew Felicity was a lawyer and so was Larry, but I didn't know they'd gone to school together. I certainly didn't know they'd lived together in their freshman year. But then, there were lots of things I didn't know about Laurence J. Winbeck the Third."

Kathy took a moment before going on. "As soon as I heard them and knew what they were about to do, I knew I should show myself, but I was fascinated. I didn't watch, but I heard it all. I had no idea Larry had so much energy in him. He'd always seemed too fastidious for down and dirty sex. But what they did was hard and fast—unlike any sex he and I'd ever had. It was over quickly, but it was like the whole place was full of steam. I stood inside the bathroom with the door half-open, lights off, and my heart was pounding."

"That must have been difficult for you to see the man you were dating with someone else," Olivia said.

"Yes and no. I think maybe I was jealous but not in the normal way. First, there'd been Dolores with her panties falling on the floor, then Felicity getting slammed on Dad's desk. I was jealous of what the women were getting and I wasn't. When would *I* get that kind of mindless passion?"

"That's what I wonder too." Elise's voice held sadness along with the anger.

Kathy looked at Elise in sympathy. "Before today I would have thought someone as thin and beautiful as you are would have it all."

"Me too," Elise said. "When I married Kent, I thought—"

Olivia cut her off. "I want to know what happened in the office."

Kathy let out her breath. "Things got worse. They lay on the carpet and began to talk."

"Yes, talk is worse," Olivia said. "What did they say?"

Kathy shook her head. "Everything was all about *me*."

"Are you going to do it?" Felicity asked. "Are you really going to work up the courage to marry your fat, bland, but oh-so-rich girlfriend?"

"Sure. Another six weeks and she's mine. But then, I have to, don't I? My dad owes too much money to old Bert Cormac for me to back out."

"Don't give me that crap! You wouldn't sell your soul for your old man. You want the house and the car and the easy job you'll get by watching that walrus walk down the aisle. Looking forward to your wedding night?"

"Cut it out." Larry sat up. "Kathy's nice. She's as naive as a child but she's okay. She's terrified of her father, but then so am I. It'll be a good marriage. Not exciting, but stable and secure."

"And you'll have a few office affairs to satisfy your lust and—"

"Hell no I won't!"

"You're trying to make me believe that you'll be faithful to that…that wimp of a whale?"

"I meant that I'm not going to have an office. About four years after the I dos, I plan to have some injury that'll make it impossible for me to sit at a desk. I already have a doctor who'll sign a certificate for me. I'm going to spend my life at the country club."

"And in the girls' locker room?"

"Now you're understanding," he said.

"Any chance your great big gold mine will throw you out and go to court? I wouldn't want to go up against Bert Cormac in a courtroom!"

"Not a chance. Kathy's so love-starved that all I have to do is smile at her and she comes running. Isn't that like you and Cal?"

Felicity laughed. "Not quite. Cal is a hard case to crack."

"But you're working on it?"

"I guess. He's not somebody who shares his innermost thoughts. I don't know anything about his past, but the sex is good, so I'll hang around awhile longer."

When someone tried to open the outer door, Kathy gasped. "We better get out of here," Larry said.

"Wait! I heard something from that bathroom."

Kathy held her breath as the door rattled again.

"It's nothing. Get your shoes and let's go out this way."

After they left, Kathy stepped into the office and opened the door to her father. When she braced herself for his sharp comment, she realized she *was* "terrified" of him. He was so loud and aggressive that she and her mom just gave in to him. It was easier.

But her father didn't snap at her. He looked at her for a moment, frowned at what he saw, but he said nothing. When he stepped away, he bent down and picked up a bracelet off the floor. "Looks like someone was in here doing something they shouldn't." He tossed the bracelet to her, then went to the far side of his desk and picked up some papers.

Kathy stood there looking at the bracelet, knowing it was Felicity's. How had she not seen the truth about Larry? She wished she could tell her dad what had happened and how it hurt her. She'd like to curl up on his lap and have him hug her and tell her that everything would be all right. But Bert Cormac wasn't a snuggle type of father—and he'd tell her she was a fool for wanting Larry in the first place.

"Mind if I break up with Larry?" she asked.

Bert gave a snort. "And save me from someday having to support the lazy bastard?"

Kathy drew in her breath. If her father had seen that about Larry, who else had? Were other people laughing at her? She was the Wimpy Whale. Maybe she should write a children's book with that title.

When her father looked up at her, he wasn't wearing his usual expression of impatience.

For a moment, she thought she saw sympathy in his eyes.

Kathy gave a little nod, then left the office, closing the door behind her.

As she got into the elevator, she realized that it hadn't all hit her yet. What she'd seen and heard weren't quite in focus. How did she handle it? Did she walk away and cry out her hurt? Or did she confront Larry and say that she'd seen what he'd done?

But Kathy didn't feel like crying. Maybe there was more of her father in her than she'd thought because all she felt was anger. Rage. It flowed through her like lava.

And that red-hot anger was making her stand up straight, and oddly, she felt rather calm.

Larry had been planning to entice her into *marrying* him. For her father's money. And neither he nor Felicity seemed to think Larry wouldn't be successful.

Those two had called her "nice." "Love-starved."

Cal and Felicity were on the dance floor. They were a good-looking couple. Cal was tall and handsome in his tuxedo and Felicity was elegant in her designer dress. She was looking up at Cal with stars in her eyes. No one would guess that just minutes before her legs had been wrapped around Larry's neck.

With a smile, Kathy made her way through the dancers. She was the boss's daughter so they stepped aside.

When she reached Cal and Felicity, they stopped dancing. Cal looked at her in such a patronizing way that she wondered what she'd ever done to make him dislike her. Felicity looked Kathy up and down, her upper lip curving in distaste.

"Sorry to bother you," Kathy said in her sweetest voice as she held the bracelet on the tip of her finger. "You left this on the floor of my father's office when you were screwing Larry. You know, maybe I shouldn't say this, but I think you should have the mole on your left butt cheek looked at. It could be cancerous."

Kathy smiled. "But I was glad to see that you two are enjoying the party so much. Good night." Turning, Kathy walked away, and the dancers—who'd heard it all—parted like the Red Sea.

Chapter Thirteen

"AND THAT'S WHY YOU WERE CRYING," OLIVIA SAID.

"Yes. Ray missed the whole thing of me with Cal and Fe-licity. Ray had put Dolores in a cab, then he went somewhere and had a couple of drinks. He'd never admit it, but I think he was looking at his life. By the time he got back to the party, I'd come down off my high and was hiding out in the office upstairs and having a good, long cry. Ray came upstairs to get some papers, saw me, and..." She shrugged.

"Sex?" There was hope in Elise's voice.

"No. He raided the office kitchen and made us a big ice-cream sundae that we shared. I think that was the night he decided to quit holding out for a romance and settle for someone who could help his career. Whatever his thoughts, we were married six months later."

"And you settled too," Olivia said.

"I took what was offered. But in my own defense, I never thought that our marriage would be less than...than *real*." She gave an embarrassed smile. "I think Dolores's words were in my head. Maybe I wasn't to get the romance I'd dreamed of, but I did think I would get Ray's passion."

She paused. "But it didn't happen. After the marriage, Ray and I got along well. He complimented me lavishly on my knowledge of the business, and he discussed every account with me. He was respectful and courteous."

"What about the personal side?" Olivia asked.

"There were kisses and some fondling, but nothing else. I told myself that Ray was practicing being a gentleman. He'd said he wanted me to teach him what I knew about the social graces." Kathy put her hands over her face. "But I kept remembering Dolores and her panties. I thought that once we were *married* that it would change, that Ray would unleash the fire inside him. On *me*."

Elise said, "Me too. I believed that marriage would make Kent and me equals. No more of his 'older brother' act."

"I thought those were beliefs of my generation," Olivia said. "I thought that you kids knew better than to believe that ancient myth of marriage solving problems."

"No," Kathy said. "We don't know any better. Haven't learned anything."

"I certainly haven't," Elise said. "I Icy! This was all years ago, so what happened to everyone? Especially to the floor gymnasts."

"Including Andy the unattainable," Olivia added.

Kathy shook her head. "You can never predict the future. I guess I believed it was the 1890s and that my exposure of Felicity's tryst would get her thrown out of society. But it elevated her. People said, 'Oh, you naughty girl, Felicity,' then laughed."

Kathy took a breath. "Larry got back together with his old girlfriend, whose family is so rich they make mine look poor. I recently heard that he had an accident and hurt his back and can no longer work for his father-in-law."

When Elise snickered, Kathy couldn't keep from smiling.

"Andy, the man I wanted, eventually asked Cheryl from accounting to marry him. She's about my size and they have two kids now."

A bit of a laugh escaped Olivia.

"My favorite is that Felicity went to a doctor about her mole. Last year she and the doctor got married."

Elise was the first one to let out her laughter, and the other two joined her.

"What about Cal?" Olivia asked. "Felicity did a real number on him. How did he feel about such a public humiliation?"

"I have no idea." Kathy refilled her wineglass. "He's not married, if that's what you mean, and he has a different date for every party. What's with you and Cal?"

"He just seems to be the one who gets left out," Olivia said. "I wonder how he reacted to that night? Anger at Felicity? Understanding? That kind of thing shows the true character of a man."

"I don't know. Like I said, Cal stays away from me. I do know that after that night he liked me even less than he did before. For months afterward, he wouldn't even stay in the same room with me. At my wedding he said, 'I hope you get what you want out of life.' The way he said it made my hair stand on end. Actually, the man kind of scares me."

"And now Ray is your life," Olivia said softly. "More or less."

"Maybe Andy was afraid to speak to you because you're the boss's daughter. Why didn't you ask him out?" Elise asked.

"I'm fairly secure about what I can do in the advertising world. I've come up with a few good ideas. But—" she motioned to her body with her hand "—I'm not so secure in a, uh, personal way."

"Oh well," Elise said. "At least your husband knows you have a brain. Mine thinks I'm a not-very-bright child."

"And mine thought I was only good for work."

"Not if you get the right one," Olivia said. "If I'd had Kit all these years I wouldn't have gone after Alan and his son." She sighed. "They would have had a life with people who made them happy."

"I wish I hadn't thought I was so powerful that I could make Kent love me."

"And I wish I'd gone up to Andy and asked him out to dinner."

The air in the room had become heavy with their regrets.

Olivia wanted to lighten the mood. "You think you young chickies have it hard? Let me tell you that when it comes to romance, there is *nothing* as bad as being an unmarried, older woman who is financially comfortable. You know how on TV and in movies when an older man's wife dies a zillion women show up with casseroles? What I didn't know is that people actually *believe* that what a financially secure widow truly wants is to take on some man to support, feed, and endlessly find whatever he's lost. 'A nurse or a purse.' That's what they want."

She took a drink of her wine. "On the day of Alan's funeral, three old men hit on me. Each one seemed to think it was *his* decision whether or not he would move into my mortgage-free house. And when I said no... The anger! None of the men wanted *me*. They just seemed to think it was my duty to take care of them. Sometimes I think I moved in with my stepson to protect myself."

Kathy put down her glass. "I have a big, beautiful husband who has such a raw sexuality that women follow him down the street. He and I are best friends, and genuinely love each other—but he never touches me. He is kind, considerate, and generous—and I'd trade it all for one really great screw."

They looked at Elise.

"Me? I'm a good girl. Obedient always. I never gave my parents any problems. When they pushed me toward marriage with Kent, I agreed. And why not? He's gorgeous and smart and ambitious. I didn't grow up fantasizing about rock stars. For me, it was always Kent. When I was eight, I started cutting out photos of the house he and I would have together. I made myself exactly what he liked. Shoulder-length hair with a headband? Check. Preppy clothes? Right. The schools that he said the woman he married should go to are where I went. I did it all. I never even questioned it. But what happened? He married me, he *likes* me, but he is passionate about Carmen. It's not possible for me to be more opposite than Carmen." She gave a pointed look at Kathy's magnificent bosom.

"Don't think these babies would solve your problems!" Kathy said. "I live on lettuce and broiled chicken, but even if I were as skinny as you, I don't think that spark would be between Ray and me."

Elise looked at Olivia, her eyes questioning. Should they tell Kathy that Ray was planning to leave her?

Olivia gave a curt nod and opened her mouth to speak, but a loud knock on the door startled them. She got up to answer it.

It was getting dark outside and Young Pete, his wrinkled old face scowling, had on a yellow slicker with raindrops on it. "I told those two to get out. They did, but they left the windows open."

Elise and Kathy were behind Olivia and looking at the old man.

When he saw Kathy, his deeply wrinkled face wadded up into a smile. "Didn't see *you* here." His voice was soft as he looked her up and down in a lustful way. He held out an umbrella. "For you."

"Thank you." Kathy took it and smiled back warmly.

With that, Young Pete turned away, seeming to be pleased by the encounter.

Olivia closed the door. "I take it that he told Kevin and Hildy to leave. I better go close the windows."

"We'll go with you," Elise said. "Someone has to protect Kathy from lecherous Young Pete."

"No! Don't! He's the best offer I've had in years," Kathy said, and they laughed. Kathy lent Elise a jacket. It was Prada, too big, but the buttery leather felt divine. "Kathy and I will close the windows," Elise said as Olivia got the house keys out of her handbag. "You don't have to go in." She explained that Olivia wanted to wait until Kit was there so they'd be together when they first saw the house.

"No," Olivia said. "I think I would like to see it. You two have made me feel good about having a man who actually wants me."

When she turned away to the door, Kathy and Elise looked at each other. Maybe Olivia had found the man, but what about the forty-some years she'd missed out on? And didn't the current problem have to do with that? Kevin and Hildy were part of her late husband.

But they said nothing. Kathy found a flashlight in a kitchen drawer and they followed Olivia across the drive to the fence that enclosed the River House. Elise made jokes about using the flashlight as a weapon to fight off Young Pete when he came after Kathy.

"Are you kidding?" Kathy said. "I'm encouraging him. Point out his house so I can sneak away later and meet him. He'll be my own personal gamekeeper."

When they reached the house, they were laughing.

Olivia had expected that when she first saw the interior of the house she and Kit were to live in, she'd feel only joy. On their long honeymoon they'd bought many lovely things. Laces in Spain, native sculptures in the Marquesas, antiques in China.

Stacy Hartman, their designer, had told them what was needed. "A chest of drawers for the linens," she'd written, then given the measurements. She would add a note about the color, a hint of blue or silver, or a red lacquer to go with a rug Kit had bought twenty years before in a market in Egypt.

It had all been fun as they'd searched for beautiful things.

When what they found didn't fit Stacy's measurements, they'd send her a photo and ask her to find a place for it. She always did.

At first, Stacy emailed them photos of the fabrics she thought would work, but she soon found out that Olivia and Kit could get something comparable in whatever country they were in. Their whole trip down the length of Italy had turned into a fabric-buying journey. They bargained for remnants of cloth that had been used in palaces. One day Olivia pulled a piece of brocade off a pile of old rugs and said she wanted it for the headboard in the guest bedroom. The fabric was dirty and faded in spots but there were no holes in it. Kit had bargained—in Italian—and they'd come away with the fabulous piece for a good price.

Two days later they went back to the store and saw that the wily old owner had tossed another gorgeous tapestry weave over the pile of rugs. Grinning, he told them that anytime he had a piece that he couldn't get rid of, he threw it on the rugs and covered it with the floor sweepings. It sold immediately. "Usually to Americans," he said, his eyes dancing in merriment.

There were a lot of things in the house that were from the years when Kit and she hadn't been together, but there was enough of what they'd bought to make Olivia feel it was her home too. But she couldn't help thinking about what she'd like to change. If she'd been with Kit through the eighties, she would have vetoed the African masks. If they'd been together during the nineties, she would have chosen different rugs. *If, if, if,* she thought. She followed the women into the kitchen.

Stacy had filled the pantry and the fridge. They made salads and threw two big pizzas in the oven.

"I want to hear about *you*, about the summer of 1970, when you and Kit were together," Elise said to Olivia.

The rain was coming down hard outside, making them feel isolated.

"I don't know..." she said. It was a story that she'd spent over forty years trying to forget, or at least to bury under the reality of her life. Kathy and Elise were staring at her. "I'm not sure I even remember it clearly."

Neither Elise nor Kathy spoke, but their eyes said that they didn't believe her. Olivia looked in the oven window to check the pizzas. Who was she trying to kid? Herself? If so, it wasn't working because she remembered every second of that summer.

She used the big wooden paddle to remove the pizzas and they all went to the dining room. "This table came from England and was said to have been owned by—"

She stopped talking because Elise and Kathy were still standing, waiting for her to begin the story of her life.

"It's your turn," Kathy said.

"Not yet," Olivia said. "We haven't heard enough about your life with Ray. Didn't you say you *worked* with him?"

"We were like business partners. He ran every idea past me and we discussed each of them. Nothing interesting. No dark-eyed gardener came to save me. And I rarely got credit for what I did. So there! That's it. I want to hear about you and Kit and the summer to remember."

"I agree." Elise sat down next to Kathy. "I want to hear all of it. From the beginning."

Olivia took the chair across from them. "The whole story would present me in a very bad light. I was obnoxious."

"You?" Elise said. "But you're perfect. You are calm and thoughtful and have great insight into people. You—"

"So help me if you say you hope to be like me when you're my age, I'll throw you out into the rain and let Young Pete have you."

"I would really like to hear," Kathy said. "And please tell us the truth about yourself. About everyone."

Olivia closed her eyes and seemed to be trying to make a decision. "I tried so hard to forget, but I never could."

She was silent for a moment. "It was 1970," she began. "Nixon was in the White House and young men were dying in Vietnam." She held up her wineglass and looked at it. The expression on her face wasn't happy. "And the Food and Drug Administration had issued a warning that birth control pills might cause blood clots, so we were reluctant to use them."

The women began to eat as Olivia talked.

"I graduated from college in the morning and took a plane to New York that afternoon. My drama teacher had arranged for me to audition for Elizabeth in a new Broadway production of *Pride and Prejudice*. I'm ashamed to say that when I got the role I felt more 'of course' than grateful. I had never had a bad thing happen to me so I had a feeling of being invincible. Nothing bad was *ever* going to happen to *me*!

"We went right into rehearsals and I loved every minute of it. I shared a tiny fourth-floor walk-up apartment way downtown with the girl playing Jane. She was from a small town in Nebraska and we were hungry for everything New York had to offer. It was a truly marvelous time and I thought my life would be like that forever.

"But then, the theater caught fire from old, worn-out wiring and was shut down for a complete overhaul. Actually, the theater needed a full remodel. The show was put on hold until September. I couldn't afford to stay in New York with no job so I had to go home."

Olivia paused. "As I said, I was obnoxious. My parents had liked the quiet of their lives while I was in college. But I returned full of New York energy, critical of boring little Summer Hill, and angry that 'my' show wasn't opening immediately."

She smiled. "I didn't know it then but my mother was a very wise woman. She and Dad put up with me for three whole days. But Mom had so accurately foreseen what I was going to be like, that she'd found me a summer job. She told me I was to be the live-in cook-housekeeper for two old men."

"What did you say to that?" Elise asked.

"I very dramatically said that I'd rather die than spend my last summer as a normal person cooking for some old men." Olivia shook her head. "You know, my last remaining time before I became an internationally renowned star."

She laughed. "It's hard to think about now, but I was the spoiled only child of older parents and you can't get much worse than that. But my mother knew that it was time for me to grow up. She handed me my packed bag and told me that Mr. Gates would pick me up in ten minutes. I was shocked! But I told myself that if all I had to deal with were two old men, both of whom I knew to be sweet tempered, I'd have time to go over my lines and perfect them."

Olivia drank of her wine. "It was on the drive over that Mr. Gates told me the job was open because Mrs. Tattington, a relative who usually cooked for them in the summer, had broken her arm. She was there with her husband and five-year-old daughter. And Dr. Everett's five-year-old son was staying with them in the Big House. Mr. Gates said it would be nice if I helped with all of them too."

"How many people is that?" Kathy asked.

"Two old men, one of whom was in a wheelchair, three in the Tattington family, and a young boy. It was six people I was supposed to take care of."

"But wasn't Kit there too?"

"Not for the first few days. The night he arrived I was so exhausted from cooking and cleaning that I slept through the turmoil. The next morning, when I was told that a nineteen-year-old boy had been added to my workload, I was furious. Volcanoes were less angry than I was." Olivia was smiling.

"I guess something changed your mind," Elise said.

"Think of the way Alejandro dresses."

"Yes," Elise said. "Shirtless."

"And nearly pantless," Olivia said in a dreamy way. "In 1970,

I'd never seen a man with less clothing on than he was wearing. And I'd never, ever in my life seen a body as beautiful as his."

She grinned. "Nor have I since."

Chapter Fourteen

Summer Hill, Virginia 1970

OLIVIA PUT THE DISHCLOTH ONTO THE BIG PORCE-
lain sink and looked out the window. It was beautiful on the
grounds of the old plantation, but when you were as angry as
she was, nothing looked good.

Behind her at the kitchen table were Uncle Freddy, Mr. Gates,
and the two little kids.

Uncle Freddy's wheelchair was beside Mr. Gates's old cane-
backed seat and the children's legs dangled off the bench. They
were eating the Campbell's soup and grilled cheese sandwiches
she had fixed for lunch. Again.

Olivia knew she should get her anger under control, but at
the moment, life seemed too unfair for her to think clearly. Everything had been so perfect. She'd had Broadway and a future
that held nothing but promise.

Turning, she looked at the four of them, their heads down
and eating in silence.

Damnation! How did she get out of this job? She was totally
unsuited for it. She'd never cooked much and wasn't interested
in learning how. These men and the children—especially little

Ace—deserved better. Last night she'd called around and found an opening at Abigail's Dress Shop. If she could find a replacement here, she could have that job.

Olivia looked at Uncle Freddy's bent head. He was an old man and she didn't want to hurt him. Beside him was his lifelong companion, Mr. Gates. The two men often told how they'd been born on the same day. "And that makes us twins," they'd say, and laugh every time. Uncle Freddy was blond and fair skinned; Mr. Gates was African American.

Same birthday but very different worlds, and everyone in Summer Hill knew the story.

Frederick Ethan Tattington had been the youngest of four sons born to an old, rich, hardworking, humorless family in Philadelphia. On his twenty-first birthday, his father did what he'd done to each of his children: He asked Freddy what he most wanted. His older brothers had each said a variation of "Own the world." Their father had set them up with businesses they could rule.

But young Freddy, handsome to the point of prettiness and beloved by them all, said he wanted Tattwell, the plantation in Virginia that the family still owned. The family's ownership in a Southern state was still an embarrassment to them. Not because of the humanity involved, but because they'd been on the side that had lost a war.

Gladly—for his father had run out of businesses to give away—he turned over the decaying plantation to his son, along with the money needed to bring it back to life.

Freddy had always been a happy person, but on his twenty-third birthday his joy was severely tested. He had three glasses of champagne as he toasted the good that was his life. Then he mounted his horse and decided to see if he could jump over a hay wagon. Everyone begged him not to do it.

He made it over the wagon but just as his horse hit the ground, one of the barn cats ran past. Rather than hurt the creature,

Freddy jerked the reins to the right. The horse tried to turn but couldn't. Freddy went flying off and hit the old stone well in the small of his back. He was paralyzed from the waist down.

His beautiful fiancée left him and his family ordered him to return to Philadelphia. But Freddy stayed where he was, and he never lost his love of life. About a year after the accident, after he'd very kindly fired three highly qualified men his family had hired to help him, a tall, thin, African American young man came by looking for work. He glanced at the entry gates and said his name was Gates, just the one name.

Freddy hired him, added the Mr. to his name, and two weeks later they were inseparable companions.

Over the many years, Uncle Freddy—as he became known to everyone—had helped a lot of people. He gave them jobs on the old plantation that seemed to devour money. And he listened to them. In fact, he lived by the belief that most problems could be fixed by people genuinely *listening* to each other.

He developed contacts in law enforcement, social services, with clergy. He learned who to ask for help with any problem.

The only aspect of his life where he wasn't successful was in keeping a housekeeper-cook. No one lasted very long. The house was too big, there were too many mouths to feed, et cetera. The longest anyone had lasted was three years. That was Margaret and she had stayed because Uncle Freddy gave her the summers off.

Three years ago Uncle Freddy's distant cousin William, his wife, Nina, and their two-year-old daughter, Ruth, came for the summer. Bill taught physics at an eastern college and Nina was a housewife. The idea was that for the whole summer, Bill would work with some local boys in cleaning up the acres around the old house and tending the orchard and vegetable garden. Nina would cook, can, and freeze anything that grew. In the fall, they'd go back east and Margaret would return from her sister's place in Alabama to a pantry full of food that she didn't have to prepare.

It had all worked perfectly for about a month, then Summer Hill's Dr. Everett Chapman came to check on Uncle Freddy. His wife had some church meeting, so the doctor took his two-year-old son Kyle with him. Nina said she'd watch the kids so the men could visit.

The children disappeared. They just plain vanished. Half the town joined in the search for them. After eight hours of looking and no sign of the children, the families, the entire town, were sick with worry.

But then the kids came down from the attic, dirty and covered in cobwebs. They were hungry.

That night there were some serious lectures and threats given to the children—but they made no difference.

The next day when young Kyle saw Mr. Gates's red truck go by, he sneaked out of the house. The child climbed in the back and hid behind the bags of cracked corn.

His parents found him at Tattwell with Ruth. "Let him stay," Uncle Freddy said.

Mrs. Chapman, who was pregnant and feeling awful, agreed that Kyle could stay for two nights. When she lost the baby, she was so depressed and weak that she went to Tennessee to stay with her mother for what came to be the rest of the summer. Kyle moved into one of the many bedrooms at Tattwell so his father would be free to take care of the medical needs of the town.

The next summer Kyle's parents were trying for another baby and after the boy sneaked off three times in two days, they agreed to let him stay at Tattwell. That was the summer Ruth said that from now on she was to be called Princess Colette, and Kyle was Ace. Her title was shortened to Letty, and the names stuck.

This was the third year the children were spending the summer together at Tattwell. Letty stayed with her parents in what had once been the old kitchen, while Ace had his own room upstairs in the Big House.

On the surface, this summer looked like the others, but three weeks ago, Nina had slipped on the bathtub and broken her right forearm. She couldn't do the huge amount of cooking that she usually did in the summer. She couldn't tend the big vegetable garden and put up all those quarts of beans and tomatoes, or make gallons of applesauce for the winter. And if all that prepared food wasn't waiting for Margaret when she got back, she just might stay in Alabama. Then what would the men do?

But what had really changed was that little Ace's mother was dying of ovarian cancer.

When Olivia was told this, she knew she couldn't deal with such grief. It wasn't something she knew about. Mr. Gates said she should just be kind to the children, but yesterday the kids had run through the clean sheets hanging on the line and knocked half of them into the dirt. She'd seen the girl wearing her favorite silk scarf—which meant that the children had been in her bedroom going through her things. Olivia asked Uncle Freddy for a key to the lock on her bedroom door but he'd laughed. None of the doors had been locked in a century or more. "Maybe not since the Yankees came through here," Mr. Gates said, and the two old men had laughed together.

All in all, the three days she'd been at Tattwell were more than she could handle. Bratty kids, old men who found everything amusing, trying to cook—something she had no aptitude for— and having no contact with the world of theater overwhelmed her. Drained her.

"Better save a can of soup for Kit," Mr. Gates said without looking up.

It took Olivia a moment to realize that he was talking to her. "Who is that?" Her frown deepened. If it was another person for her to take care of, she might start screaming.

The kids came out of their food trance. "He's tall," Letty said.

"He's strong," Ace said.

Olivia narrowed her eyes at Uncle Freddy. "Who is this?"

"He…" Uncle Freddy swallowed. "He's from Maine, the son of a relative on my mother's side. His father called me and said young Kit needed a place to spend the summer, so I…" He didn't have the courage to admit what he'd done.

Olivia put her hands on her hips and went toward him. With him in a wheelchair, she was a great deal taller than he was. "Summer? You have added a *man* to my workload? Without asking me?"

"Well," Mr. Gates said, "at nineteen, he's hardly—"

"Nineteen!" Olivia nearly shouted. "You want me to take care of a nineteen-year-old *boy*? Do you have any idea how much they eat? I'll be cooking in vats. Roasting whole turkeys for lunch. I'll have to—" She took a breath. "I'm not going to do it," she said to the two old men. "I'm going to go to work for Abigail Harding at her dress shop."

The children had stopped chewing and were looking from one adult to another, their eyes wide. This was the kind of grown-up drama they usually weren't allowed to hear.

Uncle Freddy twisted around to look out the screen door. "There he is now."

"That boy can work!" Mr. Gates said. "He didn't get here until one a.m." He glanced up at Olivia. "I guess you slept through his arrival, but then, Ace and I were trying to be quiet. Out of respect for you, Livie." He looked back at Uncle Freddy. "And the boy was up before daylight. He took a hand sickle to those old briars at the back. I've been meaning to do that for about ten years."

"Bill said he'd never seen a harder worker than that kid," Uncle Freddy said.

Olivia knew the old codgers were trying to coax her into staying, but it wasn't going to work. She glared at them. "I was told I was to cook for two people. That's all. But half of Summer Hill plops down in this kitchen and I'm supposed to serve them. And now you're dumping a teenage boy on me? Have you two thought about his being around the children? He'll have girls here and…and marijuana. It's what all the kids do now."

With each word, the children's eyes got wider. They expected that at any moment someone would tell them to leave, but no one did. "You have to tell him," Uncle Freddy said to her.

"Yes, you have to tell Kit to…" Mr. Gates waved his hand. "Tell him to eat somewhere else or you're leaving. I'm sure he'll understand."

Olivia knew they were up to something but she didn't know what. Maybe they thought that she wouldn't have the courage to stand up for herself. Or, heaven help her, maybe they thought that at twenty-two, she was the same age as the boy.

With determination in her eyes, she went to the screen door and flung it open. She was ready to confront the kid, tell him he'd have to find somewhere else to eat.

He was, as Letty said, tall, over six feet, and he was wearing next to nothing. The upper half of him was nude, while an old pair of khakis hung low on his hips. She could see the V-shape that moved downward. The pant legs had been cut off so short they barely covered his backside.

He was at the old water pump, soaping his naked chest, running his long-fingered hands over his body and through his thick black hair.

She stood in the doorway, unable to move, as he raised a bucket of water over his head and poured it over his body. She watched the rivulets make their way down.

His body, Olivia thought—or rather felt. She'd had no idea the human body could look like that: lean and muscular, with curves and planes that moved when he did. His stomach!

Muscles divided on each side like rows for planting. He had arms like a sculpture, legs with heavy thighs, calves like tree branches. The tiny bit of clothing he was wearing hung very low. She could see his hip bones.

Never in her life had she seen anything as beautiful as that man's body.

She didn't realize it, but she took a step back. Even though she was some distance from him, it was as though she could feel the raw, sexual heat of him. He was like the inner circle of a volcano and he was drawing her to him. Pulling her.

When he bent to refill the bucket at the pump, she saw the muscles in his back. They were moving about, rippling. His glorious skin, seemingly acres of it, was beginning to brown in the summer sun. The sight of him was making her mouth and her fingertips ache; the center of her was pulsating.

Without blinking, she took another step back, then another. The door stayed open and she could see him as he poured a second bucket of water over that beautiful, divine body.

Behind her, the old men were working hard to contain their laughter.

Ace started to ask what was wrong with Livie, but the look Mr. Gates gave him shut him up. Ace looked at Letty, his eyes saying, *This is getting more exciting by the minute.*

She nodded in understanding. *Yes!*

Uncle Freddy was the one who saw the wooden truck on the floor. It was in Olivia's backward path. With many years' experience in a wheelchair, he whipped it around so he could bend down and grab the truck. He tossed it to Mr. Gates, then turned the chair just before Olivia would have stepped on him.

Mr. Gates put the truck on the table, but he never took his eyes off Olivia.

She only stopped moving when her back was against the far wall of the kitchen.

Straight ahead, through the open door, Kit was shaking water off his nearly nude body. He ran his hands through his thick hair, flinging droplets into the sunlight.

Olivia's heart was pounding, her breath coming fast and hard. Had a cyclone torn through the kitchen at that moment, she wouldn't have noticed.

It wasn't until Kit stepped out of sight that she began to remember where she was. When she did come back to reality, it was with the precision of a military general. She turned toward the four people at the table, ignored the smirks of the old men, and looked at Letty. "Go tell him lunch will be served in thirty minutes." She looked at Ace. "Get me four zucchini from the garden."

The children didn't move.

"We just had lunch," Letty said.

"What zoo? I like the tigers best," Ace said.

"We're going to have a second lunch." Olivia started grabbing the half-full dishes off the table. "And before you ask, you did *not* have a first one. Zucchini are those green plants you two use for space guns. Now go!"

The kids jumped up and ran to the door. "And keep him busy!" Olivia added.

Letty paused in the doorway. "What can he do?"

"Anything," Olivia said under her breath, then louder, "Be yourselves. That should occupy him for an hour or so."

Olivia looked back at the men whose expressions were smug. They may as well have tattooed *I told you so* across their foreheads. "One word and I'll say you've already eaten."

Instantly, their faces went into angelic repose. "What can we do to help?" Mr. Gates asked.

Olivia slapped a couple of old cutting boards on the table, two knives, and a pile of onions and potatoes. "Peel and chop," she ordered. "And do it quickly. No storytelling about the good ole days."

The men didn't reply, just began cutting.

Olivia knew she was being ridiculous. Absurd, even, but... She had no excuse for her actions except the ringing in her ears, the vibrations of her body, the scrambled eggs that were her brain. It was as though something had gone off inside her. An alarm? No. More like a bomb.

She was at the kitchen window, frantically scraping carrots. Behind her were the old men and their silence filled the room. Usually, they occupied themselves by laughing at the world. But right now she could feel them looking across the table and wiggling their eyebrows.

Olivia would like to be aloof from what she was feeling, to be above it. But then, she looked out the window and saw *him*. The kids, true to form, were keeping him occupied by pestering him. Ace had tossed six zucchini at the back door, three of them broken in half, then he'd run back to be with Letty.

She was the talker, while Ace was all action. Letty had bombarded the tall young man with a thousand questions, never giving him time to answer. He was looking down at her with a smile of amusement.

In Olivia's first look at him, she'd never noticed his face. He could have three eyes for all she'd seen. But now, when she saw his face, *aristocrat* was the word that came to her. Sharp cheekbones, eyes that weren't round and open, but secretive, as though he didn't want people to see what was in his mind. His nose was large, hawk-like.

All in all, Olivia could imagine him in a full-length portrait wearing the robes of a nobleman. In a play, he'd be the king.

Olivia picked up the zucchini. What was it her mother did with them? She wished she'd paid more attention to what went on in the kitchen. There was a cut-up chicken in the fridge.

She'd meant to use it tonight but...

She grabbed the chicken, threw it in a bowl with flour and lots of pepper, and heated a deep skillet full of oil. She could bread the zucchini and fry it. Too Southern! she thought. This guy was a Yankee so he'd probably be disdainful of all things from the South. He'd—

"Tomatoes," Uncle Freddy said. Olivia didn't at first hear him.

"Tomatoes," Mr. Gates said louder. "This morning I saw Kit break off a ripe one and eat it like an apple. He said they were the best he'd ever tasted."

Olivia handed him a big enamel bowl. "You can go get some. I'll slice them."

Mr. Gates put his hand to his back. "My sciatica has been bothering me a lot today. Livie, I think you should go get them."

For a moment she blinked at the man. Go outside? Near him? She glanced down at her dress. It was old and had been washed many times. There was no reason to put on her New York clothes when all she saw were old men and kids. On the other hand, all the washings had made the cotton fabric shrink a bit—and fit tighter. Since she was a child, she'd taken dance lessons from Summer Hill's only instructor. Ballet, jazz, tap, and every kick she'd ever done showed. While it was true that he looked glorious in his little shorts, Olivia knew that in her snug dress, she was a match for him.

Uncle Freddy and Mr. Gates were looking at her in an encouraging way. They meant for her to get the tomatoes. The fact that in the three days she'd been there she'd never once stepped foot in the big garden seemed to mean nothing.

Olivia set the bowl on the kitchen counter and picked up the pretty basket the children used for gathering eggs. Props were important.

She went to the door, then paused and looked back at the old men. They nodded to her.

Olivia straightened her shoulders and went outside. She did *not* look at the young man with the two laughing children. He was holding them with his long, muscled arms and washing their faces. Since Olivia had been there, no one had been able to catch them to wash them.

With her head high and her posture showing every second of her years of ballet, Olivia entered the vegetable garden. She was acutely aware that behind her the noise had stopped. The kids weren't screaming in excited protest at having weeks of dirt removed from their smelly, sweaty little bodies.

She knew the young man was watching her, assessing her in the way she had him. As though she were playing a part, she sauntered into the garden and rather prettily skipped over a large cabbage plant. She saw that the tomatoes had nearly broken the vines. With her hands in classic ballet pose, she pulled off a few and put them in the basket.

"Hey!" Letty yelled. "That basket is for the eggs."

Olivia took a breath. It was time to face him. Turning, she looked at them. The young man, almost naked, had a child under each arm, and he was staring at Olivia as though he'd never seen anything like her in his life.

Only through years of acting lessons was she able to conceal her emotions. She had to put her feet in a ballet position to keep from swaying toward him. "Perhaps," she said slowly, "you could find another basket that I could use for produce."

"What kind of juice?" Ace asked. He was tucked under the man's arm like a sack of flour.

"Whatever you want," Olivia said with an adoring smile. Finally, she looked up at the young man. *I have to get this under control!* she told herself. "Are you the boy who was hired to help around the estate?" Her voice was as adult as she could make it.

Kit nodded but didn't speak.

"Perhaps you could tie up the tomatoes?" Again, he nodded in silence.

Olivia gave him her best smile. "Good. Luncheon will be in twenty minutes. I'll call you." She swept past him with all the dignity she could muster.

Uncle Freddy and Mr. Gates were in the doorway and she nearly tripped over the wheelchair. Behind them, the deep skillet was smoking and it looked like the fire had gone out under the other one.

"You two are going to die of gas inhalation. Get that window open! Did you turn the chicken? Why haven't you finished those potatoes?" She threw open the refrigerator door.

"Where are the lemons I bought yesterday?"

"Ace—" Uncle Freddy began.

Olivia put up her hand. "Don't tell me. Something to do with space demons." She looked at Mr. Gates. "This afternoon I'm going to give you a list and you're going to the grocery."

"Yes, ma'am," Mr. Gates said in exaggerated meekness.

"Cut it out!" she snapped, and in a flurry of energy, she went back to work.

It was nearly an hour before she covered the old table with a feast: fried chicken, sliced tomatoes, sautéed zucchini and onions, mashed potatoes, carrots simmered in orange juice. Thanks to an instant vanilla mix, she'd even managed to make a bowl of banana pudding. She told Uncle Freddy to call them in.

The children, with shiny clean faces, came into the kitchen with a look of wonder. The smells, the heat, the abundance dazzled them.

Behind them, wearing a blue cotton shirt and full khaki trousers, his hair still damp, was the young man. He had his head down, as though asking permission to enter.

The kids jumped onto the bench and reached for the platter of chicken, but Mr. Gates's look stopped them. "You know we always ask the blessing first."

Ace started to say something to that, but Uncle Freddy's glare made him close his mouth.

"Kit," Uncle Freddy said as he motioned to a chair, "did you meet Olivia?" Kit took the seat, but as before, he just nodded and didn't speak.

After the blessing, Olivia finished putting things on the table and sat down with them.

She was seated across from the boy and she couldn't help sneaking glances. Up close, he was extraordinary. He hadn't shaved so there was whisker stubble on his cheeks and upper lip. His hair was longer than the men she knew, but— She corrected herself. It was longer than the high school *boys* she saw around town. Was he an afficionado of the Beatles?

She took a small piece of chicken—shades of Scarlett O'Hara, but she didn't want to eat like a field hand in front of him.

The adults were quiet as Letty and Ace told about their latest battle against demons. According to them, this was the third army that had chosen Summer Hill, Virginia, to start their war on the world. Yet again, Mr. Gates told them to stay out of the Tattington cemetery. As he nearly always did, he said how he was going to clean up the place very soon.

When everyone stopped talking, Olivia looked up. The two men and the children were looking at the tall boy, whose head was bent over his plate. He had a healthy appetite!

At first, Olivia didn't know what they were waiting for, but he looked up at Mr. Gates and gave a silent nod. He seemed to be saying that yes, he would take care of the cemetery.

Olivia couldn't help frowning. Did the boy know how to talk? She could understand that he was shy. After all, he hadn't lived long enough to learn too much about the world, but even so, he should make an effort to try to speak in the company of adults.

When he silently looked back down at his plate, Olivia had a surge of feeling, well, something like being a missionary. She'd help this shy young man get over his fear of strangers. Help him learn how to act like a grown-up *man*. She'd—

He lifted his head. For the first time, he looked directly into her eyes.

What she saw was far away from being shy. She saw heat; she saw fire. He gave her a look like other men had tried to, but couldn't quite pull off.

His look was *not* that of a boy. His eyes were that of a man, full grown, and— She took a breath. *Experienced*. This was no fumbling virgin of a boy who Olivia was going to teach anything.

HE KNOWS, she thought. Damn him to hell and back but he *knows*.

For a full minute, a film played in her mind. Him mostly naked. Had he done that because he knew a young woman was nearby and probably watching? Ace had "helped" Mr. Gates when Kit arrived in the wee hours. Olivia wouldn't put it past the child to open her bedroom door and show her off to the newcomer. Sort of like exhibiting a prize pig.

Even if he hadn't seen her, Ace would have told about Livie being there. The child had often said that she looked like a movie star.

So this boy, Kit, had peeled off his clothes to show her the goods on offer—and Olivia had fallen for it. As she remembered how she'd acted, she could feel blood rise to her face.

She'd very nearly performed *Swan Lake* in the tomato patch. She'd almost done a Grand Jeté over the three-foot-wide squash plant.

And he'd seen it all. Worse was that he'd known it was for *him*. For his viewing pleasure.

She leaned back in her chair and glared at the top of his head. "Livie?" Uncle Freddy asked. "Are you all right?"

"I'm fine." She didn't take her eyes off Kit's bent head. She'd always thought of herself as an actress but today she'd failed. How had she not immediately realized that a tall kid who looked like him would know all about women? Back in Maine, he probably had a dozen girlfriends. All of them, no doubt, wearing flannel and rubber boots. And Yankee that he was, he probably thought Southern girls were easy.

She was sure he knew she was looking at him. Letty was asking how they could make shields to protect themselves from the latest invasion of outer space monsters.

Mr. Gates looked at Livie. "You know how to make a shield?"

Olivia didn't answer. Instead, when the young man set his glass of iced tea down, she moved the big platter of chicken just enough that the glass tipped over. The others didn't see what she'd done, so it looked like Kit had spilled his tea.

"It wasn't me!" Ace yelled.

Kit looked at Olivia. This time his eyes didn't have that know-everything look. He seemed to be puzzled, as though asking her why she'd done that.

Everyone was looking at Olivia. She was the one who usually jumped up and got a cloth to mop up spills. But she just sat there, her eyes on Kit. "I don't wait on worthless boys," she said with all the insouciance she could muster.

For a moment, everyone froze, stunned by Livie's rudeness. The tea ran off the side of the table and dripped onto the floor. Slowly, acting like he was ancient, Mr. Gates started to get up to get a cloth.

But Kit unfolded his long body, got a towel off the rack, and wiped up the spill.

The whole episode had shocked the children into silence. Again, they expected to be sent away.

After Kit cleaned up the table and the floor, he neatly folded the towel and left the house, the door closing softly behind him.

The others turned to Livie as though asking for an explanation.

But she didn't give one. She stood up and cheerfully said, "Is everyone finished?" She smiled sweetly at the children. "After lunch, why don't we go out to the big magnolia tree and I'll make you a couple of shields? Anybody want some banana pudding?"

Letty and Ace stared at her, eyes wide, barely able to nod yes to all of it.

Mr. Gates looked across the table at Uncle Freddy. Both of them had twinkling eyes. They'd lived in the same house for many years and they knew what the other was thinking. This was a time for extortion.

"That boy sure can work," Mr. Gates said.

"Best worker I ever saw," Uncle Freddy said. "I'll bet he has the cemetery spic and span by nightfall."

Livie, a bowl of pudding in her hands, looked at them. It was like waiting for the other shoe to drop. What was their point?

Mr. Gates smiled at her. "So, Livie, what kind of soup are we having for supper tonight? Maybe I should go into Richmond to a restaurant supply store and buy cans of Campbell's by the case."

Olivia's lips tightened.

"No need to do that," Uncle Freddy said, his voice exaggeratedly loud. "Olivia is going to go work in a dress shop."

"No!" Letty yelled. "Who'll make our shields?"

When Ace's lower lip began to quiver, Olivia was reminded of what the child was about to face. He knew his mother was very ill and—

Olivia's face looked stormy. She was *not* a cook. She was a woman with a great career ahead of her. She wasn't one of those earth mothers who naturally enveloped children. She wasn't—

She let out her breath and glared at Uncle Freddy. "You're going to pay someone else to clean this house. I'm not going to do it. And there's too much laundry for me to do." She turned to Mr. Gates. "You are in charge of errands."

The two old men nodded. A bargain had been struck. "What do we do, Livie?" Ace asked.

"Eggs. And no more rolling them down a ramp. And you're going to help me clean up that garden."

"And get tiger plants?" Ace asked.

It took her a moment to figure that one out. Zucchini equals zoo equals tiger. "Right. Tiger plants." She went to the back door. "The four of you can clean this up. I have to go see Nina."

"My mom?" Letty looked worried. "I didn't break that lamp. It just fell. I was a million feet away from it. In the garage."

Olivia shook her head. "I'll deal with that later. Your mother has a cookbook I want to borrow." She looked at the men. "Julia Child's *Mastering the Art of French Cooking*." She left the house.

"What's that?" Letty asked.

"Heaven," Mr. Gates said. "Pure heaven on earth. Who wants some banana pudding?"

"Boeuf Bourguignon," Uncle Freddy whispered as though it was a sacred phrase. "Did I ever tell you about the time I was in Paris?"

Mr. Gates had heard the story dozens of times, but he said no, that he'd missed that one.

Each of them was smiling as they finished their second lunch and listened to Uncle Freddy's story of a meal he'd had in Paris when he was a young man. They were all glad Livie was staying. For all that she complained and was often grumpy, there was something about the way she shot out orders that gave life to all of them. But best of all, she made things *happen*.

Chapter Fifteen

"THEN WHAT?" KATHY ASKED. "YOU CAN'T STOP there."

Elise leaned forward. "Why was he running around in so little clothing?"

Olivia stood up. "*That* is a whole other story. Anyone want some more wine? How about ice cream?"

The women followed her into the kitchen.

"You said Kit has lived all over the world and now he's in government service," Kathy said. "My guess is that's the reason he was there. He was planning to go on his first mission, wasn't he?"

"You're right," Olivia said, "but he would have died before telling anyone that. Country was first to him. I just thought he was an exhibitionist. And a predator and a—" She waved her hand. "Everything bad."

"You hated him but were fascinated by him," Kathy said.

Olivia scooped ice cream into bowls. "That's exactly what I was. And after I heard him speak, I was even more angry."

Kathy and Elise waited for her to continue.

"You ever hear a voice that sent chills down your spine? Made your hair stand on end? Revved up your heart so it was pounding?" Olivia asked.

Elise grimaced. "Does my dad yelling at me when I was six and broke a Tiffany vase count?"

"Definitely not." Olivia turned to Kathy.

"Don't look at me! Ray's voice makes me wonder what else he wants me to do."

Olivia paused as she thought about what Kathy had said. According to Ray, his wife lived for him. But Kathy complained about the lack of passion. "Did Ray—?"

"Go on with *your* story," Elise said. "You were borrowing a cookbook and making shields."

"Not just 'a cookbook,'" Kathy said. "*The* cookbook."

"Right," Olivia said. "Me, who didn't know how to make a meat loaf, was saying I was going to cook French cuisine. Of course, I wasn't *really* thinking about doing that. I was just so angry at the smirks of those old men that I would have said anything to make them shut up.

"And *him*! That boy! I was already sick of hearing how fabulous he was. I just wanted to be better than he was. At anything."

"So what did you do?" Kathy asked.

"Nearly killed myself—and him." Olivia gave a little laugh. "Kit and I had three weeks of a competition that should go down in history as the roughest, toughest..." She grinned. "The very *stupidest* war there ever was."

"Okay," Elise said, "start at the beginning. Did the cookbook or the magnolia tree come first?"

Olivia took a bite of mocha ice cream. "First came the shields. I am embarrassed to admit that in the time I'd been there I'd been so angry that I'd ignored the children. But back then you just shooed kids outside and let them entertain themselves. Parents didn't need to supervise every second of their kids' lives."

"But you'd seen Kit playing with them," Kathy said.

"Yes, and I was quite jealous. Anyway, I took a big cardboard box, some shears, string, tape, and foil out under the tree. The kids trailed behind me like baby ducks. It didn't occur to me that I was doing everything outside so that worthless boy could see what I was doing."

She paused. "It took me a couple of hours to make the two worst shields ever created. They were flimsy and the string handles I taped on the back came off, and the foil tore. The kids were nice about it, but they knew the shields were awful."

"What did Kit do?" Kathy had a hint of disgust in her voice. "If it had been Ray, he would have shown up with some handcrafted masterpiece just so he could win."

"That's sort of what happened." Olivia was looking at Kathy in speculation. "I was trying to tape some tree branches onto the back of the shields to make them stronger, when he pulled up on the tractor."

"The modern equivalent of the charging horse," Elise said. "My personal fantasy."

"I didn't know it but that morning the children had asked him to make shields for them. He'd already glued up three sheets of heavy cardboard. After lunch, he used the old band saw to cut out shield shapes."

"Is that fair? You didn't have any tools," Kathy said.

"That's what I thought too. On the back he'd bolted two wooden handles, but vertical. Beside them he'd used shoelaces to tie on wide pieces of leather."

"Ah." Kathy nodded. "So they could slip their forearms through."

"Yes," Olivia said. "They were truly magnificent shields and the children were awed by them—and by Kit. They flung themselves at him and he held both of them." Olivia shook her head. "I was so jealous! My wimpy shields were on the ground, bent and already coming apart, while his were strong and—" She waved her hand.

"What did Kit say?" Elise asked.

"Nothing. The kids were hanging off of him and he looked at me as though he expected me to praise him. *Thank* him. But I wanted to smash him on the head with the shields. Or run the tractor over him. Instead, I said, 'Go away.'"

She looked at Kathy and Elise, who were waiting for her to go on. "Kit put the children down and said, 'As you wish,' then climbed back up on the tractor and drove away."

"Like in *The Princess Bride*," Elise said with a sigh.

"Only Kit said it before that movie came out."

"And his voice gave you chills," Elise said.

"How does the voice of your young gardening Adonis affect you?" Olivia asked.

"Like hot champagne pouring over me," Elise said, sighing. "He sounds even better in Spanish."

Olivia smiled. "Like when Kit speaks Arabic! But that first time, Kit's deep, gravelly voice sent an electrical charge through me."

"And that made you even more angry," Kathy said.

"Very much so. I genuinely and truly *hated* that worthless boy."

"Who was far from being a child," Kathy said.

"Right. I was the adult but he…he was outdoing me. His work was applauded while mine was ridiculed. The children adored him but they tolerated me. My shield was bad. His was perfect. In my mind, war had been declared. I *had* to prove that I was better than he was."

Kathy opened a bottle of wine. "What did you fight with? Cooking and what else?"

"Everything. Anything." Olivia closed her eyes for a moment. "For three weeks I nearly killed myself. Remember the movie about the woman who cooked everything in Julia Child's book? I almost did it before she did. Duck a l'orange and coquilles Saint Jacques and Bavarian crème. I canned grape jam and marmalade and gallons of apple butter. I made huge pots of soupe au pistou and vichyssoise and froze them."

"I bet the old men loved that," Kathy said.

"They certainly did! Mr. Gates went to the grocery nearly every day. They began talking about food like they were writing critiques for the *New York Times*."

"And the children?" Elise asked.

Olivia smiled. "Something I could do that Kit couldn't was sew. I rummaged in the attic and found an old treadle machine and my mother cleaned out her fabric storage. I made the kids medieval-looking outfits to go with the shields Kit had made—which, by the way, I coated in silver paint. Thanks to lessons in set design, I put a blue dragon on Ace's and a white unicorn on Letty's. I got hugs and kisses for that one."

"What did Kit do?" Kathy asked.

"Worked as hard as I did. Every day, Bill, Letty's father, came by and told us what Kit was doing. He single-handedly cleared up the old cemetery. Bill told us how Kit lifted big marble headstones and reset them in concrete, and how he cleaned off the moss. And he repaired the old fence, then planted rosebushes around the whole place. Bill said that Kit had slithered on his belly through the wild blackberry vines to reach the old well house and repair the roof."

Olivia took a breath. "Bill said that between Kit and me doing so much work, he and his wife were having time for a second honeymoon. 'Nina really wants another baby,' he said. The old men laughed at that, but I was embarrassed."

"Who won?" Kathy asked.

"Neither of us," Olivia said. "It ended when we slept together."

"Ah…good ole sex," Elise said with a sigh.

"No, not sex. Sleep. And we didn't know we were together. We'd had weeks of no rest and masses of work. We were exhausted. We didn't know it, but we both collapsed under the big magnolia tree, one of us on each side, and fell asleep. Everything would have been all right if the kids hadn't seen us."

Olivia laughed. "By that time I'd fed all of them so much butter-laden food that they were having digestive problems. They were getting homesick for the bland food they usually ate. And the kids were refusing to eat anything with anchovies or garlic and absolutely *no* chicken livers. They wanted canned tomato soup and grilled cheese—and nothing green added to either one. 'Like the old days,' they said."

Olivia smiled. "Years later, Dr. Kyle—that's who Ace grew up to be—told me that Uncle Freddy said that if Livie and Kit didn't stop fighting his heart was going to burn up. Poor soft-hearted Ace started to cry. He'd never heard of heartburn and didn't know it wasn't fatal. He just thought Uncle Freddy was going to be taken to the hospital where his mother was."

"What did they do to get you two together?" Kathy asked.

"Weaving." Olivia's eyes were sparkling in memory. "While we were asleep, those loud, boisterous children tiptoed around Kit and me on fairy feet and tied us inside spider's webs. I think they thought that if they tied us to one spot we'd talk and become friends. At least that's my guess. Shall we go sit in the living room?"

"Only if you tell more of the story." Elise stood up.

"I agree," Kathy said as they left the kitchen.

Chapter Sixteen

Summer Hill, Virginia 1970

OLIVIA WOKE WHEN A BUNCH OF PEBBLES RAINED down on her body. They were followed by the muffled giggles of two kids, then the sound of their running away.

She didn't open her eyes. She knew she was lying under the big magnolia tree and that she'd been sound asleep. A stick was poking her in the back, but she didn't mind. The air was heavy with warmth and fragrance. For weeks now she'd rarely left the kitchen and she was *sick* of it! Onions, tomatoes, cucumbers. She wasn't sure she ever again wanted to see any of them.

And it was all the fault of that *boy*! The way he'd raised gravestones without any help. Tore away briars with his bare hands. Built things. Restored. Repaired.

It was all totally disgusting—and she'd had enough of him.

With a sigh, she opened her eyes and looked up at the underside of the big, beautiful tree. Uncle Freddy said his mother had planted it and that's why there was a statue of her under it. The kids said she was the queen of a planet called Athena—they'd heard the name from Uncle Freddy—and they made flower garlands to drape on her.

Olivia knew she had to get up. She had jam to make. Soup to cook. Chickens to roast. "Wonder what phenomenal things he's done while I was sleeping," she muttered.

When she started to lift her hand, she couldn't. "What in the world?" She tried to sit up, but she seemed to be tied to the ground.

She gave a sharp tug to her arm and it broke away. Lying still, on her back, she held up her arm and looked at it. There were about a dozen strands of various colors of sewing thread over her arm.

Slowly, she sat up. Each movement pulled threads away from where they were tied to clothespins that had been pushed into the soft ground.

Her annoyance changed to amazement. How in the world had the children done this Lilliputian task? She'd seen a big, illustrated version of *Gulliver's Travels* in Letty's room. Had the children tried to copy it?

"What the hell?"

It was "his" voice coming from the other side of the tree.

"I can hear you breathing," he said, "so get over here and cut these off of me."

She knew he thought she was the children. "It's me." They were the first words she'd addressed to him that weren't hostile. "Are you tied down?"

He gave a grunt of pain. "Yeah. You?"

Olivia gave a few kicks, then rolled her body to the side, and the threads broke. She stood up and walked around to the far side of the tree.

Kit was sitting on the ground, untying his ankles from purple knitting yarn. As always, he was as naked as he could get without being arrested, and there was yarn hanging off all of him.

A bit of a laugh escaped Olivia.

He looked up at her in disgust. "I know. More ridicule of the worthless boy."

Olivia held out her arms and multicolored threads hung down from them. "It's a bat wing fringe. Think the style will catch on?" Threads were also on her dress and around her ankles.

At her joke, Kit leaned back on his hands and his face softened. "Looks like they got you too."

Bending, she used her nails to loosen the knots in the yarn around his ankles. "How do you think those children did this without waking us?" She sat back on the ground a few feet away from him and began pulling threads off her clothes.

Kit was tugging at the pink yarn around his wrist and when he couldn't loosen the knot, he held his arm out to Olivia. "Hovering spacecraft. I'd believe anything of those two. I have to put cracked corn around the blackberry vines to keep them out of there. Warning them that the thorns will make them bleed doesn't do it."

Olivia was trying to get the knot undone but it was too tight. She started to break the yarn, but Kit pulled his arm away. "You'll hurt yourself." When he broke it, there was a red mark on his wrist.

She was trying to pay no attention to being so close to his nearly naked body. "Why cracked corn?"

"To lure Old Thomas to guard the tunnel I made at the cost of a lot of my flesh." He stood up.

He was speaking of the hateful, aggressive, bad-tempered old peacock that wandered about the place. Kit's glorious body was inches from hers, and he held his hand down to her. She took it, and stood up before him. It was the closest she'd ever been to him, and she could feel the warmth of his body. When he reached out as though to touch her face, Olivia instinctively stepped back.

"You have thread in your hair."

She stood still while he pulled out several strands and took some off her shoulders. He stepped around her, removing pieces of thread from her clothes. Bending, he pulled two long green strands off her ankles.

"There!" He stepped back to look at her. "You are now back to being perfect."

For a moment they stood in silence, looking into each other's eyes. "I guess I better get back to work," he said.

"Me too."

Turning away, Kit took a couple of steps, then he halted and looked back at her. "Or you and I could call a truce and take the afternoon off. I need to go into town to—"

"Yes," Olivia said. "Anywhere. *Go* is my new favorite word."

Kit grinned. "Come on then, let's move around the side. If any of them see us, they'll give us something to do."

"Or cook," Olivia said. "What about...?" She nodded at his bare body.

"I keep clothes hidden in the well house."

"Ah, right," she said. "Protected by the thorns, which are guarded by Old Thomas."

"Exactly!"

Olivia followed Kit across the acres, and when he stopped behind big shrubs and tree trunks and looked in all directions, she did too. They were like a pair of comedy spies, racing from one hiding place to another. "The yarn monsters," he called them as he pulled another piece off his arm. "*How* did I sleep through that?"

"Three weeks of sleep deprivation and nonstop work will do that," Olivia said as she ducked behind a sycamore tree.

He halted beside her. "We ought to stop."

She knew what he meant. They should stop trying to outdo each other.

When she nodded in agreement, they ran to the huge mass of blackberry vines. Most of the branches had long since stopped producing fruit and should be cut away, but they'd been neglected for years.

"You better wait for me here," Kit said as he got down on his stomach and started to go through what seemed to be a tunnel.

"Because I'm a girl?" Her hostility was back.

"I was thinking more of your pretty dress." He rolled over onto his back and motioned to the entrance. "But please, be my guest."

Olivia didn't want to go slithering on the ground, but she'd talked herself into a corner. She got down beside him, ignored the smile of delight he gave her, then worked her way through the tunnel.

At the end was a small building with a door that barely opened against the vines. Inside, it was small, with a window at one end. On a hanger on the wall was a freshly ironed, short-sleeved blue shirt and light colored trousers. Slip-on Weejuns were on the floor.

In the corner were half a dozen pillows that she knew used to be on the furniture in the Big House. A few books were on an old shelf. Here and there were artifacts that had probably been found around the plantation: arrowheads, shells, a teacup with a missing handle, a rusty sword that looked to be from the Civil War.

Kit entered in silence and gave her time to look around. "Now you see my secret hiding place. Where I escape."

She well understood the need for such a retreat. Privacy wasn't readily available on Tattwell. Between the kids and the two old men, Olivia rarely had a moment alone.

"This is great." She sat down on a pile of pillows. "I think I could go back to sleep."

Kit was smiling, pleased that she liked his hideout. "Do you mind if I...?" He motioned to the clothes.

Olivia gave her best I'm-a-woman-of-the-world shrug and picked up a book. It was a history of war from Russia's point of view. She pretended to read while surreptitiously watching him remove his skimpy shorts. He had boxers on underneath—

but she knew that since the fabric often peeped out. *Not* that she'd looked!

When he turned his back to her, she admired his deeply tanned skin. But when his boxers dipped down on one side, it took her a moment to realize that she wasn't seeing contrasting white skin. *Good heavens!* she thought. *He's getting a tan* all over. Somewhere on this old plantation Christopher Montgomery was running around naked.

He quickly pulled on his clothes, and when he looked back at her, Olivia was absorbed in the book.

She stood up. "Great," she said, "you're clean and I'm a mess. I can't go anywhere looking like this."

"I could boost you up the rose trellis to get into your bedroom." His eyes moved down her in a suggestive way.

Olivia couldn't help smiling. "Thanks, but maybe when we go into town we could stop by my parents' house. I need some clothes."

Kit's face changed to serious. "You want to introduce *me* to your parents? The lowest of the low? Aren't you afraid I'll contaminate them?"

She had to work not to laugh. "It's Tuesday afternoon. Dad will be out fishing and Mom is at her bridge club."

"I should have known." His tone did make her laugh. "After you." He motioned to the tunnel.

"How are you going to get out without messing up your clean clothes?"

"That's a secret."

Olivia got down and made her way out through the vines. The ground was damp, but her dress was already dirty so it didn't matter.

Turning, she watched Kit come out. He snaked out by using his forearms and his feet. His knees and his clean trousers didn't touch the ground. It was a movement she'd never seen before and she was startled by it. To do that, he had to be in truly excellent physical condition.

She followed him across the plantation, again going from tree to tree so they wouldn't be seen, to where the old truck was parked. Kit picked up a rock. Under it was a tin can and inside were the keys.

"The kids haven't found my hiding place yet, but I'm sure it's only a matter of time."

Smiling, Olivia got into the truck and they pulled out. When they reached the road that led into town, they looked at each other and burst into laughter. They had escaped!

"So why do you have this job?" Kit asked.

Since Uncle Freddy and Mr. Gates loved gossip, she was surprised that no one had told him everything about her. "I grew up in Summer Hill. I'm a small town girl. We take what jobs we can get."

Kit looked away from the road to glance at her. "You're about as much a housekeeper as I am a gardener. Why are you here?"

She was pleased with what he'd said, but she didn't want him to see that. "Actually, I do have another job. But the theater caught fire and it was postponed until the fall."

"Theater?" When Olivia was silent, he said, "Are you going to make me guess?"

She shrugged one shoulder.

"In Richmond?"

"Not quite." She put on her haughtiest look.

"Something local. Did you get the lead in a play about the history of Summer Hill?"

"No! I—" She saw that he was teasing her. "On Broadway."

"Where is that? Virginia? North Carolina?"

She sat in silence while she waited for him to realize what she meant.

His eyes widened in a very gratifying way. "*That* Broadway?"

Olivia smiled sweetly. "The very one." For the rest of the

drive, she told him how she'd won the lead role at the auditions, shared an apartment with her costar for the rehearsals, and finally, how the fire had caused the delay.

He pulled into the driveway of her parents' house, turned off the engine, and looked at her. "I am impressed. Really, I am. Now I see why you were so angry when I got there."

The way he said that made the blood rise in her cheeks. "I guess I was. A bit."

"Are you kidding? That first day I was so scared of you I couldn't say a word. I was afraid of what you'd do to me. Anybody who could sail over the cabbages like you did has to be dangerously strong. I was worried you might—"

Her look made him stop. Laughing, he got out of the truck.

Olivia walked away with her nose in the air, but she was repressing a smile. It was so good to hear humor. For weeks all she'd heard about this guy was how hard he worked. And she'd seen his body. She'd never once thought he might have a brain— or a personality.

As it always was, the front door to her parents' house was unlocked. Inside, she looked around as though seeing it for the first time. She and her mother had decorated it. The current style was for bright colors and wallpaper painted on aluminum foil. But they had stayed with subdued colors of sand and cream and the pink of an early morning sunrise. She still liked it, but she had never before noticed the many photos of her around the long living room.

Kit didn't say anything but began walking about the room and looking at the framed pictures. Her parents had insisted that she have a professional shot done in every costume she'd worn for a play, whether in high school or college. In one she wore a short pixie cut for Joan of Arc. She wore a nun's hood for a high school play. Her favorite was a snapshot when she had on a flat-topped newsboy cap, her face solemn. She'd been home from school for the holidays and listening to her dad when her mother took the photo.

Kit picked that picture up and looked at it for a moment before setting it down. "Beautiful and talented," he said softly, his voice even deeper than usual.

Olivia waved his compliment away as though it meant nothing, but she was quite pleased. "I'll just get my clothes, then we can go into town and…" She wasn't sure what they would do.

She hadn't meant for him to go to her bedroom with her, but he followed her down the hall. Telling him to stay out seemed too provincial. She reminded herself that she'd lived in New York, so middle-class morals were beneath her.

Her room was in the same colors as the rest of the house. The wall behind her bed was papered in a very subtle pink-and-cream stripe. She and her mother'd had a crisp exchange of words about Olivia's insistence of putting the paper on only one wall. But Olivia had seen it in a magazine and was adamant.

The pictures around the room were prints of Impressionist paintings: Renoir, Matisse, Degas.

As she opened her closet door, she glanced at him. He was standing in the doorway, looking very serious, and seemed to be studying what he was seeing. He looked like a director trying to decide if this was a good set for the scene he wanted to shoot.

With his hands clasped behind his back, he came into the room. "After careful observation, I have decided that in spite of your common ancestry and your family's lack of prominence in an unremarkable town, I will consider you as my companion for an evening. Perhaps even for dinner."

Olivia's jaw dropped nearly to her chest. Of all the— When he picked up a copy of the script of *Pride and Prejudice* from her bedside table, she realized what he was doing. He was playing a version of Darcy.

She kept the look of horror on her face. "You insult me, my

family, even my ancestry, yet you believe I will go out with you? Sir! I will *never* set foot in your company."

Kit stiffened. "You say this because of what you have been told about me. Let me assure you that it is the Wicked Children who have taken away my dignity with their purple woolen chains of humiliation."

"It has taken no chains to show your overweening pride. Your lack of garments, even to fawning about in the near nude brings your own disgrace."

Kit opened his mouth to reply, but he couldn't hold back. He started laughing. "My mother would agree with you, but I..."

Olivia waited for him to continue but he said nothing else.

He sat down on her cream-colored chair. "I was thinking of buying some bikes for those rapscallion kids. Anywhere around here I can get them?"

Olivia pulled a jumper and three blouses out of her closet and put them on the bed. "Trumbull's Appliances can order what you want, but otherwise you need to go to Richmond or Charlottesville."

"That's the same way we do it where I live."

"Oh?" she said in an encouraging way.

"Warbrooke, Maine. The town was founded by an ancestor of mine and it's full of my relatives. If we don't want to marry a cousin we have to go out of state."

"And what if you do want to marry a cousin?" She pulled out a Bill Blass pantsuit, off-white with gold buttons. She was tired of wearing worn-out dresses all the time. Maybe one evening they could use the big mahogany table in the dining room.

"That's as likely as your going out with the kid who delivers the propane."

"I don't know... Alfie's kind of cute."

"He certainly thinks *you* are." There was venom in Kit's voice. "And the guy who said he stopped by to see the old men couldn't take his eyes off you."

Olivia looked at him, startled. He was frowning deeply. "That's Ted. His father owns the furniture store. I hardly know him."

Kit didn't reply, but he seemed annoyed. He got up, mumbled something about seeing her later, then left the room.

Olivia stood there for a moment. What in the world was wrong with him? She tossed a blue jacket by Pierre Cardin on the bed, then pulled out a red jumpsuit. It had a halter top and wide legs, with a small waist. Maybe they'd have a picnic under the magnolia tree. She got out a few more items, some jewelry, a few pair of shoes, then pulled a suitcase from under her bed and packed. She took her time doing it as she didn't want to give him the idea that she was in a hurry to go into town with him.

When she finished, she sat down on the bed. She needed to think about what she was doing. She knew she was very—okay, *extremely*—attracted to him, but it couldn't possibly go anywhere. In New York, her cast mates had tried to look on the bright side of spending the summer waiting for the play to begin. A summer affair seemed to be what most of them planned. "Summer jobs, summer sex," one of them said.

Olivia had wanted to seem as worldly as they were so she'd agreed. But a summer affair with a teenager? Then what? Break his heart when she went back to New York? When he was fifty, would he talk about the famous actress who'd ripped his heart out? That wasn't something she wanted associated with her name.

The sound of voices drew her out of her thoughts. No one was supposed to be home. Who in the world had he invited into her parents' home?

She entered the living room just as her father and Kit came in from the hall that led to her father's study. Since he'd retired from banking, he'd indulged himself in his love of ancient history, even to writing a few papers.

"There you are," her dad said. He was shorter than Kit and

a bit slumped from years at a desk, but he was still handsome. "Your young man has been telling me about his life in Egypt. He's even invited your mother and me to stay at his parents' house in Cairo in January."

Years of acting lessons helped her hide her shock at hearing this. "How nice," Olivia managed to say, then added, "He's not my young man. He's only nineteen years old."

"Oh, I see. My mistake."

Olivia glared at her father. She knew when he was laughing at her. As for Kit, his eyes were also laughing. "Are you ready to go?" she snapped. "Or do you want to stay and discuss Tutankhamun's tomb—which you probably helped to build."

Mr. Paget looked shocked at his daughter's rudeness.

"Actually," Kit said, "I did see his tomb. It was opened for just a few hours and my father came to get me out of bed at three a.m. to go see it. I was ten years old and it was all very exciting."

With each word, Mr. Paget's eyes widened. "Is it...? Does it...?"

"Could you get my suitcase?" Olivia said to Kit as she went to the front door. Once she was outside, she wanted to kick herself. What was it about that boy that brought out the worst in her? When he was around, she seemed to go through every emotion. Anger, laughter, lust, a feeling that she had to win, all of it so strong that they nearly killed her. And she had to admit, sometimes jealousy. The kids, Uncle Freddy, Mr. Gates, and now her own father seemed to adore him. He could do no wrong. They seemed to think he was brilliant, entertaining, a hard worker, and now it looked like he was a world traveler. A house in Cairo! Not Cairo—pronounced K-row—Illinois, but the real one. Pyramids. Sphinx shot up by the Turks. Really! Was there no end to the boy's good qualities?

He came out with her suitcase in his hand and put it in the back of the truck. He started to go around to her side to open the door but she did it by herself.

Kit started the truck and headed toward town. But then, he pulled over beside Mr. Ellis's cow pasture, turned off the engine, got out, and opened her door. "We need to talk."

Olivia looked straight ahead and didn't move.

"If I have to pick you up, I will."

She got out of the truck, but her expression let him know that she didn't like his attitude.

There was a gate nearby and he motioned to it. They walked together for a while until they came to a pretty rock formation. Olivia had been to it many times when she was a child.

Stepping back, Kit held out his hand. He was motioning for her to sit down.

For a while, they sat a yard apart, silently watching the cows grazing in the field.

"I grew up all over the world," he began. "My father is in the diplomatic service. He worked his way up from being a kid who carried the briefcase of some major to being a traveling advisor. If there was a problem in the Middle East, he was often called in to fix it. My mother followed him everywhere—and she dragged her three kids with her. I'm the youngest so I've been to more countries, been exposed to more cultures and languages than they have."

For a while, Olivia didn't say anything. It seemed that he was saying something very serious. Should they give free rein to the strong emotions between them or pull back? Stop it before it started? "I have a career ahead of me. I've worked for it since I was a child."

"And I have something waiting for me too," he said.

She gave him time to tell her what he was going to do, but he didn't explain. She knew he wasn't going to say any more. "We'll be friends," she said, and he nodded in reply. *So be it*, she thought. Or as he had said, "As you wish." They had set boundaries. They hadn't openly acknowledged their...their attraction to each other. But in a way they had—and they were in agreement about it. Now was not the right time for either of them. They had lives ahead of them and they didn't want them interrupted. Friendship was their destiny.

"What's the big secret about Ace?" Kit asked. "And what's the kid's real name?"

She turned to him. "No one told you?"

Kit shook his head. "I've been working rather a lot so I've not had time for chats."

"Me too," she said. "But coq au vin can't compete with single-handedly raising old tombstones."

"They told me *you* were doing a better job."

Looking at each other, they laughed. It seemed that the old men had been playing them against each other. Their shared amusement cleared the air.

Olivia took a breath. "Ace's name is Kyle Chapman and his mother is dying of ovarian cancer. His father is the town's only doctor, and between patients and his wife, he can't care for the child. And besides, Ace needs Letty."

"That poor boy. He's so young."

"You're not going to look at him with pity, are you?"

"No," Kit said. "I'm going to—" He turned his head away.

When she heard his breath catch in his throat, Olivia reached out and took his hand. "I think we need to act as normal as possible."

"Maybe tie the two of them up in a tree with purple yarn?" He looked back at her and when he held her hand tighter, she pulled it away. They were too alone in a beautiful setting to risk touching.

"I vote that we give the children the best summer they ever had," she said.

"Lavish them with gifts? Christmas every day? That sort of thing?" he asked.

"Absolutely not! First of all, we need to get them back for

tying us up and I think the attic is haunted and Old Thomas is from a planet called Zenos."

With each word, Kit's smile widened. "I like how you think. I don't know about you, but I'm starving. Didn't I see a tea shop in town? Let's drink a gallon and eat pounds while we come up with some scary things to do to those brats. And I want to order some bikes."

"Can you afford them?" Olivia put her hand up. "Let me guess. You're rich."

He stood up and held out his hand out to her. "That's just one of many bad things about me. Did you bring your script? Can I play Wickham and run off with the girl?"

"Lydia is an idiot." Taking his hand, she stood up.

He leaped off the rock, then put his hands on her waist, and swung her down to the ground. "Remind me to call my dad to tell him he'll have a couple of visitors in January."

"Would they really do that? You can't imagine what it would mean to my father. Do you have to take a Jeep to get to the pyramids?"

"Ha! They're across the road from Mena House Hotel. There's a highway that runs right past the pyramids."

"He'll be disappointed."

"Don't worry. There are lots of places that will fascinate him. Egypt is magic." He opened the truck door for her and she got in.

Kit walked around the back of the truck so she wouldn't see his smile. *Friends*, he thought. That's what she wanted them to be. And if that's what she needed right now, he'd give it to her.

As for him, he'd found the woman he loved and would always love—and he was going to do whatever it took to get her. He'd just take his time, go as slowly as she needed him to.

And when the time was right... He smiled. She wouldn't know what hit her.

Chapter Seventeen

"THAT'S WHAT HE TOLD YOU?" KATHY ASKED. "THAT he planned to get you no matter what he had to do?"

"He didn't tell me then what he was thinking, but he did on our honeymoon."

"You mean recently."

"Yes," Olivia said. "Very recently."

Elise and Kathy were silent as they thought about what they were hearing. All that Olivia was telling them happened long ago. Even if they hadn't been told of their love now, it was easy to see where the young couple was headed. Yet they had spent their lives *apart*.

"When did you turn from friendship to passion?" Elise asked. "Some moonlit night? You saw naked Kit under a tree and you were so overcome with lust that you couldn't contain yourself?"

Olivia and Kathy were staring at her.

"Honey," Kathy said, "you need a man." Olivia nodded in agreement.

"I'm ready, but the only one I've seen is Ray and I wouldn't have him if—" She looked at Kathy in horror. "I'm sorry. I didn't mean to disparage your husband. He's quite nice. Lovely to look at. Olivia and I made him sit around shirtless for hours and he—" Again, she broke off. "I think I'll shut up now. Is there any iced tea? I've had more than enough wine."

Kathy looked at Elise for a moment longer, then back at Olivia, who was filling a glass for Elise. "How long did your sweet, innocent friendship last?"

"Wait a minute," Elise said. "I want to know about the children. You told us that Ace grew up to be a doctor, but what happened to Letty? Please tell me those kids grew up to marry each other."

"No, they didn't," Olivia said. "When the kids were about ten, Bill got a job in California and they quit spending summers at Tattwell. Letty married a man she met in college. You know the actor Tate Landers?"

"Sure. Who doesn't?" Kathy said.

"He's almost as beautiful as Alejandro. Not quite, but close."

"He's Letty's son." She paused. "And he recently married one of Ace's daughters."

"That's good," Kathy said. "Really great. Does the name Tate come from Tattwell?"

"Tate is short for Tatton and both names came from Tattington. His sister's name is Nina." Olivia paused for a moment. "Tate bought the plantation in memory of his mother."

"In *memory*?" Elise said. "Oh no! I think I hate knowing the future. Poor Ace and his mother, and poor Letty dying young. And you and Kit." There were tears in her eyes.

"Tell us some more good things," Kathy said. "Tell us about you and Kit being friends and the wonderful things you did for the children."

"My mother..." For a moment, Olivia had to blink away tears. All this talk was bringing up some painful memories. "My mother knew me so well. I talked to her every day on the phone. At first all I did was complain, but gradually, I began asking her how to do things. About twice a week she showed up with cooking equipment that I needed or something that would help me. Back then, I was too young and dumb—sorry, Elise—to understand how much she did."

"No offense taken," Elise said, "but we all tend to mess up our lives, no matter what our age."

"Ouch!" Olivia said, making them laugh. "Mom foresaw that two old Southern men and two little kids were going to get sick of elegant French cuisine. Before they did, she handed me a shoe box. Inside were big index cards with recipes for meat loaf, beef stew, chicken and dumplings, fish with hush puppies, et cetera. All homey things. The first time I again served them Campbell's tomato soup and grilled cheese sandwiches for lunch, I thought the four of them were going to start crying."

"What about the bikes?" Kathy asked.

"The Saturday after he met my dad, Kit and I drove into Richmond to get them." She smiled in memory. "It was a nice trip. He told me so much about himself that I didn't realize he was leaving out the biggest parts. He talked about his first year in college, about majoring in poly sci, his friends, his family. All of it. At least I thought he did. He just left out that he was planning to go undercover to infiltrate Muammar Gaddafi's new regime."

Both Kathy and Elise drew in their breaths in horror.

"Right. Back then we had no idea what the man was like. There was no hint of what was coming."

Elise put her hands over her face. "I don't want to hear the bad things. Poor Ace and Letty and now Kit."

"Was Kit hurt?" Kathy spoke quickly, before Elise could add Olivia's first marriage to the list of bad.

"Yes. It's a wonder he can still walk, but the good part was that he was declared unfit to be a soldier. That's what made him go into diplomacy. But I always knew that was his calling. I saw it that first summer."

"You have to tell us," Elise said.

"But first," Kathy said, "tell us about the children and the bikes. Did they like them?"

Olivia took a sip of her wine. "Yes and no. Kit and I agreed that if we gave them two shiny new bikes as gifts they'd be so suspicious that they might not use them. So we decorated them." She smiled. "With pond slime. Letty's bike was silver and Ace's black, but Kit and I covered them with mud and all the icky things we could dig out of the pond."

For a moment Olivia looked off in the distance in memory. "One rainy afternoon I was teaching the kids—and by that I mean all four of them—how to put papier-mâché strips over balloons. When the sun came out, Kit burst through the door in a rage. Furious! We were all shocked. He said he could no longer work in the wood shop because there was so much useless junk in there that he had to throw some out. He said the first thing to go were those old bicycles he'd found in the back. He said they must be a hundred years old. That was all the kids needed. They took off running."

Olivia sipped her wine. "Kit and I tried to get them to wash off the mud and slime but they never did. They truly loved those bikes!"

The women were silent for a moment, thinking how good it was to have given so much pleasure to children whose futures were less than perfect.

Olivia leaned back in her chair. "I knew Kit was a born diplomat the day the children killed Uncle Freddy."

As she meant, Elise and Kathy looked at her with eyes wide with horror. "Everyone was in hysterics. You see, Kit had been giving the children swimming lessons, but they were forbidden to get in the pond without adult supervision."

"And Uncle Freddy was an adult." Kathy was frowning, not sure she wanted to hear this story if it had a tragic ending.

Olivia nodded. "That's exactly what I said then."

Chapter Eighteen

Summer Hill, Virginia 1970

OLIVIA WAS HANGING SHEETS ON THE LINE AND KIT was helping her keep them from touching the ground. The washerwoman they'd hired had a sick grandchild so the task had fallen to Olivia. She had a feeling the child wouldn't be sick if it weren't change-the-bedding day.

But in the weeks since she and Kit had called a truce, they'd become good at helping each other with chores. They'd worked together to clean up the big kitchen garden. Nina had come over and mumbled about feeling guilty for not helping, but then, as always, she'd run off after Bill.

"'I'll bet thee a thousand pounds to a crown we have a boy tomorrow nine month,'" Kit said.

Olivia cracked up because she knew he was quoting from the movie *Tom Jones.*

It was a very hot day and she and Kit were dressed so differently they may as well have lived in separate countries. Olivia wore long sleeves, her collar up, and a wide-brimmed hat. Her long legs were encased in cotton trousers that reached to her ankles. Kit had on nearly nothing.

"What about your feet?" Kit asked. "They're open to the sunshine. Doesn't that scare you?"

"You laugh, but you don't know what sun does to your skin. When you're forty you'll look sixty."

"And you'll always look twenty," he said in such an admiring way that she blushed.

The old men had delighted in teasing her about the way she and Kit were now working together.

"You two have certainly become friends," Uncle Freddy said.

"I never would have thought that could happen after the way you two started out," Mr. Gates said.

"I truly believed that our Livie hated young Kit," Uncle Freddy said.

Letty was confused. "But she cooked a second lunch just for him. I thought she liked him."

"Did she?" Uncle Freddy asked. "I don't remember that."

Mr. Gates agreed. He didn't remember that either.

"It was the best fried chicken I ever had," Ace said. "How could you forget that?"

"They didn't," Olivia said. "They're just pulling your leg."

That phrase made the children's eyes widen.

She didn't want to be caught in one of their twenty-minute-long "why" sessions, so she changed the subject. "Who wants strawberry Popsicles?" She narrowed her eyes at the men, but her warning just made them laugh.

It was the next day, as she and Kit were hanging up the laundry, that he heard the screaming. When he dropped one end of the sheet, it scraped the ground.

"Hey!" Olivia said. "I just washed that. You're going to have to—"

"Quiet!" His voice was a command and in the next second he took off running.

Olivia tossed the sheet into the basket and ran after him. It wasn't until they'd rounded the trees that she heard the children crying. And there was a low moan of such anguish that it made chills run down her spine. She would have stopped, afraid of what she was about to see, but Kit didn't slow down.

When she saw the pond, she halted. To her left were the children, clinging to each other and crying loudly. To her right, Mr. Gates was sitting at the edge of the slimy old pond, his legs in the water. Pulled onto him, facedown, like some sea creature dragged up from the depths, was Uncle Freddy. All of him was wet, with nasty pond weeds clinging to him.

"Get the kids!" Kit ordered as he went to the two old men.

"He's dead." The agony in Mr. Gates's voice made Olivia shiver.

She started toward the children but they ran the opposite way, afraid of what had happened. They were very difficult to catch! She chased them past the chicken coop, through the orchard, and toward the house. "Please don't let them go in the house," she said aloud.

With all those hiding places, she'd never find them.

She managed to get Ace just as he reached the clothesline. But then, the child was crying too hard to keep running. Olivia went to her knees and pulled him into her arms. His convulsions were making her body shake.

As Olivia knew she would, Letty stopped running and came back to them. Olivia opened an arm and held her too.

"We killed Uncle Freddy," Ace wailed.

"We drown-ded him," Letty said.

She could guess what happened. The children loved to push Uncle Freddy around in his wheelchair. They'd been warned about getting too near the pond with him, but it looked like with all the adults busy that day, they'd disobeyed—a common occurrence with them.

"It was an accident," Olivia said, but then she too began to cry. Uncle Freddy and his humor, his kindness and generosity to all of Summer Hill. Gone forever. And poor, poor Mr. Gates. How was he going to live without his friend? How—?

"I can swim," came a raspy voice over them.

Olivia's head was bent over the children, the three of them clinging together so hard they looked like a human barrel.

It was Ace who first looked up.

Kit was standing over them, a weak, dirty Uncle Freddy in his arms.

"Livie," Ace whispered, a hiccup in his voice.

Olivia kept crying. Dear Uncle Freddy. And there was what was waiting for Ace with his mother! It was too much for one child to have to bear in his little life. "I know, Ace, sweetheart, it's not your fault. It was an accident."

"Olivia!" Kit's voice was stern. She was still holding the children tightly.

Letty looked at Ace, then turned to see Kit holding Uncle Freddy like he was a baby.

She let out a scream and pushed so hard that Olivia fell backward onto the ground.

In the next minute, the children were clutching Uncle Freddy's hand and laughing, crying, hiccuping.

"You're going to get sunburned." Kit was smiling at Olivia as she looked up at him in astonishment.

Behind them, Mr. Gates was pushing the wheelchair. From the look of him, he'd aged years.

Uncle Freddy, his thin, frail body limp in Kit's arms, smiled at them. "We're going to put in a swimming pool because I can swim."

"Come on, old man," Kit said, "you're getting heavier by the minute." Looking at Olivia, he nodded toward Mr. Gates. He needed to be taken care of.

She went to him, gave the wheelchair a push that sent it rolling, then picked up his arm and put it around her shoulders. That he made no comment about hugging a pretty girl scared her.

Ace's dad, Dr. Everett, was called and while they waited for him to arrive, Mr. Gates insisted on bathing Uncle Freddy. It's what he'd done since both of them were in their early twenties, and he wasn't going to neglect his duty now.

Kit helped undress Uncle Freddy and get him into the hot water, then left him with Mr. Gates, who was still shaking. "They need each other," Kit told Olivia.

As for the kids, they were so subdued by what had almost happened that they weren't making a sound. Olivia gave them peanut butter and jelly sandwiches with glasses of milk and they were in the kitchen, eating in silence.

Kit had put on a shirt and he and Olivia were sitting on the hall floor, one on each side of the bathroom door. Inside, they could hear Uncle Freddy talking. His voice was low but there was excitement in it.

"The kids didn't put the chair's brake on," Kit said. "It was all because I made them swear that they wouldn't go swimming without an adult present."

"And Uncle Freddy is an adult."

"Right," Kit said. "I should have added qualifiers. It had to be an adult who could jump in after them if they started to drown. An adult who is *not* in a wheelchair. One who is—"

She couldn't bear to hear him blame himself. "But he found out he could swim?"

"Yes. His chair rolled into the pond and when he floated out of it, he began waving his arms around. That's when he remembered how he used to swim. The exertion nearly killed him, but he did make it to the bank."

"And that's when Mr. Gates found him."

"Uncle Freddy was so worn-out that he couldn't move. A lifetime of no exercise takes its toll. When Mr. Gates saw Uncle Freddy lying facedown at the edge of the pond, he assumed he was dead."

"And the poor kids..." She started to say more but she heard voices in the kitchen. It looked like the doctor had arrived. "I'll go." In the kitchen, Ace had wrapped his arms and legs tight around his father and was crying again. Letty was at the table, tears slowly running down her cheeks.

"Come on," Olivia said to the children, "let's go pick some tiger plants."

Dr. Everett, a handsome man, midthirties, looked at her in gratitude. There were dark circles under his eyes.

She took the hands of the children and they went outside. They weren't their usual boisterous selves but wanted Olivia to push them in the swing attached to the big oak tree near the house. It was as though they wanted to revert to being a younger age.

About thirty minutes later, Kit and Dr. Everett came outside and stood by the car talking.

Then the doctor looked at his watch, waved in the direction of his son, and drove away. Olivia didn't like it that he hadn't said goodbye to Ace and her face showed it.

"It's okay," the little boy said. "His job is very important and my mom needs him."

His very grown-up words and tone made Olivia feel that her heart might break. Every Sunday someone came to pick up Ace and take him to see his mother in the hospital. When he got home, it always took Letty quite a while to get him to go outside. Livie had developed the habit of baking a chocolate cake with cherry frosting every Sunday afternoon.

When the doctor was gone, Kit turned to look at the three of them and grinned, his teeth white against his tanned skin. "Uncle Freddy is out of the tub and he wants ice cream. Anybody else want some?"

"Me!" the kids yelled and ran ahead. But Ace turned back, took Olivia's hand, and made her run with them.

That night, after they got all four kids into bed early, Olivia and Kit flopped down on the couch in the living room. He had made them Tom Collins drinks and she downed half of hers in one gulp.

"Slow down," he said. "I've had enough disasters today."

"You handled everything well," she said.

"I did what needed to be done."

"I thought Uncle Freddy was dead. He looked like it."

"He nearly was," Kit said. "He only swam about fifteen feet but it's the most he's done since his injury. All these years he should have been using an overhead bar, dumbbells. But he didn't. He—"

Olivia took his hand and squeezed it. "You were great."

When Kit picked up her hand and kissed the back of it, she jerked it away. She suddenly became aware of how alone they were. The men and Ace were tucked away in bed, and Nina had taken Letty home. Kit's and Olivia's bedrooms were across the hall from each other. Abruptly, she stood up. "I need some sleep. Today has been too much for me."

He nodded but said nothing.

She paused at the doorway. "What did you talk to Dr. Everett about?"

Kit closed his eyes for a moment. "Ace's mom doesn't have much longer. She's mostly on morphine for the pain."

Olivia stood there, her mind full of what had happened and what was going to happen, and she could feel the tears coming back. She started to turn away, to take her sadness into privacy, but Kit put up his hand, as though telling her to wait. As she watched, he opened a door in a side closet that was full of beat-up old boxes and pulled one out.

"I brought these with me from home and I think that right now we need them." He took the box to a big mahogany cabinet on one side of the room. Olivia had never been curious as to what it was, but then, it would take weeks to explore all the furniture in the rambling old house.

When he lifted the top, she saw that the cabinet was a record player and the whole bottom was a speaker. Inside Kit's box was a double stack of 45 rpm records.

She frowned. "You can't play music now. Everyone is asleep. They need their rest."

"Yes, they do. But we need joy more. Uncle Freddy is safe; Mr. Gates will recover; Ace's mother is alive. Right now, today, this minute, we have everything to be happy about."

"You're right. But just play something soft and quiet, okay?"

"You got it." He dropped a pile of records onto the fat spindle and turned the sound up full blast. To Olivia's horror, out came the raunchy, throaty blast of Steppenwolf's "Born to be Wild."

Olivia nearly leaped across the room as she tried to turn the music off, but Kit grabbed her and began to dance with her, his hips grinding provocatively against hers.

She fought him for all of about eight seconds, then she yelled, "Oh, what the hell! We're alive! No one died today!" She gave Kit a look of challenge, a sort of sex challenge. "Come on, Worthless Boy, let's see if you can dance."

"I can't leap cabbages," he yelled back, "but with sex, baby, no lessons are required."

She kicked off her shoes and started grinding. Using her hips and thighs that had been strengthened by years of dance classes, she went down to the ground and kept moving.

Kit went with her. He turned so her leg was between his and went down. And down.

When he leaned toward her as though to kiss her, she pulled back so far her hands touched her ankles. Kit stayed with her.

Ace was the first one to show up, standing there staring, his eyes sleepy. A minute later, Letty appeared in the doorway— and that made Olivia and Kit start laughing. She was supposed to be at home with her parents, but it wasn't surprising that she had sneaked out and was sleeping somewhere near Ace—and probably Uncle Freddy.

The boy ran over and pushed his way between Olivia and Kit, as though laying claim to her.

"Hey, kid," Kit said, "this is *my* girl. Get your own." Letty, rubbing her eyes, went to Kit.

The record stopped and there was a moment's silence as the next one dropped down.

It was the band Cream, named for being the Cream of the Crop: Ginger Baker, Jack Bruce, Eric Clapton. The best there was. "Sunshine of Your Love" blasted out.

Kit made another attempt to get to Olivia, but Letty and Ace thwarted him. Laughing, he picked up Letty and began dancing around the big room with her.

It was no surprise when Uncle Freddy and Mr. Gates showed up. Mr. Gates twirled the wheelchair around in a way that looked like they'd done it many times before.

What was a surprise was when Nina and Bill walked into the room. They had on swimsuit covers, but no suits on underneath—which sent all the adults into howls of laughter. Obviously, they'd been out having a moonlight swim in the nude.

"A mating couple," Kit said to Olivia as Letty's parents went to the far side of the room and just held each other and swayed.

The records kept changing and everyone danced. Jefferson Airplane, Rolling Stones, Marvin Gaye, Aretha Franklin, James Brown, Creedence Clearwater Revival. All of it played at a deafening level.

Somewhere after midnight, the oldest and the youngest gave out. Letty's parents slipped away into the darkness outside, and Kit lifted Uncle Freddy out of the chair and put him in bed. Mr. Gates took the cot near his friend, refusing to leave the room. Olivia managed to get the kids up the stairs and they fell across the twin beds in Ace's room. She left them dressed, but put them under the covers.

When Kit turned off the music, the house had a feeling of being silent, but of also being gratefully, wonderfully *awake*. The house was an old lady who'd seen wars, births and deaths, and right now she seemed pleased that everyone she loved was safe.

Olivia stepped into the hall and pulled the door to Ace's room nearly shut. Kit was standing in front of his bedroom door. He looked so very, very good. He was like all the dreams of male fulfillment that she'd ever had. More than anything in the world she wanted to touch him, feel him, put her skin against his. Their dancing, so close together, had made her very aware of him.

He was looking at her in invitation. She knew that if she made the tiniest step toward him that he'd open his arms to her, then they'd...

Before she could have another thought, she mumbled, "Good night," slipped into her own room, and shut the door firmly behind her.

The next morning, before going downstairs, Olivia had a long talk with herself about her and Kit. She knew that he was infatuated with her, that he watched her. *But it can't happen*, she thought. He would go back to his Yankee college and she'd go to Broadway and end up falling for some producer. She could bear that, but it wouldn't be fair to him. It was one thing to tell her friend who was playing Jane that she'd had a summer fling with a lusty college boy, but what happened when he showed up with a bunch of his beer-drinking fraternity brothers?

She'd probably die of embarrassment on the spot.

No, whatever happened, she needed to be the adult and not let the sight of his beautiful, gorgeous, naked body make her do something that she'd regret.

She remembered when her mother had first seen Kit. She'd dropped by to give Livie a chinois and pestle to make liver pâté and Kit had walked by on his way to the pond. As usual, he had on very little clothing.

Her mother lowered her reading glasses and watched him

walk the entire distance, until he disappeared in the trees. "Now I understand."

Her tone was so suggestive that Olivia was shocked. "Mother!"

"Dear, you may have come late in life to your father and me, but we spent whole years trying to create you."

Olivia was so stunned that she couldn't speak.

Mrs. Paget opened her car door. "Actually, young Kit reminds me of your father at that age. Don't you just love those flat, washboard stomachs?" As her mother started the engine, she said, "Have fun, dear. And I hope you do everything your father and I did." Laughing at her daughter's continued silence, she drove away.

After The Great False Alarm, as Letty's father dubbed Uncle Freddy's near death, things changed. Bill had a right to be sarcastic. Because of what happened, he got a lot more work dumped on him. In the past, he'd had the whole thirty-five acres to oversee. High school kids were hired to help, but he said that ever since Woodstock happened last year, all the kids wanted to do was smoke grass and grow hair.

Then Kit had arrived and taken over nearly everything. For the first time since their daughter was born, he and Nina'd had time to themselves. Bill smiled. Lots of time to themselves.

But since the near tragedy, Kit spent most of his time giving physical training lessons. He gave two swimming sessions a day to the children, and he spent an hour in the water with the old men. Mr. Gates had never been able to swim, but he needed to help Uncle Freddy, so Kit worked with both of them.

Kit said that Mr. Gates had some muscle on him. After all, he'd been lifting Uncle Freddy for years, but since he hated the water, that caused problems. Kit had to do a lot of coaxing. As for Uncle Freddy, Kit said that marshmallows had more muscle than he did.

Olivia learned to tell the cleaning women when they called in sick that the work would be waiting for them. Every day, she put on a swimsuit and helped Kit with the lessons. And she started a dance class that everyone—kids, old men, Kit, Bill and Nina—participated in. Livie was sure Mr. Gates was recovering when he said he'd do any ridiculous thing she came up with just to see her in a pink leotard.

On Sunday, Kit and Olivia drove Ace to the hospital to see his mother. They'd even taken her a big slice of chocolate cake. She'd been barely coherent but she'd smiled at her son, and Kit had held the boy so he could kiss her cheek.

It was taking a while, but everyone was coming back to life after the near-death experience.

One day when he was on his way to the orchard where he was going to help Kit with the mowing, Bill waved to his wife and Livie. They were sitting at the big picnic table at the side of their little house and snapping and stringing a couple of bushels of green beans. They planned to can them that afternoon and promised that they'd make his favorite dilly beans.

As Bill left, he didn't see the two girls coming down the old brick path.

"Olivia!" Betty Schneider called.

Olivia was sitting across from Nina, her back to the young woman, and she squeezed her eyes shut for a moment. "What did I do to deserve this?" she muttered. It took all her acting training to get her face under control and put a smile on before she turned around.

Betty and her friend Shirley Williamson were coming toward them. Olivia had gone to high school with the two girls. They'd been quite popular as they were pretty in a cute way and they'd had all the latest clothes. Sweaters with a padded cutout of a horse on the back, kilted skirts with brass buckles, a circle pin on every Peter Pan collar, with matching bows in their hair. They'd headed every committee, had the top athletes for boyfriends, and never did anything wrong. They were perfect!

As for Livie, she was so involved in the theater group that she just tried to get to class with no paint on her face.

"Olivia!" Shirley said. "How wonderful to see you."

To Livie's consternation, Shirley leaned forward to kiss Olivia's cheek, and Betty followed.

"That's how they do it in New York, isn't it? Or is that in France? I get those mixed up." Shirley giggled in a way that said she believed she was still cute.

Olivia stepped back. "This is Nina Tattington. Her husband—"

"Tattington? Do you own this old place?" Betty asked.

"No, my husband and I just work here for the summer."

As they were scrutinizing Nina, sizing her up, Olivia was looking at them. They were as dressed up and made up as stage performers. Betty's eyebrows had been plucked until there was little left of them, and Shirley's hair had been ironed flat. No kinky curls were left in it.

They had on skirts so tight they were like sausage casings and their blouses were open down to their bras. Their legs were encased in panty hose and their feet squashed into the pointed toes of high heels.

What do they want? Olivia wondered. Her mother had kept her filled in on the town gossip so Olivia knew that these two hadn't had the perfect lives they'd expected. Betty had married her high school football player, but they'd divorced a year later and he'd moved to California. Shirley's boyfriend broke their engagement after she'd been wearing his ring for four years. Olivia's mother said the boy had volunteered for Vietnam rather than marry Shirley.

When he got back, he'd immediately married some girl who Shirley had always considered beneath her.

As for Olivia, in high school their attitude toward her had been that she didn't exist.

She'd never been invited to their parties or asked to join them in the cafeteria. But then, Olivia had never tried to be part of their crowd. To her, high school had been a stepping-stone to where she was going to go.

Without being invited, the girls sat down at the picnic table.

"So, Olivia," Betty said, "I hear you were fired from your Broadway play."

As she sat down at the end of the bench, Olivia opened her mouth to defend herself, but she closed it. It looked like the girls were still in the territory of high school, still degrading people to make themselves feel better. She smiled. "I was, and now I'm the cleaner for a couple of old men."

Nina coughed to cover a laugh.

Olivia could give their cattiness back to them. "And what about you two? Married? Kids?"

Both of them frowned.

"I wouldn't have any man in this town," Betty said. "You were right to go to New York to get one."

Olivia was puzzled by the remark. "I didn't get a man."

"What about the one everyone in town saw you fawning over at the tea shop? We heard it was quite embarrassing."

"And we also heard that he runs around here wearing no clothes." Shirley's voice was low, suggestive.

Olivia's face lost its fake look of complacency. *They're after Kit*, she thought. *They've come here with pounds of makeup on as bait for Kit.*

"So what's he like?" Betty asked.

"I heard he's rich," Shirley said. "Your father told Mr. Wilson at the club who told my uncle that the man has a palace in Italy. Is he a prince?"

Olivia looked at them in horror. She had a vision of the two of them—and the other single females in town—parading around Tattwell in four-inch heels.

She glanced at the bowls of green beans and saw it all ending. She suddenly realized that they had created a family here at Tattwell. They had inside jokes; they each had tasks. They knew about each other. Cared. Loved. Yes, they'd grown to love one another.

And she did *not* want that to end!

Olivia dug deep under her own emotions to find the character she needed to play. She gave a little laugh, doing her best to sound as though she didn't care. "Are you talking about Christopher? He's rich? You have to be kidding! Would he be mowing lawns if he had any money? And girls…" She leaned toward them as though sharing a secret. "Christopher is just a boy, a teenager. He's not the kind of man women like us need. Really, you mustn't waste your time on a child like him."

She was glad to see that her words were succeeding. The made-up faces of Betty and Shirley began to deflate like punctured balloons. Not rich. Not old enough. Olivia decided to sell the idea. "If you were seen out and about with the Worthless Boy—that's what I call him—you'd be the laughingstock of the entire town."

At that condemnation, both of the young women stood up. "Oh. I guess we heard wrong."

Trying to control her relief, Olivia also stood. "You should have a word with the gossips who told you those lies. I don't think they had your best interests in mind."

"You can be sure we will," Shirley said.

"I think we better go," Betty said.

"Yeah, right. Olivia, we'll see you in town. Maybe."

As fast as they could walk in heels on the old brick walkway, they hurried back to their car.

With a triumphant smile, Olivia turned to look to Nina, expecting congratulations. But what she saw on Nina's face was an expression of horror. Her skin was pale, as though all the blood had drained from it.

Please, no, Olivia thought. *Don't let it be what I think it is.*

Slowly, she turned in the direction Nina was looking. Standing just around the corner of the house was Kit, a shirt on over his bathing trunks. In front of him was Uncle Freddy in his wheelchair, his usually smiling face looking sad. He wouldn't meet Olivia's eyes. Behind them was Mr. Gates and he wore a look of disgust. It was one thing to call Kit Worthless Boy within the family they'd created, but *not* to tell other people that.

As for Kit, she couldn't read his expression, but then he'd turned his face away from her.

Even under his deep tan, she could see the red of anger on his skin.

When he pushed the wheelchair forward a few feet, Olivia saw that the children were in the back, and from their looks they too had heard what Olivia said. As young as they were, their sweet little faces looked at her as though she had betrayed them, had broken some unwritten code of family loyalty.

Olivia wanted to say something in her own defense, but what could she say? Whatever her excuse, she had disparaged Kit, belittled him, put him down. She had turned a family joke into a public condemnation.

Kit took his hands off the wheelchair and started to leave. His silence seemed to say that he too had no words.

He got about ten feet away, then he turned back, and the look on his face had changed.

For the first time, all of them saw Kit's anger. His eyes were dark lights of rage. He was formidable looking.

Olivia started to step back, but she held her ground.

In just a few steps, he was in front of her and he took her in his arms. Not gently, but with a force that nearly took the breath from her.

He kissed her. His body, his lips showed the passion he'd been feeling since the day he saw her. His desire for her, from seeing her daily, being close, laughing with her, from the tears to the quiet moments of happiness that they had shared, it was all there in that kiss.

His hand went to her face and his thumb caressed the corner of her mouth as his lips opened over hers.

This was not the kiss of a boy or of inexperience. This was a *man's* kiss, a man who had seen much of the world, and tasted most of it.

It was a kiss far different from anything Olivia had experienced before. There was no fumbling. No awkwardness. No insecurity. This was the kiss of a man who knew what the hell he was doing.

Kit broke away and for a second he looked at her. His eyes had not changed. They were cold fire, angry, maybe even cruel.

He had one arm around her body, and when he pulled it away, Olivia's legs folded under her.

With a snap of his wrists, Kit let her drop.

Olivia staggered backward for a step, but she was too unbalanced to catch herself. All the dance lessons she'd had hadn't prepared her for a kiss that had pulled the insides out of her. Emotion, feelings, even sanity, were gone.

She sat down on the brick pavement hard, her teeth jolting together, pain shooting up through her.

Standing over her, Kit's face went into a sneer. "Not a boy," he said. Then he turned on his heel and walked away.

Chapter Nineteen

Summer Hill, Virginia 1970

"SORRY, BUT WE AREN'T OPEN YET," THE BARTENDER said. "Come back in a couple of hours."

Kit put a fifty-dollar bill on the bar. "I want a beer and keep the change."

"I guess I just opened." He poured a beer, put it in front of Kit, then stood there watching him brood. "So which one did you choose?"

"What?"

The bartender was wiping the counter. "I assume you're here because you're after one of the girls. Or did you come into town to see your other choices?"

Kit looked at the man like he was crazy.

"Girls!" The bartender nodded at Kit's tan. "You been in the sun so long you forgot about them?"

Kit sighed. "Girls are all I think about."

"That's normal. It's what I did at your age. So which one is it?"

Kit frowned. "I have no idea what you're talking about."

"Betty Schneider or Shirley Williamson? Last night they were in here talking about the rich, naked guy who's a relative of

Uncle Freddy. They were saying they were going out to Tattwell to meet him. You're him, right?"

Kit took a deep drink of his beer. "Rich, naked guy," he mumbled. "That describes me perfectly."

"Did they show up?"

"Who?"

The bartender glared at him.

Kit shrugged. "Yeah, there were some young women there today. I didn't talk to them."

"Didn't—?" The bartender leaned forward. "Listen, those two girls are hot to trot, if you know what I mean. They used to be the queens of the local high school but now they just want a man. Betty is the smarter of the two. Shirley's the nicer one, but she won't let you out of her sight. If you want to see what else is in this town, I can put the word out. If you come back about seven, every unmarried gal within fifty miles will be here. And a few married ones, if that's what you want."

Kit was looking at the bartender as though he were from another planet, but then his eyes changed. He smiled as though he might like being hit on by lots of randy women. "You from here?"

"Born and bred."

"What's Olivia Paget like?"

The man stepped back from the bar and looked at Kit. "You've gone that way, have you? Well, give it up. She's the prettiest girl in town but she wants none of *us*. She may have been born a small town girl but she's not one. Her heart is somewhere else." He stood there looking at Kit, whose head was so low it was practically touching the counter. "Got it bad, have you?"

"Yeah," Kit said. "*Very* bad."

"Poor guy. I fell for a girl like that. She was way above me. Let me give you some advice. Olivia Paget isn't for some kid who runs around mostly naked and cleans up cemeteries. Yeah, we heard about that."

"I think maybe I did a really stupid thing today. Livie sent the girls away."

"You mean Betty and Shirley? Why'd she do that? I can't imagine Livie taking an interest in them. When she lived here, while the rest of us were having backyard barbecues, Livie was in Richmond taking lessons for her future life—and this was when she was twelve. So why did she send the girls away? It's more like she'd laugh about them being there to check you out. Olivia has a sense of humor that can cut glass."

Kit looked up at the man, his face showing the misery he was feeling.

The bartender's eyes widened. "You don't think...? Olivia couldn't be...?" He let out a snort of laughter. "You think Olivia sent those girls away because she's interested in *you*? In some kid who mows the grass?" He gave a genuine laugh. "One thing I'll say for you, kid, you got a pair on you."

"I think the absence of a brain counterbalances my overwhelming sense of self," Kit said as he drained his beer, then left the bar.

Watching the door close, the bartender shook his head. "'Overwhelming sense of self,'" he quoted. "Keep talkin' like that and who knows, kid, you might have a chance with Livie after all." But then he thought of all the young men who'd made passes at Olivia Paget and failed.

No, not possible. Laughing, he went to the storeroom to get more beer.

It was Nina who solved it all. First, she found out where Kit and Olivia had gone in their separate runaways. She got an earful from the bartender at the tavern that was a few miles down the road. Kit had already been there and left.

As for Olivia, she was a local girl. She'd walked to the road and someone she knew stopped and gave her a ride. Nina called Mrs.

Paget, gave her a brief explanation of what had happened, then said that if she heard where Olivia was, please let them know.

Next, Nina tackled the family by giving them a piece of her mind. The two old men and the children had assumed that Olivia had betrayed them. "She was protecting the lot of you!" Nina said, and went on from there.

The children were so fascinated at seeing Uncle Freddy and Mr. Gates getting bawled out by Letty's mother they were almost having a good time.

After she finished, Nina left the house and used her ever-present coat hanger wire to try to scratch under her cast. She was *very* annoyed with all of them.

When she got home, her phone was ringing. It was Mrs. Paget saying that Livie had come home, gone to her bedroom, and shut the door. She said her husband was out looking for Kit. "And I'm packing. We're going to spend a few days at the lake cabin."

"Good idea," Nina said as she kept scratching. Her anger had made the itch worse.

An hour later, Mrs. Paget called again to whisper that Kit was there, and she and her husband were leaving the house. "We don't plan to be back for two days."

"Make it three," Nina said.

"I hope I'm not making a mistake," Mrs. Paget said.

"You aren't," Nina answered. They said goodbye and hung up.

Chapter Twenty

WHEN OLIVIA STOPPED TALKING, KATHY AND ELISE were silent, waiting for her to go on. But she said nothing.

"I want to know the rest of it," Elise said.

Olivia blinked away tears. "We had six weeks of perfection. It's a cliché to say that we had heaven on earth, but we did." She took a breath. "My parents had an ulterior motive for leaving Kit and me alone in their house. They were proud about my Broadway role, but they really just wanted me to settle down and have babies. I didn't know it, but after my dad met Kit, he did some checking and he liked what he heard. By leaving us there, my parents were matchmaking."

"Did you and Kit stay there?" Elise asked. "In the house? Alone?"

Olivia gave a little smile. "If you're asking about sex, the answer is yes, yes, and yes. Sweaty, exhausting, all-consuming, never-ending sex. At the end of three days I knew his body as well as my own."

Kathy and Elise were smiling.

"When my mother called to tell us they were returning, Kit

and I went back to Tattwell. No one made a big deal of it, but they were very glad to see us. And we felt the same way."

Olivia had to pause, closing her eyes for a moment. "For weeks we were a very happy family. We were joyous that Uncle Freddy was alive, that Ace's mother was hanging on, and Kit and I were…were full of laughter." She gave a one-sided grin. "We used the well house as our private place. Kit bent some galvanized siding to make a sort of tunnel so we didn't get torn up by the thorns, and he put lots of cracked corn by the entrance."

"So the peacock would be your guard," Elise said.

Olivia nodded. "It was a divinely happy time. All of us lived very well together. To this day, Kit thinks we didn't know it, but dear little Ace started sleeping with him. The child knew what was coming and he needed comfort."

"But it all ended," Kathy said.

Olivia took several deep breaths. "My life changed because I went to Richmond. No, that's not true. It changed because the day before, I said those words. 'I love you.' I hadn't meant to, but it was just before I was to leave and they came out. Kit kissed me but he didn't say the words back to me."

She paused. "That afternoon he nearly killed himself clearing a half acre where Uncle Freddy's swimming pool was going to be put in, and the next morning he slept late. I was so annoyed with him for not telling me he loved me that when Mr. Gates said he was taking Uncle Freddy into Richmond for his six-month checkup, I said I'd go with him."

She was silent for a few moments. "As I was leaving, I tiptoed into Kit's room and looked at him sleeping. He had scratches on his face and soft black whiskers. He looked so good that I almost stayed. But unfortunately, my anger overrode my passion. I bent over and kissed his forehead, then left the room." She turned away and whispered, "I didn't see him again for over forty years."

She looked at Kathy and Elise. "When we got back, Kit wasn't there. Clothes, books, records, everything. It was as though he'd vanished. Poof! The completeness of his disappearance almost made me doubt that he'd ever existed."

"You thought he ran away because you told him you loved him," Kathy said.

"I am ashamed to say yes, that's exactly what I thought. The kids said that Kit's father came to get him in a big black car. I thought that's what Kit had told them. I was too upset, too angry, to realize that was their childish interpretation of what they'd seen. Man in a suit equals father."

She paused. "I thought Kit had called his father and said, 'Come and get me out of here' and he came running. Uncle Freddy said he called Kit's family and they said they didn't know where he was, but I thought they were lying. None of them knew that I'd said those three little words, so how could they know anything?" Her voice was rising.

"What was the truth?" Elise asked softly.

Olivia took a few breaths. "The military came for him. That's why he was there, hiding from his nosy family, and tanning all over. He was preparing to go on an undercover mission. They knew what he'd taken with him and they made sure they got it all. But he did manage to leave a message for me in the well house. Actually, it was a marriage proposal—along with his grandmother's ring."

Olivia held out her hand to show the beautiful ring. White gold lacework with a big round diamond in the center. "I didn't see it because I was so angry that I refused to ever again enter the well house. I didn't want to hear his name, to think about him. Or…" When she looked up, her face was white. "My stupidity still angers me, and regret eats at me."

"Love is stupid." There was venom in Elise's voice. "Why does Kent love Carmen and not *me*? And why do I lust after—" She sighed. "There is no sense in love."

"I agree," Kathy said. "My husband is one gorgeous hunk but

I wanted Andy, an ordinary-looking little man who has never so much as glanced at me."

The three women were silent for a moment.

"You went to Broadway?" Kathy asked.

"Just days after Kit vanished, I was on a plane to New York."

For a moment, the women were silent, but then Kathy spoke, her voice puzzled. "You trained to be an actress for most of your life, but you left your lifelong dream and returned home."

"And married someone else," Elise said.

Olivia seemed to be considering what to say—but in the end, she didn't reply. She stood up. "I really do need to go to bed." Abruptly, without another word, she turned on her heel, grabbed a flashlight, and went out the front door.

"Wow," Elise said softly. "Forty years."

Kathy was staring at the door. "I think she left out a lot of the story."

"Like what?" Elise asked.

"Remember how she started? Nixon, Vietnam, and…"

"That no one was using birth control pills," Elise said as she began to gather up dishes to take to the kitchen, then she halted. She and Kathy exchanged looks.

"Let's leave this mess," Kathy said softly. "I don't want Livie to be alone. We can clean it up tomorrow."

"That's a good idea."

They walked back to the summerhouse in silence, each with her own thoughts. What had happened to Olivia's life was a travesty—and they wanted to prevent something similar happening in their own lives.

The cottage was quiet, and upstairs, Elise paused outside Olivia's door but she heard nothing.

That was because Olivia had had forty years to learn how to cry in absolute silence.

Chapter Twenty-One

THE NEXT MORNING KATHY WOKE TO A SILENT HOUSE. It had that feeling of people in it, but they were far away. She got up, dressed, and went outside. It wasn't full light yet, but she liked the early morning. The grass was damp with dew and it felt good on her sandaled feet.

Young Pete was raking a patch of lawn and she waved at him. He stopped and smiled at her in a way that would have made her blush if she hadn't been so pleased. With as much time as she spent with Ray, she nearly forgot how good it was to feel desirable and womanly.

She went past the yawning vacancy of Camden Hall and through the rose-covered wall to River House. For a moment she stood looking out at the stream with the curved bridge and the pretty island. She was sure most people would think how they'd love to live in a place like this, but all Kathy saw was maintenance. The ten acres she and Ray owned in Connecticut were as beautiful as this. A treat for the eyes. One of Ray's clients said it was "Serenity personified."

She'd trade every perfect flower that took so much of her

time for an apartment in New York. She'd happily exchange birdsong for the scream of an ambulance siren.

The front door of the house was unlocked and she went in. On the floor was a small box, neatly wrapped in brown paper. The label had the names of all three women on it, but no return address. *It must be from Ray*, Kathy thought. Only he knew that the women were there. Or maybe Young Pete had left it, Kathy thought with a smile.

She picked up the box, set it on a table by the front door, then began cleaning up from last night. Olivia's story of her past had made Kathy think about her own life. Ray had said she should stay here so she could have a vacation. "Enjoy yourself. Go shopping." He seemed to think that shopping cured every woman's problems. But right now, the last thing she wanted was a new blouse. What she really and truly wanted was a new *life*.

She turned on the dishwasher, then walked through the house. There were art objects from around the world, beautiful things, but as she looked at them, she thought of Olivia's story. *Regret*, Olivia had said. She regretted so very much.

"So do I," Kathy said aloud.

"So do you what?" Elise's voice startled Kathy.

"Nothing important."

Behind her was Olivia and she was holding the box. "What's this?"

"I found it on the floor. I guess it's from Ray. A thank-you gift." *I taught him to say thanks*, Kathy thought but didn't say.

"I think we should open it." Olivia began removing the paper. Inside was a note from Dr. Hightower.

This is real. Please try it.

Then her signature.

Olivia set the box on the table. It was filled with what looked to be cotton quilt batting and buried inside were three business cards. On the back, their names were handwritten in old fashioned copperplate.

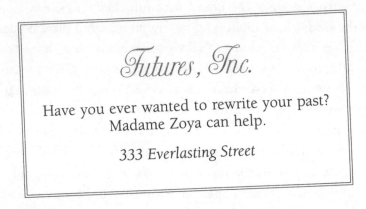

Futures, Inc.

Have you ever wanted to rewrite your past?
Madame Zoya can help.

333 Everlasting Street

At the bottom had been handwritten "now off Farm Road 77."

Olivia and Elise sat down at the big kitchen table, and Kathy opened the refrigerator to pull out a dozen oranges. There was a tall manual juicer clamped to the counter. She cut the oranges in half, pulled the handle down, and filled glasses with fresh juice.

"Lovely fantasy, isn't it? *To rewrite the past.*" Elise was smiling at the absurdity of it.

"I agree." Kathy put full glasses of orange juice on the table. "But it *is* a great thought, isn't it? So where would you go back to?"

They were ignoring Olivia as she sat there staring at the card. Her eyes were fixed, unmoving, unblinking. No one needed to ask her what she'd change. She wouldn't go to Richmond on *that* day.

"I'd go to my wedding," Elise said.

Kathy cracked some eggs and was whipping them about in a bowl. "I'd think you'd want to go back and say no when your husband proposed."

"That wouldn't work," Elise said. "If I said no in private, my parents and Kent's would drive me so crazy that I'd eventually say yes just to make them shut up. I'd have to say no in a big, huge, public way. I'd throw my skirt over my arm and run out of the church."

"Then what?" Kathy asked.

"I have no idea. I'd like to be rescued by a gorgeous man riding a big black horse, but since that wouldn't happen, I don't know."

"How about a driver and a long black limo?" Kathy began scrambling eggs. "Have him drive you to the airport, then fly somewhere. If you planned it beforehand, you could have a suitcase packed and in the trunk. You could change clothes in the back of the car."

"I like that," Elise said. "Except that I have nowhere to go."

"Maine." Olivia was at last coming out of her trance. She put the card down on the table. "Kit has lots of single male relatives in Maine. You could take your pick. I'm sure they'd compete to see who could win you."

"That sounds great!" Elise was laughing. "I'll elope with one of them and return home married to some guy who is so rich he'd please even my parents."

"What about Alejandro?"

"I didn't realize it at the time but he started working there just a week before my wedding. But even if I went back, nothing would have changed. We still live in different worlds. I don't know how they could be merged."

"What about you?" Olivia asked Kathy, who was putting a bowl of scrambled eggs and a plate of whole wheat toast on the table. "Would you go back to get your Andy?"

As Kathy sat down, she was frowning in concentration. "What would I change?" She looked up. "Does it have to be about a man?"

"No!" the two women said in unison.

"Hmmm," Kathy said. "If I went back in time—knowing what I do now, that is—the first thing I'd do is make a place for myself in my father's advertising firm. A lot of the ideas that

Ray presented were mine. The second thing I'd do is stay away from Ray. You know something? I hate living in Connecticut. I hate the big house Ray and I own. I even hate my gorgeous garden. Keeping it all going takes masses of my time—not to mention how much it all costs."

She took a bite of egg. "I'd go back to those two weeks when Ray got caught in a blizzard in Chicago. *Before* we were married. Married or not, I'd never be able to do anything with him around. Dad was crazy for those two weeks that Ray was gone. He had clients coming in from Hong Kong and..." She shrugged.

"How did it get resolved?" Olivia asked.

Kathy shrugged. "Like always. Ray came back from Chicago with a great campaign and everyone was happy. My fantasy is that I would be the one to win the hearts of the clients." Her chin came up. "And after that I'd demand that my father give me a real job, something other than playing a social hostess to him and Ray. I'd like to have a real salary and an office with my name on the door—and an apartment on the Upper West Side. Something cute with a terrace."

She sighed. "But I'll never get that. Ray is just like Kent. He believes he needs the Connecticut house to entertain clients." She looked down at her plate.

"Ray wants to divorce you," Olivia said softly. "That's why he's been going to Dr. Hightower."

Kathy's eyes widened for a moment, then she buried her face in her hands and began to cry loudly.

Instantly, Elise and Olivia were beside her, hugging and patting.

"I'm so sorry," Olivia said. "I shouldn't have told you. I'm sorry, sorry, sorry."

Kathy got up, her pretty face covered in tears, and went to the refrigerator. She withdrew a cold bottle of champagne, untwisted the bale, and the cork popped out. She poured it into the glasses of orange juice and held hers up. "A toast! At this moment I am the happiest woman on this planet."

Elise and Olivia were too stunned to speak. They managed to pick up their glasses but all they did was stare.

Kathy drank deeply, then poured more champagne into her juice. "Ray would never leave without someone waiting for him. Tell me it's Rita. Please, I hope it is. They're so perfect for each other. And if he marries her and they produce kids maybe Carl's mother will forgive him about her son." She looked at them. "If he told you about Rita, did he tell you about Carl too? Of course he did. Just so you know, Carl was a thug. Not the saint Ray wants to believe he was."

Elise and Olivia were still holding their glasses in silence.

"Drink up, girls! We have a lot to celebrate."

They took sips but their eyes showed their shock.

Olivia began to recover. "How do you know about Carl?"

"I've always known about him," Kathy said. "Ray and Dad met when Ray invaded a lunch Dad was having with a client. Afterward, Dad said Ray was either the best salesman he'd ever met or a lying thief. He told me to find out which. My report said that Ray was both of them. Dad said he was perfect for the advertising world and hired him."

Wide-eyed, Elise and Olivia sat down at the table and began to eat. "Ray said you hired his secretaries," Olivia said.

"Yes, I did." There was pride in Kathy's voice. "Both my father and Ray dump clients' social lives onto me. If some guy who owns half of Iowa comes to New York and wants Dad's agency to advertise whatever it is he sells, *I* am delegated to show the wife around. Whatever she wants to do, I'm told to fulfill her wishes. One wife wanted me to hire a Magic Mike—type dancer to visit her in her hotel room. She seemed to think I'd know how to arrange that. 'You live in New York, don't you?' she said."

Kathy took a breath. "Anyway, I'd had enough of all of it. I was married to Ray but I didn't feel like his wife. We were to the point where he'd pat me on the shoulder and say, 'Good job.' Like I was one of his colleagues. I wanted out. But you've met Ray. It was just like with Dolores. It had to be Ray's decision to end it. I knew that the only way he was going to let me go—I mean really and truly release me—was if he had someone else."

"So you set out to find her," Olivia said.

"When Ray's original secretary retired, I coaxed him into letting me find someone to replace her. I treated it like a beauty pageant. I don't know Ray's sexual preference except that he doesn't like big, healthy, curvy women like me, so I went for a variety."

Smiling broadly, Kathy took a drink of her mimosa. "I found a Scandinavian blonde who had the men in the office running into glass doors. But Ray never looked at her. Next came a cute little Latin girl who married another guy in the office. Then there was a buxom redhead."

Kathy laughed. "I nearly drove my husband crazy for over two years. Every time a girl learned how to run his office, I'd make up an excuse to get her another job."

"And you were trying to find a wife for your husband." Elise sounded as though she couldn't quite believe it.

"Yes. Ray may wear a suit to the office, and he can sit down to dinner with men who play polo, but scratch the surface and he's the guy from the streets of Brooklyn."

"And that's where Rita is from," Olivia said.

"Oh yes! She was a godsend. The answer to all my prayers. I was to the point where I thought I was going to have to ask Ray for a divorce."

"And if you did, he'd dig in his heels and say no," Olivia said. "He had to make the decision and no one else. If you asked, out of principle he'd wage a war—and everyone would lose. You, your father, Ray, the company, your clients."

"I think you understand my husband completely—and so did

Carl's mother. When Rita needed a job, she sent her to me, not to Ray. I think she figured that after years with him, I probably knew him pretty well. I had Rita come to the house for lunch and right away I saw that she was reserved enough for him in public, but underneath, she still had that street flair. I thought they'd make a perfect couple. I hired her to work for Ray." Kathy grinned. "I am very proud of myself!"

"What about Dr. Hightower?" Olivia asked.

"That was another gift out of the blue. Totally unexpected," Kathy said. "When Ray told me he was going to see a therapist, I think he expected me to talk him out of it, to say that nothing could be wrong with a great guy like him. But I didn't. I was hoping with all my might that he was trying to get up the courage to ask me for a divorce. The man has the strange belief that my entire life is him. It almost is, but not by choice!" Kathy poured herself more champagne, minus the orange juice.

Olivia picked up the card and looked at it. "Now that you have what you want, you probably wouldn't want to change anything."

"You can get your New York apartment and maybe you can make your father listen to you," Elise said.

Kathy thought about that for a moment. "I think that in this case it's like a prisoner who's released after being found innocent. All his life he would have people saying, 'Weren't you in jail? What was it like?' In the advertising world, I will always be known as 'Ray's first wife.' The one he dumped. As it is, women ask me what it's like being married to him. They sense that he's only half a step away from being some street gangster and it excites them."

"But not you," Elise said.

Kathy rolled her eyes. "When we got married, he was barely civilized. I taught him table manners, gave him ballroom dancing lessons. You know what he got me for our first anniversary?

A handbag with a lizard on it. A real lizard that had once been alive. He said his mother had always wanted one of those bags."

Olivia was the first to laugh.

"He gave me so many weird gifts that a condition I put on his secretary was that she had to do whatever was necessary to keep him from buying me *anything*. And I opened an account at Chanel."

Olivia was laughing harder. "He told me that Elise was all Chanel and Cartier."

"And who do you think taught him that?" Kathy drained her glass and leaned forward. "This thing—" she nodded at the card "—is a scam. Whoever it is will want lots of money, but I say let's go anyway. I haven't had so much fun in years. Just thinking about rewriting my past and not marrying Ray Hanran is making me feel like dancing."

"Me too!" Elise said. "Imagining running down the aisle in my wedding dress—away from Kent—is a great fantasy."

"No dancing for me," Olivia said. "It's making me feel like driving—not that it'll do any good. There is no Everlasting Street anywhere in Summer Hill and there's nothing on FM 77 but a few old houses. One of them was abandoned years ago."

"I vote for anything that might help me with my current situation. Or at least give me some hope of a solution." Elise stood up.

"I second that," Kathy said.

"Put everything in the sink and let's get in Kathy's car," Olivia said. "Mine might be recognized. Anyone have some big sunglasses and some scarves?"

"Prada and Hermès do for you two?" Kathy asked.

"No dead lizards?" Elise said. "Darn!"

They laughed.

Olivia drove, Kathy beside her, and Elise got in the back. Olivia was glad the two of them were chatting, bonding. They each had body hang-ups. Kathy obsessed about her weight, and eyed every morsel of food as though weighing it for calories and nutrition.

Whenever Kathy moved, Elise looked at her, assessing every curve. She seemed to be wondering whether being more voluptuous would help her capture love.

Olivia had to fight the urge to lecture both of them. It wasn't their body types that won or lost a man. It was *him*. The man. The women had chosen wrong—and Olivia was an expert on that. The things Kit liked about her were what Alan had abhorred. Olivia's competence, her ability to get a job done, had made Alan feel useless, had taken away his essential feeling of being a *man*.

It was after Kit returned to her life that she thought about the differences in personalities.

Kit didn't know it, but she'd asked his son about his mother.

Rowan's usually serious face softened. "Mom is lovely. She's related to Italian nobility and she's quite beautiful. She's well educated, well traveled, and can talk to anyone about anything."

"Oh." Olivia's eyes showed her disappointment. How could she compete with "Italian nobility"? And she had never been out of the US.

"What Mother couldn't do was deal with Dad's peripatetic life. He'd get a call from some government and we were to be gone in twenty-four hours. He expected Mother to organize the move and to take care of everything. But she couldn't do it. She was used to being taken care of, not the other way around."

Olivia's eyes brightened at his words. Moving, organizing, managing people were all things she could do. And more importantly, she would have loved it.

Rowan's handsome face hardened. "Dad wanted Mother to be something she wasn't, and when she couldn't be that person, he got angry."

Olivia had just nodded. She'd understood well. But understanding didn't take away the pain.

She drove past Mr. Ellis's farm. Long ago it had been sold to a developer and a few little houses had been built, with many more planned. If she could go back in time, she'd buy the land with the rocks where she and Kit had sat and talked. Someone told her that the new owner was going to blast them out of the ground. Boring houses needed boring, flat tracts of land to be built on.

Just as there was no Everlasting Street in Summer Hill, Olivia was sure that no one on earth could rewrite the past—if that's what that silly card even meant.

Kathy and Elise were now discussing the design details of Phillip Lim handbags and enthusiastically agreeing that he was someone to watch.

Olivia couldn't help smiling, happy that they were finding a common ground—and glad that for a moment they'd forgotten the bad of their lives. What concerned her was that the young women were so traumatized by what the men had done to them that they'd never recover. They were both beautiful women. Different but quite lovely. But years of being put down and found to be lacking had made them feel less than they were. How could big, lusty Ray not want to pounce on Kathy? As for Kent, he was just plain stupid.

When Olivia got to FM 77, she slowed and turned right. She knew what was down the road. There were three old farmhouses set quite far apart. The first two were inhabited by older couples, and for lack of money, the houses had been allowed to deteriorate. Last year Josh Hartman had been paid by the church to repair the roofs. She knew he had put in many more hours than he was paid for.

At the end of the road was the third house and no one had lived in it for over twenty years. It was set way back from the gravel road and had once been owned by an old man with six dogs. He'd left the house to his son, but no one could find him so the house had sat vacant.

Olivia drove down the road slowly and at each driveway she had an impulse to turn around. This was ridiculous! Why were they here? To give money to some charlatan? To be ripped off because... Because they had hope? Is that what they were trying for?

By the time she neared the end of the road, she was driving so slowly the car was barely crawling. She could hear every piece of gravel under the tires.

Kathy turned in her seat and looked out the windshield. "Are you okay?"

"I'm feeling silly. Why are we doing this?" Olivia asked.

"Why not? Getting out of the house, thinking about something positive instead of the rotten things men have done to us has to be good."

Olivia smiled. "I like your attitude."

"Look!" Elise leaned between the seats and pointed.

There was a brand-new green-and-white sign that said, EVERLASTING STREET. Olivia couldn't help giving a snort of laughter. "This is a driveway."

"Magic comes in many forms," Kathy said.

Olivia turned into the driveway that was now called a street. There were big old trees shading the way, and it wasn't until she got to the end that she saw the house.

What had once been a derelict, decaying old place had been completely rebuilt. Big windows had been added and the front section built out to form a tall bay window. The old porch enclosed the entire side of the house.

"Looks like some work has been done," Elise said. "Think it was magic?"

"Unless I miss my guess, it was Josh Hartman. He can design as well as build. I can assure you that the original house never looked this good!" Olivia turned the engine off and sat for a moment looking at the pretty house. It was a nice size, not sprawling, but not a cottage either. She was a bit annoyed that no one had told her this had been done. Stacy, their designer, was Josh's sister, so she should have mentioned that her brother was—

"You okay?" Kathy asked.

"Sure." Olivia tried to brush away the feeling of having been left out. "Let's do it."

Elise got out of the car and the others followed her.

It was very quiet around the house. Birds chirped; the wind rustled the leaves. To the right, a tall wooden fence had been put up, with an arch over the gate. Olivia went to it and glanced inside. It was a large vegetable and herb garden. Right now, it was new and raw, but give it a couple of years and it would be glorious.

"For witch's brew?" Kathy asked, lightening Olivia's sense of foreboding. "We don't have to do this if you don't want to."

Before Olivia could reply, Elise started running. "Come on, you two. Let's go."

"She's really unhappy in her life, isn't she?" Kathy said softly.

Olivia sighed. "I don't want to think about what's in store for her. This hiatus won't last long. When she's found, her parents will... I don't know what they're going to try to do. She needs a job and..." Trailing off, she looked at Kathy. "Whatever gives that child even a minute of hope, I'm all for it."

As soon as they reached the front door, it was opened by a pretty young woman. She was medium height, with lots of unruly brown hair, and she was quite thin. She had on a loose green T-shirt and black cotton trousers.

"Hello." Her smile showed even, white teeth. "You are... No, don't tell me. Olivia, Kathy, and you're Elise. Did I get it right?"

If Dr. Hightower had told her they'd be coming, it wouldn't have been difficult to guess who was who.

Olivia was standing in the back. She'd always been an observer of people. When she was acting, she liked to think how to play the character. Unless she missed her guess, this young woman was very nervous. Her bravado was forced, as though she was trying to cover some insecurity.

"You're Madame Zoya?" Elise's tone told of her disappointment.

"No, I'm not." She said it with a fierceness that smacked of defiance. "That's my aunt. I'm Arrieta Day. I..." She paused and took a deep breath. "I'm taking my aunt's place."

They were still standing in the doorway and the young woman kept glancing at Olivia with an expression she couldn't quite fathom. It was almost as though she wanted Olivia's approval—or her permission. But permission for what?

There was an awkward moment of silence, then Arrieta stepped back. "Please come in. I made raisin cookies and the kettle is on and...and..." She didn't seem to know what else to say.

They entered a large foyer with a staircase before them. To the right was a small dining room with an antique pine table. To the left was what looked to be a little library with double doors that were standing open. As for the rest of the house, it was all closed doors.

Arrieta motioned for them to go into the library. At the far end was a tall bay window with a cushioned seat. The other walls had floor-to-ceiling bookshelves that were mostly empty. The only furniture was a maple desk and four lattice-back chairs. It all felt barren, as though no one had yet moved in.

The women sat down while Arrieta stood behind the desk. "I guess you want to know how this works."

Elise nodded while Kathy and Olivia just stared at her.

"I can send you back in time." Arrieta's voice sounded almost like an apology. "You choose when and you stay for three weeks. Then you come back here. Anyone want cookies?"

"Time travel?" Kathy said. "I just thought this was a...a reading. But time travel? I don't think—"

"I'm in," Elise said. "When do we begin? How much do we pay? Will you take a rain check since I have no money?"

"Neither do I," Arrieta said, then looked a bit panicked. "I mean... I guess that would be okay. I hadn't thought about that. I may need to call my aunt and ask. Oh, and it's a hundred dollars per person."

Kathy was looking at the hope on Elise's face. She wasn't going to put logic into this and take that look away. "I'll pay for everyone. So how many times do we have to come back to you before we do the time travel?"

"None." Arrieta's expression showed that she knew Kathy didn't believe any of it. "I make you some tea, you drink it, then you go back in time. All in one visit."

"What kind of tea?" Kathy's voice was suspicious.

"It's not drugs, if that's what you think. It's herbs that help you relax." Arrieta looked around as though searching for an escape route.

Olivia spoke up. "This isn't possible." They all looked at her.

"The Butterfly Effect?" When they said nothing, she went on. "You change one thing in the past, no matter how small, and it will *all* be different."

"You can only change what affects *you*," Arrieta said. They waited for her to go on, but she didn't.

"But I want to go back to three weeks before 9/11," Olivia said. "I want to warn people. Or before Pearl Harbor. Or—"

"No." Arrieta sat down behind the desk. "We've had people try that. One man spent his whole three weeks in jail. When he tried to warn people, he was arrested for disturbing the peace. People thought he was going to set off bombs. Another man went back so he could get a second chance at being a good father. But you know what he did?"

No one answered.

"He plagiarized songs. He had a good memory for lyrics, so he wrote them down and put his name on them. Made his kids memorize them."

"So when he came back to the present he'd be rich and famous," Kathy said.

"Exactly," Arrieta answered.

"But I take it that it didn't work," Olivia said.

"When he got back he was exactly where he was when he left. All memory of the songs he'd stolen was gone. His ex-wife still hated him and his children had no use for him. It was a very sad case." She took a breath. "And writers are the worst. My aunt says she'll *never* send another writer back. They love to steal plots. One man rewrote *Guardians of the Galaxy* from memory and sent it to his agent."

The women waited to hear the results. Arrieta raised one shoulder. "The agent loved it but later, he thought the author was crazy for saying that he wrote the book before it was put on the screen. The agent dropped him."

"So we need to keep our noses to our own business," Olivia said. "Is there a way to know when we step over the line?"

Arrieta shrugged. "Only what is supposed to happen will." She stood up. "I'll let you think about when you want to go back to." With that, she nearly ran from the room.

Kathy stood up. "This is a joke." Olivia and Elise stayed seated. "You two don't actually believe this, do you?"

"I would like to go back to the morning of my wedding," Elise said softly. "Before that day I could stand it all. I had an absolute belief that after I married Kent everything would change. I thought our parents would start being pleased by me. Kent and I would have babies and talk about where we wanted to go on vacation. Ordinary, normal things. But they didn't happen." Her voice was growing louder. "After I got married, everything got *worse*. People were even less pleased with me than before. And Kent had no interest in me at all. He—"

Olivia put her hand on Elise's arm.

"Sorry." Elise looked at Kathy, her eyes pleading. "I don't care if all I do is fall asleep and dream. I'd rather have hope than just wait for them to come and get me."

Olivia got up and went to the few books that were in the many feet of empty shelves. There were some on growing herbs and a dozen about serving tea. How to run a tearoom, what to serve, recipe books. She turned to the two women. "I'm going to find out more about this." She went into the big foyer and looked at the closed doors. *The lady or the tiger?* she thought. Which door should she choose?

The clatter of silverware being dropped made her go to the door on the right. It opened into a beautiful kitchen. "Hello." As soft as Olivia's voice was, Arrieta was still so startled that she nearly dropped a teacup. "Here, let me do that. You sit down." She nodded at the table in the adjoining breakfast nook.

"I think I'm supposed to serve you," Arrieta said, but she sat down anyway.

"How many times have you done this?" Olivia asked.

Arrieta's expression answered her.

"Oh, I see. Your first time." Olivia put loose tea in the flowered pot. "Tell me about yourself."

"I'm also supposed to ask the questions."

"I'm sure that's right, but there are extenuating circumstances, aren't there?"

"I guess." Arrieta still looked like she wanted to run away.

"Did your aunt dump this job on you?"

"Yes!" Arrieta said. "I hate destiny! It sounds romantic, but it's not. It means I have no free choice but that I *have* to do something. But that's not fair, is it? A person could have a great singing voice, but she doesn't *have* to sing, does she?"

"And you don't want to charge people for hope, then give them nothing," Olivia said.

"Oh no, that's not it at all. I can sing. I mean I can send people back in time, but I'm not very good with people socially."

"Then why do you want to open a tea shop?" Olivia said quickly.

For a second Arrieta's eyes widened, then she laughed. "Aunt Primrose told me you were good at figuring out people. I have to earn a living and I like to bake and garden. With a couple of good employees, I think I can make it work."

"And meeting people will help with your destiny," Olivia said. "I can't imagine that what you say you can do is possible."

"It is. We just have to be careful who we tell about it. Dr. Hightower has referred a lot of people to my aunts—and now me."

"I'm curious. Was Ray or Kathy the original target for this... opportunity?"

"Kathy," Arrieta said. "It was never Ray. Dr. Hightower thought you should hear him tell how he treats his wife because Kathy might not say anything. She's good at keeping things to herself. But Ray is fine—thanks to his wife taking such good care of him. She's the one who has the problems."

"How did you get her here?"

Arrieta shrugged. "My aunts know lots of people so some calls were made and voilà! Ray leaves the country and Kathy goes to Dr. Hightower's house. It all worked out." Olivia didn't have to ask about Elise.

"Dr. Hightower wants to retire." Arrieta said this with an intense look at Olivia. "Rescuing Elise was Jeanne's final straw. She can't take any more and we need someone to fill her role— someone who will send the right people our way."

"I think you'll need a very special person who believes in... What do you call this? Time travel?" Olivia's tone told how ridiculous she thought it all was.

Arrieta looked at her nails. "If you returned to 1970, you

could go back to school while Mr. Montgomery was in the Middle East. By now you'd be a qualified therapist."

Olivia was too stunned by that statement to speak.

"I told Aunt Primrose that you'd *never* agree to this."

"You're making it sound like you planned for me to come into the kitchen so I could hear about this."

"Cale said you would."

"Cale? Kit's cousin? The writer? I hardly know her."

"She's friends with Ellie Abbot, who my aunt sent back. Cale said you were insatiably curious and the most capable woman she's ever met."

"Oh," Olivia said. "I had no idea. That's a wonderful compliment."

"Of course none of it would start until now."

"What does that mean?"

"You can go back to 1970, marry Mr. Montgomery, and begin to study to be a psychologist. When he comes back from his secret mission, you and your family can live all over the world, then—zap!—you return here and use your certification to help us. The aunts and me, that is. You'll help find people who need us."

It was all too fanciful for Olivia to comprehend. She just sat there blinking.

"I guess I should tell you about the memory. When you get back here, after your, uh, journey, you can choose to remember or not. My guess is that Elise won't want to remember what her family did to her. Kathy will need to remember that big, lusty Ray is a no-no. And you'll want to know everything about both your marriages because you like a full mind. Actually, you *need* to remember all about your late husband and your dreadful daughter-in-law—I met her—so you can help other people."

Olivia was trying to digest this. "Will Elise remember *us*?"

"Only the hate will be removed from her memory. Not the love."

"Can I tell Kit?"

"If you wish. Your life is your own."

"If...if I did...uh, return to the past, could I tell him I'm from the future?"

"You can, but it'll be like that man with the songs. You can tell him about computers and cell phones and 9/11, everything. But at the end of three weeks it will all disappear. You'll return here to this house and you'll be this age. You will have gone through the years together but neither of you will have known the future."

"I was trained for the stage, so how will I remember that I need to study to become a psychologist?"

Arrieta smiled. "That's exactly what I asked my aunts. They said that if you'd really and truly *liked* being an actress you would have continued to be one."

At that, Olivia gave a bit of a smile. She'd never admitted to anyone but Kit that she'd loved the first week she'd been on Broadway, but doing it over and over, night after night, had bored her.

"My aunt Primrose said that if you'd had Mr. Montgomery and been *happy* you would have gone back to school. And she believes you would have studied psychology."

"I did take a few courses in college and I loved them, but the stage seemed to be calling me." She looked at Arrieta for a few moments. "The man with the songs wasn't the only time it didn't produce good, was it?"

"No. Sometimes there are disasters." Arrieta leaned forward. "Sometimes people are so joyous to be young again that they're reckless and get themselves maimed, or even killed. They say they want to experience a different side of life so they run off with dreadful people. When they get back to the present, they nearly always choose to stay with the life they had before. Especially if they died in the second visit."

"I would think so!" Olivia paused. "But even with all the

bad, when they returned, it would release that feeling of regret. It's something that haunts me every day. I recently had a new one put onto me. I thought I was a good mother to my stepson, but I found out that he thinks I only cared about money. It's made me worry that I wouldn't be a good mother to anyone."

"Your stepson is a greedy little bastard," Arrieta said vehemently. "Sorry, but this is a small town. When Josh was doing the renovations, your stepson came here. He and his wife are planning to add an entertainment wing onto their big house. They said that Mr. Montgomery was going to pay for it."

It took Olivia some moments to fully understand what she was hearing. After all the protests that Kevin and Hildy had made about her marriage to Kit, they were actually planning to benefit with his family's wealth. That was more than Olivia could take. "All right, I'll try it—but only if you tell me how you do it."

Arrieta shrugged. "Actually, it's up to the people. I just have to think hard, and if they really and truly want to go, then it happens. I have *no* idea how. It's just something some of the women in my family can do. We—" She clamped her mouth shut, not saying any more, then she got up and put the teapot on a tray. "Are you ready to go back in time?"

"I think I am," Olivia said, and they left the kitchen.

When they were in the empty little library, Arrieta put the tea tray on the desk and handed each woman a cup. While they drank, she explained about memory.

Elise said, "I don't want to remember what my parents and Kent did to me!" Arrieta and Olivia exchanged looks. It's what they'd predicted she would say.

When they finished their tea, Arrieta took the empty cups and put them on the tray.

After a moment's thought, she moved her chair from behind the desk and sat down in front of the three women. "Shall we get started? All you have to do is tell me when you want to go back to, then close your eyes and think really hard about that time. I'll do the rest."

Instantly, Elise nestled her hands in her lap, then closed her eyes. Her whole body seemed to relax.

Arrieta looked away from Elise. "She's already there. She wanted to get out of this world so very much. But if you two don't want to go…"

"Sorry," Olivia said. Elise was smiling. She looked like she was sleeping—and like she was very, very happy. Whatever she was dreaming of, she was enjoying it. Olivia looked back at Arrieta. Whether what she was proposing was true or not, Olivia would like to again feel as happy as Elise looked. "I want to go back to exactly three weeks before they came to get Kit. I want every second I can get to change a lot of things with many people. I want—" She didn't say any more because she felt herself drifting off, floating. *Kit, Kit, Kit,* she thought. With a smile, she imagined Uncle Freddy and Mr. Gates, the children, her parents, and… She felt too good to do any more thinking. She just gave herself over to the feeling of being weightless, of not having a sad thought or feeling. She drifted. It felt like all the unhappiness of her life was being taken out of her mind, being removed from where it seemed to have settled down into her bones. She was smiling as she hadn't done since… Since the day Kit left.

Arrieta looked at Kathy. "What do you want to do?"

"Be as happy as those two look. Do I click my heels?"

"To stop talking would make a start," Arrieta snapped. "Sorry. I'm new at this. I'm not used to dealing with sarcasm and doubt and all the other bad things that go with this job that I never wanted in the first place."

Kathy was looking at her with wide eyes. "When Ray went to Chicago," she said softly, then closed her eyes. She was so skeptical about everything that it took minutes before she began to feel a release from what her life had become.

"Kathy!" she heard her father order. "Get us some coffee."

"Get it yourself," she heard herself say, and that made her smile. No one had *ever* talked to her father like that. Kathy began to smile so broadly that it was about to take over her entire body. The sheer size of the smile seemed to turn her inside out. She had no body, just an enormous, life-changing *smile*.

Arrieta looked at the three women, glad that they were where they should be, then got up and went into the kitchen to call her aunt Primrose. Everything was going well. So far, anyway.

Chapter Twenty-Two

AS ELISE POUNDED ON THE DOOR OF CARMEN'S HOTEL room, her only thought was *Alejandro*. The skirt of her big wedding dress was thrown over her arm and her fist ached from hitting on the door. She was doing her best not to think of the horror of the last four hours. "Open up!" she rasped as she looked up and down the corridor. No one was there, but then they were probably all in the church waiting for Elise to march down the aisle.

Just hours ago, she'd been sitting in the little library of that woman, Arrieta, doing as she'd been told, and thinking hard about the time she wanted to return to. When the silence continued, Elise opened her eyes, expecting to see Olivia and Kathy sitting beside her.

Instead, she'd found herself in the big hotel suite her mother had booked for her to use for the wedding. Elise was sitting on a hassock with her ghastly wedding dress spread out around her. It was like a silk cloud left over from a nuclear explosion.

To her left was a full-length mirror, and to her right were four of the six bridesmaids that her mother had chosen. They were the unattractive daughters of the two mothers' college friends. "They're all rich and they'll help you in the future," her mother said when Elise protested them.

As she glanced in the mirror, she saw the girls huddled together, whispering.

For a few moments, Elise was caught in a halfway point between then and now, and she could still feel the elation she'd had on her wedding day. She was going to marry *Kent*! The man of her dreams. And a side effect was that in doing so she'd please everyone. She had a vision of both families smiling and sharing meals together. It was going to be heaven!

But now, years later, she knew how wrong she'd been. Marrying Kent had brought her *more* under the control of the families— and made her more unhappy.

It had taken her a few moments to adjust to the transition and she heard Kathy's voice in her head, telling her what she needed to do was run away. She sent a bridesmaid to get the limo driver to come to her. He said that yes, her bags for the honeymoon were in the trunk, and he'd been told to take the newly wedded couple to a nearby hotel. There wasn't to be a honeymoon as Kent couldn't be away from work for long. Elise gave the driver a check for five grand and told him that in about an hour she wanted him to drive just her to the airport. He smiled as if this kind of thing happened all the time, and said he'd be glad to. She'd then booked a one-way flight to Bangor, Maine, on her cell phone.

After he left, her heart was pounding, but she was also exhilarated. She was going to do it! She looked at her left hand. No wedding ring. On impulse, she asked one of the girls where Carmen's room was, making it sound like she truly cared about the help. Cared enough to strangle her, she thought, but kept smiling. When the girls didn't giggle or exchange knowing looks, Elise was relieved. At least it didn't seem as though they knew about Kent and Carmen.

It was only by accident that Elise found out that the limo driver had betrayed her. Just as she was about to leave for her triumphant scurry out of the church, one of the bridesmaids burst into the room saying that there had been a bomb threat. They all came to a halt. The girl had reached the conclusion that there was a bomb because Elise's father had called a security company and they'd come quickly.

"There are men with *guns* standing in front of the church doors. And you should see the limo! There's a guard in the front seat and one in the back. And I just saw two more security men waiting for the elevator. I think they're coming up *here*."

For a moment, Elise's heart seemed to stop. When it began again, it was in her throat.

Think! she told herself. *What would Olivia do? She wouldn't stand for this!* Elise thought. *She'd probably say she wasn't going to—*

Okay, Elise thought, *I'm not Olivia and never will be.* But she knew of one place where it was guaranteed that no one would look for her.

Turning, she smiled at her bridesmaids and said that she'd like to be alone for a while. "To pray," she added, knowing that that would clear them out quickly.

She closed the door behind them, waited about two minutes, then opened it and ran out. There were some hotel guests in the hall who ooohed and aahhed at the bride in her big white dress. Elise grabbed all forty pounds of the skirt and hit the stairs just as the elevator dinged.

Kent had rented his pregnant mistress a suite at the top of the hotel. No doubt he'd told Carmen that he *needed* her there. That he couldn't get through the wedding to the bland Elise without the lusty, fiery Carmen nearby. Oh yes, if people were looking for Elise, the *last* place they'd look was in Carmen's room.

She pounded on the door harder. What if Carmen was gone? What if—?

Finally, Carmen opened the door. Her pretty face was nearly

green with morning sickness and it got worse when she saw Elise. "What are you doing here?" Her voice was a sneer.

Elise pushed her way into the room. "I'm running away and you're going to help me do it." She shut the door behind her.

"I'm just the gardener's sister," Carmen said. "I can't—"

Elise glared at Carmen's stomach. "Do you really want to go that way? You *want* to turn me over to them so I can marry your boyfriend?"

Carmen's only reaction to that revelation was a couple of blinks. She put the chain on the door. "Your father called in men with guns. You're in a *lot* of trouble."

When Elise sat down on the bed, the dress billowed up so high that she got a mouthful of it. Sputtering, she said, "I'm not going to be bullied into a marriage that I don't want."

The green look was beginning to clear from Carmen's face, and for the first time Elise thought of it from her side. She was here to attend the wedding of a man whose child she was carrying. Elise's voice softened. "I need to borrow some clothes and you have to help me find a way to get out of here."

Carmen's lips tightened. "My clothes won't fit you." She gave a pointed look at Elise's much flatter chest.

"You're going to be catty *now*?" Elise said. "Really?"

Carmen gave a shrug, as though it didn't matter what she did. For a moment, they stared at each other. Then Carmen picked up her cell and called her brother. She told him, in Spanish, that he needed to come to the hotel right away, that it was an emergency. She listened, then hung up.

"My brother will be here soon," Carmen said. Neither her eyes nor her voice had softened. She was still looking at Elise as though she were the enemy. Not Kent, who was playing the women against each other, but Elise.

She started to say she'd heard the call, but it dawned on Elise that this was years earlier. No one knew that she'd learned to speak Spanish. Nor did anyone know that she and Alejandro were friends. The first time around, they didn't meet until after she was married. "So Diego is coming for me?" she asked.

"No. He's out of town. My younger brother, Alejandro, will be here as soon as he can, but it'll be at least an hour. He's one of the men who's been working at your father's house for a month." She looked Elise up and down in contempt. "If you plan to sneak out, you need to change now. My brother has to work for a living. He doesn't have all day to wait for you."

Elise was trying to steady herself as she grasped the facts. Alejandro was coming for her!

She turned away from Carmen, pointed to the buttons down the back of the dress, and reluctantly, Carmen began unfastening them. When the dress was unbuttoned, Elise managed to step out of the thing and let it drop to the floor. She was glad she'd worn her yoga pants.

Reverently, Carmen picked the dress up and put it on the bed.

As Elise took a robe off a chair, she looked at the way Carmen was smoothing the dress. It was as though she was imagining her own wedding. Softly, Elise said, "What is it that you like about Kent?"

Carmen didn't turn around, and when she spoke, her voice was quiet. "He makes me laugh. He's generous, always doing things for me." She straightened her shoulders, then turned to look at Elise. "And the sex is great."

Elise stifled the hurt that she felt. "He sounds like he is truly in love with you."

"Yes, he is. And I'm in love with him."

Elise nodded toward the dress on the bed. "It must have hurt to see him planning his wedding to marry me."

Carmen grit her teeth. "I wanted to kill you. No offense."

"None taken." Elise went into the bathroom and closed the door. For a moment she leaned against it and tears came to her eyes. Generosity, laughter, fabulous sex. She'd seen none of those in the years she'd been married to Kent.

She pushed away from the door and wiped her eyes. What was wrong with her? Why couldn't she just stand up to all of them? Why couldn't she look into her mother's eyes and say she was *not* going to marry Kent? *Not* going to spend her life with a man who didn't love her?

But then what? Elise had no money. She had a useless education that had prepared her for being a wife to an executive. She'd studied art and poetry, and done lots of exercise to keep herself fit. If she defied her parents, she knew of no one who'd risk their wrath to take her in until she could get on her feet. And that thought terrified her. What could she *do*?

In the shower, she washed off the quarter pound of makeup her mother had insisted on. She was trying to combat the "blandness" of Elise, meaning her blonde hair and eyebrows and lashes. What her "family" was planning to do to her wasn't fair. Where were those parents who said, "We support you no matter what you want to do?"

She got out of the shower, dried off, put her underwear back on and the thick hotel robe, then began to blow-dry her long hair. Okay, so now she had a second chance, but what had changed? Her parents were going to be so angry that they would cut her off completely.

Maybe she should have asked Arrieta to go back to when she entered college so she could major in business. But then, when the three weeks were up, her old self would probably still believe she was in love with Kent. What was she going to do? Write herself a letter about her future? No, she needed the years of marriage to show her that Kent wasn't who she thought he was.

Her thoughts were interrupted by a low rumble of a sound that she recognized.

Alejandro's voice. He was here!

Elise looked at herself in the mirror. With no makeup on, she was pale, but she knew Alejandro liked that.

With her hand on the doorknob, she took a deep breath. She

reminded herself that at the time of her wedding she'd never met Carmen's brother. She needed to act that way now.

Quietly, she opened the door. Carmen and Alejandro were on the far side of the room so she couldn't see them, but she could hear them clearly. They were talking rather loudly in Spanish.

"You want me to take care of her?" Alejandro's voice was disbelieving.

"I want you to look after her for two or three days, that's all. Is that too much to ask of my own brother?"

"You're up to something, aren't you? You..." He paused. "You want me to do what? Seduce her? So you can steal her husband?"

"He is *not* her husband." Carmen sounded angry. "You don't have to do anything with her. Just feed her. She's so skinny she probably eats a peanut a day. Just keep her hidden for a few days, then put her on a plane to wherever she wants to go."

"What the hell am I supposed to do with her? Can she dig flower beds? Spread mulch?"

"No," Carmen said. "She can't do anything. Kent says she is an absolutely useless person!"

Elise leaned against the door, her eyes closed, trying to take in the hurt.

Carmen's voice sweetened, was cajoling. "I know you don't like this whole thing, but Kent and I love each other."

"He's *marrying* someone else."

"He was, but after this humiliation I don't think he will. And Kent may lose his job because of her. Why did she have to destroy everything? Stop looking at me like that. You've seen this girl. She's so shapeless I'm not sure she's a woman. And Kent said she's really cold. There's nothing between her and him except business and she knows it."

"If she wants the marriage, then why did she run away?"

"Who knows? Maybe she wants more money. I know she thought that by coming to me I could get Kent to forgive her."

Elise gasped at that great lie. "What was that?" Alejandro asked.

"Nothing. It was in the hall. Will you do this for me or not?"

"I don't know. Where's she supposed to stay?"

"I'm staying with Diego, so she'll be with you. In your bedroom."

"What?" Alejandro half yelled.

"Shhh! She'll hear you. Not that she'd understand, but she'll hear. If you think I'm going to sleep in the same room as a crazy woman, you're wrong. She ran away from her own wedding. Who knows what she'll do next?"

Elise stepped back into the bathroom and silently shut the door. *You're afraid to go to sleep around me?* she thought. So much for her compassion for Carmen. It looked like it wasn't reciprocated.

She stood up straighter. *Right now*, she thought, *I need to think about how to take care of myself.*

Since she'd seen the extent of what her parents and Kent would do to get her under control, she had to act wisely. She knew that if she showed herself to them now she'd either marry Kent or be taken away to…to… She didn't like to think about that.

She needed food and shelter until she could figure out what to do. Surely there was someone in her life who could help her. She just needed time to think about it all. Even if she could get to Warbrooke, Maine, she didn't know if she'd find help there. It was years before she'd met Olivia, and years before she got back together with Kit.

"One day at a time," she whispered. At the moment, she needed to take care of the necessities, like food and shelter, and the rest would have to follow.

She opened the door again. Carmen and Alejandro were still arguing. "You're sure she doesn't speak Spanish?" he was saying.

"Absolutely. She's American. She can barely speak one language, certainly not two. And it's none of my business but if I were you, I wouldn't let her know you speak English. Kent says she's the world's biggest whiner. She complains all the time. She says no one ever pays any attention to her or spends enough time with her. You're so softhearted you'll probably begin to believe her. You might even fall for the skinny girl."

"After the mess I just got out of? I'm staying away from all females. I'm going to let Mom choose a wife for me. Some village girl with a hairy upper lip."

Carmen laughed. "I'll believe that when I see it."

Elise had heard enough. She started to step into the room, but on impulse, she let the robe fall to the floor. One thing she knew about Alejandro was that he was physically attracted to her.

She had on a lacy white demi-cup bra that exposed the top halves of her breasts. Her matching panties curved across her— thanks to frequent gym visits—very firm derriere.

Loudly, she flung the door open. "Carmen!" she said as she strode across the room to the closet, not looking at the two people standing on the other side. "Which of your clothes should I wear? Everything is either too big or too short for me. Your jeans wouldn't reach to my calves. It's a curse having such long legs." Elise pulled out the smallest skirt and held it in front of her in a way that exposed her tight stomach. The upper half of her was nearly bare.

Turning, she saw Carmen and Alejandro staring at her. Carmen's frown was so deep she could plant wheat between the furrows. Alejandro was looking at her in stunned silence.

Was there anything more gratifying than seeing a beautiful man dumbstruck by desire? Elise had never seen it on her husband's face. And Alejandro had always kept himself under control. She'd seen twinges in his eyes but never this down and dirty look of *lust*.

"Oh!" Elise said, trying to sound innocent. "Sorry. I didn't

know anyone else was here. You must be Alejandro." She pronounced it as Alex-andro. "Did I say that right?"

She held the skirt up in a way that it covered nothing as she
went forward to hold out her other hand to him to shake.

He just stared at her.

"Is he okay?" Elise said in a false whisper, and realized she
was channeling Tara.

Carmen was still frowning. "He doesn't speak English and
he doesn't greet naked women."

"Oh." Elise pulled the skirt to her, but covered very little
of her well-toned body. "I. Am. So. Sorry." She spoke slowly
and very loudly. "Welcome. To. A-mer-ee-ca." She was almost
shouting. Elise looked at Carmen and whispered, "I'll just be
a minute, then we can go." She gave another glance at Alejandro, as though to say it was too bad he wasn't a fully function-
ing human being, then she walked back to the closet—with the
skirt in *front* of her, exposing her entire back half to their view.

With a warm smile at the two of them, Elise grabbed a handful of Carmen's clothes, and disappeared into the bathroom.

"I'm a dead man," Alejandro said, and collapsed into a chair.

Chapter Twenty-Three

THANKS TO ALEJANDRO, IT WAS EASY GETTING OUT of the hotel unnoticed. Outside the suite was a pretty young woman with a cleaning cart. Smiling, he told her in Spanish that Elise was the runaway bride everyone was looking for, and she needed a disguise. He unnecessarily added that the two of them were eloping. The young woman smiled back, her eyes dreamy with romance, and unlocked a closet that held a maid's uniform.

Alejandro motioned for Elise to put it on, then stood outside the door while she changed. When she came out, he frowned. The uniform was for a much shorter woman so it exposed a lot of her legs.

However, as they rode the elevator down, no one so much as looked at either of them. He had on dirty jeans, an old T-shirt, and a baseball cap, while she was dressed as a maid. They were anonymous to the world.

When they reached the bottom, he led her through the kitchen. A lot of the staff knew she was the missing bride, but they didn't tell. But then, Alejandro kept saying that they were in love and she was leaving her heartless gringo ex-fiancé to live with him in Mexico.

Elise didn't speak, pretended she didn't know what was being said, and stayed close to Alejandro as he led her outside.

They hurried through the parking lot to his truck and when she saw it, she couldn't help a laugh. She'd forgotten that it was big and black. Was it the source of her black horse fantasy?

Alejandro looked at her in question, silently asking why she was laughing.

Elise waved her hand. It didn't matter. When she got into the truck the short skirt rode up so high she may as well have been wearing just her underpants. She started to pick up a shirt that was jammed behind the seat and cover herself, but when Alejandro kept glancing at her bare legs, she didn't.

As he started the engine, she realized that she needed to get him on her side. Carmen had lied about her—or rather, she'd repeated what Kent had said, so Elise wanted to counterbalance that.

First, she needed to see if Alejandro was going to keep up his lie about not speaking English. Turning, she looked at him. He was even more beautiful than she remembered. Cut cheekbones; black, black hair; whiskers that she longed to touch.

"I'm Elise," she said, then waited for him to introduce himself. But he didn't. He acted as though he didn't know what she'd said.

She had to look out the side window for a moment. Maybe their friendship hadn't happened yet, but damn! To flat-out lie was a low blow.

She took a breath. "I know you don't know what I'm saying, but I need to talk to someone. Sorry, but you're it. First of all, I apologize about the Welcome to A-mer-ee-ca. I got that from *West Side Story*. I was really angry at Carmen and I guess I took it out on you. And I also apologize for running around in my underwear but I wanted to make your sister angry." She smiled. "I think I succeeded."

There was no reaction from him. "Okay, where do I begin? I only recently found out that your sister and my—" She hesitated. *Not* her husband. Not yet. "That my fiancé and your sister are a couple. I knew Kent wasn't madly, passionately in love with me, but I thought he would be. I've been after him—kind of like a boy band groupie—since I was a kid. I really believed I could *make* him love me."

As Alejandro turned onto the expressway, he glanced at her. For all that he was pretending not to understand, his eyes were skeptical.

If the circumstances had been different, she would have exclaimed that he'd understood her. But now she just wanted to talk. However, she did glance in the visor mirror. An advantage of going back in time was that she was four years younger than she was yesterday. It wasn't much in age but there'd been a lifetime of experience in those years.

"Anyway," she said, "I was shocked when I found out about your sister and Kent. I guess you know that she's pregnant." When he kept looking straight ahead, she tapped his shoulder with a single finger. He looked at her and she said, "Carmen," then pantomimed a big belly.

With an expression of disgust, Alejandro nodded. Yeah, he knew.

For a moment Elise wondered what she would have done if she'd actually known about Carmen before she got married. The way she felt back then, she probably would have married Kent anyway. But she'd always been absolutely *sure* she could make him love her. "I planned to run away to the airport, but the limo driver betrayed me."

She told him about giving the driver a check and that he must have gone directly to her father. Alejandro said nothing, but the muscle in his jaw was working furiously, and his neck was turning darker. Elise smiled. Even if he was lying about the language, his rising anger was making her feel good. It was nice to have someone on her side!

"The security men scared me," she said. "I knew that if I didn't get out of there I'd end up saying vows to Kent. Then what? He has two lives? Me in one house, Carmen and the baby in another? I knew who'd lose in *that* tug of war."

When she looked at him, Alejandro turned just enough that she could see sympathy in his eyes. *Good!* she thought. At least she was showing a different side to the awful things Carmen had said about her.

But Elise didn't want to go too far, didn't want to make Alejandro feel too sorry for her. That could lead to something that she didn't want right now. She planned to spend just a few days with her almost-husband's lover's family, then get out. There was no way Carmen would hold out for more than forty-eight hours before she blabbed to Kent.

As Elise looked at Alejandro, she could feel the heat of him. It hadn't happened yet, but she remembered the closeness they'd had before. Laughing together, telling each other about what they did during the day. He'd told her about the American woman who'd demanded more than Spanish lessons from him. He said he'd accepted a summer job from his brother on a whim, thinking that he'd last about a week. But he'd liked the physical labor, had liked the US. "But I don't like your winters!" he'd said, and they laughed together.

Elise reminded herself that none of that had happened—but she had no doubt that if she let it, it would repeat itself. The very last thing she needed now was to attach her life to another man. To in essence say, "I am yours. Do with me what you will."

No. What she needed was to find a place to put her own feet. In two days—three tops—she'd go to Warbrooke, Maine. She had no connection there, but she needed to con her way into

Olivia's future family. Maybe they could help her with legal matters. Help her find a job.

Alejandro stopped the truck. She hadn't paid attention to where he was driving, so she was surprised that he'd pulled into a shopping mall parking lot. In front of them was a Nordstrom's.

He turned off the engine, got out his wallet, pulled out four one-hundred-dollar bills, and held them out to her.

Elise's heart nearly stopped. She'd gone too far and he was throwing her out. But no, he motioned to her maid's uniform. He wanted her to buy herself some new clothes.

She took the money from him because she needed it, but she didn't get out of the truck. "I think you're a very nice man, but your sister hasn't exactly been a friend to me." She gave a bit of a laugh at her joke. "Oh well, if we were held accountable for our relatives, I'd have to take on the sins of my parents. Sorry, but I'm in a bad state right now. And sorry you got stuck with me." She extended her right hand to him. "Thank you."

Alejandro took her hand in his. "Amigos."

"Yes," she said. "Amigos." She got out of the truck.

In the store, Elise rushed to buy some jeans and leggings and T-shirts. When she went back outside, he was there, waiting for her, and when she smiled at him, he smiled back. For a moment he was the Alejandro who was her friend.

She got into the truck, and when she handed him a leftover hundred-dollar bill and change, he looked surprised. In the years of her marriage, she'd had to learn to economize. But then, her husband was supporting two families.

Alejandro's cell rang, he answered. "Yeah, she's with me," he said in Spanish. "No, you can't stay with him. You have to come back tonight." He hesitated. "I don't give a crap if your lover is upset. You're needed at home."

He turned away from Elise. "Because I don't want to be alone with her. No! She isn't useless and I want you to stop saying that." He paused. "I have to go back to work. Do you remember what that is? Or are you too busy with…with *him*?"

Elise kept her face turned away so he couldn't see her expression. It looked like Carmen was with Kent, and Alejandro didn't want to be left alone with Elise.

He hung up the phone, started the truck, and got back on the highway. Minutes later, he pulled into the cracked concrete driveway of a little house on the outskirts of the Long Island neighborhood where Elise had lived with Kent. She assumed the house was rented for the summer. It had that forlorn look of being unloved and neglected. *Like me*, she thought.

Inside it was nearly bare. There was a little living room with beat-up old furniture, and a kitchen to the side. An old table and chairs was by the back door.

There were two bedrooms, but she was glad to see that there were also two tiny bathrooms. It seemed that Alejandro and his brother had one room, Carmen in the other. But that was to change.

Alejandro was staring at her.

Oh, she thought. She wasn't supposed to know that she was to take the twin bed in his room. "No, no, no," she said. "I didn't dump one man to get another one."

She saw that he had to work not to laugh at something he wasn't supposed to understand.

She pointed at his bed, which was neatly made up and had one of his shirts tossed across the foot. Alas, he was wearing another one.

He was still staring at her.

Elise pointed at the bed. "Carmen?"

He shook his head and pointed toward the other bedroom. "Carmen there."

For the second time, Elise thought that if she hadn't known he spoke English, his unaccented words gave him away. "I get it," she said. "Carmen the Coward. She's knocked up by *my* boyfriend so she's afraid to go to sleep in my presence."

Alejandro shrugged, as though he didn't understand what she was saying, but his eyes were sparkling.

"So how do I tell you what I mean?" She pointed at his bed and said, "Carmen," then went to the bed on the far side of the room and pointed to herself. She pantomimed sleeping, then waking and tiptoeing to the other bed—where she put her hands around Carmen's throat and started strangling her. Then she stabbed her. Then she pulled Carmen's body off the bed by her ankle and slammed it on the floor three times.

When she stopped, she looked up at Alejandro and gave him a sweet smile. "Is *that* why she doesn't want to sleep in the same room as me?" That needed no translation. Laughing, he nodded yes.

She followed him into the kitchen and watched as he pantomimed having to return to work. But no matter what he did, she acted as though she had no idea what he meant. After the fourth time, he narrowed his eyes at her and she smiled.

With a snort of laughter, he nodded at the dirty dishes in the sink, motioning for her to leave them alone. He opened the refrigerator door to let her know that she could help herself.

She pointed to her wrist, where she usually wore a watch, to ask what time he would return. He shrugged that he didn't know, then he showed her how to work the dead bolt on the front door. But he still didn't leave.

"Go!" she said. "I'll be fine. As long as Carmen doesn't show up, I won't murder anyone."

As he left, his eyes were twinkling.

Elise closed the door, bolted it, then sat down on the old couch. *Now what?* she thought. Where did she go from here? Yes, she had escaped marriage with Kent, but what had that accomplished? How was she going to do something in just three weeks that was so fabulous that it would change her life forever?

When she got back to Olivia and Kathy, she wanted to tell them that she'd... What? Had a silly little thing with Alejandro where they pretended to not speak each other's languages?

Or was this time in the past to be all about sex? Would she be able to tell Olivia and Kathy that she'd at last had some truly great sex? But they were four years in the future. How was she going to fill four whole years? Even the Kama Sutra wouldn't take *years*!

For a moment she blinked back tears of self-pity. Out of one mess and into another.

She was in a dreary little house that had a dirty kitchen with the breakfast dishes in the sink. "Too bad I had to come back as myself," she muttered.

Something they don't tell you in college, she thought, is that when you get married you need a degree in domestic engineering. With what her father paid Kent, they should have had a lot of household help, but they didn't. She hadn't known that the cause was Kent supporting Carmen and their child. All Elise knew was that she'd done most of the work herself.

She got up and went into the kitchen. There are always choices and right now she knew that she could feel sorry for herself, roll in misery, or she could—

Make myself useful, she thought, then set about cleaning up the kitchen. There was an old washing machine inside a closet, and piled on it was a tall stack of filthy, muddy clothes from the men. She started a load.

The rest of the house needed dusting and sweeping. She found a broom but no vacuum cleaner. When the first load was done, she saw that there was no dryer. In the weed-infested backyard was a broken turnstile of a clothesline. Kent's mother had insisted that all bedsheets be hung outside so that's what Elise had to do for her husband. That his mother's two maids hung out her laundry didn't matter, just so Kent's sheets smelled like sunshine.

Those thoughts made anger go through Elise. No doubt he

was with Carmen right now, whining about how Elise had humiliated him. Poor man, everyone would think. Such a saint!

She picked up a rusty can that was hidden in the scrawny weeds, then another one. Within minutes, she had a pile. When she went back inside, she got some plastic bags, put another load in the washer, then went back outside and hung up the first load.

By the time she'd done enough physical labor to calm her anger, the backyard looked a great deal better. She swept the little patio area, pulled some weeds, then did more laundry and hung it out.

"Boxers," she said aloud as she slipped a clothespin onto the line.

Inside, she made herself a sandwich and thought that she should sit down and relax.

And think about her life? *Not* something she wanted to do.

On the end of the kitchen counter was a laptop and a box full of papers. They were receipts for supplies and plants. Each one was marked with the name of the job they'd been bought for. Her parents' name was on six bills. It looked like her mother had replaced the roses in the south garden.

Elise moved the box to the table and began sorting them into piles by job. That done, she wondered what Diego's bookkeeping system was like.

She glanced at the laptop. A computer was as private as a woman's handbag, but still…

She put the computer on the table and opened it. Maybe it had a password and she wouldn't be able to get into it. But it didn't. The background was a photo of Diego's wife and two kids—number three hadn't been born yet—and there was a folder for his landscaping business.

Elise hesitated for just seconds before she began entering the bills in their proper places. She was tempted to double what her parents owed but it wasn't her name on the invoice.

Once the bills were complete, she set them up to be sent via emails to the homeowners.

Smiling, feeling that she'd accomplished a few things, she began looking for groceries to see what she could cook for dinner. Alejandro would be hungry when he returned.

The cooking courses she'd taken in an attempt to please Kent were coming in handy.

She went online, found a recipe for chili and corn bread, and got busy.

Chapter Twenty-Four

"IT'S THE FAULT OF BOTH OF YOU!" DIEGO SAID IN Spanish as he unlocked the front door. "You and Carmen did this together. Now what am I to do with her? Hide a rich girl until the law finds us? She—" He broke off when he stepped into the little house. It smelled clean and something good was cooking.

He flipped the switch to turn on the lamp in the corner. The clothes that had been thrown on the furniture were gone. The floor was clean and there was no longer a layer of dust on everything.

Turning, Diego looked at Alejandro in question, but he shrugged. He had no idea who'd cleaned the place. Diego's eyes said it couldn't have been the rich girl.

In the kitchen a pot of chili bubbled and beside it was a pan of corn bread.

"Look at this," Alejandro said. He'd opened the computer to check email and seen that that month's bills were ready to be sent out.

Diego opened the door to the closet that held the washer. No dirty clothes.

It was dark out, but Alejandro opened the back door and turned on the light. All the trash that had come with the house had been picked up. There were two full garbage bags by the gate. He went to the clothesline and removed the three pairs of socks hanging there.

"Useless, huh?" he said, and pushed past his brother to go into the house.

He found Elise in the bedroom, stretched out on the bed, a five-year-old magazine on her chest. She was sound asleep.

He sat down beside her and gently removed the magazine. "You did a good job today," he said softly in English. "And you showed us that you're worth a lot—which I knew. The moment I saw you, I knew that...that you were different."

He smoothed her hair back from her face. "I will carry the vision of you in that white underwear with me all my life." He couldn't help it as he ran his hand down her arm. She seemed so fragile, so beautiful—and so unattainable.

Before Alejandro came to the US, his sister had gained his sympathy with her story of being in love with a man who was being forced into a marriage with a coldhearted rich girl.

He'd arrived in the US believing every word she'd told him.

But then he'd started helping Diego, and Alejandro had seen Elise from a distance. To him, she was beautiful beyond belief. Carmen kept saying that she wasn't womanly, but he didn't see her that way. He'd heard her mother berate her, correct her, complain about her. All her father seemed to say was, "Get me another drink, would you, kid?"

Alejandro had made sure Elise never saw him watching her, but then she seemed to be living in a bubble of happiness about her coming wedding.

He had been torn between loyalty to his pregnant sister and

wanting to warn this innocent girl of what she was getting into with her marriage. As it always did, family won out.

As he pulled the spread over her, he thought how he liked having her nearby. And he was *very* glad that she had cleaned and cooked today. Such things went a long way to winning over his stubborn brother. Diego took care of a lot of people and hiding his boss's daughter was making him nervous.

Elise had wanted to be up to make breakfast, but the smell of bacon frying woke her. She had a frantic moment of fear that if she didn't pull her weight she'd be abandoned. And what then? She had no doubt that her father still had men waiting for her at the airport. The moment she presented an ID, sirens would probably sound, and men in white coats would take her away.

She leaped out of bed, took a three-minute shower, put on her only other set of clean clothes, and went to the kitchen. Diego and Alejandro were sitting at the table digging into plates of bacon, eggs, and toast. Very American.

"I'm sorry I overslept," she said to Diego. He was shorter than his younger brother, and heavier. He was handsome but not in the same class as Alejandro. "But then, yesterday was traumatic." She glanced at his closed bedroom door. "Did Carmen come back?" Elise put two pieces of bread in the rickety old toaster.

"No." Diego kept his head down, not able to meet her eyes since they all knew where his sister was.

As Elise waited for the toast, she looked at the top of Alejandro's head. Hard to believe, but he looked even better in the early morning light. In that moment, she was pretty sure she was the only woman on earth who'd ever wished she *wasn't* faithful to her husband.

When the toast popped up, she got a plate, sat down across from them, and looked at Diego. "I wanted to ask about your brother. No! Don't look at him. I don't want him to know we're talking about him. Is he okay? I've heard him talk on the phone to Carmen, but when I'm around he's silent. Does he hate me?"

Diego gave a bit of a grin. "He thinks you're pretty."

"Does he?"

"Yeah. *Real* pretty."

Elise tried to keep her face straight. "But he thinks I'm useless, right? That's what Carmen says I am."

Diego frowned. "You did a good job here." He nodded at the house.

"I'm glad you like it. Where are we going today?"

Diego's frown deepened. "We're going to the Bellmont house, but you're staying here."

Elise took a moment before she spoke. "I know their daughter, Tiffany. I went to school with her. Poor thing. She's not too bright, but she married well. But then, it's hard to understand who men will like. The man I was to marry doesn't like me, but he does like your— Oops! Sorry to bring up the bad."

Alejandro lowered his head, but she saw his smile.

As for Diego, he was staring at her. He'd been married for years so he knew when a woman was after something. Elise was putting guilt on him for a reason. "You can't go. The law is after you."

"For running away from my own wedding? I don't think that's an offense that can be prosecuted." She batted her lashes. "I'll help with the work."

Diego snorted.

"I can plant fluffy ruffle petunias." When he looked blank, she said, "It's from a movie. *Cross Creek?* It doesn't matter. Diego, please. I'm scared here. What if Carmen rats me out? Kent would be here in a minute. Then what? We have a threesome fight? Think I could win against Carmen? Will she—?"

"Let her go," Alejandro said in Spanish. "She can sit in the truck and listen to music. It's just for a few days, then I'll take her to the airport."

Diego glared at his brother. "I heard about what you said at that fancy hotel. You'd like to take her away to Mexico, wouldn't you? She's not for you! She'll marry some other rich guy, not some teacher of horny women."

Elise ate her toast and worked not to enter into the conversation, but it was interesting to know who was on her side.

"I want her near me so I can protect her," Alejandro said. "Those men looking for her had guns."

"And who do you think they wanted to shoot? Her? She's the bait her greedy parents used to attract some guy they can control. Do you think this girl's father will give his daughter away to some Mexican gardener?"

For a moment Elise stopped eating. This was horrible, but on the other hand, it was nice to hear that she *was* valuable to her father.

When she spoke, she tried not to sound as though she was shocked by what she'd just heard. "Mrs. Bellmont likes really gaudy colors, and she's so vain she expects people to read her mind. If you're thinking of putting in pale flowers she'll get angry. Remember that ghastly red mulch you put on my mother's flower beds and she made you remove it?"

She didn't wait for Diego to answer. "My guess is that made you think all the women in the area would hate that mulch. But Mrs. Bellmont would love it. The gaudier the better. I could tell you what to buy so she'll be happy with your job and not fire you as she did her last three gardeners." Elise finished her toast.

"What if she sees you?" Diego asked. "I don't want any trouble."

"No offense, Diego, but has Mrs. Bellmont ever looked at *any* of you?"

Alejandro looked at his brother in silence, but with an I Told You So expression.

Diego grimaced. "Get a hat out of the closet and cover your face."

Elise tried to keep the triumph out of her smile.

That night Elise had never been so tired in her life. All day long, she'd hauled flats of plants, planted shrubs, small trees, and what seemed to be thousands of bedding plants.

Every minute, Diego and his men had watched her, all of them expecting her to refuse to go on. But she never quit.

She made only one mistake and it was a big one. It took just three hours before Diego's six workmen saw that she spoke Spanish. But she couldn't help it. They told a joke and she laughed. She begged them to please not tell Alejandro. Since they knew he was pretending that he couldn't speak English, they loved lying to him. Besides, they liked the tall skinny girl who worked as hard as they did.

At lunch, she rode in the truck between Diego and Alejandro when they went to a drive-through restaurant. "I hope you know that this stuff is awful for you," she said as she bit into a hamburger the size of a dinner plate and dripping three kinds of sauce. "Ooooh. Curly fries. What a treat."

That night she took a shower, pulled on a huge T-shirt of Diego's and the white yoga pants she'd worn under her wedding dress, then collapsed into bed. She slept so soundly that tornadoes wouldn't wake her.

The next morning she awoke early. There was a bit of light coming through the bedroom curtain and she could see Alejandro asleep just a few feet from her.

In the two days she'd been there, she'd never seen him in the other bed, but now, she lay there looking at him. His eyes were closed, his whiskers dark, his lashes soft against his cheeks. The light cover was off one bare shoulder, which meant that underneath there was a lot of naked skin.

She wondered what he'd do if she slid into bed with him.

She imagined saying nothing, just taking the two steps across the room, moving the sheet aside, and getting into the narrow bed with him.

What would it be like to kiss him? He had the most beautiful lips, so full and luscious looking.

When she looked down at his neck, she could almost feel her lips on his warm skin.

Yesterday he'd opened a big bottle of water and drunk half of it at once. Water had run down his chin, his neck, and onto his T-shirt. Elise had been planting some red geraniums and she'd stopped to watch him. Her mouth and hands seemed to dry out.

Miguel, one of Diego's workmen, had seen her looking. "You better make your claim," he said in Spanish, then nodded across the garden.

Tiffany Bellmont, a little dog in her arm, was also watching Alejandro.

Elise suppressed an urge to throw her sharp-pointed trowel at the girl. Why was Tiffany looking at Alejandro? She was married. And like her mother, she was a snob. If she wanted Alejandro, it was for only one thing.

Miguel and the two workmen beside him laughed at the expression on Elise's face. He said she'd better be careful or her jealousy would set her hat on fire.

"I'm not—" she began, but stopped when Alejandro turned to look at her. She gave a cough as she glared at Miguel, who grinned back at her.

Now Elise was looking at what she could see of Alejandro's body and imagining the feel of it, the taste of it, the— She quit thinking when she realized that his eyes were open. Slowly, he held out his hand to her in invitation.

Yes! she thought. She would go to him and for the first time in her life have sex with a man who *wanted* her. A man who *desired* her. Who—

She couldn't believe what she did, but she threw back the

cover and ran out of the room. In the living room, she leaned against the wall, her heart pounding, and tried to understand what she'd just done. This is what she wanted, wasn't it? This is what she'd complained to Olivia and Kathy about. So far in her life, she'd missed out on great sex. Maybe later, after she got away from Kent and their parents, she would find someone to have it with, but right now there was this beautiful man. So why was she turning down his invitation?

Because she *liked* Alejandro, that's why. To him they'd just met, but to her, she'd laughed with him, shared his hopes and dreams.

And damn it! She wanted more than just wham! Bam! Be quiet so Diego doesn't hear.

She wanted… What she couldn't have, she thought.

She heard the shower running in "their" bathroom. Yesterday after lunch, he'd insisted that Diego stop at a big drugstore and let her go inside to buy some toiletries. Alejandro had gone in with her and paid for everything.

Her toothbrush was in a glass with his. They used the same container of toothpaste.

His razor—which he didn't use often—was next to her pink one.

Elise tried to calm herself—and to stop thinking. As she pushed away from the wall, she noticed the rolled-up papers on the coffee table and wondered what they were. When she unrolled them, she saw that they were a garden plan for Mrs. Bellmont.

It took Elise about two minutes to see that it was a rip-off design from an estate she'd seen in England. An elegant, tranquil English garden was the last thing someone as flamboyant as Mrs. Bellmont would want.

She looked at the bottom. Ah. Right. Designed by Leonardo. The delicate little man who was all the rage of the neighborhood. Her mother had said she wanted to get Leonardo to redesign her garden. "And put in some stainless steel sculptures?" Elise had said, but her mother's put-down look had silenced her.

Diego came into the room, yawning.

"Are you going to do this garden?"

"If I get the job," he said. "I hate that guy. He never tells what kind of anything he wants and I have to guess. He'll write, *Red Flowers*. What does that mean? He doesn't even tell how tall they have to be."

"So when the client doesn't like them it's your fault," Elise said.

"That's right." He was going into the kitchen. "You want some eggs?"

She rolled the plan back up. "I'll make breakfast. You sit down and tell me about Alejandro." Her face turned red. "I mean, tell me about Leonardo from your point of view."

He knew she hadn't made a mistake; she wanted to know about his brother. "He doesn't have a girlfriend and nobody thought he'd stay here to do work that gets his hands dirty. But some girl in her underwear was walking around a hotel room and he hasn't been the same since."

It wasn't until he got to the end that she realized he'd said it all in Spanish. His eyes were sparkling.

"Very funny," she said. "Don't tell him."

"When not talking to you is making my little brother so miserable? I wouldn't dream of it." They heard Alejandro in the bedroom. Diego lowered his voice. "Are you going to break his heart?"

"He broke mine this morning when I had to say no to him," she whispered back. "Besides, your sister wants him to seduce me so she can tell Kent on me. I want to be sure I'm not just a part of that plan."

Diego gave her a look of sympathy. "Family, right?"

Elise gave a laugh, then turned and started breakfast as Alejandro entered the kitchen.

★ ★ ★

They went to the Kendricks' house to weed the flower beds and put down new cedar mulch. Elise was given the job of deadheading the roses. She put on a big canvas sling bag, used some little cutters, and began clipping.

What she was really doing was watching the men. The minute they moved to the front of the house, she planned to make her escape. The Kendricks' house was just across the back lane from her parents' place, and the little cottage where she was to live after her marriage.

She'd promised Diego not to do anything that might get them in trouble, but if she were caught, there might be repercussions. Her father would demand to know who had helped her run away.

What Elise wanted to do was slip into her parents' house and get some clothes. And there was cash hidden in her room. If she was to make her escape to Maine, she needed to buy a plane ticket.

It wasn't until after lunch that she saw her chance. When she told Diego that she'd work on the bed by the back fence, he nodded. The second the men went around the corner, she made her move.

There was a wide service lane separating the houses. It was where the landscapers, cleaners, and delivery people parked their vehicles. Garbage was picked up here. No big green bins were ever put in front of the houses.

Elise knew that her parents' house would probably be empty. Even if they had people looking for their missing daughter, she doubted if her parents would interrupt their routine. Her mother's beauty and massage appointments took up a great deal of her time. Then there was clothes shopping and what Elise called "gossip meals," where the women told all the salacious things they'd heard about each other. Her mother would certainly go to those to try to prevent the truth from being told about Elise and Kent.

She went out the back, crossed the lane, then slipped through the gate that was behind the house she'd lived in with Kent. As she ran past it, she paused for a moment. She'd never been happy in that house and it had never seemed like hers.

It was when she turned back that she saw Alejandro. He was standing there watching her.

Even when she rasped, "Go back!" he didn't move. She didn't dare speak any louder in case someone was in the house and heard her. "I need some clothes." She was wondering when he was going to stop this lunacy of pretending that he didn't understand her.

He made a gesture for her to go ahead, letting her know that he wasn't leaving.

Turning away, she ran across the garden to the side door of the house. She knew where a key was hidden and she knew the alarm code. *Please*, she thought, *don't let them have changed it.*

Alejandro stood beside her as she punched in her father's birth date, then held her breath. No alarm sounded. When she looked around again, Alejandro was nowhere to be seen, but when she reached the big, two-story foyer, he was standing at the foot of the stairs.

How does he know his way around the house? she wondered.

When she reached her bedroom, he was already there to open the door, and she frowned. "As soon as we see Diego, you're going to explain how you know where my bedroom is."

With a smile, he shrugged that he had no idea what she was saying.

Frowning, as she was growing tired of the game, Elise went to her big walk-in closet. She needed to pack some things, but she didn't want to take so much that her parents would report a burglary.

Alejandro leaned against the closet doorway. "I wish I could talk to you," he said in Spanish. "I wish I hadn't listened to my sister and started all this about the language. But then, I'm afraid of what I might say if I did talk to you."

When he stopped, Elise looked at him. "Go on. Talk," she said. "I'm nervous and your voice calms me." She made gestures to show what she meant.

"Right now I'm very glad you can't understand me," he said. "Because I remember things. About us. But that's not possible."

For a moment, he watched her going through her clothes, her back to him. "If you could understand what I'm saying, you'd think I'm crazy. Sometimes I feel like I can see the future. But no! It's like I can see things that have already happened—but I know they haven't."

He took a few breaths. "Yesterday I saw you pick a damask rose, and I also saw you cutting a dozen of them while I held a long basket. You said it was from England and it had a funny name."

A trug, Elise thought but didn't say. She was moving the hangers of clothes but not really looking at them. She was listening to every word he said.

"I know what you look like when you cry. I know that I wanted to hold you, but that I couldn't. It was forbidden to get too near you, but I don't know why. You looked like someone should hold you."

Alejandro ran his hand through his hair. "I don't know why I'm telling you all this. Are these dreams? Are they the imagination of a sick man? It's just that they're so *real* that I can't get them out of my mind."

She wanted to tell him that what he remembered hadn't yet happened—and now never would—but then he'd think she was the insane one. She pointed to a suitcase on a top shelf. "Go on talking," she urged.

As he pulled the suitcase down, he said, "You always did like my voice. You said so. But no, you didn't say that because we've never spoken."

When Elise put a dress with blue-and-white flowers in the case, he said, "I know that dress! It has a blue jacket to match it."

He sat down on the hassock in the corner. "How did I know where your room is? How do I remember your wallpaper? I said it was pink and you said it was peach."

She looked at him. It was exactly what had actually happened. He had been sprawled on the hassock, his long legs stuck out across the floor.

Just as before, she had a thought of kneeling between his legs and… Quickly, she looked away.

Alejandro put his head back and closed his eyes. "How many times have I seen that look?" he said softly. "Never, but yet I've seen it a thousand times." He opened his eyes. "Want to hear something funny? In every one of these…visions, dreams, whatever they are, I'm half-naked. Maybe they're my wishes coming alive."

He paused, watching her put things in the suitcase. "But yet, as clear as these dreams are, I never feel your skin on mine. I've tried to. This morning…" He let out his breath. "This morning I wanted you. Like I wanted to live, I wanted you. When you ran away, I felt that my heart might break. I wanted to feel your flesh on mine, my lips on your skin. Me inside you."

He took a moment to breathe. "But that vision isn't there. It's as though I'm condemned to wanting you but to never having you—not even in my mind."

He gave a scoffing laugh. "Diego says that when it comes to women, I'm an idiot. He says I should marry a girl from home and have a bunch of kids, and that will calm me down. His wife has a pretty sister and…" He trailed off.

Elise turned away so he couldn't see her. She didn't know how it could be that he remembered what hadn't yet happened, but then, she certainly did. But her memories were different.

When she'd been near Alejandro, she'd also been married to Kent—and endlessly trying to please her husband.

But now she didn't have that conflict. Kent didn't rule her life—and never would. She looked back at Alejandro. His eyes, so dark, so full of desire, were pulling her to him.

Not yet, she thought. *I need more.* More of what, she didn't know.

Abruptly, she left the closet and went into her bedroom. She needed to get the cash she'd saved and hidden under the top drawer. Beside the money was her passport. Since she and Kent were only going a short distance away for their honeymoon, she'd left it at home. She was glad to see that it was in her maiden name, not her married one.

As Alejandro put her suitcase on the bed, he continued speaking in Spanish. "Ah, good. You have money. Now you can get away from us. I could drive you to JFK or LaGuardia. Your dad can't cover those airports. You can go anywhere you want to. Somewhere far away from my family who has caused you so much pain." He smiled. "You know something? I'm *glad* Carmen ran off with that cowardly—and very stupid—man you were going to marry."

Elise didn't know when she'd heard such honesty—and if anything was missing in her life it was truthfulness. Smiling, she removed a little art case from a drawer and put it in the outside zipper compartment. Maybe she'd help Diego figure out the plans for the Bellmont job.

As she dropped a handful of necklaces in the pouch that contained the cash, they heard voices downstairs.

Immediately, Elise went into panic mode. Her mind filled with that horrible trip in the trunk of Dr. Hightower's car. In this version of her life, that hadn't happened but it *could*. All the players were there. Her parents could—

After a glance at her panicked face, Alejandro closed her suitcase, threw it out the window, put his arm around her, and led her to the window.

She looked out. The bedroom was on the second floor. "You're kidding, right?"

He went out first, stepped sideways onto the low roof of the one-story sunroom, and held out his hand to her.

Elise didn't hesitate when she took it—nor did she look down. When she was halfway onto the lower roof, he jerked her arm and pulled her to him. For a second he held her against him, then released her. Still holding her hand, they ran across the steep roof. At the far end was the big rose trellis. Alejandro went down first, then held his arms up to her.

As she got to the last steps, he grabbed her waist and pulled so hard that she flew backward. Smack into his arms.

When she caught her breath, he was grinning at her. She couldn't help but put her head against his chest. How warm he felt! She could feel/hear his heart beating.

"My father has a shotgun," she whispered, but she didn't lift her head from his chest.

Nor did Alejandro move.

"Bang, bang," she said, but without much energy. She was content to stay where she was. Maybe forever.

Her words finally reached him. He was holding the missing daughter of the homeowner. He was the gardener.

He dropped her feet to the ground and took her hand.

Alejandro sent her toward the back gate as he broke away to get her suitcase from below the window. When they were in the service lane, he tossed the case inside his truck. His big black truck.

Elise said, "Not a stallion but second best."

As they went through the gate to the Kendricks' place, Alejandro looked at her in question.

"It's my fantasy to be rescued by a man on a big black horse.

I even practiced the jump with my trainer. He rides fast toward me, then leans down and grabs my arm and pulls me up. I know how to do that."

He gave her a blank look of not understanding what she'd said. Annoyed, she looked away.

"Where the hell have you two been?" Diego yelled as soon as he saw them.

"Breaking and entering," Elise said. "My parole officer is going to be furious."

Diego threw up his hands. "You want to get paid, you work."

"I get paid?" Elise said. "Wow. Somebody give me the pruners."

Chapter Twenty-Five

DIEGO WAS SUSPICIOUS OF BOTH OF THEM, SO FOR THE rest of the day, he never let them out of his sight. He worried that they didn't know what kind of rage Elise's father was in—and what he would do to the people hiding his daughter.

Elise worked doubly hard that afternoon. But every time she tried to pick up something like a heavy flat of geraniums, Alejandro's arm would appear over her head. "Thanks," she'd mumble, then get the next one off the truck.

Visiting her parents' house had made her think about the past and what had happened to her. She kept thinking about what she was supposed to achieve. How could she change her life in just three weeks? She remembered what Kathy said. "Does it *have* to be about a man?" It was as though all three women had the same goal: Change the man; change your life.

But surely there was more than that. There had to be a different way. Absently, she watched Alejandro spray water from a hose over his head and saw his sweaty T-shirt plaster itself to his magnificent body. She wanted him, yes, but then what? What happened after sexual urges were satisfied? Not that she knew from experience, but there had to be a time when even the most beautiful of men ceased to set you on fire. There had to be nights when you just wanted to go to bed and snuggle up with a book by your favorite author.

She needed something in her life besides a man.

When Elise heard laughter, she came out of her trance. Miguel and the other men were laughing at Alejandro. They were telling him in Spanish that he had to work harder to impress the girl because she was looking at him but she wasn't *seeing* him.

Elise had to turn away so Alejandro wouldn't see her roll her eyes. "You idiots!" she said under her breath, and they laughed.

That night, Elise was sweaty, dirty, and very tired, but she knew that supper had to be made and clothes run through the washer to be hung out in the morning. "The second shift" it was called and it nearly always fell to women.

Diego nodded toward the computer. "Your boyfriend stole Carmen so you get the bookkeeping job. Tomorrow is payday."

"*My* boyfriend?" she sputtered. "I was the victim in all this! You guys should—" She saw Diego's teasing smile. Alejandro was turned away, but he too was laughing. "Very funny."

The two men cooked while Elise sat at the kitchen table and tried to figure out the software to do the payroll. After she subtracted the wholesale price for all the materials, there wasn't a lot of money left. It took a while to calculate the government's cut, but when she did, the paychecks were appallingly small.

She took the cold beer Alejandro handed her and leaned back in her chair. "This is disgusting," she said. "That little twerp Leonardo copies someone else's design and gets paid six figures. We kill ourselves doing the actual work and we barely get a living wage."

Alejandro said in Spanish, "Then you should make a better design." Diego translated.

"He's a plant expert, not me. All I've done in garden design is draw a circle on a piece of paper. And I only did that because

I wanted—" She stopped. The men were looking at her hard. How did she know about Alejandro's knowledge of plants? "Besides," she said loudly, "Mrs. Bellmont wouldn't listen to me. What do I know about gardening?"

"You know as much as that little thief does," Alejandro said, and again Diego translated—while frowning at his brother.

"She wants some famous name to do it, so she can brag to the other women." Elise stood up. "Maybe I should say my name is Caliente and that I have a degree from some made-up school in Italy."

The two men were staring at her.

"What?" She looked down at herself. Her clothes were too big and she'd already pulled sticks out of her hair. "What's wrong?"

"A rich man's daughter," Alejandro said. "Bryn Mawr."

"I understood that name." She didn't wait for Diego to do an unnecessary translation. "Bryn Mawr isn't exactly known for garden design. I studied a lot of art history. The closest I ever got to learning about garden design was studying Monet's water lilies."

The men were still staring at her.

Elise's voice was rising as she tried to make them understand. "Mrs. Bellmont would never look at anything I proposed. She and my father can't stand each other. He said that one time she made a pass at him, and after he turned her down, she..."

The men had their backs against the kitchen counter. They were waiting for her to see what they did.

"A woman scorned," Elise said. "It's quite possible that Audrey Bellmont would love to hire the daughter of a man who humiliated her."

Alejandro and Diego smiled at her. A seed—a big one—had been planted. Elise got the drawing pad and pencils out of her suitcase. Where did she begin?

Diego put a plate of refried beans and rice beside her. "We go back to the Bellmonts' on Friday. You have two days to come up with something to show her."

"But I don't know how to do this," Elise said. "I've had no training. I don't even know the size of the garden."

Diego picked up the rolled plan off the countertop. "It's all here. Just change it."

"But—"

"Eat, then get to work," Diego said.

Elise had an overwhelming sense of "I can't" and "I don't know how." Alejandro said, "I hate the fishpond," and Diego translated.

"Me too," Elise said. "Her dogs would eat the poor fish. One time my mother said that Audrey Bellmont wanted to be a professional dancer but she got married instead so she gave it up."

Again, the men were looking at her.

"A dance pavilion," Elise said. "A concrete form. Round. Then a building of lattice where she can sit. In the back, it has mirrors and a ballet barre." She picked up the pad and began to sketch. She knew just where it could be built in the garden.

Hours later, when she fell asleep over her sketch pad, it was Alejandro who carried her to bed.

"I'm dirty," she murmured, half-asleep.

"You can shower in the morning."

She was too sleepy to notice that he spoke in English. "Pink astilbe. No! Red firecracker plants. What are those funny-looking ones that curve? They're thick and fuzzy."

"Coxcomb."

"Right." She yawned. "You have to choose the plants. What grows on Long Island? Isn't there some kind of wild orchid around here?"

Her eyes were closed and Alejandro kissed her forehead—then wiped his mouth. She was indeed quite dirty. She was barefoot but otherwise fully clothed, but he didn't dare remove anything. Smiling, he went to his own bed. He was glad to see that the scared look was beginning to leave her eyes. Maybe it was on its way to being permanently gone.

The next morning, Elise was at the kitchen table when the men came in to breakfast.

She still hadn't showered.

Alejandro leaned against the counter, drinking coffee and smiling at her. He looked at Diego. "Tell her I'll come by for her at noon and take her to get whatever she needs."

"You tell her," Diego said, and went outside to begin loading the truck.

But Alejandro said nothing as Elise was engrossed with the drawings, and the men left her there. At noon, Alejandro returned to the house. Elise had showered and put on some of her own clothes. As she got into the truck with him, she started talking. "I have no idea if my plan is any good or not. I've not seen anything else like it. Worse is that I can't remember exactly what my mother said about Mrs. Bellmont. Maybe it was sarcasm and she never was a dancer. I'm planning what I call a Dancer's Garden, but she may hate it."

Elise sighed. "Anyway, I think the cabana should be wired so there can be music. I found some sculptures online for copies of Degas's ballerinas. I like coming around a corner and seeing something beautiful. Mrs. Bellmont has over two acres so I could do a lot with that."

She put her head back against the seat. "The truth is that I don't know what I'm doing." Alejandro just smiled at her as he pulled into a parking lot in front of a used bookstore.

It was one of those places that had lots of old hardbacks on shelves, on the floor, stacked on chairs. Nothing in the store had been cleaned in years.

"Perfect!" Elise said as she got out of the truck.

Inside, he held the books as she picked out ones on garden design and a few on dancing.

"It's a good thing you can't understand me because I want

to tell you that you are the most beautiful pack mule ever put on this earth."

Alejandro did his best to look blank, but she saw his smile.

After he paid for it all—and the books were wonderfully cheap—he drove her to an office supply store and she got paper, pencils, and a scale ruler.

When Elise awoke on Friday morning, she lay quietly in the twin bed and listened to Alejandro breathing. Usually, she woke thinking of pouncing on him, but today she wanted to slip in beside him so he'd hold her and say encouraging things—in his choice of language. In Swahili for all she cared. She just needed someone to tell her she *could* do this. Could push herself onto Mrs. Bellmont, who she remembered as a rather bad-tempered woman—like her mother.

Elise closed her eyes for a moment, thinking about how she was the product of two very aggressive parents. Win at all costs! had been their motto. And that included their daughter.

They'd never seen a reason for Elise to make any decisions of her own, from her clothes to her friends, her education, even to her husband. As a child, Elise had realized that the easiest way to deal with them was to just give in. They loved her, didn't they? They had her best interests in mind, didn't they?

It was only after she found out that her parents had always known about Carmen that she doubted everything.

When Alejandro turned in the bed, she looked at him. Sleepy-eyed, whiskery cheeks, he was one fabulous-looking man. He raised his eyebrows in question.

"I'm scared," she said. "If I reveal myself to Mrs. Bellmont, what if she calls my father? He hired security guards. What if he shows up with them?"

Alejandro shook his head, then threw back the sheet and went to her. He took her shoulders and pulled her out of the bed to stand in front of him. For a moment, he put his forehead to hers, his hands tight on her shoulders.

She took a few deep breaths. "Okay, I get it," she whispered. "Be strong. Have courage. Believe."

He put his hand under her chin and lifted her face to look into his eyes. For a moment, she thought he was going to kiss her. But he didn't. He spun her around and pushed her toward the bathroom.

Laughing, she shut the door behind her.

By the time she got out, showered and cleanly dressed, Alejandro and Diego were at the breakfast table. Her drawings and notes had been stacked up neatly, all ready to go.

"I was thinking," Diego said in Spanish as he looked at his younger brother. "Since Carmen seems to be staying away, you should move into the room with me. Give our guest some privacy."

Elise's hands froze on her drawings.

"No," Alejandro said mildly but with all the firmness of a rock talking.

She looked away so they wouldn't see her smile. She was becoming used to waking to the sound of his breathing, to seeing him smile at her. To sharing thoughts and feelings—and adventures—with him.

Friendship, she thought. It was completely undervalued as an aphrodisiac.

Diego got them in the truck and he was silent as he drove toward Mrs. Bellmont's house. Alejandro sat with his arm behind the seat, sort of around Elise, but not.

Elise suddenly realized that all her fears were for herself. What might happen to *her*. But it dawned on her that the success or failure of this venture would also affect them. It must be in their minds that she could, well, dump them. She could get the design job, then hire one of the more glamorous landscape companies, the ones with the green vans with gold lettering on the sides. Their workmen wore nice uniforms.

"You're not going to let me down, are you?" Elise asked.

"What?" Diego asked.

"If I get this job, you aren't going to tell me it's too big for you, that you don't have enough men or tools or whatever, are you? I'm not going to be *alone* in this, am I?"

Alejandro seemed to know what she was doing, but then he knew his brother well. Diego always worried that everything good was going to turn bad.

One of Elise's hands was on the truck seat and Alejandro squeezed it.

"I have thousands of cousins at home," Diego said, "and I'll bring as many as I need to help. And I know men who do concrete. You want handmade tiles for your little house? I can get them."

"Yeah?" Elise said. "What else can you get for us?"

The silence in the truck was broken as Diego began to talk. He hadn't let on that he was seeing this as his big break, but it all came out as he talked nonstop on the way to the house.

When they got there, Alejandro got out, put his hands on Elise's waist, and swung her down. "Gracias," he said.

"Too early for that! I haven't yet done anything to earn thanks."

Alejandro just smiled, and they went to the back to get tools out of the truck.

Elise wanted time to go over her sales pitch, but Mrs. Bellmont was waiting for them—and she seemed to be in a bad mood. She was telling Diego to take out some flowers that she didn't like.

"When Leonardo gets here, all this will have to go. Just clean it up now and he'll oversee everything later. Whenever he bothers to get here," she added.

When she started back toward the house, Alejandro gave

Elise a push, then a glare. "Okay, okay!" she said, and took her
drawings from him.

All the workmen were watching her. Miguel's usual laughter was gone.

"How did I get the job of savior?" Elise muttered, and Alejandro grinned. When she started toward Mrs. Bellmont, he pulled
her baseball cap off to let her blonde hair fall to her shoulders.
She shook her head to loosen her hair, put her shoulders back,
and strode forward.

"Mrs. Bellmont?"

"Yes?" She sounded angry. "What is it?" Turning, she saw
Elise and her eyes widened. "You're— Oh good heavens! Ev-
eryone is looking for you." She glanced at the men behind her.
"You haven't been with *them*, have you?"

Elise didn't answer that. "Is it true that you used to be a
dancer?"

Mrs. Bellmont blinked a few times, then smiled. "Why, yes,
I was."

"I thought so. It's in the way you move. I wonder if I could
show you—"

"Why did you run away from your wedding?" Mrs. Bellmont
demanded. "The rumor is that you have mental problems."

The memory of that ride in the trunk of Dr. Hightower's
car came back to Elise. And how Kent had lied about the pills
he gave her. But as she looked at Mrs. Bellmont, she knew
she couldn't tell the truth. To tell on Carmen would hurt her
brothers.

"I found out that Kent is gay."

"No!" Mrs. Bellmont said. "That gorgeous young man? But
then, that should have been a giveaway. You poor thing. How
did you stand it?"

"I couldn't, so I had to run."

"And this?" She waved at the men behind her, who were only
vaguely pretending to work, and her eyes fixed on Alejandro.

"Sex," Elise said. "Wild, never-ending sex. Alejandro doesn't speak a word of English and I love that about him. He's the perfect antidote to Kent and his…well, his nothing."

Mrs. Bellmont gave Elise a speculative look. "You're not at all how your mother describes you, are you?"

"If you mean bland, with no personality, no, I'm not like that."

For a moment they looked at each other, then Mrs. Bellmont nodded at the big drawing pad Elise was holding. "I take it you have something you'd like to show me?"

"I do."

"Will it enrage your father?"

"Beyond all understanding." Elise was beginning to smile. "And my mother too." She lowered her voice. "And it will get rid of that annoying little Leonardo and his silly little fishpond. You go with my design for your garden and you can invite students from Juilliard up for the weekend and dance with them."

"OMG as the kids say, but you sound just like your father trying to sell something."

"Take that back!" Elise snapped without a smile.

Mrs. Bellmont laughed. "Come inside and let's talk." Turning, she walked to the house.

Behind her, Elise gave a double thumbs-up to the workmen. Diego and Alejandro were smiling hugely at her.

It was two hours later that Elise left Mrs. Bellmont's house. As she went back toward the men, she nodded with every step. "We got the job," she whispered. They were all standing in front of her in silence, waiting for her to elaborate. "She liked all of it. The building, the dance floor, the sculptures, everything. It's a six-figure contract and we're going to need— "

Elise took a breath. "How the hell do I know what we need?" She looked at Alejandro. "I BS'd my way through all of it. I told her that what I didn't know, you guys do. Have any of you ever built a twenty-foot-long dance pavilion?"

For a moment, they looked at her blankly. They weren't builders! Then Alejandro jumped up on the flat top of a low wall and went into the stance of a flamenco dancer. He stamped his left heel a few times.

"We don't need a dancer, we need a builder!" Elise said. Alejandro looked so puzzled that they all burst into laughter.

"Down!" Diego yelled at his brother. "There's work to be done." He stopped for a moment, then turned and put his hands on Elise's shoulders and kissed her cheek. "Thank you."

It was the first time in her life that Elise had been congratulated on something she'd done. Like all the other kids in school, she'd been given trophies no matter what they achieved, but this was *real*. So okay, her position as her parents' daughter got her inside the door, but it was her ideas that had won the job.

"Hold on!" she said, then stuck out her cheek and tapped it. "All of you. Now!" Grinning, one by one, the men kissed her cheek—except Alejandro.

Miguel said he didn't think it would be good to set the garden on fire before they even began, so Alejandro better not touch her.

At that, Alejandro grabbed Elise, bent her over his arm and… And kissed her cheek. "Damn!" she said when he released her, and everyone laughed some more.

All day, as they worked, there was a sense of excitement in the air. For years, Diego and his men had put up with bad designers and inept homeowners who told them what to do and how to do it. But in just one morning they had changed status. This was going to be *their* job!

That night everyone piled into Diego's rented house. Someone brought a little barbecue grill and others showed up with beer and tequila. Diego called his wife at home in Mexico and told her he was going to be hiring more people—and maybe in the fall she could come here to live.

All in all, it was a glorious party and Elise didn't fall into bed until midnight. Alejandro stood over her smiling. "You've done a lot for all of us," he said softly, his Spanish sounding beautiful in the moonlight that came through the window. He started to turn away, but looked back at her. "About that promise to just be friends... I'm ready to go back on it."

A very sleepy, not fully sober Elise put her hands up in invitation.

Alejandro took them and kissed her palms, but then put them down and stepped away. "Only when you're fully sober and know exactly what you're doing. I'm concerned that once you and I start, it may *never* end, so you need to be really sure of what you're doing. As for me, I know *exactly* what—who—I want. Good night." He left the room.

The next morning, as Diego was driving to the job, he couldn't stop grinning. All morning he'd talked endlessly about their new business. Elise sat in the middle, Alejandro beside her, both of them so sleepy they could hardly sit up—or maybe they wanted an excuse for her to lean against him.

The ride was long since Diego had a job in the country. He'd been trying to branch out from just lawn care so they were repairing a stone wall today. Earlier, he'd told Elise that she was to talk to the owner's wife.

"And say what?" Elise asked, yawning. Diego glared at her.

"I liked it better when I was an honored guest," she mumbled.

Diego threw all her drawing supplies into a beat-up old shopping bag and put it in the front of the truck, where it was now between Alejandro's boots.

When they pulled off the road onto a long driveway, Elise sat up. She needed to look about the place, see what she could suggest adding, or taking away. Besides the planning, if she was going to do this, she needed to learn to sell things. Like Ray, she thought. Ray who she'd never met but actually had. The confusing idea made her smile.

It looked to be a ranch. To the right was a barn next to a pasture with a few horses. In the distance was a long, low house nearly hidden in the trees. The whole place reeked of wealth.

"Do you ride?" Elise asked Alejandro in English. She was still hoping to catch him in his lie of not speaking her language.

Diego answered. "He's played polo."

"Really?" She leaned back to look at him as though appraising his body—which she was doing. "For some team owned by a rich woman? What else did he do for her? Manicures? Hairdressing?" She was batting her lashes at him innocently.

Alejandro's lips twitched as he repressed a grin and he turned away to look out the window.

"Picks out her clothes for her," Diego said. "He likes to buy shoes."

"For him or her?"

"They share them." Laughing, Diego stopped the truck and got out. His smile showed how happy he was. "Come on, you two. Let's get to work."

"Tell her I'm good at riding things other than horses," Alejandro said in Spanish.

"Tell her yourself," Diego said. "Better yet, don't talk, just work." He took the bag of drawing supplies out of the truck and handed them to Elise. "Here she comes. Sell yourself."

"I'm not sure—" Elise began, but Alejandro put his hands on her shoulders, straightened them, then gave her a shove forward.

The woman was tall, with lots of dark hair and her face was so perfectly cared for that it was hard to guess her age. But she wasn't young. She had on tight jeans and a cotton shirt that fit her trim body well. She walked past the two men to Elise. "You must be the designer I've heard so much about."

"Me?" Elise said, then caught herself. "I mean, how nice. From which of my clients?"

Diego and Alejandro were standing over her like guardians of a temple.

"Audrey Bellmont couldn't say enough good things about you. A dance pavilion. What a clever idea! She can invite gorgeous half-naked men and call it dancing." She looked at Alejandro. "You might get an invitation."

The smile left Elise's face and she took a step toward him.

The woman looked at Elise and nodded in understanding. This man was taken. "I'm Eva Foster, and as soon as I get the men settled, we'll go inside and talk about something I'd like to do in the back. My husband's going to hate it, but he'll get used to it."

Elise stood to the side as Mrs. Foster spoke to Diego in Spanish, and unless Elise missed her guess, that was her native language. Cuban, maybe?

Mrs. Foster told Diego about the wall and clearing away some brush toward the back.

Then she looked at Alejandro and asked if he knew which end of a horse to saddle.

Elise watched as he gave Mrs. Foster a slow, easy smile that made her take a step toward him.

"If I get too close, your girlfriend will tear my hair out," Mrs. Foster said softly in Spanish.

"She's not mine," he replied. "I dream of it, but she says no. I think maybe she's afraid of me. I'm too much for her."

Elise couldn't help it as she narrowed her eyes at him.

Alejandro smiled back at her innocently. Supposedly, Elise had no idea what he'd said.

"One of my stable hands is out today, so saddle the black for me. As soon as I'm done with young Elise here, I have to go across the river." She spoke in Spanish to Alejandro. "Want to go with me?"

Elise was unabashedly watching him. While it was true that there was nothing between them, at the same time, it was far from true.

"I apologize, but my heart is with someone else," Alejandro said. "I'm just waiting for her to gather her courage and accept what I offer."

Mrs. Foster laughed. "Ah... I've been there. But alas, it's your loss." She turned to Elise and said in English, "Shall we go? I have a guest who is dying to meet you. He says he owns a huge garden and needs a designer for it. Think you can handle a big job?"

Elise was still hearing Alejandro's words in her mind. His heart? How could that be?

To him, they'd known each other a very short time. They'd never had so much as a conversation. How could he talk of hearts when they didn't *know* each other?

On the other hand, she'd known Kent since she was a child and look how that had turned out.

When Mrs. Foster walked ahead, Elise stayed where she was, standing close to Alejandro. She wanted to say something to him. Spanish, English, she didn't care which. But no words came to her mind.

Instead, with her eyes straight ahead, she reached out and entwined her fingers with his. It wasn't a full handhold, just fingertips.

Like her, he kept looking forward, but there was promise in their hands. It was time for them to be together.

When Mrs. Foster started to turn back, Elise dropped Alejandro's hand and hurried forward, the shopping bag held tightly.

This is it, she thought. She was really and truly starting a new career. She'd never thought about being a garden designer, but she liked the idea. And she'd have Alejandro, Diego, and Miguel and the men. Maybe even Carmen would help.

Mrs. Foster opened the door to her house and stepped back to let Elise go in first.

On the threshold, Elise paused to look at Alejandro. He was standing exactly where she'd left him. There was an expression on his beautiful face that she'd never seen on a man before— or at least not directed at her. True, there was a look of lust, of sexual excitement, but also of… Elise took a breath. Love? Was that what she was seeing in Alejandro's dark eyes? Was it possibly how she was looking at him too?

She wasn't only starting a career. This was a new *life*!

Reluctantly, she turned away and went into the cool darkness of the interior. It took a few moments for her eyes to adjust— and when they did, she didn't believe what she saw.

Her father was standing at the end of the big living room— and coming swiftly toward her were two of his hired guards.

"Elise, I'd like you to meet—" Mrs. Foster began. But Elise was already headed for the door.

She wasn't fast enough. The guards grabbed her, one on each arm, and pulled her back into the room.

"What the hell is this?" Mrs. Foster yelled. "I'm calling the sheriff."

One of the guards, still holding on to Elise, took the phone from Mrs. Foster's hand.

"Get out of here!" Elise said to Mrs. Foster in Spanish. "Get Alejandro to go after the sheriff."

"Really, Elise," her father said, his voice sounding long-suffering. "Such dramatics. Where did you pick up that awful language? You sound like the cleaning woman. We just want to get you some help." He turned to Mrs. Foster. "I apologize for the subterfuge, but this is my daughter and she has some serious mental problems. I need to get her to a doctor. Immediately!"

"Oh my goodness!" Mrs. Foster said. "I had no idea. The poor thing." She looked at Elise with sympathy. "I'll get the bastard for you," she said in Spanish, then turned back to the men. "Do you need a car?"

"No," Elise's father said. "We brought one." In the distance they could hear sirens. "What did you do?" he yelled.

Mrs. Foster seemed genuinely puzzled.

Elise's father looked at his daughter with a sneer. "If you think those illegals you've latched onto can get you out of your family duty, you'd better think again. Take her to the car!" he ordered the men.

As soon as they were outside, Mrs. Foster ran to the landline phone in the kitchen and called 911, but she was told that the sheriff was already on the way.

Outside, Elise was trying to keep her dignity. The two guards were holding tightly onto her arms and leading her toward a big van with a third man as a driver. Even though she could hear the sirens, they were still too far away to reach her before she was taken away by her father.

She knew that what her father was doing was illegal, but how was she going to get away? She knew from experience that telling people she wasn't insane got her nowhere. People tended to believe the calm, well-dressed, successful man, and not the girl who was hysterical with fear, her hair, clothes, and face a mess from days of tears.

When they got within a few feet of the car, she saw Diego. He looked worse than she felt. It was as though he was watching all the hope of his life being taken away from him.

Without Elise's planning, there would be no big, new jobs. His family wouldn't come to live with him. And there was sadness for her, that she was being put through this ordeal.

Elise looked away from him, her eyes searching for Alejandro, but he was nowhere to be seen. With his disappearance, all hope left Elise. Like a great whoosh, the belief that all this would somehow repair itself fled. She'd been sent back in time, but her stay had accomplished nothing. She'd have to spend the two weeks she had left battling her father—and he'd win. Like he always won. This time, there'd be no Dr. Hightower or Arrieta to save her. This time—

At the sound of a horse's hooves, Elise halted. She looked up to see Alejandro—beautiful, dark-haired Alejandro—riding an even darker horse.

In an instant, she knew what he was planning to do. She'd told him of learning how to jump onto the back of a galloping horse and he was using it.

"What the hell is that crazy bastard doing?" one of the guards yelled.

The other guard clamped down on Elise's upper arm and tried to pull her out of the way of the animal coming toward them. He was much stronger than she was and she knew she couldn't stand up against him. She bit his hand. She twisted and clamped down with all her might.

The man jerked his hand away. "He can have you!"

Both men jumped away as Alejandro came at them on the huge horse. He didn't slow down but leaned far over to one side and held his arm down to Elise.

As she'd trained to do, she grabbed his arm and leaped upward.

Alejandro pulled so hard that she went sailing through the air and landed in the saddle behind him.

She flung her arms around him and buried her face in his back.

He never so much as slowed down as he urged the horse forward. They went around the side of the house, past chickens and dogs and a couple of workmen. He didn't begin to slow down until they were on the side of a hill that looked down over the ranch.

As he halted the horse and leaned forward to stroke its sweaty neck, Elise stayed with him. She didn't loosen her grip around his chest, or remove her face from his back, or even open her eyes.

"You can look," he said softly in Spanish, his hands on hers. They were so tight on his stomach they were sure to leave a bruise.

"Sorry, but I can't speak Spanish," she murmured in Spanish.

"And I can't speak English," he said in English. "Look!"

Smiling, relieved that the charade of language was over, she opened her eyes and looked down the hill. There were four cars with SHERIFF printed on them, and her father was being put into the back seat of one of them. The three guards were in the other cars.

Standing to the side, angrily talking to a man in uniform, was Mrs. Foster. "You called the sheriff?" Elise asked Alejandro.

"No, I didn't. It's my guess that he did."

Elise looked where he was pointing. Standing to the side, leaning against a silver car, was Kent. The sun glinted off his blond hair.

Just as her father got into the sheriff's car, she saw him say something to Kent. Elise had an idea that her father was ordering Kent to find her.

"That's not possible," Elise said. "Kent would never call in the law. He worships my father. He'll do *anything* for him. Marry me, give me sleeping pills, have me committed to a mental institution, chase me all over the country, threaten to—"

Alejandro turned in the saddle to look at her. The things she was saying hadn't happened.

The cars, with their prisoners, began to slowly move down the long driveway. Mrs. Foster went to talk to Kent, then she turned and pointed up the hill to where Alejandro and Elise were sitting on the horse.

"I have to talk to him, don't I?" Elise said.

"Yes."

There was determination in Alejandro's voice, but she also

heard fear. She hadn't seen Kent since she escaped their wedding. The first time around, she hadn't known that you can't force someone to love you. You can't do enough good deeds or virtuous tasks to inspire love. At least not the kind of all-consuming, passionate love that was needed in a marriage.

Alejandro held her arm and helped her get down from the horse. When she looked up at him, he wouldn't meet her eyes. *He's worried that I'll go back to Kent*, she thought—and couldn't help smiling.

He dismounted, but gave his attention to the horse.

"I guess I better ride down," she said, and he nodded. "I'll talk to him and…and tell him that I'm *so* sorry for running away and would he please, please take me back. I'll do anything—"

In one quick move, Alejandro whipped about, pulled her into his arms, and kissed her.

She'd spent a lot of time imagining kissing him, but the reality was much better than her fantasy. His lips on hers sent feelings that she didn't know existed through her body.

His strong arms pulled her close and she could feel his muscles against the softness of her.

But as good as the kiss was physically, there was something else. There was an emotion that was flowing between them. It was something deeper than just touching. It was as though their inner spirits—their souls?—were speaking to each other.

His lips left hers and he held her, her cheek against the cloth of his shirt over the dip just under his collarbone. It was as though the space had been created to fit her head.

Is this what love feels like? she wondered. *This union? This merging?*

She couldn't help but think of Kent. She had wailed and whined and gnashed her teeth over the question of WHY. Why had Kent chosen Carmen over her? What was wrong with her? What did Carmen have that she didn't?

The answer was, Nothing.

Love wasn't scientific. It was… *This*, she thought. It was this union between two people. This bond.

When she looked at it from a distance, she knew Kent was a better match for her than Alejandro was. He'd grown up in a different country, spoke a foreign language. His experiences had been very different from hers. Nothing was the same between her and this man. Logically, a union between them made no sense at all.

Elise pulled away to look at Alejandro. They'd never been this close before and she touched his cheek. His eyes were worried, and she knew that what happened after today was *her* decision. "The woman does the choosing," she'd heard said. "The man can ask but it's the woman who chooses."

Part of her wanted to tease him and laugh, but the larger part didn't want him to suffer. "I want a baby," she said. "I've waited long enough to have my own family. I know the fashion is to live together first but I want—"

She broke off as he again kissed her. This time it was a kiss of sweetness, of promise.

When he broke away she thought she saw tears glistening in his eyes.

"Okay," she said, "help me up. I have to go straighten Kent out, then I'll be back and we can start baby making."

The tears left Alejandro's eyes and that invincible attitude that made a man what he was came back to him. Now that he was sure she wasn't going to leave him, he took charge. "Like hell!" he said. "Babies yes, but you're not going to be alone with him." He clasped his hands to give her a leg up into the saddle.

"Kent? You think *he* might harm me?"

Alejandro mounted behind her. "Carmen said—"

"Don't talk to me about your sister! She—" Alejandro was kissing her neck. "Are you doing that so Kent sees you?"

"Why else would I do it? Certainly not for my own pleasure! Oof!"

Elise had gouged him in the ribs with her elbow. They were down the hill now and she could see Kent waiting for her. Unbidden, all the old feelings of being intimidated by him came back to her. How hard she'd tried to please him! And how completely she'd failed!

"You'll do all right," Alejandro whispered as he nibbled her ear. "You need this for you, not him." She nodded because she knew he was right. "I will be close by. You're safe."

For a moment she leaned back against him. He did make her feel safe. And loved, she thought. She almost turned to tell him so, but now was not the time. First, she needed to cut some old ties.

When they were in front of the house, he held her arm as she got down, then he rode away.

Kent was waiting for her. He looked younger than she remembered, but then he hadn't had years of being married to one woman while loving another.

"Did you turn me in to my father?" she asked.

He gave a curt nod. "Carmen didn't mean to tell me where you were, but she did. I was worried about you."

"So you told Dad to come after me with armed guards?" She didn't try to keep the anger out of her voice.

"I didn't know he was going to do that."

"Did you call the sheriff on him?"

"No. Carmen did. Your dad was so angry she was afraid her brothers would be hurt." For a moment, he looked at his feet, then up. "I want to make sure that you understand what you're doing. If you and I don't marry, we'll lose everything. There'll be no company partnership. Your father even owns the house we're to live in."

"But you have Carmen. And you're going to have a child." She didn't mean it to, but there was bitterness in her voice.

Kent gave a little smile—the one that used to make her dizzy with what she thought was love. "I needed to have some *fun*. You can't begrudge a man that."

This time, his smile had no effect on her. "What none of you thought of is that I want to have fun too. I need laughter in my life. I want what you have with Carmen." She paused.

This isn't what she wanted to say. "Kent, why don't you tell them all to go screw themselves? You've been a victim of our selfish, greedy parents as much as I have. They've manipulated you too. Walk out. Leave them. Marry Carmen and live with her and your children and be happy. Maybe not rich, but happy."

With every word she spoke, Kent's eyes widened. "Are you sure you're the kid next door? You don't sound like her. That girl is absolutely perfect—and obedient. She's like a porcelain doll. Unreal."

Elise didn't like that image of herself, but she knew it was true. But then, you can't be a sassy, back-talking girl around people who you know don't love you. "That's who I tried to be, and now it's wonderfully freeing not to have to be her." She looked at him. "From what Carmen says, you two really love each other."

"Yes. I can be myself around her. I don't have to pretend to be some perfect hero."

"If that's supposed to transfer blame to me, it's not working."

He gave her a genuine smile, not one with feigned patience, as though she bored him. "You know, if you'd been like this before, I wouldn't have needed anyone else."

For the first time in her life, Elise saw him clearly. She *had* created a myth. In her mind, she'd made him into a hero and had expected him to be that person. No wonder he preferred a woman who yelled at him when she didn't like what he did.

In that moment, she released everything. All the years of longing for something that didn't exist, disappeared. Vanished forever.

Kent seemed to realize what had happened as the smile he

gave her was tinged with a bit of regret. Everyone wanted to be a hero to someone! "So you're going off with him?"

Not far away, in the shade of a big tree, Alejandro was still sitting on the black horse—and he was scowling at her. She'd taken quite long enough. "Yes, I am. He's a good man and…" She wasn't going to mention the word *love* to Kent.

"Carmen has nothing but good to say about both her brothers. She wanted me to help them get jobs."

"I don't think you have to worry about that. We're helping ourselves."

"So it's 'we'? Already?"

Elise glanced at Alejandro and he'd quit scowling. To her astonishment, he'd begun to unbutton his shirt. "I have to go," she said quickly. "You'll do whatever is necessary to get Dad out of jail?"

"Eventually. First, I might talk to your mother about her future grandchildren."

"If you mean you and Carmen, are you forgetting that without me you aren't related to my mother?"

Kent glanced at Alejandro. His shirt was now open all the way down to his washboard abs. "I predict that our kids will be first cousins." He nodded toward Alejandro. "Think you can handle him? You haven't had much experience and he looks serious."

Elise remembered what Kit had said to Olivia. She gave a snort of derision, then quoted, "'With sex, baby, no lessons are required.'" Turning, she looked at Alejandro. As he sat there with his shirt open and high up on a big black horse, all she could think about was him.

When she smiled at him and gave a nod, she knew just what he was going to do. With his head down, he urged the horse into a gallop and headed directly toward Elise and her former fiancé. Kent cried out in warning as he jumped back so far that he landed on his rear end in the dirt.

But Elise didn't move. She just lifted her arm and as Alejandro thundered by, he grabbed it and pulled her up into the saddle behind him. She put her arms around him, her head on his back, and smiled.

"Amigos," Alejandro said, making her laugh. Yes, friendship was an excellent aphrodisiac.

Chapter Twenty-Six

Summer Hill, Virginia 1970

OLIVIA KNEW IT WOULDN'T WORK. IT COULDN'T POS-
sibly actually *happen*. But the idea of going back in time was a
wonderful concept. Ever since she'd seen the business card, her
mind hadn't stopped working. All the things she'd do differently
kept running through her thoughts. She would prepare for the
life she wanted, not the one she'd had, but the one with Kit.

As she'd driven the women to the house on—she smiled at
the absurdity of the name—"Everlasting Street" she'd told herself it was all ridiculous. But that didn't quieten her mind. When
she talked to that young woman, Arrieta, that should have reinforced that it was all a made-up fairy tale.

Instead, it was as though she had been energized. Her foremost
thought was that if after three weeks she forgot what had happened, then she'd have to fix things so they couldn't be changed.
She'd make them legal. Permanent, meaning marriage, and if
she was to study psychology, she'd have to enroll in college.

Three weeks before Kit had been picked up by the military
would probably be sometime in July, but she wasn't sure of the
date. The children had been there and those dear old men, and

Bill and Nina, and… She took a breath. Her beloved parents were still alive. But back then, she and Kit hadn't noticed anyone else. They were young and in love, and they'd sneaked away at every possible opportunity to have glorious sex.

Olivia closed her eyes tighter. She never wanted to open them, didn't want to see Arrieta's face, didn't want to hear her say, "I don't know what went wrong." That's what all charlatans said, didn't they? Then they asked for more money.

And there'd be poor Elise, crying because all hope of escaping what was coming with her father was gone. How did one prove sanity when you had people who supposedly loved you telling the world that you were flat-out crazy?

Kathy was facing a life of being labeled as Ray Hanran's castoff. After having met him, Olivia was sure that no one would believe that Kathy had been the one to want to get away from him. No, everyone would believe she was inadequate. Couldn't hold her man. That was going to destroy her self-esteem.

Olivia squeezed her eyes very tight, knowing that she was deepening the lines that radiated out across her face. Ah, old age. The things you have to worry about.

"The cat broke them," said a child's voice.

"It was a demon cat," said another child. "Green with purple spots that glow in the dark."

"And it flies," the first child added.

Olivia didn't open her eyes, but at the memory of those deliciously familiar voices, the tears started coming. She let them find their way out and run down her cheeks.

"We're sorry," Ace whispered.

He always did have a soft heart, Olivia thought. Her face was wet and she was much too scared to open her eyes. Had she wished so hard that she'd conjured them? Like in some voodoo spell?

"Livie!" It was Letty's voice of command. She had always been the leader of the two children.

Olivia swallowed hard and very slowly opened her eyes. But

they were so full of tears she had to blink several times before she could see.

She was sitting under the big magnolia tree on an old oak chair that had been left outside for years. In her lap was a bowl of green beans that she'd been snapping into pieces. To her right was the garden, lush with vegetables that were to be harvested. She could see the corner of the house. It needed to be painted.

In front of her were the two children, Ruth and Kyle, aka Letty and Ace. Letty had on her look of defiance, her dark brows drawn together, while Ace looked a bit guilty for not telling the truth about the broken eggs in the basket.

How beautiful they are! Olivia thought. Why hadn't she remembered what extraordinarily good-looking children they were? She could see Tate, the child Letty would someday give birth to, in the girl's face. Under her sweetly rounded cheeks were Tate's sculpted cheekbones.

As for Ace, he was blond and blue-eyed, and he'd grow up to be an excellent doctor. He cared about every one of his patients, about all of Summer Hill.

"What's wrong with you?" Letty demanded. Her pushiness was covering her guilt that she and Ace had yet again broken every egg they'd collected.

Slowly, Olivia put the bowl of beans on the ground.

The children were watching her odd behavior and she could read their minds. Were they going to be punished with no brownies, or would Livie run off with Kit and forget about their latest transgression?

When Olivia stood up, she gasped. There was no stiffness in her joints, no catch in her left knee from where she'd hurt it while trying to slide a washing machine out of the way.

She took a quick step to the side. Her body was all suppleness and grace, easy of movement. Lifting her arms, she did a pirouette. Laughing, she held out her hands to the children.

They were puzzled, but Letty dropped the basket of broken

eggs, nodded to Ace, and they took Olivia's hands. She danced all the way around the tree with them. "Can I still sing?" she wondered aloud. When growing up, when she'd been absolutely, totally *sure* how her life was going to go, she'd taken voice lessons.

Arrieta had said that songs and stories wouldn't be remembered, so she started singing "Let It Go" from the movie *Frozen*. The children quickly picked up the tune and the words. Letty yelled the lyrics with great feeling. Ace sang his line about not minding the cold with a funny little flip of defiance. And when the three of them belted out the title, the rooster and the peacock joined in so loudly they sounded like barnyard musicians. Livie and the children leaped and twirled and sang at the top of their lungs.

It wasn't until the fourth chorus that Olivia saw that Uncle Freddy and Mr. Gates were at the edge of the shade and watching them in astonishment. Abruptly, Olivia halted.

When she'd been young, she'd thought the men were very old, ancient even. But now she saw them differently. Late seventies, early eighties. Not that old. And they looked healthy. She knew that both of them would live another eleven years— and they'd leave the earth within months of each other. She also knew that at their funerals the town would hear of all the good the men had done. All the fruits and vegetables that Olivia had paid no attention to had been given to anyone in town who needed them.

Uncle Freddy had quietly helped several high school students get into college. One of the reasons he hadn't been able to keep a housekeeper-cook was because his big house was an unofficial way station for people in abusive situations. At his funeral there were a dozen weeping women telling how Uncle Freddy had helped them escape terrible lives. As for Mr. Gates, he was the one who made sure everything got done.

When she'd been twenty-two and angry at the world for delaying her plan of becoming a Broadway superstar, Olivia had been unaware of what was going on with these people. All she'd cared about were her own wants. And Kit. And more Kit.

But now, at her age, she had learned that people don't exist alone. She hadn't been aware of it when Kit abruptly left, but the grief hadn't been hers alone. It had been deep for all of them.

Olivia stood there, holding tightly on to the small, precious hands of the children and she began to cry. Not ladylike tears, but bawling. She dropped to her knees, put her hands over her face, and cried hard and loud.

It was when Ace began to cry too that Olivia pulled him into her arms. "I'm happy," she said. "I'm very, very glad to be here. I love all of you so much." She pulled Letty to her.

"Did someone die?" Letty whispered in fear.

Olivia knew the child meant Ace's mother, who would hold on until the fall. "No! Everyone is alive and well and happy."

"Are we going to play records and dance some more?" Ace's voice was full of hope.

"We can." Olivia started kissing the children's sweet, dirty, sweaty faces.

Ace looked to Letty to see if that was okay, but she was looking at Olivia in speculation. Usually, Livie was either grumpy or hurrying so she could run off with Kit. She never had time for something as silly as dancing around a tree.

"Got any of that sugar for us?" Mr. Gates asked.

With her arms around the children, she looked at the men, Uncle Freddy in his wheelchair, Mr. Gates with his hand on the back. Livie stood up, again marveling at how easy the movement was, and went to them. She hugged Mr. Gates, gave him big, loud kisses on both cheeks, then did the same with Uncle Freddy.

She stepped back, took the children's hands in hers, and said, "Who wants mac and cheese for lunch?" When they looked blank, she said, "Macaroni and cheese?" and they nodded. It was 1970, and the US hadn't yet started shortening every word. *Invitation* to *invite*, *vacation* to *vacay*, *mayonnaise* to *mayo*, *tarpaulin* to *tarp*, et cetera. All those would come with the invention of the cell phone.

"Kit's working in the orchard," Mr. Gates said softly, bringing her back to where she was.

For a moment, Olivia had to fight the urge to run to him, but she didn't go. She might have a young body, but her mind was old enough to have learned that *all* people are important.

She was still holding tightly to the children's hands. "I think that this afternoon I should make you two some stuffed animals. You need to see what you're battling. My mom—" Olivia had to pause a moment to catch her breath. Her mother was alive! "My mother can come over and help us sew them. But you have to tell us what the space creatures look like. And I think we need to get Kit to make laser guns out of a couple of flashlights. We'll use wire and plastic wrap."

"What's a laser?" Letty asked.

"A gun." Ace's eyes seeming to twirl around in circles.

Livie looked at Uncle Freddy. "Is there a camera around here somewhere? I'd like to take a thousand photos of everyone and everything. Tate and Nina will want to see—" She broke off. They didn't yet exist.

"Who is Tate?" Letty asked.

Olivia started to say nothing, but if going back in time was true, then forgetting was also. "He's your son, and he's a movie star. Nina is your daughter and she has a little girl named Emma who looks very much like you."

"Yuck," Letty said. "I'm never going to get married."

"I am!" Ace said. "And I'm going to have a hundred children."

At that, Olivia laughed even harder and skipped with the children toward the house.

Mr. Gates watched them for a moment, then said, "I don't know what got into her but I like it."

Uncle Freddy was frowning. "Bill's father was called Tate, for Tattington. If Letty did have a son, I could see that she'd name him Tate. And Nina could well be her daughter's name."

"Little early to be planning her kids, isn't it?" Mr. Gates began to push the chair to the house. "Livie's been around those children so long that she's becoming as fanciful as they are."

"It's almost as though she's a different person." Uncle Freddy's voice was soft, thoughtful.

"At least she seems to *like* us," Mr. Gates said. "You think she and Kit had a fight and she's trying to make him jealous?"

"No," Uncle Freddy said, "I don't. But something has happened to her! I sure wish I knew what it was."

"Whatever it was, if it gets us… What was it? Mac and cheese? I'm all for it."

As they rolled past the garden, Uncle Freddy pointed to the yellow squash. "You better take a basket of those over to the Willis house. How's their new baby doing?"

"Poorly. It's mewling a lot."

"Then go buy some chickens to take to them. My guess is it's the mother who needs strength."

"That's what Dr. Everett says. Mind if I take some berries too? The kids can pick them this afternoon."

"While Livie and Kit are in one of their secret meetings inside the old well house?"

"That would be a perfect time for picking," Uncle Freddy said. "Besides, the kids don't need to hear what goes on in there."

"To get them out of earshot of *that*, I'd have to take them to Richmond."

The mutual laughter of the two men could be heard all the way inside the house.

When Olivia saw her mother, she started crying again. As though she were a toddler, she collapsed into her mother's arms and the tears came from deep inside her body. "I love you so much."

Tisha hugged her daughter back, and when she held her away, she too had tears in her eyes. "Let's help the children, shall we?"

All Olivia could do was nod.

Her mother had brought her Bernina sewing machine, and the kids helped them find a plug in the baseboard of the old house. Tisha said that the whole place needed a complete remodel.

"Tate will do that," Olivia said before she thought.

Instead of asking questions, Tisha said, "I hope he does." But then she was smiling in a way that Olivia thought she could tell her about 9/11 and she'd still smile. It made Olivia think with regret about how she'd so rarely told her mother that she loved her.

It didn't take long for them to set up the process of making some stuffed animals. Tisha had sewn all of Olivia's clothes as a child, and several things she'd taken to New York had been made by her mother. At the time, Olivia had been contemptuous of them. *Homemade* was a derogatory word.

The children soon learned that it was Mrs. Paget who could make whatever they wanted. She put an attachment on her machine and sewed purple eyelet circles to fulfill Letty's fantasy of a spotted creature.

Olivia loved watching them. When she'd been married to Alan, his mother had been adamant that Kevin was *her* grandchild, that he was no relation to Tisha Paget. At the time, Olivia had been too busy and too young to think about how her mother had been deprived of that special bond of the only grandchild she'd ever have.

It was Ace who pulled the men into the sewing. Reading glasses were found, lights turned on, and everyone was put to work.

As Olivia sewed the easy, basic seams on the old treadle machine, she began to feel, well, youth coming into her body. As the minutes ticked by, she felt herself changing. At first it had been enough to move easily and fluidly. And her mind had been full of seeing old friends and knowing their futures. In eight years her mother would call her father to dinner and when he didn't answer, she'd find him slumped over his workbench, dead. Tisha Paget would live another eighteen years. She'd dedicate herself to the community and the church—just as Olivia had done after Alan died. The difference was that her mother had enjoyed her role. But even after Alan's death, Olivia had been too weighed down by guilt to enjoy much of anything.

"She's doing it again," Ace whispered loudly to Uncle Freddy.

They all looked at Livie as yet again there were tears running down her cheeks. She wiped them away with the back of her hand.

Suddenly, Olivia knew that it was time to see Kit. She stood up. "I, uh..." She couldn't think of what to say. Turning, trying to look as dignified as possible, she left the room, walked through the kitchen, and went outside.

The sun and the air felt good on her body. She had forgotten how restless she'd been as a young woman. Over the years, she'd regretted how snappy and rude she'd been that summer she stayed at Tattwell. Why couldn't she have been kinder to the children? To the old men? Why had she been so obsessed with Kit? At times even her career had been forgotten. Later, when she went back to New York, all she could think about was *him*. By then she was angry at him for having left her, but still, Kit was everything.

She walked into the garden. How beautiful it was! When she reached the big old magnolia tree, she leaned against it and closed her eyes, letting herself remember the time the children had tied her and Kit up. Remembering the first time he'd kissed her. He had been angry, but what a kiss it had been! "Not a boy," he'd said.

No. Not a boy. She hadn't known it then, but he'd been facing what would become a heroic act of risking his life to help his country. Certainly not the act of a boy.

With her eyes still closed, she breathed deeply of the soft, fragrant summer air. She could feel her body tingling. Lips, breasts, between her legs.

Over the years, she'd forgotten that feeling. She'd found pleasure in a good book, an afternoon movie, an hour away from running appliance stores. And recently, after she and Kit had married, there'd been sweet and tender sex. But it hadn't been that hard, pounding, have-to-have-it-or-die sex of their youths.

Right now she felt *that* coursing through her body. The desire for it. Wanting it. Craving it. *Needing* it. As much as she had to breathe, she needed to feel skin on hers. Lips and tongues. She wanted her hands and mouth on the male hardness of Kit. She only wanted *him*.

When she opened her eyes, she wasn't surprised to see Kit standing there. Alive, breathing, young. She'd remembered him as beautiful, but the reality was much, much more than she remembered. He had on practically nothing, exposing skin that was a luscious golden brown. He was all lean muscle.

She looked down at his bare feet and went upward, savoring every inch of him. The bulge that was barely covered by his low-slung shorts was growing. Big and pressing against the cloth. Hungry.

When she reached his face, she saw a heat that she barely remembered. This *is why teenagers are all over each other*, she thought. *We adults forget this surging, pulsing, utterly uncontrollable desire.*

She could feel her body moving toward his. It was as though a rope had been tied to the middle of her and he held the end of it.

He didn't speak, just gave a quick movement of his head. The rope was pulled.

Part of Olivia knew she was a rational being. She'd been an adult who'd cautioned young people against following their "base instincts."

"You just have to say no," she'd told teenagers at church. How pompous she'd been!

As she followed Kit to wherever he was leading her—and she didn't care where it was—had someone tried to stop her, she would have used a gun on them. What she was feeling was as primitive as a fight for survival.

When they were at the back of the property, Kit halted and put his hand out to her. Taking it, she felt his touch through her entire body. She threw back her head and laughed from pure joy. She was here and now and the man she would love forever was with her.

Kit smiled, but he asked no questions. Instead, he began to run. He left Tattwell, stepping over the old fence, then led them through the woods that used to surround the plantation. Olivia knew that in the eighties a developer would plow most of the big trees down and build some boring little houses.

With a jolt, she realized where he was leading them. "River House," she said. Kit was silently asking if that was all right.

Olivia hadn't believed that her happiness could be increased, but it was. *This* was the day they'd sneaked over the stone wall to Camden Hall. Today they'd make the memory that Olivia had repeated with Elise. I mustn't forget to leave my bra behind, she thought, and laughed again.

At the sound, Kit tightened his grip on her hand and began to run faster. When they reached the wall, Olivia knew how to get over it. The first time, Kit had been the one to figure it out, but this time she already knew and she couldn't wait. Back then, it had been under twenty-four hours since they'd last made mad, passionate love. But this time, it had been over forty years.

She ran along the wall, ducking under overhanging branches until she reached the big limb that went over the side. She bent her leg for Kit to give her a boost up, then he vaulted up behind her. When they stood up, for a moment she thought he was going to kiss her, and her eyes flickered in anticipation.

Smiling, knowing what she wanted, he caught her about the waist and stepped past her to walk along the tree. But he didn't kiss her.

"I'll get you for that," she said.

"That is my hope." His tone was so suggestive that Olivia's gasp made the leaves move.

When they were on the other side of the wall, Kit silently jumped down and held up his arms to catch her. As he swung her down, it was her turn to put her lips close to his, then turn away. He laughed in delight.

She knew where they were going, so she took his hand. To reach the bridge, they had to walk through water that was a lot deeper than it would be when she and Elise went through it. On the island, the ruins of the little building were still there, surrounded by trees and pretty flowers, all of them left over from when the estate was loved and lived in.

Stopping in front of the little building, she turned to Kit. As she started to say something, he grabbed her to him, his mouth coming to hers with all the passion they both felt.

In an instant, her clothes were discarded and his shorts fell to the ground. Before she could take a breath, he was inside her. Strong and fast, as only all-consuming desire—and youth— could make it.

Long, hard thrusts, so deep she thought they were hitting her heart. She was no longer a living, breathing person but something primitive, all feeling, with no thoughts.

It didn't take long before the first round ended, then Kit picked her up, her nude body against his, and laid her down on a mossy bit of ground.

They made love again, taking their time, kissing and touching, stroking and caressing.

Exploring their young, beautiful bodies that were so full of energy and need.

When they fell back from each other, sated at last, the sun

was low in the sky. This time around Olivia'd had a lifetime of being responsible for other people's food and clothing and transportation, and with Alan, supporting the families.

"We should go," she said softly, but she didn't move. Her head was on Kit's bare shoulder, her leg between his. Oh! The sweaty skin, the happy exhaustion. How had she forgotten all this?

"What's happened to you?" Kit asked. "You're different. What's done this to you?" There was worry, maybe even fear, in his voice.

She took a long, slow breath to give herself time to think. If she was to make this permanent, that meant marriage. But how could she ask him to marry her? Should she tell him she knew about his secret mission that she wasn't supposed to know about? Or tell him that it was possible she was carrying their baby? If it was true that she'd forget their alternate future, for the rest of her life she'd wonder if he married her because he felt he had to. "When are you going to leave Summer Hill? I was wondering because I have to go to New York soon."

"About that." His arm tightened around her. "I was thinking about… You see, I have something coming up but I don't know exactly when it will be."

When he said nothing else, Olivia looked at him. "That was clear. Now that we have that settled, we can go home. I need to cook—"

He didn't let her go. "I'm here in Virginia for a reason."

She was trying not to enjoy herself at his expense, but she was. Kit had told her how much he regretted not telling her about the mission he was to go on, and how difficult it had been to keep the secret from her. He'd said, "Back then, I thought my country was more important than you were. I was a fool!"

"And what would that be?" she asked. "Did Uncle Freddy's family send you here to put some muscle on him?"

Kit didn't smile. "I'm going away."

"Oh? Anywhere interesting?"

"Olivia," he said slowly, "I was wondering if you'd…"

She drew in her breath. Was this it? The moment she'd regretted not having for the last forty-plus years?

"Marry me before I leave."

She drew in her breath at his words. This was different. It hadn't happened the first time they did this. If it had, what would she have said?

Whatever the reason, this was what she wanted, but… There was something missing.

For one thing, where were the words of "love forever"? She felt herself hesitate. "We're very young, you especially. And you have college to finish and—"

He rolled over so he was looking down at her. "I'm with the military. I can't tell you any more than that, but they'll come to pick me up and I'll be away for a year. If you and I are married, they'll tell you where I am. They'll send my paychecks to you. They'll—"

She lifted her head to kiss him. "Is this the only reason you want us to marry?"

Kit lay back down beside her. "You know how when you go to a car dealership and right away you know which vehicle you want? Maybe it wasn't the one you thought you'd want but when you see it, you *know*."

"Are you saying I'm like a used car?"

Again, he didn't smile. "The day I saw you in that tight green dress and you sailed over the cabbages and ordered everyone around and cooked a second lunch just for me and—"

"You knew that?"

"You think the kids could keep that a secret?"

She laughed. "Of course they wouldn't."

"But it didn't matter how you felt about me. Even if you truly believed I was a worthless boy, I still knew. You're the one I want."

Olivia lay on the sweet-smelling grass, looking up through

the tree leaves to the sky, smiling. Kit had told her all this on their honeymoon, but how she wished she'd known it earlier. And why was it changing *now*? What had made him ask her this time around? It didn't make sense. It was as though he *remembered* that they had been separated and he was trying to prevent that. "When?" she asked.

"Six weeks? Is that too soon?"

The military would come for him in half that time. "So you do know when they'll pick you up?" She could feel the tiny stiffening in his body. He didn't want to tell her more.

"No, I don't. They said it would be in the fall."

"What happens if we aren't married before they show up?"

"Nothing," he said. "I'll go away and you won't hear from me until I knock on your front door a year later."

It will be three years, Olivia thought, *then more time for him to recover from a vehicle turning over with him in it*. She wanted to be there while he healed. She turned to face him. "Okay. Six weeks."

Kit blinked at her a few times. "You're saying yes? You *will* marry me? I never in my life believed—"

She lay back down. "Me neither. Especially with this unromantic marriage proposal. No ring, no one knee, no—"

She broke off because Kit had sat up and was now on one knee in the traditional proposal stance—which was awkward since they were both completely naked.

He picked up his shorts, put his fingers into an inside pocket, and withdrew what Olivia knew was his grandmother's ring. It was so beautiful in its old-fashioned setting.

As she sat up, she modestly put her arm across her bare breasts, and held out her left hand. Kit slipped the ring on her finger.

Olivia couldn't think of anything to say. This was how it *should* have been. This was what should have happened. Was supposed to be. If this had happened then a lot of misery would have been avoided.

The sound of a dog and a man telling it to be quiet reached

them. "Young Pete!" she said in alarm. "I forgot about him. He has a shotgun."

Just as he'd done before, Kit reacted immediately. He went into army camouflage mode, slapping mud on his face and across his chest. He put a branch in his hair, then began yelling as he ran. Olivia stood back, laughing at the sight—but then, with a jolt, she remembered Arrieta saying that sometimes people died in the past. Shotguns were serious. She grabbed their clothes, ran across the bridge, and headed for the wall. Just as in the past, Kit was there to pull her up and help her over. They ran through shady forest until they were well out of sight and hearing of Pete and his shotgun. Laughing, they couldn't help but make love on the grass.

It was later, as they were dressing, that Kit saw that Olivia's pretty pink bra was missing. "It's all right." Smiling, she thought about what Young Pete would do and the repercussions.

She looked back through the trees. They could just see the top of Camden Hall.

A wave of something very like homesickness went through her. Kit had bought the beautiful River House for her as a wedding gift. It was to be their first home together. With a sigh, she said, "I love that place. I think if I could live anywhere in the world, it would be there."

Kit was buttoning his shirt and he tried to cover his frown, but she saw it. "If that's what you want," he said softly.

Olivia's hair seemed to stand on end and anger ran through her. She did *not* like his tone! "I wasn't asking you to buy it for me, if that's what you think I was hinting at. Here! I think you should take this back." She was tugging on the ring but it wouldn't come off. It always did fit tightly.

Kit pulled her into his arms. "I think our lives are going to be bigger than this town. I might be like my family and live all over the world. Think you can handle that? Cairo in January? Wait until you see Bali. And Java. And—"

She pushed away from him, her annoyance showing. "That sounds great. But didn't your family have a home base in the US?" Before he could answer, she stepped away. "I think we better get back. I need to cook dinner."

Behind her, Kit was frowning. Something was off with Olivia but he didn't know what it was. She was so odd today that it was as though she were a different person. As she'd run from a man with a shotgun, she'd been laughing. She seemed to think there was no real danger, that it was all a great joke.

And she'd said yes to his hurried marriage proposal. The Olivia he knew and loved would have made him work for it. Would have told him no a dozen times before she said yes. But this Olivia seemed to… Well, she hadn't seemed surprised at his proposal. And the way she'd said yes sounded as though she was checking something off a list. Marriage seemed to be as equally important as telling the kids to wash their hands.

As for the house, he knew a hint when he heard it. Before, she'd been contemptuous of his background. But today, she seemed to want him to buy her an estate. Did the fact that he could afford such a large place have anything to do with her acceptance of his proposal?

No, not possible, he told himself. There had to be another reason for the way she was acting.

He caught up with her before they reached the broken fence at Tattwell, and he held her arm. "If something were wrong, you'd tell me, wouldn't you?"

"Yes, of course. It's just that I have a lot of things to do." *I have to get Alan and his mistress together*, she thought. *I must make up to Kevin for what I did to him as a child! I have to arrange for my future.*

With every second, what she must do was becoming stronger in her mind. With a weak smile, she peeled Kit's hand off her arm.

"Tonight—"

She cut him off. "I think you and I should cool it for a while with the sex. I wouldn't want to get pregnant."

Kit was astonished at her words. "You know I always use protection."

"I really do have to go. I have people to feed." Turning, she ran ahead of him toward the house.

Kit watched her run. "'Cool it'?" he whispered. "Who are you? And what did you do with my Olivia?"

Chapter Twenty-Seven

WHEN OLIVIA GOT TO THE HOUSE, SHE SAW THAT HER mother had cooked dinner for everyone.

She heard a TV on and was glad to be able to escape unnoticed. She went to her room and stretched out on her bed. She needed time to *think*—and remember. She'd spent a glorious afternoon with Kit and she had a ring on her finger, but had she truly changed the most important thing? Soon after the military came to get Kit, she went back to New York. She'd starred in a few performances of *Pride and Prejudice*—to excellent reviews—then found out she was pregnant.

Olivia hit the old pillows with her fists. Memories that she had repressed for so many years were coming back to her. Finding out she was expecting had been the low point of her life. To her mind, her life was finished. She'd gone from being on top of the world, to standing at the bottom of a dark pit.

It was Dr. Everett, Ace's father, who she'd called, crying hard as she told him her predicament. He'd arranged everything. She was to spend the months at a facility for unwed mothers in Jacksonville, Florida. She was to give the child up for adoption. Back then, unmarried mothers were looked down on. Olivia didn't want to do that to her child or her family. She'd made Dr. Everett swear not to tell her parents. Since he well knew that her father's heart wasn't strong, he agreed to tell no one.

During those months at the home, she hadn't been alive. She'd existed, her belly growing, but she hadn't felt part of the human race.

The pregnancy had been easy, but the birth was long and difficult. When she woke up from the anesthesia, her child—who she never saw—was gone and a doctor told her that she'd never have any more children. In the '70s, doctors didn't tell patients the details of what happened to their bodies. It was considered too complicated for them to understand.

But Dr. Everett didn't keep his vow of secrecy. Not fully, anyway. He arranged for Estelle Latham, a high school classmate of Olivia's, to adopt her child. Since Estelle had recently miscarried, she told everyone in Summer Hill that she'd given birth to the pretty little girl.

As soon as Olivia had recovered enough physically, she went home to Summer Hill.

That was when she found out that her entire personality had changed. She no longer had any goals. She felt that she didn't, well, didn't deserve them. Her feeling of being invincible, that nothing bad could happen to her, was gone.

For a while she stayed with her parents. They tried to get her to talk to them, but she wouldn't. They assumed it was a love affair gone wrong. Truthfully, they were so glad to have her back that they didn't pry too hard. Uncle Freddy offered her a job with him, but Olivia couldn't bear to see the place or the people.

She got a job at Trumbull Appliances, and soon afterward married Alan and took on the care of his son. Olivia never told him about her baby, just that she couldn't have children. He'd said that was all right with him, but several times over the years he'd given a great sigh and said he would have liked to have a daughter. Olivia's response had been to work harder.

She didn't know that she often saw her daughter. Estelle's husband, Henry, got a job in a bank in Pennsylvania and they moved, but they returned to Summer Hill at holidays and they attended the same church.

Olivia had never allowed herself to really look at the child since she was about the same age as the daughter she'd given away. But no matter how hard she tried to forget, she didn't— and she was changed by what happened. Changed from deep within her.

I went from being full of myself to apologizing for my existence, she thought.

It may have been over forty years ago, but now that she was back in her young body, she could feel that hope for the future. With each hour she was again feeling like she could set the world on fire.

She did *not* want to repeat what had happened before!

That night she couldn't sleep. It was late and she knew the children got up early and she needed to cook their breakfast, so she had to sleep. But she kept thinking about it all.

When she'd first seen that card from "Madame Zoya," aka Arrieta Day, and the idea of going back in time had presented itself to her, she'd known exactly what she'd do. First, she'd get Kit to marry her. But if she changed that one thing, she'd have to change other things.

She'd have to make sure that Alan got with the love of his life, Willie. That was imperative. She owed them both that. After her talk with Arrieta, Olivia knew she'd have to register to study psychology at the University of Virginia.

It had all seemed so simple. If she changed what had happened to her, she'd have to change the lives of the people she'd been with.

But now that she was here, something was happening to her.

She wasn't just in her young body, but her young *mind* was taking over.

Last year she'd been a sixty-plus-year-old woman and a lot had happened since she'd seen Kit. For one thing, she'd had years of running a business. During ordering, overseeing shipments, and arguing with deliverymen, friendships and enemies were made. She knew nearly everyone in Summer Hill, and most of all, she'd lived with Alan and his son.

All those people, places, and happenings had dulled the pain of her past. With tremendous daily effort, she'd blocked out the loss of the baby she had given birth to—and given away.

But now things were different. With every hour, youth was seeping back into her. It wasn't just a lack of pain in her joints but all that *energy* was returning to her. In her sixties, she'd looked forward to an hour to sit down and do nothing. In her twenties, a free hour was a time to do something exciting. Laugh, dance, argue, make love. Go. Do. Create.

Right now she was feeling anger. When Kit had returned to her life after years of being away, she'd been understanding, forgiving. After all, she'd seen and done a lot in that time.

And besides, Alan's dislike of her had taken the edge off Olivia's spirit.

She flopped onto her back and looked at the ceiling. Moonlight was coming into her room and she could see the shadows of tree branches. Over the years, she'd asked herself why she hadn't done the sane and sensible thing of contacting his parents when she found out she was pregnant. Back then, Olivia thought her parents were old, and therefore fragile. Ha! There is *nothing* fragile about old age! It took strength and stamina just to get out of bed each morning.

But here she was, and she didn't feel sane and sensible. She felt angry.

Worse, her anger at Kit was increasing by the minute. She'd made herself repress memories of what had actually happened.

When she'd been alone at the maternity home, her only hope had been that Kit would show up. She told herself that maybe he hadn't been terrified when she'd told him she loved him. She'd fantasized that he'd somehow find her and tell her the reason he'd left. The death of someone he loved usually won out.

What was bothering her now was that Kit had seen her on Broadway. He'd been in New York just before being shipped out to Libya. With a government camera in hand, he'd sneaked out a bathroom window and paid a scalper's price for a ticket to see her on stage. He said he greatly regretted not speaking to her.

Not speaking *to her!* she thought.

She turned over in the bed. What kind of man was he that he could spend a summer as they had done, then just walk out and leave? He could have taken five minutes to speak to her that night in New York, tell her he had to do something for his country, tell her how he felt about her. And she would have told him of her condition. If he'd arranged for her to go to his parents, their lives would have been changed forever. Hers, his, their daughter's. Her parents wouldn't have died thinking they had no grandchildren. If Kit had just *spoken* to her!

It was well after midnight before Olivia fell asleep, and she woke often. Every time she opened her eyes, she thought of her miserable months in the maternity home. Dr. Everett had paid for it, and later she'd paid him back with interest. Plus, every time he had a patient who desperately needed a range, a refrigerator, a new sink, or heat, Olivia had supplied it. She felt she owed him for helping her, and too, she wanted to pay it back by helping other women in need.

The loneliness, the tears, the fear, all came back to her. Kit could have stopped all that pain, could have prevented the tragedy of what happened. If he'd just spoken to her that night. Was that too much to ask of him?

The children came into her room at 6:00 a.m. They wanted to know which Olivia she was going to be today. Was she going to cry some more and dance with them? Or was she going to dump hot dogs and beans into a bowl, then run off with Kit?

Olivia opened her arms and they snuggled with her. Last year Letty's son had finally been cast in a role as something other than a heartthrob and he'd received great reviews. And Ace would get his wish to have many children.

"Tell us a story," Letty said.

"A new one. Like the song yesterday," Ace said.

"How about if I tell you about taming a dragon? Once upon a time, there was a skinny little boy named Hiccup."

Olivia felt a little bad at stealing a story, but since it would be forgotten, she figured it was all right. When she saw a foot peeping around the corner, she told Uncle Freddy and Mr. Gates to come in.

It was when she was at the part where Hiccup was making a saddle for his dragon, Toothless, that Kit appeared at the door. He had on a tiny pair of shorts, his long, lean body exposed. Yesterday the sight of him had sent her into an explosion of de-sire. But today, she frowned at him. He was lounging against the door frame in a way that said he knew everything about her. Knew what she was thinking, what she wanted. And what she absolutely, positively *must* have was HIM.

Olivia looked away and went back to her story. By the time she got to Hiccup refusing to kill a dragon, Kit was gone. She couldn't help it, but she breathed a sigh of relief.

She made pancakes for breakfast and she did her best to shape them into dragons.

At about ten, she drove Uncle Freddy's old car into town to see her father. It was time to begin setting in motion the things that she needed to do.

She went to the Summer Hill Bank, where her father was president. The sight of him was as deeply felt as it had been with her mother. It took her a while to get her emotions under con-trol before she could speak. They talked for over an hour before he had to go back to work. On the way out, she made arrangements to meet with Willie, a teller, and the woman Alan would love so much. As Olivia drove back to Tattwell, she felt good about what she planned to do.

In the past, she'd always been impatient, hurrying onto the next thing, but this time around, she was content to spend her time with the children and the dear old men. She led their exercise class and at the end she gave a dance recital for them— or for her as she wanted to feel what her young body could do.

In the late afternoon, she saw Kit in the vegetable patch, pulling weeds.

He glanced up at her, smiling, but when he saw her turn away, his smile disappeared.

I have to fix this, she thought as she went inside the house. She didn't feel pregnant but it was possible that she was carrying his child. *We're to get married before the three weeks are up. He's my destiny. Without him I'll end up with a man who hates me. My child will...*

She couldn't bear to think of what she knew would happen to her without Kit.

But was that true? Kathy had asked if they had to build their futures on a man. Right now, Olivia had the same question. The first time around she'd let her emotions and her pride get in the way. She hadn't asked for help from anyone. But what if she did? What if after Kit left she asked her parents to help her? She knew without a doubt that if it came to it, her parents would move to another state. They would allow no shame to come onto their daughter or their grandchild.

She was a twenty-first century woman standing in 1970. If she was expecting—oh, for a drugstore pregnancy test!—she could handle it. She used to think she had no help, but it had been there all along. Her parents, Uncle Freddy and Mr. Gates, Dr. Everett. They were all there and ready.

As she prepared an early dinner—chicken with apricots, a

recipe that Letty's son's wife had taught her—she began to feel better. When she'd been presented with the idea of going back in time, all she could think of was getting together with Kit. But now that she was here she saw that she had *choices*. What a fabulous word, she thought. Choices! There wasn't just one man available and, even more important, the twenty-first-century woman had learned that a man wasn't necessary to a woman's happiness.

She was singing a Lady Gaga song and dancing around the kitchen when Kit came in. He had showered and put on a full set of clothes. Since they were alone, he slipped his arms around her waist and kissed the back of her neck.

Olivia twisted out of his grip. "Someone might come in."

"Would that be so bad? Kissing is something engaged couples do." He gave a pointed look at her empty finger.

"Housework," was her explanation for why she wasn't wearing the ring.

"Is dinner early because you're going out tonight? And might I ask where?"

She had no intention of telling him the truth. "I'm going on a date. With Willie."

"Ah," Kit said as he picked up a carrot stick and crunched it. "Isn't she the girl who works at your dad's bank?"

Olivia didn't answer him, but was annoyed that he knew.

"She called and said she was looking forward to going to the sale tonight and she asked me what she should wear. I told her high heels and tight jeans. She certainly does have a good giggle. And, oh yes, she really needs a new toaster."

When Olivia didn't comment, he sat down at the table and watched while she put bowls of food out. "So when do we leave for our date?"

"It's *my* date and you're not going."

"I think we should do things together. With our clothes on. Get to know each other outside the darkness."

"Does that include my knowing about you running around naked in the sunlight to get a full body tan?"

If Kit was surprised by her knowledge, he didn't show it. He just smiled. "What car do you want to use? Bill and Nina are staying home tonight so we could go in theirs. I'm not sure Uncle Freddy's old Packard is up to the two-mile journey into town. Or we could take the pickup. Maybe—"

"I have things to do." Olivia modified her tone, made it less strident, less angry. After all, Kit hadn't yet done the things she was furious at him for doing. When he said nothing, she stepped in front of him. "I'm not trying to be rude, but I really do have some very important things that I need to do and I can only do them alone."

"Ah," he said again.

"Stop saying that! We'll go out tomorrow. I promise."

Kit got up and went to the door. "I'll get Bill's car and meet you in the front in fifteen minutes. We wouldn't want to miss a minute at—where was it?—Trumbull's Appliance Store's semi-annual sale. I'm sure this will be a very exciting date."

He was out the door before Olivia could say another word. This was something she hadn't imagined. How was she going to get Alan and his Great Love together if Kit was hanging around? He liked to be in charge, in command. He liked to give the orders.

She called the kids to dinner and the men followed. They all wanted to know why she was dressed up and where she was going. She told them. Letty asked if she could go too; Ace asked if she'd bring back some ice cream; Uncle Freddy said the Summer Hill Bakery had blackberry pies; Mr. Gates asked her to find out how much a new stove would cost.

Olivia grabbed her sweater and ran out the door before they gave her more to do. Kit was leaning against Bill's Chevy and cleaning his nails with a pocketknife.

"You want to drive? I wasn't old enough to learn until last week."

With an eye roll at his lie, she got into the passenger seat.

They were barely out of the driveway before Kit said, "Why is it so important for you to go to this sale tonight and why did you ask someone you hardly know to go with you?"

"How do you know she isn't my best friend?"

"I can't see you being pals with someone who giggles and flirts with a stranger over the phone. Not your type at all."

Olivia had to agree with that! When Alan was dying, she got to know Willie well. Makeup, clothes, and who was going to pay her bills were her main concerns.

"You're not going to tell me what you're up to, are you?"

"I'm not 'up to' anything. Willie is new in town. I saw that Trumbull Appliances is having a big sale, so I invited her to go with me. Now are you satisfied?"

"Not in the least. Why did you *really* invite her to go with you?"

Olivia threw up her hands. "You are an exasperating man! Okay. I think she and Alan Trumbull would like each other. Happy, now?"

"Happier," he said. "What are you planning to buy? I think our washing machine was used during the First World War."

Kit was parking the car in the alley beside the bank. In a few years, the town would tear down three lovely old buildings to put in a parking lot. She started to reply to him, but the Caldwell family walked by. Six years from now, their house would burn down and Mr. Caldwell would die saving his youngest daughter.

"Are you all right?" Kit asked.

"Fine," Olivia whispered. Mr. Deavers and his wife went by. They would lose their son in Afghanistan.

"Livie?" Kit pulled her into his arms and stroked her back. "What is it? What's wrong?"

"I don't like knowing the future."

He pulled back to look at her. "You can talk to me, you know. Tell me what's wrong."

She moved away and leaned back against the seat. Patty Ferris was walking with her high school boyfriend. When she dumped him to marry Sue Collier's fiancé, there would be a lot of anger. But Patty would have three kids and be very happy, and Sue would leave town in a rage, go to law school, get her degree, and also be very happy.

"The future isn't all bad," Olivia said. "Sometimes good things happen."

"Glad to hear it. Why do you really want Willie to meet the Trumbull kid?"

"So they can give Kevin and Alana a happy life. Or maybe it's to ease my guilty conscience." She opened the car door. "Why don't you go have a beer somewhere while I do this?"

"I wouldn't miss it for the world. Got any more people you want to match up? Uncle Freddy could use a girlfriend."

She stepped out of the car. "How about you and Betty Schneider?"

"Not a bad idea. I hear she's had a lot of experience."

"More than you," Olivia shot at him.

"If you want to believe that, go right ahead."

She couldn't help smiling and by the time they reached the appliance store, Olivia realized that Kit had teased her out of her bad mood. But the idea of seeing Alan again, even of seeing the appliance store, bothered her. She must have been attracted to the man at the first. She could tell herself that it had all been baby lust. She'd just lost her child, and there was Alan with a baby who needed a mother. At the time, it had seemed perfect.

But surely there had been some male-female attraction. Over the many years of living with him, it had disappeared, but it must have been there at the beginning.

Kit took Olivia's arm in his. "Whatever you're so worried

about, I'll be right here." He opened the glass door and they went inside.

"Olivia!"

She turned to see Estelle Latham standing to the side. Her new husband, Henry, was bending over a washing machine. For a moment, Olivia felt her knees weaken. This was the couple who would adopt the child Olivia gave up. They'd name her Portia after Livie's mother's given name, and even keep the nickname of Tisha. They would eventually take her away, and return years later with a teenage granddaughter. "I haven't seen you in ages."

Olivia was holding tightly onto Kit's arm or she might have fallen. Estelle was waiting to be introduced.

"Hi, I'm Christopher. Kit. I work at Tattwell and Livie let me drive her into town."

She was glad for his tactful explanation, for not blurting about the engagement. But then, it was a small town. People probably knew what was going on with them.

"Henry's here to get us a new washer and I'm pushing for a dryer. I'm fed up with hanging clothes on a line."

Olivia still couldn't speak. If she was pregnant, then so was Estelle. Only she would lose her baby in a car crash on a slick, rainy road. *If I could prevent that,* Olivia thought, *maybe Estelle wouldn't need to adopt.* It wasn't easy, but she willed her body to stand up straight. She let go of Kit's arm. "Could I see you for a moment?" She looked at Kit. "Could you...?"

"Occupy myself?" he said cheerfully. "Sure. I'll look at blenders."

"Livie!" Estelle said as soon as they were alone. "Is that him? Everyone in town says you two are a love match. But what about Broadway? You worked so hard for that. I'd hate to see you give it up. Will he—?"

"Estelle, I had a nightmare about you. It was really horrible."

"I'm so sorry. That must have been awful. But—"

"You were expecting a baby and about six months along.

You and Henry were in Pennsylvania visiting his parents and you were driving in a bad rainstorm. A big truck skidded and ran into your door. You lost the baby and you could never have more children, so you adopted a baby girl. But you didn't tell her she was adopted until she found out when she was seventeen and she was really, really angry at you and Henry."

Estelle's eyes were saucers. "Oh. I, uh... I..."

"It was such a vivid dream that it was almost real. I haven't been able to get it out of my mind. You must swear to me that you won't ever drive in a rainstorm. Especially not in Pennsylvania when you're pregnant."

"I am," Estelle said. "Expecting, I mean. But only Henry knows—and Dr. Everett, of course. I haven't even told my mother. And we are planning to go to Pennsylvania in a few months. Henry might get a job there."

Olivia couldn't think of anything else to say. She just took Estelle's hands in hers and held them so tightly they hurt. Her eyes were pleading.

"I promise," Estelle said. When Olivia didn't let go, she said, "I swear. On all that's holy, no driving in the rain until our child is safely delivered."

Olivia released her hands and Estelle slipped her arm through Olivia's. "I had no idea you thought so much about me. Thank you. Uh-oh. Here comes Alan."

Olivia looked across the many people and the appliances with their big sale signs to see Alan Trumbull coming toward them. He was a good-looking young man. Not particularly tall, but he had nice hair and big brown eyes. She knew that he would keep his body trim. *All that golf*, she thought, then couldn't help her anger.

"Now you've done it," Estelle said. "He's going to give your handsome Yankee some competition."

A customer stopped Alan to ask a question about a refrigerator. *He won't know or care*, Olivia thought, and sure enough, Alan stopped, but he frowned in annoyance. She looked at Estelle. "What do you mean?"

"Alan Trumbull has had a crush on you since high school."

"That's ridiculous."

"Of course you never knew. You were the queen of the Drama Society, a princess on stage, and Alan was just a guy who played a flute in the band."

"Alan played the flute?"

"According to the bandleader, he wasn't very good. We girls said it was just so he could sit at your feet while you were on stage."

Olivia was looking at Estelle in disbelief. "Are you sure of this? I don't even remember Alan in high school."

"My point exactly. The day you left for college, that night we girls held a pity party for Alan in that tavern out by Tattwell. Poor guy was miserable."

Olivia was looking at Estelle in shock.

"Uh-oh, here he comes—and your pretty boyfriend is right behind him."

Alan stopped in front of Olivia and stared at her in silence.

Her stomach clenched. She knew that look so very well. He wanted her to *do* something, *fix* something. There was a problem so of course Olivia was to take care of it. There had been times when she'd been so overwhelmed with child care, running a home and the stores, that she'd nearly burst into tears. Never, ever, *never* would he tell her what he wanted. He'd just stand there and stare until she figured it out.

Kit put his arm tightly around Olivia's shoulders, his fingers digging into her skin. "I'm Christopher Montgomery," he said. "And you are?"

Alan didn't so much as glance at Kit, but kept staring at Olivia's pale face. "Good to see you again, Livie. Why don't we go somewhere and talk?" His tone was so proprietary, so full of ownership, that she took a step forward—as though she meant to obey him.

But Kit didn't release her. "We have some work to do." He led her to a corner of the store. "What the hell was that about?" Kit demanded. "Old boyfriend? That guy acted like he *owned* you. Why didn't you tell me you were coming here to see him?"

Between the emotion of seeing Estelle *and* Alan, Olivia felt like she might collapse. She couldn't think clearly, and right now the past and the future were all one. "I never went on a date with him, but I was married to him for many years. It hasn't happened yet, but it looks like he remembers it anyway."

Kit was staring at her, speechless.

When she looked up at him, her eyes were bleak. "Now you see why I didn't want you to come with me. What I have to do is beyond anyone's power to understand, much less accept. I have to go. I need to find Willie, who will someday be the mother of his daughter, Alana. They haven't met yet so I need to introduce them to each other."

Kit was still looking at her without comprehension, and she turned away. As much as she dreaded it, she knew she had to do things to make the future right.

Habit, she thought. What was that saying about doing something three times and it will become a habit? How about doing it over and over for more than half of your life? The store with all its appliances in the ghastly "harvest gold" and "avocado green" was as familiar to her as breathing. As was Alan. All it took was one lift of his eyebrows and out of habit, she knew what he expected of her.

Why hadn't that girl Arrieta warned her that this might happen? *Probably because she didn't know*, Olivia thought.

Her fear, one that was seeping into her like some flesh-eating parasite, was that if she wasn't successful at drastically changing things in the three weeks she'd been given, that she'd repeat her past mistakes. When she no longer remembered a world of computers and cell phones, would Alan look at her in that way that said she belonged to him and she'd go with him?

She glanced at Kit. In the future, she'd spent only a year with him, but she'd had a lifetime with Alan. Habit was a very, very strong pull.

Kit took her hand in his. "It doesn't matter what I think or believe," he said softly. "Tell me what you need and let me help." He smiled at her. "Please."

Olivia took a few breaths and squeezed his hand. Willie was just coming in the door and looking around. "I need to get Alan and her together."

"Now you *are* talking fantasy. You want scrawny, flabby Trumbull to look at her when *you* are in the room?"

Olivia couldn't help smiling—but then it's how she'd always felt. Vain, yes, but Willie wasn't especially pretty or built or smart. Yet Alan had liked her better. "Thank you," she said. "So how do we do it?"

Kit smiled at the *we*. "Empty the earth of all people so only those two are left. They might notice each other but I'm not sure."

In spite of the trauma she'd felt since entering the store, Olivia laughed. Alan was wearing that expression she knew so well, that he *expected* her to follow him.

But Kit's sarcasm, and the way he was holding her hand so securely, was giving her courage. "There's a storage room," she whispered and Kit bent down to hear her. "Down the hall to the left. If we lock them in there for a while they might realize that they like each other."

He nodded in understanding. "Think the girl will go with me if I ask her to?"

She was so grateful for his help that when she looked up at him he seemed to have starlight encircling his head. "I think she'll believe she's died and gone to heaven."

"Keep looking at me like that and I'll show you what you can do with a vibrating washing machine."

"How do you know that?" she snapped.

Smiling, Kit let go of her hand and went toward Willie, who was looking lost.

"I'm glad you sent him away," Alan said. He was looking her up and down in a way she'd always disliked. "I knew that as soon as you returned to Summer Hill you'd come see me."

Has he always been this arrogant? Olivia wondered. She knew he was after they were married, but if he'd done this at first, she wouldn't have married him. No. At first he'd been quiet and unassuming and helpless, she thought. And she had jumped in and taken over. "How have you been?"

"Better now that you're here."

"Alan," a customer said, "I was wondering about—"

"Ask a salesman," he said quickly.

The tone he used sent Olivia back in time. After they were married, Alan would snap, "Ask Olivia." Behind him, the door opened and in came a pretty young woman Olivia had only met once. She was Kevin's mother. During the birth, a blood clot had erupted and she'd died instantly.

"I thought you were going out with Diane." Olivia nodded toward the young woman.

"I was but, now that you're here, I'll let her go."

Olivia had a flash of panic. What about Kevin? Did he have to have Diane as his mother? If Alan and she didn't marry, would Kevin be born?

She saw Kit across the room. He was walking with Willie and listening to whatever she was saying. Behind his back, he pointed toward the end of the hall and Olivia shook her head. They had the wrong woman! In spite of all Kevin's ingratitude, Olivia had helped raise him and she couldn't risk that he'd cease to exist. Willie was going to have to take care of herself.

She smiled at Alan. "I seem to remember a big closet at the back of this building."

With a smile that said he'd won, he led the way.

When they passed Kit, she said, "Not Willie, get Diane."

Kit took only seconds to recover from his confusion, then he went back into the store.

Fifteen minutes later, Olivia and Kit were walking away and smiling. She held up her hand to him but he had no idea what she meant. "It's a high five." She showed him how to slap hands. Behind them, they couldn't hear the yells of the two people they'd just locked in the big closet.

As they got back to the showroom, Kit halted. "Are you feeling better?"

"Much," she said. "Thank you."

"So why'd you stay married to that jerk for so many years?"

Considering that she was twenty-two years old and had never been married, what he said was absurd—and funny. "Great sex," she said.

"Anything you'd like to teach me?"

She slipped her arm in his. "I don't think I need to teach you anything."

His eyes turned hot. "How about if we leave this place?" He nodded down the hall toward the locked door of the closet. "Unless you want to release them now."

"No, I'll call later. I think they need a few hours together. We can—" She broke off because she saw Mr. Trumbull sitting in his office. He'd unexpectedly died of a heart attack the year before Olivia returned to town, and she didn't really know him. But she knew he'd had the reputation of being an honest, hardworking man—and he and his son never got along. Their arguments were legendary.

"I need to do something." She tapped on his door, then opened it.

Mr. Trumbull looked up. "Why, it's pretty little Olivia Paget, isn't it? And who is your lucky young man?"

"Christopher Montgomery, sir." Kit held out his hand to shake.

"I just wanted to say that my father speaks very highly of you," she said. "He says you were a war hero."

Mr. Trumbull smiled, obviously pleased at the accolade. "Not a hero, but I did my part."

Olivia picked up a little framed photo of Mr. Trumbull in his army uniform, his chest adorned with a long line of medals. "Didn't you give Audie Murphy a run for his money?"

Mr. Trumbull looked like he might blush. Audie Murphy was the most decorated man in WWII and he went on to star in some movies.

Kit was standing to the side, waiting to see what she was up to.

"I hate to be a pest, Mr. Trumbull," she said, "but Uncle Freddy wants a new stove. I was wondering if we could get some prices on something gas, thirty-six inches? I'd ask the salesmen but you know Uncle Freddy, he only trusts you."

"Sure." Mr. Trumbull got up. "I'll just be a few minutes. Anything for Uncle Freddy."

As soon as the door closed, Olivia went to her knees and started using her nails to pull at the cheap, thin paneling on the wall. "Hand me that letter opener, would you?"

Instead, Kit knelt beside her, put his hands on the paneling, and pulled up. The thin wood came away on one side.

Olivia put her hand inside and reached up as far as she could. She withdrew a long, narrow wooden box.

"What's in it?"

"It's full of Mr. Trumbull's war medals." She hesitated, then thought, *Why not tell?* "Alan did it. He was sick of hearing how his dad was a hero, so he stuck the box of medals behind the paneling, then messed up the office and said there'd been a robbery. I found it years later when I remodeled the office."

"How about if we let Mr. Trumbull think he found it?" Kit slipped the box back behind the paneling, but left the nails sticking out.

"I don't know what happened to Alan," Mr. Trumbull said

as he returned to the office. "He was supposed to be helping on the floor tonight."

"Oh, you know Alan," Olivia said. "If there's work to be done, he disappears."

Mr. Trumbull looked at her in shock, then laughed.

"I bet he's out playing golf," Olivia said.

Mr. Trumbull laughed harder. "I shouldn't think it's funny, but his mother—"

"Believes Alan can do anything," Olivia said. Behind her, Kit was doing something with his foot.

"He's a clever boy but…"

"He'd rather spend time figuring out how not to do something than to do it," Olivia said.

Mr. Trumbull was still laughing. "Oh, Livie, I had no idea you knew my son so well. Why don't you come over for dinner some night? Get to know all of us better?"

She stopped laughing. It was as though he was matchmaking her with his son. She knew how lazy he was, therefore she should *marry* him? Scary concept!

"She's taken," Kit said loudly. "Mr. Trumbull, I seem to have stepped on a nail and I can't move my shoe. I'm caught on a corner of the paneling and there seems to be something under here. Would you mind giving me a hand?"

Chapter Twenty-Eight

AFTER THEY LEFT TRUMBULL'S, OLIVIA WANTED TO go home, but when Kit took her hand and led her down the street, she was glad. She was feeling full of energy at what they'd just accomplished. Maybe—possibly—she had broken the tie between her and Alan. Whatever happened now, she might not find herself back with him.

The drugstore was still open and they sat down at the counter. The soda fountain would be removed in the mideighties to make room for gaudy racks of big-name cosmetics.

"Hamburger or hot dog?" Kit asked. "Coke or Tab?"

The old names made her smile. With the health consciousness of the twenty-first century, she hadn't had a Coke or a hot dog in years. "Dog and a Coke."

Kit got a hamburger and a Coke.

When their orders came, Olivia couldn't help staring at it. By twenty-first-century norms, there was very little food on the plate. No side of coleslaw swimming in high calorie mayonnaise, no beans in brown sugar, no fried potatoes. She hadn't noticed it until now, but people ate about half as much as they did in the modern, tech world. "And to burn it off, all we do is sit behind a computer," she murmured.

"What did you say?" Kit asked.

She brought her attention back to the present. "I'd like mustard and pickle relish," Olivia told the girl behind the counter. She would marry a young man from Richmond, move away, have two kids, go through a horrible divorce, then return to Summer Hill and eventually marry Dave Harrison and be very happy. "How is Dave?"

"Who?"

"Dave Harrison. Sings in the choir at church? Oh, sorry. I thought you two were together. I know he likes you a lot."

"Does he? He hasn't said anything to me. Besides, I have a boyfriend."

"I know. He lives in Richmond. But later..." Olivia took a bite of her hot dog. "You know, you're so good with people that you might try selling houses. I bet you'd be really good at it. I'd buy from you."

The young woman took a step back from Olivia, looking at her as though she were crazy. "I, uh... I have to go check on supplies." She practically ran from the room.

Olivia looked at Kit, waiting for him to ask her questions, but he didn't. Instead, he said, "You think she'd sell us some ice cream for Ace?"

"That girl would sell us the drugstore and leave town five minutes after she got the money."

"And you've had experience in buying houses from her?"

She avoided his question. "Did you know that hot dogs are made of ground-up animal hooves?"

Kit looked at his burger for a moment and she could see the muscle working in his temple. He seemed to be trying to decide what to say next. Finally, he turned to her. "Tell me or not, but whatever you need help with, I'm with you."

Olivia thought she'd never loved anyone so much in her life

as she did this man in this moment. "I think of things as I see people."

"Then we'll have to go find them," he said. "Since we've both worked seven days a week for a month now, I think we deserve some time off. Think the kids can feed themselves for a couple of days?"

"Ace and Letty, for sure. Give them a loaf of bread and a jar of peanut butter and they'll be fine. The other kids, I don't know. Maybe Nina can babysit."

They laughed together.

On the drive back to Tattwell, Olivia sat next to Kit—no seat belts in the car—and he put his arm around her shoulders. When they got back, he kissed her good-night, but he didn't ask to go into her room with her. Behind him, she could see Ace's little blond head above the covers. His last visit to the hospital to see his mother had been the worst yet. The child needed comfort, and Kit was his security blanket.

She went into her own room. The bed seemed big and lonely. If Kit had asked to spend the night with her, she would have said no. Maybe. That he didn't ask bothered her.

She went to sleep right away, but she had nightmares. She saw burning houses, car wrecks, multiple funerals, and three suicides. When she awoke, she was in a pool of sweat—and her lower back was aching in a way it hadn't done in years. It took her a moment to remember what caused that particular pain. She went to the bathroom and sure enough, she had started her period.

Instantly, tears came to her eyes. She was *not* pregnant. All of the horror that had happened wasn't going to. If Kit left her now it wouldn't be so traumatic. She wouldn't have to go to an unwed mother's home, give her child up for adoption—and for the rest of her life she would NOT feel that she deserved nothing good to happen to her.

She went back to bed and put her hands behind her head. This changed everything! Broadway was still open to her. Last year she'd been in a local play and she'd forgotten how much she loved being onstage. That the play had been put on by Kit so he could win her back didn't count.

Freedom of choice was a wonderful thing, she thought. The entire world was open to her. Careers, travel, men, anything was possible.

Smiling, she tried to go back to sleep, but every time she closed her eyes, the dreams returned. Except they weren't dreams. She was remembering things that had happened in her dear little town. She'd lived in it all her life and she'd always been involved with its people. As she grew older, people began to depend on her. After Alan died, after she sold everything to pay off the debts of Kevin and Hildy, she became a sort of matriarch for the entire town. "Go to Olivia. She'll know what to do," seemed to be a motto. Because of her position in town, she knew a lot of secrets.

When Letty and Ace threw open her door before daylight, she felt worse than she had when she went to bed. As with children throughout time, they wanted something new and different to occupy them.

"My kingdom for an iPad," she mumbled. "DVDs and the latest movies to keep them *all* busy."

Kit, in shorts and T-shirt, was standing in the doorway. "Who wants green pancakes?"

Squealing, the kids ran to him, and Olivia gave him a look of thanks. Twenty minutes later, she was downstairs and telling Ace he was named Harry Potter and Letty was Hermione and they were at wizard school. Everyone ate in silence as Olivia told the story.

After the dishes were washed and the oldest and youngest were gluing together pointed wizard hats and painting sticks to be magic wands, Kit told Livie that Nina would look after them so they could go out.

At first Olivia thought he meant that they'd go somewhere

and make love. But there was no way on earth that she was going to let him touch her. She wasn't going to tempt destiny so that when he went away she was left behind carrying his child.

As for the marriage… If she wasn't expecting a baby, there was no need to rush into that. Maybe she would go to Broadway and try it again. She'd see Kit when he returned.

He saw the way she pulled away from him. He didn't comment but she felt him stiffen. "You said it helped with what you need to do if you see people. I thought we'd go to town and look."

"Yes, thank you," she said formally. Arrieta had said that she could only change things that related to her, to Olivia. But how far did that extend? In her little town, tragedies affected everyone. If she could help just one person, she'd feel she'd accomplished something great.

Besides, Olivia was *not* from the ME generation. She picked up a pen and a spiral notebook off the phone table and she was ready.

She directed Kit to drive her around the streets of Summer Hill as she thought about the owners. There were several people she hadn't met, but she knew the majority of them.

There were few families that hadn't been struck by that awful word *tragedy*. Some of them no one would know about until the next generation. A man abuses his children and they do it to theirs. A girl molested as a child goes berserk when she's an adult.

There were accidents that could have been prevented, diseases that if detected earlier wouldn't have killed.

Olivia and Kit rode in silence as she made notes. How could she prevent these coming catastrophes? She knew that as she was now, if she went to the authorities and reported rape, incest, abuse, she wouldn't be believed. Her youth and inexperience would be against her.

Besides, she thought with a grimace, it was the times. In the 1970s if a woman accused a man of rape, *she* was put on trial. She had led him on, entrapped him. If she'd worn a low-cut blouse years before, she was considered a slut and the man was innocent. Olivia wanted to scream that every item in every store was packaged attractively but if you stole it, you were prosecuted. Why were women considered less than a stick of deodorant?

Kit reached across the seat, took her hand, and squeezed it. "If you want to talk, I'm here."

"Thank you." She pulled her hand away as she looked at the next house. The Nelsons, a lovely family. When little Lisa was fourteen years old, she would slit her wrists and die before she was found. In the school locker room, some girls had stolen her clothes, then let the boys in. Lisa didn't think she could live with the shame. How did Olivia stop something that wouldn't happen for years?

For the next three days, Olivia lived in a haze of trying to prevent the horrors that she knew would happen. She called people— using the annoying rotary dial phone—and wrote letters—with a typewriter, no less. Using every lie she could imagine, she said she had a dream, a premonition, she saw something, someone told her something. Whatever she could think of to warn people, she said it.

She was aware of the people around her at Tattwell, but only vaguely. Kit seemed to be taking care of them. He allowed the youngest pair to bother her twice a day to ask for more about what Letty was calling *The Story of the Girl Wizard*. She wanted to hear how smart Hermione was, and Ace wanted her to tell how brave Harry Potter was.

Uncle Freddy made them laugh when he said he wanted to be Voldemort, the personification of evil.

After only minutes, Kit ushered them all out and let Olivia get back to her phone and typewriter.

"But even if I do this, will it all be forgotten at the end of three weeks?" she said aloud, her head in her hands.

It was on the afternoon of the fourth day that she fell back in her chair and was ready to admit defeat. When she was an older woman, people listened to her, but when she was barely out of her teens, they dismissed her. She was hung up on, yelled at, called a liar. Three people reported her to the police. The sheriff called and cautioned her. He said that what people did in the privacy of their own homes was their business.

"It's going to take forty years to show people that that's not true," she said.

"Then, Livie, you call me back in forty years and I'll listen to what you have to say. Until then, leave the residents of Summer Hill alone." The sheriff hung up.

In the end, Olivia ran away. She'd had days of trying to prevent disasters, tragedies, accidents, and crimes, but she didn't seem to have made any progress.

She ran through the kitchen and out the back door. No one was about, but she didn't wonder where they were. All she could see were the visions in her mind. Funerals, mothers crying, fathers in a rage, people in handcuffs, neglected children, abused children.

She often told people of the peacefulness of their dear little town, of the almost-nonexistent crime. But over the years many things had happened. When she looked back over that long expanse, there was time between the bad. Years would go by and nothing bad would happen. But now she saw it all. A lifetime of preventable misery was screaming through her mind.

But she couldn't do anything about it!

The feeling of helplessness was sucking the energy out of her.

She ran through the garden and stopped at the big magnolia tree. Why had she been sent back in time if she had no power to change anything? Forget the big horrors, the wars and bombings. She couldn't even prevent the suicide of a girl who was going to be bullied at school.

Closing her eyes, she leaned back against the old tree. Last year she'd ridden in a little red truck with her friend Casey past this tree. Olivia had told how Alan had lied and cheated, and how he'd taken away the business that Olivia had built. Casey was the wife of Tate who was going to be the son of five-year-old Letty. Olivia had talked to people who didn't yet exist!

When she opened her eyes, Kit was standing there, a garden hoe over his shoulder. As always, he had on next to nothing.

But she didn't feel lust for his beautiful body. What she felt was anger. All of this was *his* fault. Her life with Alan was because Kit had left her alone and pregnant. She had come back in time with the idea of having a life with Christopher Montgomery. But she wasn't pregnant, so there was no *need* to have to spend her life with him. She was utterly and totally *free*!

She knew that what she was feeling, all her anger and frustration, was on her face.

When Kit first saw her standing there, he smiled, but one look at her glower and he put on what Olivia called his "diplomat face." It was a mask he hid behind so no one would know what he was thinking—but Olivia did. Today the mask covered his extreme disapproval.

"Let me know when my Olivia is back." It was the voice he'd someday use with trumped-up dignitaries who he wanted to put in their place.

Olivia broke. Like a glass vial full of some nasty, smoky, green poison, she snapped.

She didn't say a word, just ran'at him with all her force.

Surprised, Kit tossed the hoe to the side and caught her just as her head hit his torso.

He grunted as she nearly knocked the breath out of him.

"It's all *your* fault!" Yelling, she began hitting him with her fists on his bare chest. "You did it all! You left me when I was carrying your baby. You—"

He grabbed her shoulders to hold her out to look at her. "Are you—?"

She swung her right arm with all her might and hit him in

the jaw. When she saw blood on his lip, she was pleased. She'd certainly shed enough blood for him! "This morning I found out that I'm not, but I was back in 1970. And I was *alone*! You saw me at the theater in New York, but you said nothing. I had to go away to Florida to have our baby. Estelle raised her. When our daughter finally met us, it was horrible."

Olivia stepped back from him and put her hands over her face. "She hated us. Our daughter had a good life—Estelle and Henry were good to her—but she couldn't bear the sight of *us*. Of you and me. She didn't know she was adopted until late, and she didn't understand why we had given her up. Why we didn't *want* her."

Olivia began to cry. "I told you I loved you but you left. I thought you were scared. You told no one where you were going, not even your father."

She looked up at Kit and saw that his face was white under his tan and his lip was bloody. "Oh, go away. How can you understand what I'm going through? You're just..." Her mouth hardened. "You're just a worthless boy."

Kit's jaw muscle was working, but he gave no other sign that he was reacting to her words. "As you wish," he said, then gave a bit of a bow. He put his shoulders back in that way that meant he wasn't going to talk about the subject anymore, then he started walking away from her.

Olivia picked up a round rock from the ground. It looked like one of the stones the children had collected from the creek. Unlike when she was with Elise, her throwing arm was in good shape. She pulled back like a pitcher and let go. The rock hit him hard on his perfectly toned rear end. "I hope Gaddafi finds out who you are and shoots you." She turned away toward the house.

Kit caught her before she had gone two feet. He grabbed her shoulders, put his nose to hers, and glared. "What do you know?"

She twisted out of his grip. "I tell you I was pregnant and

gave our child up for adoption and that means nothing to you? But the mention of a Middle East dictator gets your attention? Go to hell!" She started back to the house.

Kit stepped in front of her. "Cut out the melodrama and tell me what you know and who told you."

She moved around him.

"Olivia!"

Halting, she looked at him. "Don't use your diplomat voice on me! I'm not some third world despot who will be over-thrown next week. This—" She motioned to his all-over tan. "This is to make you look more Arabic. The military, specifically some guy you said was wider than he was tall—you called him a cartoon bear—is going to pick you up in just over two weeks. They'll give you twenty minutes to pack and leave. And you *do* it! To hell with us and your family. You only cared about Muammar Gaddafi."

When Kit opened his mouth to speak, Olivia knew what he was going to say. He was going to tell her that she was saying the name wrong. Always the perfectionist! She leaned toward him, her face red with anger. "Don't you dare say it!"

But he had no idea what she meant. "Actually, his name is—"

She put her hands over her ears and screamed so loud the pea-cock screeched and the children came running.

"Go!" Kit ordered them, and the kids and the bird obeyed. When they were alone again, he looked back at Olivia. "You must tell me what this is about. Do I talk in my sleep? Is that how you know about…about my mission?"

Her arms were stiff at her side, her hands in fists. "No! You tell me when we finally get married—over forty years from now. But by that time I'm so beaten down by life that I would marry Gaddafi if it meant escaping my stepson and his wife."

Kit's face was losing the hard, unbending look that he would perfect as he aged. "Did you agree to marry me now because you thought you were expecting our child?"

"Yes!" she said. "I did. I thought I had no other choice in this unenlightened era when a single mother is considered—at best—an object of pity. This time is hardly better than the Puritans'."

"Thought," he said softly. "Past tense."

"Yes. Past. Done. I now know I have choices. I have freedom. I don't have to marry vain little Alan Trumbull just to get his kid because I lost mine. I don't have to see our daughter's eyes when we tell her we're the parents who…" The energy her rage had given her was vanishing. "Who gave her up."

"Come with me." Kit's his voice was soft and gentle. "I want to show you something."

"I don't want to go anywhere with you. I hate you! You lied to me. You *left* me."

"I know." He took her hand.

Olivia was feeling too bad to do anything but go with him. She'd had days of little sleep and endless misery. No one would listen to her or believe her. Even on small things like saying they needed to check the gas lines in the basement, she'd been told to mind her own business. And through every hang up, every warning, she'd thought how all this was happening because of Kit. Was it worth it? *Must* her future depend on *him*? Wasn't there another choice? An alternative?

Tears of anger were blocking her vision, but she saw that he had led her to the pond.

On the side were the big towels they brought out for their twice-daily swims, but no one else was there. She had an idea that the men were keeping the children inside. *Away from* me, she thought. *Me and my bad temper.*

Kit gave her a very sweet smile. "Feeling better?"

She wiped her eyes with the back of her hand and nodded. "I am, but it doesn't change anything."

Still smiling, Kit made a lightning-fast move as he bent, picked her up, then twirled around and threw her. Like a human spear, Olivia went sailing through the air to land in the deepest part of the pond. The force of Kit's thrust sent her underwater. She hadn't been expecting the plunge and she fought hard to get to the surface.

When she came up, Kit was there beside her, treading water.

"You bastard!" She started swimming to the bank, but Kit caught her ankle. "Let go of me!"

"I have some cousins who—"

"Yeah, I know," Olivia said angrily. "We're married, remember? I know your whole family." Her skirt was wrapping around her legs and she didn't like treading water.

"In the year twenty-something, right? But that couldn't be. The world ends at the year 2000."

"It doesn't even screw up the computer clocks. I need to get back to feed the kids."

"You haven't thought about any of us for the last few days, so why bother now? As I was saying, I have some cousins, a bunch of earth-bound creatures, who say we Montgomerys are part fish. I can stay out here all day, and we will, until you agree to tell me everything."

"Okay, I'll tell you." She started toward the bank, but again he caught her ankle and pulled her back to him. She closed her lips tight and didn't speak.

"At first, I didn't mind it when you called me a worthless boy. I knew you were overwhelmed with lust for me, so—"

"I was no such thing!"

"It's all right as the feeling was mutual. I figured you'd come around eventually."

"Ha!"

He went underwater and came up on the other side of her. "You did come around. And around." He paddled in a circle, surrounding her. "And around. And around."

"Okay!" Some of her anger was leaving her. "The sex was good. I admit it. But there's more to being together than sex."

"Trust? Honesty? Sharing things?"

She glared at him. "Like you told me what you were doing for your country? You know what you told me?"

"In the future, you mean? When we're married?" He was laughing at her.

"Yes! Then. You said you were an idiot for thinking that your country was more important than I was."

Kit stopped paddling and he lost that smirky expression.

Olivia smiled. "Sounds like you, doesn't it? Just so you know, you don't get back from Libya until three years later and it's in a medic plane. Takes you a year to recover and the military no longer wants you."

Kit looked so devastated that she almost felt sorry for him. Almost. She swam to the bank, got out, and grabbed a towel.

"I want to hear it all," he said from behind her.

"You won't listen. No one does. In the last few days I've concocted more lies than I have in my whole life. I was trying to save lives—except that it was all a lie. I…" She sat down on the ground, the towel around her shoulders, and looked out at the water. When she spoke, her voice was quiet. "You and I were so *polite* to each other. We made a pact to never talk about all the bad we'd been through, all that we'd missed by being apart."

"When was this?" Kit sat beside her and began rubbing her back with the towel.

"After we were married. By then, you were so famous and—"

"Please no," he said.

"Not like George and Amal famous but—" When he looked confused, she waved her hand. "You're famous inside the political world. You solve problems for whole countries. It's just that you couldn't solve your own life. You greatly disliked your first wife. Rowan said…" She didn't finish.

He'd stopped rubbing. "I married someone other than *you*?"

The disbelief in his voice was so honest that she looked at him. His lip was bleeding again. "After Libya, you came here to Summer Hill. You saw me but you thought I was married and had had another man's child. Your pride didn't allow you to ask anyone in town the truth. But…" She looked back at the pond. "But then, I still hated you for leaving me. I'm sure that if you had shown up, I would have pushed a refrigerator over on you."

"I would never leave you," he said. "If they came to get me, I'd let you know where I was."

"You did. Sort of. You left a note and the ring in the well house, but I didn't see them. I couldn't bear to go back…back there."

Kit put his arm around Olivia and pulled her head onto his shoulder. "I want to hear it all. From the beginning. Every word. What happened the day they came to get me?"

"I went to Richmond," she said. "I was angry at you because I'd slipped up the day before and said I love you. You said nothing in return. You were silent."

"Because I didn't love you?" he asked.

"I thought that then, but no." She took a deep breath. "You had your grandmother's ring and you were going to ask me to marry you before you left."

He was nodding in understanding. "But while you were in Richmond, they came to get me. When you saw that I was gone, you were so angry that you didn't see the note I'd hidden in the well house. Do I have that right?"

"Yes."

"What did the note say?"

"You asked me to wait for you, to marry you, and to go to your parents."

"But as I understand it, your pride—and that temper of yours—as well as your lack of faith in me, kept you from seeing the note."

The last of Olivia's anger left her. It hurt too much to blame herself for what had happened. It was one thing to joke about her stupidity in not believing in him, but another to see how many lives she'd hurt with her stubborn pride.

"I could have called," he said. "I'm sure they let me call my parents before I left. My dad has a lot of power in parts of the world. I *should* have called. And sneaked out to send you a letter."

She knew that he was taking the blame onto himself. Blame for something that hadn't happened yet—and now never would.

"Who is Rowan?"

"Your son. He's an FBI agent and you want him to be with pretty little Stacy, who is one of Ace's many daughters, but she likes Nate Taggert better. You've been *very* upset about that."

Kit was looking at her in shock. "These things sound *real*."

"They *are* real. You bought River House for me because you and I had such a good time there. Besides, I have to open an office. I should register at the University of Virginia to study psychology." She looked at him. "But if I don't marry you, I don't need to do any of that."

He kissed her forehead. "Of course you'll marry me. Otherwise our daughter won't have a father. So let's start at the beginning. I left you a heartfelt note and a beautiful ring and you were too stubborn to look for them. Go on from there."

Olivia started to protest, but as he so often did, Kit was trying to make her laugh. "We came back from Richmond and you were gone," she began.

"Wait! About..." He ran his hand through his thick black hair. "In the future am I...?"

"Bald?" She at last gave a bit of a smile. "Your hair is as thick as it is now, and it's a magnificent shade of silver gray. You are always and forever a beautiful man."

"To you or the rest of the world?"

"To me. Other women find you repulsive."

Kit snorted in laughter. "Okay. Go on. Tell me all the horrible things I haven't done to you. But if you can find time, I'd like to hear about the computers you keep mentioning. And who is Google? We've been hearing you complain about how much you need him. Should I be jealous?"

"I was..." Olivia started to tell him of the pain she'd been through as she carried his child, about what Alan had done to her, about... But she stopped. He was right. It no longer mattered what had happened in the past. It was *now* that was important. And this time around, she didn't want to do everything *alone*. She didn't want to bear a child alone. Didn't want to have to deal with men like Alan and have to cope with her stepson and his wife. And right now, she didn't want to continue trying to deal with the 1970s. *Keep the music of these years*, she thought, *but ditch the I-don't-get-involved attitude.*

She wasn't sure what this new future held, but it was as Kit said the night after Uncle Freddy hadn't drowned in the pond: *"Right now, today, this minute, we have everything to be happy about."*

When she spoke, it wasn't about what had happened to make her life miserable. "You are a great lover of technology," she said. "I like emails but you love all of it. You text and twitter and emoji, whatever. When my laptop makes me so angry that I want to drive a car over it, you fix it in about ten minutes."

He stretched out beside her. "I think I like this story better than Harry Potter. Does this one have any music?"

Olivia laughed. It didn't matter that some stories were real and some made up. If they hadn't happened yet, they might as well all be fantasy.

"Mind if the kids hear this one?" Kit asked. "Maybe you can tell them more about their future lives. What about Ace's daughters? How many does he have? Oh, wait. Better not go there. Too many women."

"He doesn't go to bed with the mothers."

"Please tell me they didn't fix *that* in the future." He gave a low whistle, and like the Munchkins appearing in the Emerald City, the men and the kids came into view. "Come on," Kit said. "I'm not sure, but I think our Livie is back. Who wants to swim while she tells us about the future?"

"Do they ride dragons?" Ace asked.

"Hang gliding," Olivia said. "You'll do it in Namibia."

"Do they have great stories?" Letty asked.

"Yes, and your son will tell them in movies."

"How about food that cooks itself?" Uncle Freddy asked.

"Microwave ovens can cook a chicken in ten minutes."

"I'd like a car that drives itself," Mr. Gates said.

"A voice on GPS tells you how to get anywhere." Olivia shrugged. "Work still needs to be done on that one."

Standing there in her wet dress, Olivia looked at them. She couldn't save the town, but maybe she wasn't supposed to. Maybe she was just supposed to change this one tiny part of the universe. Perhaps these people, here and now, were everything. Maybe it wasn't the length of life but what happened while we were here. Whatever the truth, she wasn't going to waste another second going over what did, didn't, could have, would have happened.

Ace yelled that he was Harry Potter riding Toothless, and Letty shouted that she was Hermione on Stormfly. Uncle Freddy started singing "Let it Go" and the others joined him.

On the second chorus, Kit gave Olivia a look that said that later they could make love. Shaking her head, she held up her naked left hand. Her eyes said, "You're not touching me without a ring on my finger." If she wasn't pregnant now, she was sure she would be the next time they rolled around together—and *damned* if she was going to do all that over again!

Uncle Freddy and Mr. Gates had seen the gesture and they were trying to hide their laughter.

"I'm Voldemort and I'm riding Skullcrusher," Uncle Freddy yelled, and Mr. Gates pushed the chair as they chased the screaming children.

Olivia stepped back and looked at the family around her. Kit was whirling the children around in an attempt to simulate a dragon's flight. Mr. Gates was turning Uncle Freddy's chair on one wheel. The air was full of laughter and song.

Now, she thought. *This is what truly matters. This one, perfect, happy moment.*

Chapter Twenty-Nine

WHEN OLIVIA OPENED HER EYES, SHE HAD NO IDEA where she was. As she stared at the desk with the empty bookshelves behind it, memories began coming back to her. Alan and Kevin and Hildy. No! It was Kit and Tisha and the boys. It was Summer Hill and washing machines and huge delivery trucks. No! It was embassies around the world.

She lifted her hand and looked at it, saw the lines and the spots on her skin that all the sunscreen in the world couldn't prevent.

Beside her were Kathy and Elise, still in their chairs, their eyes closed, both of them smiling. Wherever they were—whenever—they looked happy.

As Olivia got up, her joints seemed to creak, and her body felt stiff and slow. *Age,* she thought. Gradually, her mind began to unclutter. Her life with Kit was getting a bit clearer than her life with Alan. A vision of her father riding a camel came to her. He learned to cross his legs on the saddle and push to make the animal keep its head down and go forward. Her mother used to giggle in delight at her husband's gorgeous new thigh muscles. As their daughter, Olivia should have been embarrassed, but she wasn't. But then, her mother said that marriage to Kit had changed Livie into an old soul.

Kit said he'd made her grow up. Olivia said that having to deal with his life wore her out so much that she'd become old early.

Smiling at the thoughts, she stretched, trying to flex her muscles, taking note of the changes in her body. Her stomach was bigger, the skin more loose. She put her hand on it and closed her eyes for a moment. Having four children had stretched her. How she'd complained to Kit! But of course she'd really wanted reassurance that he still loved her even if the beautiful twenty-two-year-old body was gone. He always proved it by making love to her. Like his hair, that part of him had never faded in strength.

She opened the office door and leaned against the jamb. Too much was in her mind! Giving up Tisha was clear, but so was holding her daughter as her family and Kit's looked on. A top hospital and staff had been able to save Olivia's reproductive system after the difficult birth. At the time, Kit was still in Libya, but they managed to get word to him that his daughter and wife were well.

Right now her memory of tears was mixed with thoughts of joy. Thoughts of traveling with Kit were intertwined with memories of trying to manage appliance stores. Kevin's inactivity even as a child was twisted around the blazing energy of her and Kit's three sons.

When Olivia opened her eyes, Arrieta was standing there looking concerned. "Are you all right?"

Olivia pushed away from the door. "I think I will be, but my mind needs to settle."

"Come and have some tea. I made some cream cookies."

Olivia sat down at the table and sipped her tea. Her head came up. "My father! He didn't die at his workbench!" She began to remember. "I threw a fit and made him have his heart checked. Kit's family got him really good treatment. It's slowly coming back to me." She ate a cookie. "Kit and I own the whole Camden estate. It was a wedding gift from his parents. And the cottage is my office. Oh! I have a degree in psychology. I see patients." She smiled. "After our little wedding, my parents were very happy when I told them that until Kit returned I was going back to school to study psychology. My father said that half of the world was crazy so I'd always have work." She couldn't help the tears that came to her eyes. "I miss them so much!"

She put her hands to her head. "If I think of a person or a place, the memory comes to me. But my life with Alan is still clear. Did he marry Diane and have Kevin? Did she die? What about Willie? What happened to all of them?" She rubbed her forehead. "I seem to remember that Trumbull Appliances was sold. I think it's now a furniture store." She was thinking hard. "Wait! Alan and Willie did get married. I was in Richmond then, living with my parents and I was hugely pregnant. I was very pleased to hear of the wedding. Mom said she didn't know I knew them, and I didn't. Not in that life."

Olivia looked up at Arrieta. "They divorced! Now I remember. Willie left Alan and married the man who built those ticky-tacky houses near us at Camden Hall. Kit said he wished he'd bought that land in memory of…" Olivia smiled. "Of our naked scurry across there. Young Pete still has my bra in a frame in his house. I wonder if Elise's is there too? Did that happen with her? Or was that wiped out like my marriage to Alan was?"

"Beats me," Arrieta said. "I'm new at this." She gave Olivia a hard look. "But you need to know everything since you're going to take over Dr. Hightower's job."

"Oh," Olivia said. "There is that memory buried under all of them. I don't know if I can do that."

"You have to," Arrieta said. "And you have to keep what you do a secret. The reason I moved here is to be near you." She look so frightened that she might pass out.

Olivia got up, put her arm around the girl, and led her to sit down. "Everything will work out—you'll see." She glanced at the door. "How long will they stay in their trance?"

"Until I pull them out. I just think very hard and tell them to come back and they do. But those two are so happy they could stay forever. They don't *want* to wake up."

"But I did?"

"I don't think you've solved everything in your life. Aunt Primrose told me this might happen. When people only go back a few years, it's easier, but you went back a long time—and you had two complete lives. It's harder for you to sort things out."

"I don't understand why Alan and Willie didn't stay together. You should have seen them in the hospital when he was dying. She cried incessantly. She kept begging me to find a way to cure him."

"How could you do that?"

"I don't know," Olivia said. "They seemed to think I could do anything." She paused. "I need some answers. I know where Willie and her second husband live. I need to go see her. Now. Can you...?"

"Can I keep them asleep until you get back? I'll try, but they'll want you to be here after they wake up. Elise especially. That girl has grown to love you."

"It's mutual."

"Take your time. Do what you need to."

Minutes later, Olivia was driving down FM 77 toward the town. Willie and her husband lived in a huge house on the out-skirts. Olivia had seen the house only once, and it had been the talk of everyone. *It's like that awful place Kevin and Hildy lived in,* Olivia thought. But now that was in a time that had never hap-pened.

As she drove slowly through the town, she remembered when Kit had driven her around.

She'd looked at each house and thought of who lived where and what had happened to them. Even though she'd tried to warn people, the same tragedies nearly always happened. And right now she was thinking of them as her failures.

But at the end of the street, she pulled the car over and turned off the engine. The yellow house on the end had *not* been the scene of unspeakable tragedy. The girl who'd grown up there had *not* slit her wrists because she'd been bullied at school.

At first the memory was vague, but as Olivia looked at the house it became more clear. She and Kit and Tisha were in Summer Hill on vacation. Olivia had her degree then, but she hadn't practiced much. They were by the lake with a picnic lunch when she saw a girl being teased by two others, and the girl looked like she was going to cry.

Olivia didn't know why she was so drawn to the situation, but she knew she had to step in. The girl, Lisa, had parents who were too busy, too extroverted to see what was being done to their quiet, introverted daughter. Olivia invited the girl to join them and after that day, they started corresponding. When she was back in Summer Hill, they talked.

On the day that would have been when Lisa committed suicide, Olivia knew she had to get to the school. She didn't know why, but she ran to the girls' locker room just in time to keep the boys out, and she got Lisa's clothes back to her.

After that, Olivia had long professional talks with the principal about those bratty girls, and with Lisa's parents.

Today, Lisa was married with two children and she taught elementary school.

Olivia sat in the car for a few moments to let the memories sift through her brain. *It's like waiting for the cream to come to the surface*, she thought. Maybe she hadn't been able to save everyone, but at least she'd succeeded with a few.

When she pulled in to Willie's driveway, she wondered what she'd find. For those three weeks when she was in 1970, Kit had enjoyed tales of the internet and cell phones and overnight delivery with the passion of a drug addict. But he'd deeply disliked what she'd told him about her marriage—and he disagreed with it all. "I pushed my way into his life," she said. "I *needed* a child. I was starving. You can't sympathize because you're not a mother."

"It's true that I don't understand men who don't support their family," Kit said.

Olivia couldn't make him see that Alan was a different type of person. He wasn't as strong as Kit. And Alan hadn't had the advantages that Kit had. Nothing she said made him understand.

She rang the doorbell, then waited, her heart pounding. When Willie came to the door, Olivia was pleasantly surprised. Willie no longer looked like she'd never done an exercise in her life. She was trim and had on makeup and her hair was soft and sleek. She was in her late sixties now but she looked good.

"Olivia Montgomery!" Willie said. "How nice to see you! How's your family?"

"Fine. And yours?" She was trying to dredge up what she knew from her two roads of memory. Willie and Alan. Willie and her contractor husband. Willie and... "Alana is your daughter. And you're Kevin's stepmother."

"Oh heavens! What's he done now? He didn't try to sell you anything, did he? Sorry. Where are my manners? I just made some iced tea. Come in and have some."

Willie's kitchen was pretty and bright and clean, and they sat at the little breakfast table with frosty glasses of tea.

"Now..." Willie said, letting Olivia know she was ready to hear whatever she had to say.

"I know we don't know each other very well, but—"

"Don't you remember that I met Alan through you? That you invited me to that appliance sale?"

Olivia remembered it well but she didn't get them together. "Diane—"

Willie laughed. "That's right. You and the man you married locked Alan and Diane in that closet together. I thought that was really funny. When Mr. Trumbull opened it, they were kissing. I thought what a great guy Alan was to turn something bad into good. He married Diane and after she died..." Willie shrugged.

"You were there."

Willie's face changed. "To my great loss." She got up to get some cookies. "Have some. I can't eat any as I gain weight just smelling them."

"You married Alan?" Olivia encouraged.

"Yes, I married the lazy jerk." Willie waved her hand. "I shouldn't speak ill of the dead, but after what I went through with that man I can say anything. But you don't want to hear about that."

"I do!" Olivia said. "I want to hear every word."

"See this?" Willie motioned to her huge, new house. "*This* is what a man is supposed to provide for a woman. A home." She wiggled her left hand to show a big diamond ring. "*This* is what he's supposed to give her. But Alan didn't do anything. He was a parasite! You'll never believe this, but he expected *me* to do all the work of running that appliance store. And his mother was just like him. They were like twin sci-fi creatures that latched on and tried to suck all the juice out of me."

She grabbed the sides of her hair and pulled. "It still makes me so angry I want to scream." She let go of her hair. "Alan came up with grandiose schemes of more stores and how *he* was going to do all the work. So his mother bought a store, then Alan went off to play golf. One time I got really angry and demanded that he show me his golf clubs. The bastard didn't have any. I'm not sure but I think he was having an affair and he expected *me* to support him and his mistress!" She leaned forward. "Right after our daughter was born, I got out!" Willie grimaced. "When I think of that man! Do you know how he met his third wife?"

She didn't wait for Olivia to answer. "Alan had a girl who worked in the office. She was really good with numbers and people. A real find. One day he came to me—by that time I was working for my current husband—and said he wanted Alana for the day. I thought that was weird since he didn't pay much attention to her, but I don't look a gift horse in the mouth, if you know what I mean."

"I do," Olivia said softly, eyes wide.

"Alan took our daughter to work and did his helpless act. He was soooo good at that. You ever know a man who did that?"

"Yes," Olivia said. "Intimately."

"So anyway, Alan told her I was a lazy ex-wife and he had no one to help him, et cetera. Six months later they were married. She divorced him two years after that. I know all this because she came to me to apologize for all the bad things she'd thought about me."

"It wasn't me," Olivia whispered.

"You?" Willie said. "You can't mean you and Alan. I can't imagine *you* would ever fall for a do-nothing like Alan Trumbull."

"Only if I had a trauma in my life so horrible that it made me feel like I deserved to be treated badly."

Willie looked at her for a moment. "That's right. You're a psychologist, aren't you? Maybe I should make an appointment and talk about how bad Alan made me feel. He had me believing I didn't deserve more than he gave me—which wasn't much of anything."

"What happened to Kevin?"

"Poor kid. He's very much like his father. Married a couple of times, but they didn't last long. No kids."

"Was one of them a girl named Hildy?"

"Wow! You've got a good memory. He dated a big girl named Hildy when he was in his twenties. But by that time the appliance stores were failing. When she dumped Kevin, he was real upset about it. Personally, I think she wanted a man with money."

"Do you know what happened to her?"

"Wasn't she in that play you guys put on last year? That was *great*! I can't believe you got two big-name movie stars here to little Summer Hill. You want some more tea?"

Olivia stood up. "I want to go see my home," she said. "I want to remember all the good. And most of all, I want to forgive myself."

Willie was looking at her as though she wasn't quite sane. "Sure. I'll show you out."

As Olivia got into her car, all she could think was that Alan's misery wasn't her fault! Her ability to do things, to manage multiple appliance stores, to run a house, take care of a difficult child, all of it were things he *wanted*. But he'd made her feel…

Olivia had to pull over to the side of the road to bury her face in her hands and let herself cry. But it was a good cry, one of relief. She had carried so much guilt in her! During all those years she was married to Alan, she'd felt that she'd ruined his life. If she hadn't gone after him, he would have found a sweet girl like Willie. They would have been a family and been *happy*.

But that wasn't true! Alan got the woman he'd loved for so many years—but without Olivia supporting them by working six days a week, they weren't happy. Willie said Alan was a parasite. But wasn't that what Willie was too? The only thing she'd said about the husband she had now was that he could provide her with a good house and rings for her fingers.

Olivia looked out the windshield. She'd tried hard to give people what they said they wanted. Alan said he wanted more stores, more of her being a wife to him. By that he meant running the house as well as the stores. Taking care of Kevin, rescuing Kevin, trying to make Alan feel like a man.

Olivia began to smile. Willie was right in that Olivia would never have fallen for a man like Alan. He and his stores had been her punishment for the guilt she felt at losing her daughter.

But that hadn't happened! For a moment, she closed her eyes and remembered seeing her beautiful daughter grow up. Tisha had been a quiet child who loved being with her parents wherever they went. For years, they were a happy threesome, content to follow Kit around the world. He'd come home and tell them they were to move to Yemen—or Dubai or Morocco.

Usually somewhere in the Middle East, as that was Kit's area of expertise. He'd leave it to his wife and daughter to pack up and move. It was what Rowan said had been dumped on his mother and she couldn't handle it. But Olivia had loved it!

Irony, she thought. Kit had loved what Olivia was good at, while Alan had hated it, been jealous of it. When she'd done something big in her life with Alan, he'd sneered at her, then said something meant to put her down. But with Kit, when she accomplished some huge task, he'd thanked her, praised her, whirled her around in his arms, and made love to her.

At the thought of the life she'd had with Kit, she smiled broadly. The smile started inside her, under her rib cage, then spread outward. Gradually, it took over her body—and that smile pushed out the guilt she'd carried all those many years she'd lived with Alan. Gone was the guilt about her daughter and the penance she'd paid for it by allowing Alan to endlessly punish her.

When the smile finally reached her lips, she knew she was a different person. No more guilt. Best of all, there would be no more looking back. *No more regret.*

Olivia started the car. She wanted to see her home. For all their travels, little Summer Hill, Virginia, had been where they called home.

When she pulled through the gate, she saw Young Pete and he gave her a half smile. She remembered how Kit and the caretaker had bonded as they worked together on the big estate. Kit's early job at Tattwell had come in handy. Whenever he had a big decision to make, he grabbed the garden tools and went to work.

She parked by Diana's Cottage—but that name was gone. By the door was a brass plaque that said DR. OLIVIA PAGET

MONTGOMERY. PSYCHOLOGIST. As she touched the corner of it, more memories came back to her. Wherever they lived,
she'd kept up her certification because she *knew* it was important. She hadn't remembered Arrieta and her ability to change
the past, but Olivia had been fierce about keeping up with her
training. One time Kit had been quite unpleasant about her returning to the US to take some courses. He couldn't go with
her, so he'd used all his skills of persuasion to get her to stay. His
argument was that she could let her credentials lapse and renew
them later. But Olivia had stood her ground and told him no.

He'd mumbled that only dictators were as unbendable as she
was. She took that as a compliment.

She opened the door and went inside. The living room, where
she and Elise had sat with a shirtless Ray, was her waiting room,
and where she met with groups of people. She had clients who
drove in from Charlottesville and Richmond to attend Saturday-
afternoon sessions that sometimes lasted for hours.

The downstairs bedroom was where she sat with individual
clients. Unfortunately, in the closet was a four-foot-tall stack
of boxes of tissues.

She went upstairs. Just hours ago, these two bedrooms had
been where she and Elise stayed, where Elise had closed the windows in fear of being found out. Now that room was Olivia's office. Bookshelves, her desk, and filing cabinets filled it. She knew
that to refresh her memory she would go through every folder,
listen to tapes, and review the videos. Her clients deserved that.

The room where Livie had stayed was still a bedroom. When
Kit was away, she often slept there, surrounded by files and tapes.
A few times, women had used the room, hiding from some hor-
ror that had happened in their lives.

She went back downstairs and out to the back. The little
walled-in area was now a garden and she knew that in the summer she often held group sessions there.

Leaving her office, she walked across the lawn, past the huge expanse of manicured grass in front of Camden Hall. This morn-ing, when she and Kathy and Elise had run off in the car to some woman they were sure was a charlatan, the big house had been empty. No one had lived in it for years.

In 1970, Olivia had only spoken to Kit of the house once. His reaction, like she was after him for his family's money, had upset her so much that she'd not mentioned it again.

But Kit had remembered. The night before their tiny wed-ding, he'd slipped into her bedroom at Tattwell and handed her an old shoe box. He hadn't said anything, just let his dancing eyes speak for him.

She assumed it was a gag gift, something silly to make her laugh. Inside were some wadded-up scraps of fabric that had been used to make animals for the kids. In the middle was a big steel ring with half a dozen keys on it.

"What's this?" she asked. "If these are the keys to your heart, they're too small."

He kissed her for that, then stretched out beside her, took the ring, and held up a big, rusty key. "This is to the gate, although I've been told it's never locked." He began to flip through the keys. "This is to Diana's Cottage, Camden Hall, River House, and—" He broke off because Olivia was staring at him. "Isn't this what you wanted? Dad had a hard time getting the place. It's been empty all these years because the family couldn't agree on which one of them owned it. They settled it by no one being allowed to do anything but pay for the upkeep. Dad had to get a friend of his to go to Burma to get one of the owners to sign the deed." He looked at her. "Please tell me you didn't change your mind."

"I don't know what to say," she whispered.

"Tell Dad he's the best there is and that you'll name a kid after him and he'll be happy forever."

"What's his name?"

"Tulloch," Kit said.

Olivia put the keys in the box, the lid on, and handed it back to him. "It's not worth it."

He laughed. "It's a good Scottish name, but using it in the middle will be fine."

"Christopher Tulloch Montgomery the Second might work."

When she groaned, he kissed her. They would have made love but Ace opened the door. Behind him was a sleepy Letty. As always, they'd thought she was home with her parents. All day the children had been quiet. They were worried about the wedding, afraid Olivia was going to leave them.

"Kit is going away but I'm staying right here," Olivia told them again.

"You're going to New York," Letty said. They were standing at the foot of the bed.

"No, I'm not." Olivia opened her arms to them and they crawled up to her, Ace on one side, Letty on the other, Kit on the end.

"I vote for a story," Kit said.

"With dragons," Letty said.

"And knights," Ace said.

"I guess I could tell you some about Khaleesi and her baby dragons." All three of them snuggled against her.

"Sorry, George," Olivia whispered to the author, then began. "Once upon a time there was a beautiful young woman who was to marry a huge and terrifically gorgeous young man who wore black around his eyes but very little clothing. And he rode an enormous black stallion and was the ruler of a fierce tribe of more beautiful men and—"

Kit lifted his head to look at her, but Olivia just smiled and went on with the story.

They all fell asleep, wrapped around each other, and only woke when a flashbulb went off. It was morning, her mother had arrived to help Livie dress for the wedding, and she'd taken a photo of them.

Olivia looked up at the big house and knew that that picture was in a pretty frame on a side table in the well-used living room. One thing she'd done in her time in the past was to see that lots of photos were taken. Her new father-in-law had sent her an excellent camera from Japan and she'd begun photographing everything. Camden Hall was full of albums and pictures in frames.

She didn't go into the big house but kept walking toward the wall that separated River House. Three of the times she'd been here had turned into a naked escape over the big outer wall. First was with Kit, then Elise, then with Kit again.

I think I'll keep my clothes on this time, she thought. When she reached the river that ran in front of the house, she stopped. It was extraordinarily beautiful! She and Kit had owned the place for years now and she was remembering all the work they'd put into it. When they were in another country and saw a garden they liked, they copied what they could at River House. Twice, Kit had torn everything out. Both times, he'd been having trouble with some diplomatic negotiations and the hard labor of gardening had helped him think.

For years, Kit and she and Tisha had lived in River House. Camden Hall had been empty most of the time, too big for the three of them, so they'd saved it for guests and parties. Every year Tisha had a party that included most of Summer Hill. Kit went all out, with animal rides, and friends of his flying in from whichever country Tisha wanted to show to the kids. One year they'd had a demonstration of yak milking.

For years after Tisha was born, there'd been no more children. Not for lack of trying on their part! They went to doctors but they could find nothing wrong with either of them.

"*N'shalla,*" Kit said. "It's God's Will."

Every chance they got, they returned to Summer Hill, and they'd filled River House with treasures from around the world.

Then when Olivia was nearing forty years old, one day she

couldn't bear the sight or smell of lemons. She thought she was coming down with a cold, but her Egyptian housekeeper put her hand on Olivia's flat stomach and laughed.

Declan was born seven months later, Rowan a year after that, then last was Tully.

During her pregnancy with Rowan, Olivia had been worried. She didn't know why, but she kept thinking that something would be wrong. One night she'd cried and said, "He won't be the same."

Only now did she understand her concern. In her other life, Rowan had had a different mother. And the second time, he *was* different. He'd always looked like his father but this time he had some of Olivia's blonde coloring. And her humor. Previously, he'd been a very serious young man. Taciturn. Almost cold. But then he'd been raised by warring parents.

The same but different, Olivia thought.

With the arrival of the boys, their lives went from quiet, orderly peacefulness, with Kit being the center of it, to… Olivia smiled. To complete and utter chaos. After the sweet calmness of Tisha, the boys were a shock. Noise, laughter, tumbling fights, accidents, broken everything. Rules were considered a challenge. They seemed to truly believe that whoever disobeyed the most won.

She and Kit left their fragile treasures in River House and moved into Camden Hall—and put bars on the upstairs windows. Kit lightened his workload but they still moved often—and Olivia and the children followed him everywhere. The boys adapted to new languages and grass huts and camel hair tents with extraordinary ease.

As for Tisha, when she turned eighteen, she opted to stay in the US and go to school. She said she'd had enough of roaming the world. But no one was surprised when she married a young man who wanted to go into diplomacy. Their daughter Lori inherited Olivia's acting talent. Kit had always felt that he'd cheated Olivia out of a great career on Broadway, so he bought an old warehouse in Summer Hill. He made it into a theater and last summer he put on a play starring their beloved grand-daughter. He even conned his famous actor cousin into playing the lead. It had been an extraordinary success, even changing the lives of several people.

For a moment, Olivia looked at the differences and the same-ness of the two lives. Almost always, deaths had occurred at the same time in both lives. The same people had married and divorced. She'd been worried that changing one thing would destroy good things, but it hadn't. There had been some bad happenings, like when Kit's father went out sailing and never returned. Every death had nearly killed her, but when Olivia looked back, it had all been nearly the same.

Except for Alan, she thought, and again she felt that all-consuming smile flow through her. The great guilt she'd car-ried for most of her other life was finally gone.

She was especially proud to remember that she'd changed one life drastically. Just as she'd done the first time, Estelle had mis-carried, but without a car wreck—and again, she was told that she could have no more children. At the time, Olivia was preg-nant and living in Charlottesville with her parents and going to school. She didn't understand it then, but when she was told of Estelle's miscarriage, she became hysterical. She and Estelle had never been close, but Olivia knew she *had* to help. She called Dr. Everett and he gave her the number of the unwed mother's home in Jacksonville. In the end, Estelle adopted a little girl and it was Olivia who urged her not to keep the adoption a secret. It took a while to get Estelle to go against the beliefs of the era, but she did. And that allowed her and Henry to end up adopt-ing six more children.

"Hi."

Olivia turned to see Kathy and Elise sitting on the terrace of

River House. They were both smiling in a way that made her sure that they had achieved what they wanted to.

Elise ran her hand over her protruding stomach. "This is my second."

"I have two children," Kathy said. "And you'll never guess who I married."

"Calvin Nordhoff," Olivia said.

"Spoilsport!" Kathy said.

"Is anybody hungry? I am!" Elise said. "Let's go inside and I'll make tacos and we can talk." Her eyes sparkled. "My sister-in-law, Carmen, gave me her recipe."

"Did she give you her brother too?" Olivia asked.

"In exchange for Kent. I got the better deal. *Much* better!"

Olivia and Kathy laughed, but then Olivia said, "Wait a minute. I thought you wanted to forget the past."

"Changed my mind. If I forget, then I might slip back into trying to please people who don't exactly have my interests in mind. Alejandro laughs when I mention things that never happened, but he doesn't mind."

"Speaking of which, how did your family take your marriage?" Kathy asked.

Elise snorted. "After Kent got Dad out of jail, he thought it might be a good idea to listen to what all of us had to say. But then, Kent was threatening to leave Dad in there if he didn't."

"Jail? I can't wait to hear this." Olivia looked at Kathy. "And what about you? Are you okay?"

"Better than I thought possible."

"I want to know what happened to Andy," Elise said to Kathy as she opened the door. "I want—" She broke off as she looked about the house. When they were in it before, everything had been so perfectly, professionally laid out.

Now the house had that lived-in feeling that a family gave it. There were still art objects from the world, but they were interspersed with cheap trinkets and many photos of laughing people.

Elise picked up a picture of three good-looking young men. "Wow! Who are these beautiful creatures?"

"My sons." Olivia's tone told of her deep, deep love for them.

"I want to hear every word," Elise said. "From both of you." She looked at Kathy. "How's Ray?"

"Married to Rita, thanks to me. And you know what? She gained so much weight after her last baby that she's bigger than I ever have been. But Ray is still mad about her and can't keep his hands off of her." She took a breath. "I learned that, contrary to all those diet people promising happiness if you just get a flat belly, love can't be weighed. It isn't given or denied based on the bathroom scale."

Olivia and Elise were smiling at her.

Kathy looked at Olivia. "Did you get your ex with his mistress?"

"In a roundabout way, I did, but—" She looked at Elise's pale face. "Let's feed this young lady, then spend the rest of the day talking. I think we have a lot to tell."

"Wait!" Kathy said, then looked at Elise. "I need to know something. Did you get pulled onto that black horse?"

"Oh yeah," Elise said. "Repeatedly. Our son runs so fast that Alejandro says we *made* him on the back of that horse. I don't think that's true, but there was that one time when…" She trailed off dreamily.

Olivia put her hands on Elise's back and pushed her toward the kitchen. "Food first, then stories."

Chapter Thirty

WHEN THE WOMEN WERE SETTLED, THERE WAS A MU-
tual agreement that Elise should go first and she had them laughing about walking in front of Alejandro in her underwear.

Her story took hours. The best part was at the end, when Elise
finally stood up to her mother. The two mothers sat on a couch,
the fathers in chairs, and Elise stood in front of them. Kent was
beside his wife. For the first time, he was on Elise's side. Come
what may, he'd decided to take a stand. "When you two were
in college," Elise said, "you concocted a plan that you'd marry
men who were either rich or aristocratic, and you did so. Later,
you decided that your kids would marry each other." She used
her height to loom over the two women. "Did you even once
think about what Kent and I wanted?"

"You adored Kent," Elise's mother said.

"Probably because that's the *only* thing I ever did that got approval from you."

"We don't have to listen to this," Kent's mother said, but he
clamped a hand on her shoulder and made her sit there.

Since Elise's father had spent three days in jail and was now facing possible prosecution for an attempted kidnapping, his attitude had changed. He sat quietly and listened.

Elise went on with her tirade. She told all four of the parents that they had to give up their snobbish racism or they were going to lose their only children.

She didn't dare look at Kent when she said that because he was still terrified of losing his job. He wanted it *all*, the money and Carmen. As for Elise, she was so happy with her new life she could walk away from them and their money—and they knew that.

In the end, the parents conceded. Carmen and Kent were going to move into the house on the property of the parents and Kent was allowed to keep his job. But then, unlike his father, he was an asset to the business.

The parents offered to buy Elise and Alejandro a big house nearby, but they declined.

She knew that taking it would put them under obligation to her parents. And besides, she knew them. Her mother would show up every day with "suggestions" about how Elise should live her life.

After a lot of talk, she and Alejandro, Diego and his wife and children, and three of their employees, decided they were going to move to Fort Lauderdale so they'd have year-round work.

When Elise finished telling her story, she turned to Kathy. "Your turn."

They opened a bottle of wine—club soda for pregnant Elise— and went into Olivia's pretty living room. They snuggled up on the well-worn, comfortable chairs and couch and waited for Kathy to begin.

Kathy took a sip of her wine. As she was curled up in a chair, she was glad that she looked the same as she did before she went back in time. But inside she was *very* different. "As I said, I at last figured out that body type doesn't matter as much as I thought it did. With the way the media bombards us with skinny, skinny, skinny, it's all I could think about. Diet books, diet pills, and sneers. Lots and lots of sneers. I seemed to have been considered evil for not being thin."

She grimaced. "Dr. Oz had a show where some big women came onto the stage and the audience was told that no applause was allowed. And why? The only 'sin' the women had committed was eating an extra helping of barbecue. I've seen child molesters on TV talk shows who were applauded because they said they were going to do better. But overweight women were given less courtesy and kindness than criminals."

Kathy took a deep drink of her wine. "You know that commercial for toothpaste where the men ignore the skinny girl and lust for the one who has a curvy body—and white teeth?"

"I *love* that ad," Elise said.

"That was mine. The guys in the office booed it, but women across the globe loved it."

"So tell us what happened," Olivia said. "How did you get your ads on TV and billboards?"

"And in print." Kathy's smile of pride told a lot. She put down her glass. "I got angry. I didn't know so much of my father was in me. But then, I was on a very limited time budget and I knew what awaited me if I didn't change things. Besides, Dad was yelling at the man I wanted."

"This is Andy?" Olivia asked. "The one you did *not* end up with?"

Kathy nodded. "When I woke up, I was sitting in Ray's office. It took me a while to figure out where I was and when. I looked at Ray's calendar and saw that he was in Chicago—and it was before we were married. It took me quite a while to adjust. First of all, there was my body. It was different."

Olivia spoke up. "If you want different, you should go from your sixties to your early twenties. Now *that's* a shock!"

Kathy smiled. "I had forgotten that Ray's obsession with having a body like some California beach boy had soaked into me. When I was growing up, Dad and his energy weren't around, so it was just Mom and me and we were readers. We liked quiet pleasures. But then I married Ray. He worked out and he got me to do it too."

"Alejandro is more of a reader, but his sister and I like to—" She broke off as they were staring at her.

"This is the Carmen who made your life so miserable?" Kathy asked.

"This time around she didn't steal my husband and besides, she's not bad at helping to run the business. This isn't about me." She looked at Kathy. "Go on with the story."

"So anyway," Kathy said, "I was sitting at Ray's desk and thinking how soft I was and that I needed to go to a gym when I noticed a pile of folders on the bookcase. I was pretty disoriented and not sure what to do. I picked up the folders and started looking through them. They were Ray's ideas for future ad campaigns."

"And you knew which ones would work," Olivia said.

"I did. At first it was just a joke. I kept saying, 'Yes, yes, no, no,' that sort of thing. It was fascinating knowing the future and which ideas the clients were going to like. And I knew how the client would change them. Ray had put a star by one of the ideas, but I knew that the client was going to hate that one, but he'd love the one in the corner that Ray had drawn a line through."

"What did you do?" Olivia asked.

"Actually, I think I was afraid to go outside and face everyone. It's a lot of responsibility to think that in just three weeks you have to do something so fabulous that you change your entire life."

"I agree," Olivia said. "I tried to save the entire town—and I had to work to keep myself from writing President Nixon and warning him that…" She waved her hand. It was all too much to tell.

"I had no problems at all," Elise said. "Three weeks was plenty of time to escape my megalomaniac parents, my greedy fiancé, and, oh yeah, find a career. And while I was at it, I was supposed to make the man I adored, but who didn't remember our time together, fall in love with me."

"But you did it," Olivia said.

Such a look of pride came onto Elise's pretty face that the room seemed to grow brighter. "I did, didn't I?" she said softly. She looked back at Kathy.

"Ray's office was quiet and since no one paid much attention to me, I knew I wouldn't be bothered. I pulled some paper out of the printer tray and began making sketches of how I knew the ads would be. There were two that had flopped, and afterward we knew why, so I fixed those."

She smiled in memory. "It was wonderful. When Ray's secretary came in, I had papers everywhere."

"Who was his secretary?" Elise asked.

"Back then, he still had Martha. I knew she wanted to retire, but Ray wouldn't let her. He kept giving her raises and begging her to stay. I asked her to find out where Rita Morales was and to ask her to come in for a job interview as her replacement. She was so pleased I thought she was going to cry."

Olivia laughed. "Great idea! So what about Cal?"

"I'm coming to that," Kathy said. "Martha went through all the papers I'd done and she knew they were good. She didn't say a word, just unlocked one of Ray's desk drawers and pulled out a two-foot stack of folders. They were clients of other firms who Ray wanted to win. He was trying to come up with ideas he could show them that would entice them to come to Dad's firm."

"And you knew every campaign that would win them over," Olivia said.

"Yes, I did," Kathy said. "Martha plopped the folders down in front of me and put my cell phone on top. 'Record the jingles you make up,' she said, then left. As I went through them—and most of them Ray and I had worked on together—I realized that it was more about choice than creativity. The ideas that were eventually used were there but we'd presented the wrong ones."

Kathy looked at them. "She called Bob from the art department and he came up and sketched out storyboards. And she called in Dave and he brought a keyboard and put music to the jingles that Ray and I had discarded."

Kathy smiled. "It was a wonderful day! We didn't leave the office until after two a.m. We were exhausted, but we had some good-looking campaigns to present to my father."

"How did he take your presentation?"

Kathy got up and went to the window to look out for a moment, then turned back. "Sorry, but it still makes me angry. My father—" she swallowed "—refused to look at them. It was the next afternoon and he was in a bad mood—as he always was when Ray was out of town. He had an office full of men and he was telling them their ideas were garbage. I was standing there with Martha, Bob, and Dave behind me, our arms full of storyboards and recordings. That man, *my father*, gave a snort of derision, then waved his hand for us kids to go away. And we did. We backed out of the office like the cowards we were.

"'That's that,' Martha said. 'Ray will have to show him what we did.'

"'And take credit for all of it?' I said."

When Kathy said no more, Elise and Olivia stared at her.

"What did you do?" Elise asked.

"Let me guess," Olivia said. "You used what you'd learned from Ray and attacked."

"Exactly!" Kathy said. "I'd gone back in time to change things, but that man just dismissed me like I didn't matter? Not this time! It turns out that I really *am* my father's daughter because I lost my temper. What was really making me angry was that half the good ideas Ray presented were from *me*. But my father only wanted to hear them if they were filtered through a *man*."

"The worship of the penis," Olivia said. "I see it in my work all the time." She saw the shock—and interest—on the women's faces. "Sorry. This time around, I'm a psychologist."

"Disappointing," Elise murmured. "I thought you were speaking from experience."

Olivia laughed.

"You're right," Kathy said. "That's what it was. I went back into my father's office but then I turned coward. You can't break a lifetime of fear in just seconds. But then I saw Cal. He was smirking at me. I could take what my father handed out but not *him*. Why did he always look at me with contempt? What had I ever done to make him so nasty to me? The whole thing with Felicity hadn't happened and never would, so what was his problem?"

Kathy took a breath to calm down. "That's when I really and truly lost it. Because of Cal, not my father. I slammed all the papers down on Dad's desk, leaned over him, and *made* him look at them. After a flash of surprise, he showed no more emotion. But children know their parents. He was shocked, stunned. Not by *me*, but by how really, really good my ads were. They were finished products that I *knew* would work. The next year, one of them won a People's Vote prize for the third-best ad of the year," Kathy said. "Is there any more of this white wine?" She sounded as though she was finished with the story.

Olivia looked at Elise. "Shall we sit on her?"

"I've heard of something called waterboarding. I think it's a torture, so I say we use it."

They looked back at Kathy with laser glares, and she smiled. "Okay, so things changed between Cal and me."

After she left her dad, Kathy went back to Ray's office—and her body began to shake. Anger had given her strength when she'd faced her father, but now that was draining away and fear was filling her. When she'd finished her presentation, he'd said, "What title do you want?"

She knew what he meant. He was *never* going to say that he liked her campaigns. Praise was not something Bert Cormac gave. But what he did give were jobs and bonuses.

When she realized that her father had just offered her a real, actual *job*, it was as though all the energy suddenly drained out of her. She was leaning over her father to the point where their noses were almost touching, and she stood up straight.

The room was still full of her rage. She could feel it, and it was an anger she hadn't possessed before she married Ray. Marriage to him had changed everything inside her.

Suddenly, she could see her marriage more clearly than she'd ever been able to. His ferocious ambition, his obsession with body image, his insatiable work ethic, had all seeped into her. It was Ray who'd pulled her into the advertising firm. His mantra had become "Kathy can do it." He'd volunteered her to plan company parties, arrange schedules, whatever was needed. At home, he'd started handing her ads and having her rewrite copy. When she made a suggestion, he'd listened.

By the second year of their marriage, they were discussing his every ad campaign. By the third year, she was as involved in his work as he was. In the fourth year, he began plopping accounts down on her home desk and telling her to take care of them—and she did.

When she met Elise and Olivia, Kathy had been married for six years, and she was as involved in her father's advertising firm as any of his employees.

But Kathy wasn't paid. Or acknowledged.

Ray thanked her. Praised her. But he didn't offer to try to get her a job in the company.

When she mentioned it, he said, "Baby, you know that what

is mine is yours. Go buy yourself something nice. Something sparkly."

As she stood in front of her father, his desk stacked high with papers and boards and tapes of recordings, it hit her that everything with Ray hadn't happened yet. There was no reason for the rage Kathy had just shown. Sure, her father had dismissed her, but then to him, she was a girl who only planned office parties and entertained clients.

And to the men sitting in her father's office, she was just the boss's pretty, plump daughter who sometimes brought them homemade muffins.

The face Kathy wanted to see was Andy's. He was the man who got away. Her father had just offered her a job so maybe she and Andy could work together. Had he been impressed with her?

Kathy turned around slowly to look at the men in the chairs behind her. A couple of them seemed to be admiring. Impressed. But Andy, he was disgusted. Repulsed. His upper lip was curled into a sneer and he wouldn't meet her eyes.

She thought of the woman Andy would eventually marry. Yeah, Cheryl was built like Kathy, but she was so gentle and sweet that the whole office took advantage of her.

Kathy didn't pick up any of the papers she'd slammed on her father's desk, didn't look at another person, just went to the door and opened it. None of the men held it for her, not after the unfeminine display she'd just made.

The distance to Ray's office seemed long, but she made it and was even able to close the door behind her. But she was standing there shaking—and she didn't know if it was from fear of having at last stood up to her father or from having seen the disgust on Andy's face.

Okay, she thought, as she walked to Ray's desk. She'd achieved one of the things she wanted, which was to get herself into her father's company. She was *not* going to think about what happened when the three weeks were up and she no longer knew about the future. How was she going to live up to what she'd just done? Maybe she shouldn't have—

"Don't turn coward now."

She turned to see Cal Nordhoff standing in front of the closed door. She hadn't heard him enter. Kathy dropped down into Ray's chair. "Go away."

"And miss the aftermath of that display? Never!" He went to a cabinet, opened it, and poured vodka and tonic water into a glass and held it out to her.

"No thanks," she said, but when he didn't put it down, she took it and drank half of it in one gulp. "Shades of *Mad Men*," she muttered, not knowing if the show was on the air or not.

Cal smiled. "Are you Peggy, but you look like Joan?"

Kathy almost smiled at his allusion, but she didn't. "Why are you here? To tell me I'll never make it in a man's world? That my father and the other men will eat me alive?"

Cal's handsome face lost its smug look and he seemed genuinely puzzled by what she'd said. "No, not at all. I was glad of what you did, and I think it's about time. You've been helping your dad for free for too long."

It was Kathy's turn to be puzzled. "I've never done anything." Since this was before she'd married Ray, that was true.

"You're kidding, aren't you?" Cal sat down on Ray's black leather Chesterfield sofa and looked at her. "You aren't aware that Bert Cormac owes you for his own personal market research?"

"I know he asks Mom and me what we think of products, but I've certainly never made a presentation to him."

"Not that you know of, but ole Bert tells me. 'Kathy likes this one,' he says. 'She thinks the blue they used in the package is off. Let's present it in a darker shade.'"

She knew exactly which campaign he was talking about. Her father—thankfully—stayed in his apartment in the city most of the time, but when he came home he talked only of advertising. And he always brought home cartons of products and asked what they thought of them. When he left, she and her mother sighed in relief.

"Kathy, pretty girl," Cal said, "you've been part of your dad's advertising business since you were on a bottle. He told me he experimented in formulas with you. One of them made you throw up."

She was leaning back in Ray's big leather chair, the one that had been custom-made to fit him, and thinking about what Cal had said. "Why do you always sneer at me?"

He couldn't hide the shock on his face. "I didn't know you saw that."

It was true that before she married Ray, she hadn't noticed Cal at all. Between Larry and Andy and her fear of her father, she hadn't seen much else in her life. But she had an idea that it was only after her marriage that Cal had really begun his looks of contempt. And with Ray's boundless energy around her, she didn't have time to dwell on why one of her father's employees didn't like her.

In fact, if it hadn't been for Olivia asking about Cal, she probably wouldn't have been so angered at the way he'd smirked at her in her father's office today. And if she hadn't been enraged, she might have slunk out without presenting the ads.

She watched him go to Ray's bar, pour himself a whiskey, then go back to the couch.

"So who are you going to settle for?"

"You mean which account?"

"No, which man? You've got four men hanging around you."

"You know, I'm not liking this conversation. I want you to leave."

"It's not your office," Cal said. "First there's that skinny kid. What's his name?" Kathy didn't answer.

"Three last names. Laurence Winbeck. That's it. He wants your daddy's money. Then there's Andy Donaldson."

Kathy drew in her breath. No one knew she was interested in Andy. Ray thought she had a crush on *him*.

"Andy says he's playing hard to get so he won't be accused of going after the boss's daughter."

"He *says* that?" Kathy whispered.

"Only to a company VP who takes him out to lunch. After two martinis he enjoyed telling me what his goals in life are." Cal snorted. "He'll never make it in advertising. Blabs too much truth."

Kathy was frowning. "Why would you do that?"

Cal didn't answer her question. "Then there's Ray."

Kathy's lips tightened.

"Oh, I see that you *do* know about Ray's interest in you. He's catching on that clients like tablecloths and that those two forks have different uses. He's beginning to think marriage is a business proposition. You could give him what he doesn't know, and in return, he'd give you the privilege of being near his glorious self."

Kathy couldn't help it but that image made her give the tiniest bit of a smile. "That's three men. Who's the fourth?"

"Me."

All Kathy could do was blink.

"Didn't know that, did you?" He got up and walked to the window to look out. "Those men want you for how you can advance their lives, for what you can give them. But me? I want *you*. I like your brain, the way you think. You're smarter than you give yourself credit for."

Turning, he looked at her—and his eyes were hot. *Like something out of a movie*, she thought. Cal looked as though he might throw her across the desk and tear off her clothes.

No man had ever looked at Kathy like that and it made her heart leap into her throat.

He took a step toward her. "I like that glorious, lush body of yours." He took another step. "I like *women*." He was standing beside the desk and he gave her a look up and down that made her feel like she might melt into the leather of the chair.

When he held out his hand to her, she started to take it, but she glanced at the door.

"I locked it," he said, his voice throaty. "And I told Martha we weren't to be disturbed no matter what she heard."

She took his big hand in hers.

Chapter Thirty-One

"OMG," ELISE SAID. "THAT'S... OH! THAT'S WONDERFUL. Great. I love it!"

Olivia was smiling in an I–told–you–so way.

"Don't you dare take credit for this!" Kathy said to Olivia, but she was laughing. "Cal and I would have happened eventually. It's just—" She stopped. "No. It never would have happened. After being married to Ray, I would have been too scared to even think about marriage again."

She picked up her wineglass and twirled the stem in her hand for a moment. "I didn't know how bad my life with Ray was. The comparison I had was my parents, and my marriage was a lot better than theirs." She looked up. "When people ask about a bad marriage, the only thing they really want to know is, Does he hit you? If the answer is no, then you're put into a category labeled SAFE. Whatever else is done to you is okay."

She paused. "Ray never yelled at me, was never unkind. But he beat me down in a way that killed the inside of me. He didn't mean to because he truly loved me, but he wasn't *in* love with me."

Kathy smiled. "Cal and I fight. We have arguments. He thinks he knows everything in the world and I have to stand my ground to make him even *hear* me."

When she looked up, she was smiling. "But we make up in bed. Fabulous sex. The kind out of novels. And out of bed we're kissing. And hand holding. And cuddling while we watch TV. Every day he lets me know that I am *loved*. Good moods and bad, I know he loves me."

"I know what you mean," Olivia said. "Reliving our lives made the dynamic between Kit and me change. When we got married when we were older, even though I loved him, under the surface I still harbored a lot of anger and resentment that he'd ruined my life. I loved him but I hated him too. But I was so afraid that rage would come out that I kept my mouth shut. I didn't talk about the bad that had happened to me. We were only married for a year and it was sweet, but I was afraid that if I let my anger out, it would destroy everything."

She paused. "And there was the guilt. I was a woman who'd given up her child. The guilt ate at my soul. When I went back, I yelled at Kit, cursed him, but he was still there. He didn't go away. I don't know whether he believed me or not, but he helped me." She smiled. "And also, when I met him so many years later, he'd had a lot of time of being a big shot and he kept that attitude. He decided things, gave orders. All decisions were his."

"And now?" Kathy asked.

"Now we've lived together all that time. I saw him go from being a mostly naked boy to counseling presidents. If he gets too uppity, I know how to stop him." She smiled. "To me, he'll always be that worthless boy."

"And you had children," Elise said. "Alejandro was made to be a father."

Olivia laughed. "I have to say that the boys took any hint of pomposity out of their father. One time Kit unexpectedly got caught in what was escalating into a desert war. He was freaking out because Tully was with him. Our son felt his father's fear and threw up on him. An absolute gusher. It was so human, so *normal*, that everyone stopped screaming and started laughing. It was easier to negotiate with laughing men than with rage so the problems were solved. Kit said it should be named 'Tully's War.'" When she looked up, there were tears in her eyes—but they were tears of happiness.

Elise looked at Kathy. "How is Ray doing?"

"Last year he left Dad's firm and started his own. He's doing well."

"Did he leave because of Cal?" Elise asked.

"I think so. Dad started spending time outside work with Cal, then when I gave him a grandson, Dad kind of became another person." She took a breath. "He's thinking about retiring."

Olivia's eyes widened. "*You* are going to head the agency, aren't you?"

Kathy's smile was slow. "I am. Dad's been spending time with Mom and they're so mad about our kids that…" Kathy trailed off and gave a shrug. "I'm happy. That's the highest, most important thing I can say. *I am happy.*"

"Me too," Olivia said.

"And me," Elise said.

They smiled at each other, leaned back, and sipped their drinks. There wasn't anything more they needed to say.

Epilogue

IT WAS EARLY MORNING AND OLIVIA WAS LYING IN the bed. Kit had already gone downstairs.

She opened her eyes enough to see that it wasn't quite daylight so she closed them again.

Only yesterday they'd returned from... From what? Their life experience? None of them were yet used to their new lives.

Last night at dinner Elise had teased Alejandro that Olivia's sons were so gorgeous that she might trade him in. Alejandro was a sweet, gentle man who looked at his wife with so much love that it was almost embarrassing. He didn't seem to be worried that she was going to run away.

Kit had insisted that everyone spend the night in Camden Hall. "It's too big and empty now." His voice was wistful.

Minutes later, Cal arrived with their two boys, Elise's son and husband joined them, and within seconds they were running and yelling—and Kit was smiling happily.

Elise and Olivia were curious about Cal. He was a big man and even when he was silent, he commanded attention. When he spoke, his deep voice made people turn to him. Olivia could see why Kathy had once said that she was afraid of him.

"He's a bit like Ray except without the thug element," Elise said.

Olivia laughed. "Your son is climbing the curtain."

Elise took off running, but Alejandro got there first and lifted the boy away.

After dinner, which the three women cooked together, they caught the kids and got them into the biggest tub in the house and washed hair and sweaty little bodies.

By the time they were done, Olivia was exhausted—but in a good way. Part of her missed her young body, but another part was so content with what she was *now* that she didn't want for anything.

When Kit came to bed, he smelled of expensive whiskey and illegally imported cigars.

She snuggled into a spoon with him.

"I feel like I haven't seen you in years," he whispered. "And today I kept thinking of Uncle Freddy and Mr. Gates. Tomorrow, Alejandro and Diego and I are going over to Tattwell to work on the cemetery." He chuckled. "Remember the first time I cleaned that place up? You—"

She turned in his arms to kiss him. "I remember you wore tiny shorts and absolutely nothing else."

"Yeah?" He was kissing her face. "Did you like what you saw?"

"Of course not. You were just a worthless boy and I was on my way to becoming a Broadway star."

"And you danced for me in a cabbage patch." He slipped her nightgown off her shoulders.

They made love slowly. It didn't have the fire of youth, but it held memories of a life together and of shared experiences. Most of all, it held a love that couldn't be broken even across time. They fell asleep together, clasping each other tightly—as they had done for over forty years.

It was morning now and Olivia didn't want to get out of bed. She wanted to snuggle under the covers and think about what she'd seen and felt in her three weeks in the past. The faces were so fresh in her mind and she wanted—

She broke off as something moved against her leg. Did someone let a dog in the house?

She lifted the cover to see a sleeping child with his head toward the bottom of the bed.

When she flipped the coverlet back, to her surprise, the big bed was full of children. They ranged from three years down to a baby in a soggy diaper.

Olivia sat up in bed and tried to identify them. Elise's boy, Kathy's two. The blond head of Liam, her grandson. He and his dad must have arrived in the night. She thought a couple of them belonged to Diego.

Like puppies, the children began to stir and Olivia slid back down in the bed. They gravitated to the warmth of her, piling on her and on each other.

It's my fantasy, she thought, the one she'd told Ray and Elise. *Well, not really.* But she could see the connection. She'd often dreamed of being woken up by kisses from "men" with different skin colors. This experience, however, wasn't at all sexual— instead, it was simply full of happiness. These children weren't men but they were all male and there was a lot of variation in skin color.

She could feel them beginning to wake up. "Whoever kisses me the most gets chocolate chip pancakes."

In seconds, she was overrun with the biggest, wettest kisses ever given. Olivia laughed and hugged and asked for more.

And that's how the parents found their children—all of them in bed with Olivia and kissing her. Cameras and cell phones flashed and beeped as the scene was recorded.

Later, everyone said that the photos were proof that Dr. Olivia Paget Montgomery was the happiest person on the planet.

She agreed with all her heart.

★ ★ ★ ★ ★